Queen's Justice

LUCILLE J. KNIGHT

If you have a few minutes, please let other readers know what you thought of this book by sharing an honest review on Amazon and Goodreads!

To all the strong, independent princesses.

Trigger Warning

This book contains violence, mild gore, captivity, and also consensual sexual interactions. An effort has been made to keep erotic scenes tasteful.

CONTENTS

BROTHER'S FALL

CRISP WINTER AIR BIT at Thunar Bonecracker's lungs. He took a slow, deep breath and then released it in an annoyed sigh. He shifted on the barrel he was sitting on, feigning a sore bottom to buy himself a few extra moments to consider his next move. The worn out cards in his thick gloved fingers were the farthest thing from a winning hand. No matter how long he stared at them, they weren't going to improve, but he was far too stubborn to simply yield.

"What's the matter, Commander?" The burly man across the makeshift table gave him a sly grin, revealing three golden teeth that gleamed in the afternoon sun. "Want me to fetch a pillow for your *august* bum?"

Thunar immediately caught what he was referencing and shot him a withering glower. It was no secret between he and his three comrades why the General's son was stationed at what was considered the worst post in all of Hamdralg.

Nobody liked being assigned to the surface towers, of which there were four along the borders to the human lands of Dunneth and Hamdralg's neighboring Sarven kingdom, Dwenenar. For this reason, troops were rotated home every three months and the duty spread through the ranks so that the same individuals weren't always stuck with the unpleasant assignment.

Not a single warrior was exempt from the rotation, though recent rumors had led many to believe that with his family connections Thunar was being given special treatment. Wanting to quash the suspicions, no matter how unfounded they were, Thunar had agreed to volunteer for the next rotation. His squad wasn't too thrilled, all of them had been stationed at one outpost or another when they were still recruits, hence the more blatant ribbing that he was being subjected to now.

"No thanks, Gredif," he grated, his green eyes flicking back to the cards he was holding. They were still lousy. Cursing under his breath, he pushed on, tossing a couple of the thin, wafer crackers that served in place of currency into the pot.

By the way Gredif was smirking, Thunar knew he had lost, but he stared his comrade in the eye regardless. He had never been a good loser, but he was an even worse quitter. They laid out their cards together. Gredif's grin turned incredibly smug at the sight of his leader's terrible hand.

"No wonder you're cranky," he chuckled, reaching out to collect the pile of crackers. "Lucky for me, though, it was Hadran's turn to make supper!"

The other Sarven seated at the table with them just shook his head. He had long since grown accustomed to being teased about his awful cooking and even then, he was mild mannered enough that it had never bothered him to begin with. "Better watch it, Gredif," he rebuked softly, "I might forget to make enough for you."

"Ha! You won't hear me complaining if you do," he chortled back, "I've got all the crackers!"

Trying to hide his frustration at being beaten, Thunar rose up from the table, which was little more than a board set on top of a barrel and moved to join the fourth member of their party. He was staring out over the parapet, gray eyes keenly surveying the snow-covered landscape below.

The tower was only about fifteen feet high; being built on the crest of a wide hill aided a great deal with the vantage from the roof. Any approaching traveler would long since have been noticed, an army would never pass unseen. Heading toward Hamdralg's gates, you would be hard pressed to distinguish the watch tower from the backdrop of the Beldrath mountains, but should you alter course to the southeast, it became well defined against the rolling hills that gave way to the plains of Dunneth.

"All is quiet, Commander," Ulreth assured, reaching up to scratch at his dirty-blond beard. His eyes never stopped searching. Of all the men, he was the most vigilant, taking their post here far more seriously than most.

The Sarven had not known full-scale war since the civil conflict that resulted in the founding of Dwenenar several thousand years ago. They had made peace with the other nations, the elves in the western forests and the neighboring humans of the plains long before that. There were rumors of recent unrest from the new human minister, but as a warrior Thunar had little desire to keep appraised of politics.

As General and leader of the army, that was his father's realm and Thunar trusted completely in Baran the Crusher's ability. One day he would have that responsibility, of that nearly everyone was certain, but until then he was just like every other soldier, which is exactly what he had come out here to prove.

"Commander!" Hadran drew his attention away from the view. "The supply wagon approaches from Hamdralg!"

The news brought a grin to Thunar's face. "Then we should go down to meet it." He motioned to everyone except Gredif. "It's your turn to watch," he commanded, his smile turning mischievous when the man started to splutter and he added, "Don't worry, I'm sure the crackers will keep you company."

Snorting and shaking his head, Gredif resigned himself to the order and took up position where Ulreth had been standing just moments before. Behind him, the other three Sarven, led by Hadran who had been closer to the door, started the descent through the tower.

The spiraling, stone staircase wound its way to the ground level, where a cluster of bunks, barrels, and weapons lined the circular wall. It was cramped with barely enough room for four men, let alone their provisions and armaments, but every squad stationed at one of the watch posts had to make do.

The chance to see a new face every few weeks was exciting in and of itself, but this particular delivery was special for the sole reason that Thunar's younger brother, Thane Stoutforge, would be accompanying it. There was no doubt in his mind that Thane was the best blacksmith in all of Hamdralg, which was why he had specifically requested him to come and make repairs. At least, that's what he would have told anyone who asked.

By the time the three men made it to the thick timber door, the supply wagon was coming to a stop just outside. The pair of woolly muskox pulling the heavily laden cart grunted their relief as two Sarven clambered to the ground. The driver gave Thunar a curt nod, while Thane rushed from the back to embrace his older brother.

"I hope the journey was not too taxing," Thunar proclaimed, clapping the younger man on the back.

They were almost matched in size. Thanks to Thane's work at the forge, he possessed the same strong shoulders and torso as his warrior brother, but it was clear that the elder of the two had been built specifically for battle. Thunar was broad and tall, with massive hands and trunks for arms. He stood a head taller than most Sarven men, including his brother.

"It was fine," Thane answered, glancing at Ulreth as he approached with a wrapped parcel that radiated the most pleasant of smells. Hadran must have also caught a whiff while aiding the driver in unloading the wagon, for he was not even a whole pace behind his comrade.

"This wasn't on the supply list, Commander," the blond Sarven held the package up, breathing deep the scent coming from within. "But it sure smells good..." Hadran nodded his enthusiastic agreement.

Thane solved the mystery before Thunar could comment. "Mother sent it." He smirked a bit. "She's afraid you're not getting enough to eat."

Snatching the lovingly wrapped package from his subordinate's hands, Thunar hastily pulled back the wax paper, his mouth watering as he imagined the sort of delicious treat that would be nestled inside. Sure enough, there were a dozen perfectly squared spice cakes that, judging by the scent alone, were going to be incredibly delectable.

Almost reverently he reached inside and lifted one of the cakes out. He was about to bring it to his lips, when he caught sight of his comrades staring hungrily. The last thing he wanted to do was share, his first impulse was to hoard the rare treat, but he knew by the amount included in the parcel that his mother had intended this gift to be for everyone. Since it was his fault they were all here, the least he could do was let them all partake in a taste of home.

"Okay, okay," he shook his head with a crooked grin as he passed one to each of them, "but that's it for now. Eat it and get back to work."

"Speaking of..." Thane cut in as the two warriors bounded off like boys, mouths full of spice cake. "What was it that you needed to have fixed? Jedris wants to head out as early as possible in the morning. Since there's still a few hours of light, I'd like to get started."

Thunar stopped chewing and tried to give his brother a grin, but his mouth was stuffed with cake. It took him a couple moments to get the spongy, moist morsel under control so that he could reply. "About that..." He swallowed, brushing crumbs out of his whiskers. "It's a funny story actually," he started to say, but that's when the afternoon erupted into chaos.

There was a loud scream from the tower above them, followed by the limp body of Gredif as though someone had hurled him over the parapet. He landed with a sickening crunch on the hard earth, just feet from where the two brothers were standing. Trailing behind him was a rain of blood splattered crackers. Before any of the remaining Sarven could react, a bone chilling shriek rent through the air and creatures from nightmare attacked out of the sky.

The clang of metal against metal and the fierce battle cries of Sarven warriors echoed through the chilled winter air in a blood stirring cacophony. The warriors stood together, five strong against a hellish foe that numbered a mere four, but the fiends were winning. What should have been easy odds to calculate in their favor had taken a severe turn for the worse only moments after the unexpected attack had come.

In a very short time, Hadran had fallen alongside Gredif, their blood pooling out from their lifeless bodies and clinging to the boots of those who still fought the seething creatures.

Ten minutes ago, the band had been laughing and jesting, sharing spice cake that was now strewn upon the ground and stained with blood. The comrades that lay dead had only moments ago been perfectly fine, but not one of the warriors let such thoughts enter their minds. They were focused on the battle, sending up a cheer when the first of their horrific assailants crumpled beneath the crushing blow of a massive hammer. It was now four Sarven against three of them.

Thunar's triumphant howl turned to a jeering snarl as the behemoth of a man raised his bloodied weapon and spun to face another of the nightmarish foes. She, at least it resembled the lithe form of a woman, had dropped from a position above him, her gray, leathery wings rustling as a shiver ran down her scale-blotched skin. A pair of silver horns protruded from just above her temples, peeking a few inches above her ratted black hair. She was as tall as he was, her seething pink eyes gleaming with blatant malice as she drew back her dark lips to reveal yellowed fangs.

"I will savor your flesh!" she taunted in a low growl, raising a black-bladed sword in one of her taloned hands.

"Sorry to spoil your plans," he brandished his hammer, a crooked grin baring his teeth, "but my wife wouldn't approve."

Hissing, the fiend took a second to gather herself, intending to lunge at the warrior and knock him to the rocky ground before he could stop her, but she didn't get the chance. A scream of agonized fury tore from her throat. The broad blade of an axe cleaved into her exposed back, just between her wing joints, severing her spinal cord.

She collapsed, her legs and lower body now useless, but she didn't stop trying to fight. Her hand shot out, grabbing Thunar's shin, claws piercing through boot and pants to prick at his skin. She tried to pull him down and had his stance not been solid, she might have succeeded.

Without mercy or remorse, he raised his hammer and threw all his strength into the downward blow. It made a sickening crunch, splattering vermilion blood across his legs as it smashed the struggling, snarling beast's skull like a melon. For a fleeting moment he was thankful for once that he was responsible for washing his own clothes, as his wife greatly disliked finding blood on them.

The thought of her brought a grin to his thickly bearded face, which he directed to the man still standing across from him. "Little brother." His green eyes glittered as they caught the other Sarven's dark brown gaze. "Here I thought working the forge might have dulled your edge," he teased, turning so that his back was to his brother's.

Thane huffed at him in response, taking the jibe with far more grace than he might have were they not in the midst of a battle. "I can't let you have all the glory," he shot back, using the only course of rebuttal available to him. Being the younger son was never easy, but when you had a perfect brother, it became downright hard.

Around them, the battle raged on. In the brief time it had taken for the brothers to kill the third fiend, her accomplices had slain the other two warriors. It wasn't skill that gave the beasts such an edge; it was sheer ferocious hatred and an obvious lust for killing.

They refused to fight outright, resorting to games and nasty tactics to keep the upper hand. One foe in particular was fond of snatching a victim from the ground, flying high into the air, and then dropping him to his death. With a glance, Thunar was relieved to see that she wouldn't be pulling that trick anymore. The delicate membrane of one wing had been ripped, the tattered leather now hanging free.

It pleased Thunar that only two of the creatures were still alive, but it was an unacceptable trade off that the Sarven numbers had dropped to match theirs.

"Well, if your intent is to keep some for yourself, you might want to try killing with the first blow next time!" Thunar was still beaming mischievously, not about to let his brother see the worry that had crept into his chest.

Thane didn't get a chance to respond this time, his eyes were on the last two creatures, who had been hanging back, watching the pair of Sarven as though they were attempting to solve an especially troublesome riddle. Whatever they were plotting, neither man liked it in the least.

"Watch yourself, little brother." The warning barely had a chance to leave Thunar's lips before the fiends shot toward them.

The injured one launched herself at Thunar, who drew his hammer back to strike her, but she unexpectedly grasped onto the haft. Struggling to wrench the weapon free, he tried to kick her, but she nimbly avoided the blow, flashing bloody fangs in a sinister grin. She was much stronger than her slender build suggested, and no matter how he tugged or pushed, she would not be shaken loose.

Behind him, Thane was equally occupied, attempting to strike the hellish female even as she flitted out of his range. He was very much aware that she was trying to lure him away and so far had not fallen for the bait.

Each time she danced out of reach, he let her go, refusing to expose not only himself, but Thunar as well. It became clear after a few minutes that she was growing frustrated by his lack of cooperation, and she finally gave up the tactic in favor of a more direct approach.

Abruptly she hopped around to flank him, hurling the dagger that had been in her hand. Thane wasn't fast enough to face her and even if he was, the chance of actually deflecting the projectile was slim. In the heat of the moment, he didn't consider why she had even moved in the first place, not when she could have certainly killed one of them. As Thane rolled to dodge the weapon, it passed harmlessly, missing both of the Sarven and clattering to the ground. A second later he realized, far too late, that the vile creature had not made a mistake. He had.

Thunar, aware that his brother had moved and fearing the worst, forcibly dragged the snarling hag around so that he could catch a glimpse of what was happening. A cold jolt shot through his stomach as he saw Thane beneath the other fiend, fighting her to the best of his ability, though she had pinned him on his stomach and knocked his axe out of reach. He knew their mother would never let him hear the end of it should he let his baby brother get killed, but that was not the only motivation driving his actions.

Sharply twisting the haft, he slammed the butt of it against her head, stunning her long enough that he was finally able to tear his weapon from her claws. Without a second thought, he sprinted to Thane's aide, swinging the hammer in a desperate blow that caught the almost gleeful creature just above her shoulder blade, shattering the bone. She fell away from her prey, revealing the deep gouges that her talons had ripped into the flesh on Thane's back – purely for the fun of inflicting pain.

Once the younger Sarven scrambled out of the way, hurrying to reclaim his axe, Thunar readied the blood-stained hammer for a killing blow, but a sudden lance of pain stopped him. The other foe had recovered, claimed the forgotten dagger and was standing behind the warrior with its blade buried in his side. Before he had the chance to react, to attempt to fight her off, she'd withdrawn the weapon and began repeatedly thrusting it into his back and ribs.

Dimly aware of a voice shouting his name, of metal scraping against stone, Thunar felt his hammer slip out of his fingers as the pinching shots of pain wracked his body. It took all of his willpower to attempt to push her away, but she clung to him with the same unsuspecting strength as she had to his weapon only moments ago.

He heard another savage scream and initially mistook it for one of the creatures until the strong arm clinging to him went slack and his assailant's body toppled away. The cry had come from Thane as he cut her down, her body preceding Thunar to the ground only a second before he collapsed beside her lifeless form.

The hot rush of blood pouring from half a dozen stab wounds made it difficult for him to focus. He weakly shook his head to clear it so that he could track where Thane had gone, still afraid that harm might befall his brother.

It didn't take him but a moment to find him, standing rigidly above the now terrified hag as she tried in vain to escape the clearly enraged Sarven. Thunar watched with satisfaction as the axe rose, its blade glistening with fresh blood, and then fell in a fluid motion, cutting short a defiant wail as the last foe's head was severed clean from her body.

Letting his axe clatter to the ground, Thane didn't waste any time going to his brother now that there was no longer an immediate threat. He was pleasantly surprised to see Thunar grinning, and he hoped that meant the injuries weren't so bad. Crouching down beside him, his hope was dashed with a single glance at the wounds and the sheer amount of blood beginning to pool. He did his best to prop him up, then hurriedly tugged his shirt off and pushed it against the spot with the most holes.

Thunar grit his teeth at the sudden pressure, growling as another wave of pain washed over him. "Rough hands... curse of being a blacksmith, aye?" He couldn't help but chuckle, though he soon regretted it as all it brought him was more discomfort.

"Shut up," Thane snarled, his gruffness almost convincing were it not for the worry in his dark eyes. "Save your strength, you'll need it for the trip home." He said the words with all the confidence he could muster, unwilling to accept that the possibility of his brother surviving a journey anywhere was very unlikely.

"Thane." The name was spoken far too solemnly.

He didn't answer, instead he continued to fuss with the nearly soaked shirt, knowing the flow of blood had to be stopped if there was to be any chance of saving his brother.

It wasn't until Thunar put a hand on his arm and said his name again, more gently this time, that he finally looked up. Suddenly his mouth was incredibly dry, his chest tightening painfully, and he felt like he was trapped inside a very bad dream.

"Not a lot of time left," Thunar said softly, blood flecking his lips as he spoke.

Thane shook his head adamantly, squeezing his brother's broad shoulder. "I won't accept that. You have a family that needs you." He trailed off, the reminder sending an unexpected pang of guilt through his belly. Thane hadn't married yet; there was nobody waiting at home for him, no wife or children to mourn his death. The thought that their places should have been reversed, that he should be dying and his brother surviving to return home, caused his heart to ache with regret.

"You must live," he continued after a pause, speaking as though will alone would be enough to mend the mortal wounds. "Fight now, fight so that you can watch your daughter grow up, so that you can teach your son to be as mighty a warrior as his father and grandfather. For if you are not there for them, then who will be?"

A faint smile touched Thunar's face. "You will, little brother. I could always count on you..."

Thane opened his mouth to reply, intending to tell him that wasn't good enough, that he could never compare to their father, but there was something in his brother's tone that stopped him. He wanted nothing more than for Thunar to pull through, to live, but the acceptance in those green eyes told him more than words ever could. Death was coming to claim him; the least Thane could do was hear his final words.

It took every ounce of his strength to let go of hope, to lay his palm over the blood-stained hand that was still resting on his arm and simply listen as Thunar's voice grew ever softer.

"Live, brother. Live the days that I will not." Thunar struggled to form the words, his strength swiftly waning, but he held on for a moment longer. "Tell Makira," he forced the words past his reddened lips, "my final thoughts were of her." He smiled again, his mouth barely moving as his eyes fell closed and he all but whispered his wife's name one last time.

"Thunar?" Thane gave him a slight shake, though a part of him knew it was in vain. "Thunar!" He squeezed his brother's limp hand as hot tears stung his eyes and an echoing agony rang in his broken heart. There was no point in fighting the crushing weight of grief and so he did not hold back the urge to weep. Gently resting his forehead against his brother's, Thane could do nothing else in that moment but mourn.

REFUGEES

HAMDRALG'S SMITHING DISTRICT BUZZED with the sounds of ringing metal, shouting voices, and roaring equipment. This quarter of the city was always hottest and loudest, filled with smog from the myriad of forges that were the very heart of Sarven crafting and reeking of the musky sweat of a thousand laboring men.

From jewel cutters to weapon and armor smiths, and everything in between, there was nothing you couldn't find or commission to be made from one of the many shop keepers or crafters. The quality was like nothing you would ever find elsewhere. Not even among the elves, whose works were always smooth and elegant, could match Sarven metal smithing, let alone surpass it.

Grim thoughts hung in Thane Stoutforge's mind as the clang of his smithing hammer pounded out a steady rhythm. Sweat slicked his caramel skin, his black hair soaked and clinging to his muscled back. Even the band wrapped around his head to prevent perspiration from dripping into his eyes was drenched.

He'd spent far too much time at the forge in the months following his brother's death, preferring the depths of his mind, no matter how dark, to the sight of his grieving sister-in-law. Not that you would ever be able to tell. She was a Sarven woman and more than that, she was a warrior's wife and a mother. If she wept for her fallen husband she did so in privacy, where her children would not see her weakness. Somehow her strength only made it worse. That she had never spoken a harsh word or shown him anything but kindness made the gnawing guilt in Thane's heart all the more potent.

'I should not have even been there...' The fact rolled from the back of his mind unbidden, but somehow knowing the perfect moment to rear its ugly head. Such a truth was even harder for him to bear, the knowledge that mere happenstance had resulted in his presence at the watch post on that day. He'd been sent on short notice to do some routine repairs, though he secretly suspected that his brother Thunar had simply missed home and wished to hear news of the family from a direct source.

The ringing hammer faltered, still drawn back to the high point of its arc. Thane's muscles tensed as his grip tightened around the wooden handle. Flashes of that battle assailed him, images of flowing blood and broken bodies strewn across a courtyard. The sight of home baked spice cake, delivered at a mother's behest, scattered about the spot where only a few minutes before a man had been inspecting the treat. They were ruined, blood having pooled around them, though who that blood belonged to, Thane could not have said.

It had required all his stamina to take care of the shattered Sarven bodies, to wrap them in cloth and safely store them in the watch post's cellar until they could be retrieved. He couldn't leave Thunar's body behind, and so when he was ready to return home, he carefully loaded the bulky form onto a small cart. No honor was extended to the mysterious attackers; he stacked their monstrous bodies in the courtyard and left them to the scavengers.

A shiver ran down his back, making the still healing lacerations across his shoulder blades itch. Grappling his thoughts free of those troubling memories, he forced himself to focus on the piece of steel that he'd been shaping. It was horribly deformed where he'd gotten carried away, bent in much farther than it should have been along that edge of the blade. Because of this he would have to reheat the metal in order to fix his careless mistake. He puffed out an annoyed sigh and decided before he did that, he needed to take a short break.

Putting away the unfinished sword and storing his tools in their proper places, he was just reaching for a towel to wipe his hands and face off, when an auburn-haired bear of a man burst through the back door. His burly, armored chest was heaving, sweat pouring off his face and trickling through his long, bushy beard as he struggled to regain his breath.

Thane stepped to him immediately, directing him to a broad stump beside his workbench that served as a stool and then offering him a ladle of clean water from a bucket near the door.

The guard choked down a few gulps between rasping intakes of air before finally croaking in a thick Sarven accent, "Ran all the way down... got summons, from Historian..." He took another swallow, draining the ladle and then swiping a bead of sweat off his bulbous nose. "They need ya in the throne room... *Now*."

Trepidation churned in Thane's belly. He wasn't sure what to think about being called to the palace, even if it was at the behest of Historian Bodrin, who so happened to be his uncle. Whatever the reason, he would not figure it out standing there, of that he knew for certain. His feet it seemed had already come to this conclusion and were nearly to the open door, giving him just enough time to shout instructions for the guard to lock up once he'd recuperated from his run two levels down.

Setting a pace that was hurried, but conservative, Thane dashed down the mostly empty streets, heading for the great stairs that connected to the districts above. Had the summons come a few hours later, when the other workers were crowding the road on their way home, it would have easily taken twice as long to reach the wide, ornate steps. Climbing them two at a time, he launched himself upward, refusing to contemplate what he was rushing toward and thinking instead of what route he would take through the merchant square, which was always bustling.

By the time he reached the top of the first flight, placing himself in the common quarter, his legs were starting to ache from the exertion and new beads of sweat were showing on his forehead. Swiping the back of his wrist across his brow, he paused for a moment to take in a few deep breaths, before sprinting off again.

He circled around to the second staircase, dodging past a mother and her three energetic boys, then weaving through a surprisingly thick crowd that was headed in the same direction. The traffic wouldn't have been so strange had the women been carrying sacks or baskets to hold their purchases, but from a few stolen glances, he noted that their hands were empty.

How odd.

"Uncle Thane!" The familiar voice of his nephew, coming from a few steps behind him, brought Thane to an abrupt halt, much to the relief of his calves and lungs. "Are you going to help the refugees? I hear there's hundreds of them!" Varan wasted no time in launching his questions, oblivious to the pain that passed over his uncle's face.

The young man looked just like his father, with black hair and sharp green eyes that always caught him off guard, making him believe for the briefest of seconds that he was looking at a young version of Thunar. Though the lad was nearly thirty years old, he was still considered by Sarven culture to be a teenager, as proven by the sparse patch of stubble on his square chin and upper lip. Ever his father's son, there was no doubt that given another ten years he'd be starting tavern brawls and flirting with any pretty woman that moved. The thought made Thane's heart ache and it took all of his strength to keep his face impassive.

"What refugees?" he ventured, ignoring the nagging urgency of his summons in favor of granting his nephew a moment of indulgence.

"From Dwenenar," Varan didn't hesitate to provide what answers he could, "They claimed to have been attacked."

This news put a frown on Thane's face and although he was curious, he couldn't put off the Historian any longer. Patting the youth's shoulder, he started to hurry away, but paused to call back over his shoulder, "No sneaking off, head back to your mother." He was almost certain the lad made a face at him, but he would obey, even if his plans were contrary to his uncle's instructions. Not because he feared repercussions from Thane, but most likely from his grandmother, who the older Sarven knew from experience did not tolerate misbehavior.

Up he ran, his pace quickening after the delay and when he came to the next landing he didn't stop like before, he jogged off into the mass of curious Sarven. As he made his way through the crowd, he caught snippets of gossip, swift moving rumors confirming what Varan had already told him. Until he heard such things from a reliable source, he was hesitant to believe much of anything he learned in this manner; these sorts of whispers had a way of becoming inflated.

It was strange that so many citizens of Dwenenar were here. Not that there was any sort of contention between the two nations nor a concern of distance, it was simply that the two kept to their own territories. It wasn't unheard of for dignitaries to visit the other's capitol or for travelers to stop in outlying towns, but for a large mass of people to come seeking aid was very strange.

These considerations carried Thane the rest of the way to the palace, which spread from the exact center to a third of the level. He didn't travel here often, having little cause to come to the merchant quarter let alone the palace itself. This was the world of his father and brother, dedicated warriors and in Baran the Crusher's case, an honored General and adviser to the king himself.

Had he not been in such a hurry, he may have lingered before the thick iron gates, hesitant to cross the threshold onto the royal grounds. As it was, he hurried inside, not even having to break stride to inform the guards he was expected for they had already recognized him and unbarred the entrance.

At the top of the stone steps, he allowed himself to slow to a walk, feeling that to run through these sacred halls would be incredibly disrespectful of all the great kings and royals who had once tread within them. He'd made it no further than the entryway when a young woman, no doubt a servant, approached and guided him with a sweep of her arm down the right corridor.

Following behind her, he was painfully aware that he'd forgotten to grab his shirt or taken the time to wash away the grime that coated his skin. His mother would be appalled if she saw him right then. Thane could hear her scolding him, saying that she knew for a fact he hadn't been raised in a stable and the mental image of her stern expression brought a faint smile to his face.

He had always been closest with his mother, maybe because he knew that while Thunar had been their father's favorite, he was Ravika's. Though she never would have said so aloud, especially now.

His elder brother had always pleased their father through no obvious effort, while Thane had futilely strove to gain even a moment's notice from the stern man. Even on the day where Thane officially became a man, the one time he was certain that his father would show him at least a glimpse of pride, he had come up short.

Every Sarven was given a secondary name upon reaching adulthood, usually bestowed by the parents, that would follow them for the rest of their days. Until their forty-sixth year, they possessed only a birth name, for it was considered improper to claim one's clan name, a name which extended to a wide range of relatives that sometimes even included distant cousins. Like most young Sarven, Thane had been excited, hoping to be granted a fierce and powerful name, but when his father announced that he was henceforth to be Thane Stoutforge, he had been deeply displeased.

"They're waiting inside for you, Master Stoutforge."

The aide's words jarred him back to the present and he realized that they'd come to a halt outside the king's throne room. Swallowing the lump that had formed in his throat, he gave her a sluggish nod, his feet taking him passed her and his arms pushing open one side of the double doors just enough that he could slip inside.

Nervousness tightened in his gut as the door closing behind him seemed to echo endlessly. He felt like a child, sneaking into a room of the house he wasn't supposed to be in, afraid of being caught, but excited to explore the forbidden. That mix of emotions kept him rooted a couple paces inside, gazing down the narrow passage to the dimly lit hall beyond. As far as he could tell from his current vantage, it looked empty.

Taking a deep breath, Thane forced himself to start moving again, the knowledge that he was meant to be here, requested to be here, driving away the sensation of wrongdoing. He was just coming to the end of the narrow walkway, stepping into the expansive section of the main room, when a voice startled him.

"There you are! I was afraid that guard had gotten waylaid!" Bodrin was hurrying toward him, his words light enough, but the expression on his face somber. Seeing him always made Thane uncomfortable, not because he didn't like his uncle, but because he was Baran's identical twin. Though he had to admit, it was quite nice to look into his father's face and see an expression other than disappointment. "Straight off the forge I see." Bodrin put a hand on his shoulder, steering him to the left. "Well, no matter, I'm glad you came with haste. The others have already gathered in the war chamber."

"Of course," Thane started to say, finding it unfortunate that this would not be a private meeting; he wasn't at all dressed for speaking to dignitaries. He was about to make a comment to that effect when the sound of raised voices distracted him. They were coming from behind the door ahead of them. Right now the speaker was someone he didn't recognize, but he sounded very upset. Not for the first time, Thane couldn't help but wonder what was going on. His trepidation surged higher as possibilities swirled around in his mind.

Bodrin led the way inside, drawing an annoyed huff from another of the room's occupants. "Where did you wander off to?" That voice belonged to the last person Thane wanted to be trapped in a room with, but he followed the Historian anyway. He pushed the door closed all but a crack before turning to see the faces staring in confusion at his presence.

Baran the Crusher flashed a seething glare at his twin, more than mere annoyance in his piercing green eyes. "What fool notion made you summon this whelp?" he rumbled, his braided beard, the color of red flame, swaying in rhythm with his words.

"Prince Javrin says they were attacked by strange, reptilian creatures, which is exactly what Thane described," Bodrin answered calmly, more than three hundred years of dealing with his brother having inoculated him to the General's swift temper. "He's the only man in all of Hamdralg with insight; he should be here."

Thankful for the vote of confidence, Thane still couldn't help but wish his uncle hadn't thought to include him. Not only because he hadn't exchanged a single word with Baran since returning with Thunar's body, but also due to an overwhelming discomfort at being made to recount the battle yet again. He'd lost track of how many times he'd recited the story, trying to keep his expression neutral while detailing the final moments of a great warrior as though he'd had no connection to him.

Standing before the small gathering of nobles, all he wanted to do was turn and leave. If such an action would not shame him and his family as well, he very well might have. Instead he remained stoic, never glancing in his father's direction and doing his best to follow a conversation he'd missed the beginning of.

"That sounds like a legitimate reason to me," came another voice. "What do you think, Prince Javrin?"

Thane immediately recognized King Ulthrac, standing in the center of the room with his arms folded across his beard-covered chest. Age had turned his whiskers to steel gray and formed his equally grayed hairline into a deep widow's peak, but his blue eyes were clear and sharp, boring into the half-clothed, dirty blacksmith with a mixture of humor and annoyance. The latter seeming more due to the interruption than Thane's presence.

"He is welcome to stay," Prince Javrin interjected swiftly. "May we please get back to the matter at hand?" His dismissive tone suggested that he didn't care one way or the other, but there was disapproval in his gaze as he glanced over the dirty craftsman.

While the conversation resumed, Thane took a moment to study the prince, curious to get an idea of who he was. Javrin seemed to lack the muscular bulk that was common of Sarven at his age. He was certainly no older than Thunar had been. The prince was tall and broad across the shoulders, but there was an out-of-place grace to his form. His hands reflected this more than his lack of physical bulk. Not a single scar could be noted as they moved in coordination with his words, slender fingers and manicured nails blatantly displayed. His golden hair was carefully styled and his clothing far too clean and neat for a man whose people had just been driven out of their homes.

All of this brought Thane to the obvious conclusion that the Prince of Dwenenar was not a warrior. He seemed a vain man who cared more for his appearance than his own people, a summation that made Thane nearly wrinkle his nose in disapproval.

"...Prince Jalrik was injured in the retreat and the king died with the rear guard as they attempted to buy the stragglers a chance to escape," Javrin finished, his expression one of sorrow.

Ulthrac was shaking his head, his face a mask of sadness and disapproval. "What stone-brain let him do that?"

"King Guldorn did as he felt was right." This did not come from the prince, but from the doorway, drawing everyone's attention as a woman strode boldly across the threshold. "He died a hero's death, giving his life so that the people of Dwenenar might live." She spoke with great clarity as she swept further into the room, radiating an air of authority and grace that only a woman could possess.

If Ulthrac felt surprised at the sudden appearance of a woman in his war chambers, he did an expert job of hiding it. "I meant no disrespect to your father, Princess Jorna, or the sacrifice he made," he gently explained, "but surely there were other men willing to go in his stead?"

"Aye, there were many willing hearts, but you knew Guldorn, he was a stubborn man. Besides..." Her eyes glittered as she came to a stop before the Hamdralgian King. "I am certain that you would have done the same, the two of you were never so different."

A sheepish grin formed on Ulthrac's wrinkle lined face and he chuckled, conceding the point to her. "Well spoken, lass."

Shifting uncomfortably, his thick arms crossing over his massive chest, Baran, ever a traditionalist, failed to hide his disapproving expression. "Come now, Ulthrac, this is no place for a girl."

"Tell that to Halgra the Boulder, Champion and General in the last age," Bodrin barked, eagerly taking the opportunity to disagree with his brother. "I'm sure if you had, she'd have broken every bone in your over-sized body..."

Thane's mind was swift to drift away once the bickering started. He was mesmerized by Jorna, by her presence as it filled the room. He watched her pale lips as she spoke, his eyes falling to her fair throat and down the voluptuous curves of her strong body. Her muscular arms were bare, adorned only with bands of silver and, in fact, this was the only wealth she displayed. The dress that fit snug against her lithe frame was simple, the skirt slit all the way up, showing the pair of pants and weathered boots beneath. Her long, platinum hair flowed freely down her back, tangled and lacking the shine of having been recently washed. With a surge of inexplicable delight, he also noted that her clothing was stained with grime and flecked with fine droplets of blood.

So she is the warrior...

Suddenly he felt her gaze on him and instinctively raised his eyes to meet her cold, gray-blue stare. He was well aware that she was inspecting him, taking in his appearance and state of under dress as she attempted to puzzle out who he was and why such a man had been included in this meeting.

She finally asked, "Who is this?" The question was spoken softly and still it silenced the heated debate as though she'd shouted above their arguing din.

"Ah, my apologies," Bodrin quickly answered, clapping Thane on the back. His fingers brushed one of the scabbed wounds, which made it itch more than hurt. "This is Baran's son."

Realization danced in her gaze and she bowed her head in Thane's direction. "Yes, Thunar Bonecracker, I've heard of you."

The words slammed into Thane like a blow to the gut, but it was nothing compared to the hurt that ached in his chest at Baran's loud snort. "That is not Thunar." His voice held a bitter edge. "My first-born died in battle, not three weeks ago. He fell to the same hellions that conquered Dwenenar. *That...*" He pointed at Thane, the gesture feeling like an accusation. "...is Thane Stoutforge."

Though he tried, Thane was unable to keep a wince of pain from flashing across his face at the way Baran said his name. Part of him knew it was just angry words. His father was famous for saying things while enraged that he didn't truly mean. The other part of him, the part that blamed himself for Thunar's death, feared that Baran would never forgive him for being the son that lived and that cut deeper than any blade ever could.

"My apologies," Jorna said this as though she were speaking to Baran, but her eyes were on Thane. "And my condolences." She spoke soothingly, calming the flustered General and even managing to ease the tension in Thane's chest. For the briefest of moments there was grief in her eyes, the same grief that he had been struggling with himself and he felt his heart go out to her. A second later, she blinked and the pain was gone, buried out of sight.

Slowly the conversation dragged on as the two siblings took turns explaining the events that led to the attack and downfall of their city.

As he had expected, Thane was urged to tell of what transpired at the watch post. This time, with Jorna's sympathetic gaze to bolster him, the recount was not so taxing.

All the same, he was grateful when the meeting came to an end, though a not so insignificant part of him was sad to say farewell to the Dwenenari princess. The chances of seeing her again were slim, unless his 'expertise' was needed once more, but he doubted they would call on him again; he had already shared everything he knew and therefore his usefulness had run dry.

Following Bodrin out of the room, he glanced over his shoulder to catch a final glimpse of Princess Jorna before he turned his thoughts to home and supper.

THE PRINCESS

JORNA HAILSTONE WATCHED THANE as he turned and left the chamber, her eyes falling to the still healing lacerations on his back. He had said little about being injured in that battle, but through the brief recount of how the creature had gotten the better of him, his words had been laced with guilt. She had glimpsed his spiritual wounds then, but to see what would become physical scars, permanent reminders of his perceived failings that day, stirred her sympathy for the man to new heights.

Excusing herself with a polite bow, she followed after the blacksmith, leaving Javrin behind with the king. She did not see the disapproving frown on her brother's face, but it pursued her until she was out of his sight.

There was no sign of Thane in the throne room and Jorna quickened her pace, hoping that she had not missed him. When she stepped into the hallway, she saw him lingering there and once again her eyes were drawn to the half dozen cuts that marred his back. She felt a twinge of sympathy for all he had endured, the least of which were his physical wounds.

At first, she wasn't sure why he had paused; he'd seemed very relieved to be dismissed and for that she could not fault him. It was the sound of raised, arguing voices around the corner that gave her a sudden understanding. Baran and Bodrin were bickering again, and Thane was waiting to avoid being caught up in their conversation. She didn't blame him.

"Master Stoutforge," she called out, approaching slowly. "Might I have a moment of your time?"

Twisting at the sound of her voice, Thane peered at her with a guarded expression, though she might have bet her kingdom's wealth that for a split instant she saw a gleam of pleasant surprise in his gaze. "How could I refuse the request of a princess?" he stated, the tone of his voice almost teasing.

Inwardly she cringed at the title, which had never fit the person she saw herself to be. The term was far too delicate for a Sarven woman, especially one who practiced the shamanic arts as she did. To Jorna, the word provoked the image of a young, gullible damsel that was incapable of doing anything that might muss her clothing or hair. Of course there was no way for him to have known that she disliked the word for her rank and so she bit back a tight rebuke.

Instead, she offered a gentle smile. "I wanted to apologize for mistaking you earlier. It was not my intention to be insensitive—"

"Please, you did nothing wrong," he interjected before she could say anything further. "It was an honest mistake and for that no one could fault you, least of all me."

This was not a response she had expected and so for a moment all Jorna could do was stare up at him, touched at his surprising benevolence. She wouldn't have thought less of him if he had been upset with her, but she could see that he genuinely felt there was nothing to forgive. She, however, saw things differently.

"Perhaps that is true of this instance," she pressed, choosing her words carefully. "All the same, I feel the need to apologize for what happened at the watch tower and to again offer my condolences. I believe that you were attacked so that those horrid creatures were free to march on Dwenenar without fear of being spotted by Hamdralg's sentries."

He nodded, not quite meeting her gaze. Had he already suspected this was the case?

Jorna reached out to put a sympathetic hand on his arm, but re-membered it was bare and thought better of the action. No matter the intent, such a gesture would have been inappropriate given he was not properly clothed. For a common woman, it might not have mattered, but as a princess she must remain aware of how her actions might be perceived.

"Given what you have lost, my words mean very little," she contin-ued. "However, should you ever require a favor, you need only ask and I will do everything in my power to help you."

Watching Thane's face, Jorna could tell he was struggling with her offer and she feared that all she'd done was make matters worse. While she'd spoken his head had lowered, his gaze falling to the floor between their feet, preventing her from reading his expression. For several long moments there was a dreadful tension in the air and Jorna had to fight back the urge to fidget.

Finally he began to answer, but what he had to say was once again far from what she expected. "You are kind and compassionate, my lady, but you owe me nothing." He raised his face, showing her the gentleness in his brown gaze. "It does you credit that you would worry about a simple blacksmith such as I, when you have endured so much more. I have never met your father, but I heard he was a great man. I am sorry that you lost him."

Something passed between them, a quiet understanding shared by two grieving hearts. Jorna opened her mouth to thank him, but a wave of emotion choked her and she quickly shut it again, fearing what might come out if she attempted to speak. For a brief moment, she let her mask fall away, allowing another person to see the extent of her sorrow. She saw the same pain reflected in Thane's expression and somehow found comfort as well.

Forgetting herself, this time she did place a hand on his arm. The firmness of his bicep stirred emotions deep within her that she had always been careful to hide. It wouldn't do for the king's daughter to show weakness her mother had often told her, and so Jorna had learned to maintain control of her feelings. But for a fleeting moment, in Thane's presence, she couldn't carry her grief alone for a second longer.

Thane touched her hand with his fingertips and a spark of understanding passed between them that caused warmth to spread throughout her spirit. Their eyes met. Jorna parted her lips to thank him for his kind words, but the moment was abruptly shattered as a stern voice called her name from behind.

In an instant, she collected herself, pulling her hand away from the blacksmith and blinking away the tears in her eyes. She saw that Thane had done the same, his expression becoming hard and unreadable. When she turned to face her brother, there wasn't a single trace of grief to be seen.

"What is going on here?" Javrin demanded, his smooth features darkened by a contemptuous scowl. He stopped just beside Jorna, turning his glower fully to the blacksmith.

"I was apologizing to Thane for mistaking him as Thunar." Jorna frowned up at her brother, annoyed and shocked at his rather rude behavior. He had always been a touch pompous, but his open hostility toward someone who had done nothing to wrong him was unacceptable, no matter how unusual it was.

Javrin narrowed his gaze into a sharp glower, unperturbed by the sheer size difference. The blacksmith was a whole head taller and at least double his girth. Had it not been for his royal arrogance, the young prince might have thought twice before provoking such a man.

He clearly wasn't worried about repercussions from Thane, for he reached out and took a firm grip of his sister's upper arm. "You are a princess, you do not have to apologize to anyone," he snapped, giving her arm a rough tug. "Now come along, we have important matters to discuss."

Anger flashed in Jorna's eyes for a brief instant, and she yanked her arm from his grasp, despite the discomfort it caused. She did not appreciate being ordered around as though she were inferior to a man and incapable of making her own decisions. Javrin should have known better as their father had never treated her or any woman in such a manner. Had he seen the way his son was acting now, he would have been appalled.

"Mind yourself, brother," she scolded, her firm tone making it clear she would not be bullied. "This manner does not suit you."

They stared at one another for a long moment in a clash of wills, neither one wanting to back down. In the end though, Javrin grudgingly folded. It was plain that doing so brought him a great deal of frustration, but he managed to fix a more neutral expression to his face as he turned to Thane.

"Pardon my outburst," he grated. "You understand that these are trying times for us and that I have a strong need to protect the only family I have left…"

Thane didn't look at all swayed by the forced apology. Lucky for Javrin, the blacksmith was not as volatile as some Sarven. "Forget it," he grunted, flicking his gaze to Jorna briefly, before turning and walking away.

Once he was out of earshot, the prince blew out a flustered sigh and flashed his sister a frown. "Why must you shame me in front of the commoners?" he pouted.

Jorna raised a dubious eyebrow at him. "Why must you always be so arrogant?"

Letting out a snort, Javrin didn't pursue a further answer, nor did he offer one. He started down the hall, pausing only to check that his sister was following. As they walked, he turned the conversation to business, keeping his voice low so that they were not overheard. "You should know, I have not told Ulthrac about the book yet. Thankfully, the weight of our news has kept them occupied for now."

"Yes," Jorna agreed with a nod, keeping pace with her brother quite well considering she was several inches shorter than him. "We should not wait too long before mentioning it, just long enough to ensure that the people will be safe here. When Ulthrac has made good on his promise to grant aid, I will seek an audience and request assistance and supplies to retrieve the book."

Javrin came to an abrupt halt, appearing annoyed again. "But who will look after Jalrik until he awakens? I am the elder sibling and the prince, why would—"

"Come now, Javrin, you know I was entrusted with the book's protection." Jorna was tired of having this argument with him. Several times they had discussed this on their journey to Hamdralg and come to the same conclusion. She was the book's guardian, it was her duty to keep it from falling into the wrong hands, and that meant it was her place to reclaim it. No matter how difficult the task might be. "Besides, as you said you are the eldest, that means you must remain here and look after Jalrik and our people. You must lead as king now."

This softened his manner once again, bringing a smile to his face. "I don't know why I keep bothering to disagree; you always convince me in the end."

Sharing his smile, Jorna slipped her arm under his and together they continued through the hallways. Long ago when they were young children, they had come here with their father, back before their mother had fallen ill and passed away. Jorna had always been impressed with the stone palace, with its solid granite walls that were adorned by vibrant tapestries and the smooth marble floors covered by soft, velvet rugs of deep blue. There was strength and history in these halls. She could almost feel the presence of the ancient kings lingering in them, granting unseen power to their living kin. It was a silly notion, but a comforting one.

"Jorna..." Her brother's voice pulled her focus away from the past. "Are you certain you wish to do this? I could never forgive myself if something were to happen to you..."

They stopped outside the door to Jalrik's quarters and Javrin turned to face her. She could see the concern in his blue eyes, but she refused to let it change her mind. Gently, she touched his cheek, giving him a reassuring smile. "You worry too much, brother," she said simply. After all their discussions, there simply was nothing left to say.

Blowing out a sigh he leaned down and kissed her forehead. "Then the matter is settled. I only hope we won't regret this."

Jorna knew it was difficult for him to trust a woman's abilities. He had always viewed men as superior, though she didn't know where he had come by such a notion. That he was putting faith in her now was a good sign. She hoped that with time he would come to realize that women had their strengths as well.

Bidding him goodnight, she slipped into the solitude of the quiet chambers, finding that she was quite relieved to finally have a moment of privacy. Since Jalrik's injury had left him in a coma, there was nobody here to impress, nobody to prove herself to. Within the confines of these rooms, she could relax and simply be Jorna. But the quietude came with a price. There was no one to see her sorrow and that meant no one to comfort her.

Like an abrupt shift in the wind, her mind fluttered to the moment she'd shared with the blacksmith, and she couldn't help but wonder what it might feel like to have such a man to comfort her. His strong arms and calloused hands made her imagine that his grip would be a little rough, but his firm body would feel warm, his tight embrace soothing. Even though Jorna was alone, a deep flush colored her soft cheeks and she quickly stopped herself before the ridiculous line of thought could wander any farther. She shook herself, regaining and then holding her composure a little while longer as she stepped further into the room.

Thane Stoutforge was completely banished as she paused to take in the splendid accommodations that were no doubt the best Hamdralg had to offer visiting dignitaries. The stone floors were covered with dark green rugs and on the walls hung a set of vivid paintings. Pushed back against one wall was an opulent, stuffed chair with rich fabric the color of a deep, dark forest. There was a moderate table in the antechamber, with two wooden chairs settled at either end and an emerald and gold table runner draped along its length. A brass bowl held an assortment of fresh fruit, grown in the agricultural sector with the aid of magical sunlight, the secret of which had been acquired from the elven Vaear in the original peace treaties of the last age.

After taking a moment to check on Jalrik, Jorna carefully removed her soiled clothing, kicking off her boots and placing them beside the chair. The dirty dress and pants she folded neatly and left on the edge of the table. Making her way to the bedchamber, she went about washing and changing into a clean sleeping gown, before returning to the main room to put her undergarments with the rest of her clothes.

She immediately discovered that the servants had already collected them and left in their place a generous tray of fresh pork, fried potatoes and a sizable portion of cheese. Next to the platter sat a flagon of the finest mead and a small plate with a large slice of fresh cobbler. Food was the last thing on her mind, but Jorna knew better than to turn away supper. She would need all of her strength for the coming days and so she seated herself at the table and ate a fair serving of what had been made available.

With her evening routine completed, she found herself at a loss. There was nothing left to be done for the day, her time was free and yet she could not think of a single thing to do. When once she would have filled the final hours before bed by doing activities with her family or even just reading alone by the fire, she found none of those things interested her anymore.

Jorna moved back to the bedchamber, sealing herself inside to best preserve her privacy. The hearth crackled gently across from the bed, filling the room with a warm, comforting glow, but it granted her no relief from the emotions that weighed on her heart.

She sat heavily on the edge of the four-poster bed where Jalrik lay as though sleeping. "I miss Father," she whispered to the unconscious figure. Her fingers absently caressed the thick doublet spread over the silk sheets and then finally, she let her sorrow and grief take control.

Alone, she wept. Shedding tears for all those who had lost their lives and for those who had been forced to leave their homes behind, but most of all, she cried for her father. More than anything she longed to hear his reassuring voice, to once again be able to seek refuge in the safety of his arms. In a hoarse whisper, she called out to him, a part of herself hoping that he would somehow be able to answer, but there was no reply. The only sound in the empty room was the sound of her heartbroken sobs.

4

GOLDSTEEL'S BOOK

Jorna's boots whispered across the velvet carpet as she approached King Ulthrac's raised throne. Nervousness wiggled in her belly as she stopped at the bottom of the blue lined steps that lead up to the impressive stone seat that Hamdralgian kings had ruled from for countless generations.

It was not often that Jorna felt small in the presence of others. Standing there, surrounded by the memory of those same kings, whose many visages were displayed in intricate tapestries around the vast hall, she couldn't help but feel a sense of how fleeting this moment was compared to the endless rampage of time.

There was such power in this room, an ancient power forged out of the years and the experiences of all that had passed within these magnificent walls. It took her a second to remind herself why she had requested this audience and with the solemn reminder of duty to keep her focused, she bent gracefully into a respectful bow.

The young shaman waited for the king to greet her before straightening to her full height once more and offering pleasantries of her own. She extended the formal greeting to his two advisers, the twin brothers who were always stationed beside their king. Baran on the right was the General over Hamdralg's army, while on the left was Bodrin, who as Historian oversaw all academic matters. For once they weren't arguing and Jorna couldn't help but wonder how long that would last.

"What can I do for you, Jorna?" The king's voice was soft and kind, contrasting with his regal bearing. A bearing that was only heightened by the awe-inspiring backdrop of the city's blue and gold banner that boldly brought out the gilding of the stonework throne.

"The people of Dwenenar owe you a great debt, my Lord, for all that you have done to shelter us in our time of need." She'd had three weeks to prepare this speech, to decide exactly what words to use to plead her case and as such she spoke with the utmost clarity, her voice filled with confidence. "It is with a heavy heart that I must reveal a terrible truth and in doing so beseech you once more for aid. Many things were left behind in the fall of Dwenenar, but none so precious as the book of Grefjein Goldsteel. Which as you know, contains the secret of strengthening and forging gold into magical arms and armor. I mus—"

"Goldsteel's book was lost?" Bodrin cut her off, his face suddenly ashen. Of the three, he was probably most familiar with the subject and therefore knew exactly what was at stake. The secret did not just allow for gold to be more durable; it changed its properties, giving the crafted item special power and resilience.

"Where is Javrin?" It may have taken him a second longer to react, but Baran was surely imagining an army of the bloodthirsty fiends clad in Goldsteel armor and wielding Goldsteel weapons. "He must account for this and for not telling us sooner!"

Raising her chin, Jorna allowed the General to make it halfway down the stairs before saying sternly, "Javrin's duty is to our people, *my* duty is to recover the book." She stood strong against his piercing gaze, knowing that to flinch now would cause her to lose what little respect she had with him.

To her benefit, Ulthrac was not so quick to take action. He leaned back on the throne, raising a hand to scratch thoughtfully at his chin whiskers. "Well, go on then, what else have to you say?" he prompted.

Jorna kept her expression neutral, though she was both surprised and relieved that he was willing to let her continue. Her father had always spoken highly of Ulthrac, but while the two kings had often seen eye-to-eye, she had feared her interactions with him would be different. After all, she was not Dwenenar's king or even its prince, she was a princess and a shaman. It would have been well within Ulthrac's rights to disregard her and do as he wished. That he chose to hear her words was a testament to his patience and wisdom.

"We did not have time to retrieve anything from the treasury, even the book, but it is safe." She was quick to allay their greatest fears.

Jorna knew the thought of such a secret in the hands of an unknown but already powerful enemy had certainly clenched her heart with terror and she imagined they felt the same way. What she was about to tell them was the only thing that allowed her to sleep at night.

"There is only one person alive who can open the vault that contains Goldsteel's book and I am here in Hamdralg. There is no way for those *creatures* to reach it or force their way in, but even still, we would be remiss if we did not make haste to recover the book."

Bodrin frowned at this. "You're certain? Stone can be broken, Princess."

"The door is magically sealed and has safeguards in place to protect against tampering," Jorna answered without hesitation, letting them see her confidence on the subject. "I'm the only one who knows how to properly and safely open it."

"Let me guess," the General snorted, "you want us to send our army to reclaim your city?"

"Not at all." Jorna shook her head, allowing a crooked little grin to tug up one corner of her soft lips. "I desire only the strength of one warrior and supplies enough to get us across the mountains."

At this Ulthrac frowned, leaning forward to peer down at Jorna as though she'd abruptly sprouted a second head. Before he could give voice to whatever he was thinking, Baran began to speak. "It is very dangerous to travel across the Beldrath range, especially in winter. If the giants and saber cats don't kill you, then the frostbite most certainly will!"

"Aye, afraid I'll have to agree with Baran; you wouldn't survive a single night in the wild drifts, especially as winter has fallen." Bodrin shook his head ruefully.

Waving them both to silence, Ulthrac stared at her for a very long moment as though sizing her up. She could feel his blue eyes piercing through every inch of her mind, reading in her gaze all the aspects and virtues that had formed her into the woman she was. Then, with a blink, the inspection was over. "It is a bold risk to be sure. The underground passages would certainly be safer and faster."

Jorna nodded slowly. There was no point in denying that what he said was true and so she wasted no time in providing her answer. "There is no certainty that the tunnels near Dwenenar are not being watched. For this quest to be successful, it will require great care and stealth. A journey over the Beldrath *is* more perilous and that is exactly why any fiends that remain in the city will not expect it."

The knowledge of hidden entrances, of which there were several leading into the mountain from the surface, she did not reveal. Only the royal family knew of their existence and how to access them and she felt it was wise to keep this information secret, even from her allies.

"Hmm..." The king scratched at his chin whiskers again, appearing deep in thought for several long moments before sitting up abruptly and motioning to Jorna. "If you please, Princess, I would like a moment to discuss this matter with my advisers. This is a weighty decision; surely you agree that it would be unwise to make it without due contemplation. But fear not, for it must also be dealt with in a swift manner. Please, wait outside the hall and we will call for you shortly."

Without question or hesitation, she respectfully bowed and swept out of the chamber. There was no need to press for an immediate answer. She could understand that Ulthrac and his advisers would not be pleased at the notion of sending a woman with just one warrior to retrieve an artifact so important, but unless they sent an army, there simply was no other viable option. There was little doubt in her mind that he was a wise and fair king and so she remained confident that he would agree to her plan, even if he wasn't entirely happy with it.

Even still, the time she spent waiting in the hallway felt endless. In reality, she was only there for about twenty minutes, but with each second that ticked by, she began to feel more and more anxious. It took all of her willpower not to show any visible sign of relief when Bodrin came to summon her back inside. Once his back was turned though, she allowed herself a faint smile. It faded the moment she saw the somber expressions on Baran and Ulthrac's faces. Had they decided against her?

A twinge of nervousness squirmed in her belly as Bodrin took his place to the king's left. Only when the Historian was settled did Ulthrac begin to speak. Time seemed to stop as he slowly opened his mouth, taking a deep breath, his whiskers shifting against his wide chest and then finally, the verdict came.

"It is no light matter that you have brought before us, Jorna Hailstone. As such, the decision was not an easy one to make. Were this an ordinary foe, we would disregard your request for a single warrior and send an army to crush the invaders. The secret of Goldsteel is worth a strong response, however..." He leaned forward, his eyes locked with hers. "Given the circumstances, such brash action is simply reckless. We must look to our own borders so that we will be prepared should these foul creatures darken our lands as well, but still, something must be done about the book..."

"Yes, my Lord," Jorna agreed earnestly, so on edge that she dared not breathe.

Her intense expression must have humored him, for Ulthrac suddenly released a soft chuckle as he settled back against his throne. "Relax, Princess, we have ruled in your favor; you will get your warrior and your provisions."

This time she allowed her relief to show as she bowed low, gracious words forming on her lips. But before she could begin to utter her immense gratitude, Baran took up where Ulthrac had left off. "Don't get too excited, lass," he said gruffly, "There are stipulations."

"What sort of stipulations?" Jorna straightened, allowing a touch of concern to tighten her brow.

"I was getting to that," the General grunted, shifting his shoulders in annoyance. "First off, we're granting you just two months to complete your quest. In that time, we will have fortified the city and evacuated the rest of the outlying towns. Once Hamdralg is secured, if you're not back, we will assume that you failed and send an army to reclaim Dwenenar. Is that clear?"

Jorna showed her agreement by nodding; there was nothing wrong with having a contingency plan should her mission be unsuccessful.

Though she greatly hoped it would prove to be unnecessary.

"Given the dire and dangerous circumstances of this matter, we will not order any of our warriors to accompany you," Bodrin began to explain their final terms. "Instead Baran will speak with a handful of his best men, if they are willing, then they will be gathered together. From that selection you may choose a champion, and at dawn tomorrow your supplies will be ready for you to depart."

"Very well, is there anything else?" Jorna hoped not.

The three men exchanged a glance and then Ulthrac shook his head. With nothing else to discuss, Jorna departed from the throne room a few minutes later, leaving them to make the necessary arrangements. She had no desire to get involved in the finer details. Her part was to choose a warrior based on his abilities and then reclaim the book.

A sudden thought brought her to an abrupt halt halfway to Javrin's rooms. Soon she would leave the safety of Hamdralg, travel hundreds of leagues at the turn of winter to sneak back into her conquered homeland and reclaim an artifact at the very heart of the fallen city. Any relief she'd felt at being granted her request was washed away.

Until this moment it had seemed a simple task, but now the immense weight of what she was about to do sat on her heart like a massive stone. If she failed, the secret of Goldsteel might be lost forever, or worse, claimed by an army of nightmarish monsters.

King Guldorn would have not backed down from this challenge and Jorna, determined to honor her father's memory, refused to let fear and doubt sway her now. She would find a way to overcome whatever obstacles lay ahead. For her father. For Dwenenar.

Blacksmith's Ire

Thane's belly grumbled as he worked, reminding him it was nearly evening and that meant almost time to enjoy the hearty supper his mother and sister-in-law were no doubt preparing at that very moment. Despite its insistence, he barely noticed his hunger. He was pounding away at the beginning of an axe blade, his thoughts running free as they often did these days. Now at least his mind wasn't wringing every drop of agony out of the battle that had claimed his brother's life. Instead, it was focused entirely on the Dwenenari princess.

Their brief conversation together had stuck with him over the last couple of weeks, distracting him as he worked. Ever since Thunar's death, he felt as though a powerful inferno had been scorching him from the inside out, slowly and painfully consuming him until her cool gray eyes had quelled the blaze, and now he longed to feel her soothing gaze upon him once more.

For the first several days he felt a strong impulse to seek her out, if only so he had the chance to steal a few moments of her time, that he might have more memories of her to keep him company in his ruminations. He quickly swept such desires away, reminding himself that he had no place in her world. He tried with marginal success to forget about her as she had no doubt already forgotten him.

That was when his mind really got away from him. Stronger and stronger the voice in his head pressed, but he always managed to convince himself that bursting into the palace in order to see her would be nothing short of sheer folly. There were few social barriers separating them as he came from a prestigious family. Her brothers might disagree, but his parents would have no grievances about him courting someone from Dwenenar. That she was a princess would only sweeten the deal in Baran's eyes.

Mostly, in matters of love and marriage, the Sarven were an open people. They didn't place many restrictions on who you could or could not be with based on wealth or rank. No, that was not the problem at all; the problem was nothing that could be controlled by anyone except Thane himself.

The steady thrum of his hammer abruptly stopped as he realized that he'd once again lost track of his work. "Damn," he muttered the curse as he discarded the deformed metal into the slack tub, wiping sweat from his face with the back of his arm.

Knowing that there was no point in continuing to work in his present state of mind, Thane began to clean up for the night, returning his tools to their proper places and cooling down the forge. He left the misshapen axe head where it was, deciding that he could figure out what to do with it in the morning. When everything was in order, he tugged his shirt on over his head and left through the storefront.

No sooner had he entered the housing quarter that a crowd of gossiping wives caught his ear. Had one of them said something about Jorna Hailstone or had Thane gone completely mad? Slowing his pace so that he could eavesdrop without appearing to, he kept his head down and his eyes on the road as he passed by them.

"...no husband of mine is going off alone with an unwed princess," one of them said shrewishly. "Maybe in Dwenenar it's acceptable for a young woman to run off alone with a man, but here in Hamdralg we've got standards!"

"That's absolutely right," another chimed in, "but you know how it goes, Drekna. When a woman flaunts herself like that, there's always some idiot-brained man willing to make a fool of himself for her!"

"I heard it was for some secret quest, something dangerous." The third voice was meek, as though this woman was hesitant to disagree with her fellows. "My brother was going to volunteer, the General even asked him, but with another baby coming any day, he refused. He said the stakes were too high, let some other fool without a family to feed take care of it..." The rest of what she was saying and any responses she might have gotten faded away as Thane continued down the street and turned the corner.

Thane frowned at the remarks, displeased for some reason that he couldn't put his finger on. Was it the negative words against her character? The manner in which the women tore at her, suggesting she had anything but pure motives, certainly frustrated him. But no, it was the idea of a bunch of arrogant brutes vying to be alone with Jorna that made his shoulders tense. For some reason it simply didn't sit right with him, but in spite of the unease in his gut, he wasn't about to get involved.

It wasn't the danger they had implied. He could hold his own in a fight and might even call himself somewhat good thanks to all the time spent training with his brother, but he was not a glory seeking oaf. He was a simple, common blacksmith and that's exactly the way he liked it. So why had his blood suddenly turned hot?

Shaking the feeling away, he did his best not to dwell on it, forcing himself to instead focus on the path home. A few minutes later, he was quite relieved when the sight of his parents' house came into view. It was customary for unmarried, adult children to continue living with their parents until they found a spouse. Even then, it wasn't unheard of for a young couple to take their time finding new lodgings, especially since locating a place that would be adequate for a family was not always so easy. Often times houses were passed down, usually to the last sibling to marry, who also typically inherited the honor of taking care of the elderly parents in their final years.

In the case of a widow, such as Makira, she would continue to live with her husband's parents or Thane's family, should he ever marry. At least until her children were grown and then it was likely that she would dwell with one of them. Nobody would ever view her as a burden though. The Sarven viewed caring for family as a matter of honor and duty. Makira, and other women like her, would be welcomed and loved by their spouse's relatives as if she were blood.

As soon as the front door was opened, Thane was assailed with the powerful aroma of roasted meat and fried spuds. The smell instantly chased away all other thoughts except filling his complaining stomach. Making his way to the kitchen, he saw right away that everyone was already present.

As usual the room was in complete chaos. Makira was having marginal success at keeping Varan and Kesra from picking at one another. Baran was grumbling that his meal was late again, causing Ravika to curtly inform him that next time he could cook and see how well it turned out. This was the same conversation his parents had been exchanging since he was old enough to remember and somehow, it never felt tiring.

"Ah Thane, you're just in time." Makira was the first to notice him come inside, but her attention was abruptly diverted back to her children as Kesra squealed indignantly that her brother had dabbed gravy in her hair.

The greeting was enough to alert Ravika that her son was home, which brought a broad grin to her square face. Leaving Baran to finish making his own plate, much to his dismay, she hurried around the table, pausing only to deliver a warning thump to the top of Varan's head.

When she reached Thane, she wrapped her arms around him in a tight hug, squeezing him until he almost couldn't breathe. He would never admit it to anyone, but being greeted by his mother each evening was largely the highlight of his day, despite having his bones crushed.

"Come on then, boy." She released him from the shattering embrace and ushered him to his spot at the table. While he was settling in, she began to prepare a plate for him, piling it high with excessive portions of meat, potatoes, and brown gravy. On top of it all she laid two large rolls before placing the overwhelmed dish in front of her son. "Tuck in, love." She kissed the top of his head, patting his shoulder as she moved to take her own seat.

Now that everyone was sitting down, Ravika the last as always, the conversation immediately picked back up. "You know that's the problem with this one." Baran's bellowing baritone seemed louder now that Thane was sitting across from him, though to hear his father speak he wasn't even in the room. "You never make him do anything for himself! You've pampered and spoiled him like a wee girl!"

"Oh, just stuff your gob, you old goat." Shaking her head of long, black curls, Ravika glowered a warning at him.

Baran started to ignore it, opening his mouth to continue the tirade, but the increasingly stern expression on his wife's face made him hesitate. Before he could decide one way or the other, speak or remain silent, Varan changed the subject to the one thing Thane was not keen on discussing in the least.

"We heard about the princess's quest, Grandfather," he burst excitedly. "Everyone is talking about it! Is it true she's going to decide a champion?"

The General shook his head, his mouth so full that he had to swallow some before he could release a disapproving grunt. When he could speak, he began in a sneering tone, "That girl hasn't a lick of sense! I pity whatever man gets chosen; he'll most certainly be following her to his death!"

"You shouldn't underestimate her," Thane retorted before he could stop himself. The words had simply tumbled from his lips, catching everyone at the table by surprise.

He instantly wished that he had kept silent and allowed his father to rant in peace, but his temper had flared unexpectedly. He knew better than to draw attention to himself when Baran was in one of his moods, especially when he had already singled him out for ridicule. The thought of sitting there, listening idly as Jorna was disparaged, made his stomach twist into knots. His father was simply wrong. Thane remembered the strength he'd seen in Jorna, the power of her presence, and he knew without a doubt that her honor was worth defending.

Baran, however, didn't appreciate being challenged. He bristled, his beard seeming to puff out like the tail of a feral cat defending its territory. "Is that so?" he boomed, his eyes gleaming angrily. "What do you know of Jorna Hailstone, boy?"

The older Sarven stared him down until Thane finally broke and cast his gaze away. Baran seemed about to dismiss his son, but then realization struck him and his lips twisted into a mocking grin. Ravika had already made the connection and immediately tried to change the subject, but Baran was like a dog who had just been given a meaty bone and he wasn't about to relinquish it.

"Don't tell me you actually fancy her!" Baran's laughter shook the room. "What makes you think she would be interested in someone like *you*?"

Thane dared not look up, afraid that if he raised his face the whole room would be able to see the embarrassed flush that darkened his cheeks. He tried to console himself that at least his father wasn't disparaging Jorna anymore, but being made fun of for admiring her was one of the most unpleasant moments he'd ever had to endure.

"Uncle..." Kesra's soft voice drew his attention and bought him a slight reprieve. "If you really fancy her, then you should volunteer! I bet she would pick you! And she would certainly fall in love with you if you were her champion!"

The notion was touching, but it was an opinion that nobody else at the table shared. Baran only laughed harder, ignoring the furious glares coming from not only Ravika, but Makira now as well. "I'm sorry, lass," he choked, reaching over to pat her cheek fondly, "I'm not laughing at you. It's a lovely idea, but Thane is just a blacksmith. He's not a proper warrior, certainly not a champion..."

"Baran, dear, you're being an ass." The affectionate moniker was said with a distinct lack of affection. "Stop," Ravika ordered coldly.

Her attempt to end the discussion backfired, however, as it only sparked his temper to life again. "You know I'm right! He's achieved nothing with his life, he has no ambition, no stone in his belly and still you praise him for it!" Baran shook his head in disgust, his tone taking on a higher pitch as he mimicked Ravika's voice. "Oh my sweet darling, you're the best in all the land! You make Mama so proud!"

"I don't sound like that!" Ravika shot back fiercely, her dark eyes smoldering with increasing annoyance. "Now shut your gob, you've spouted your bile. Leave the boy alone!"

The fire-haired man growled, his green eyes narrowing angrily at being told to shut up. "I'm the man of this house. I'll rant and rave all night if I please!" He only grew louder as she made to rise. "And there's nothing you can do to stop me!"

For once Ravika was looking down at her husband who was normally much taller than her. "Baran, old man, you better not try my patience or so help me I'll knock your head so hard it spins backwards." She didn't raise her voice, she didn't have to. She spoke with a passion that left no room for argument, her eyes staring intently, burning into her husband's face, and daring him to challenge her again.

Baran should have known not to trifle with her, should have seen that he was pushing too hard - Thane certainly saw it, having learned long ago that his mother didn't make idle threats - but he blundered on despite the warning signs. "That's right, take his side, as usual," he bellowed. "Keep coddling the poor little baby and making excuses for his failings. Just ignore that you've made him soft!"

Through it all, Thane remained silent, watching as his parents argued back and forth. He was running what Kasra had said over and over again in his mind. Despite his efforts to dismiss it as folly, the urge to try was sounding better with each snide thing his father said. Secretly he wished nothing more than to impress Jorna, but his desire to prove Baran wrong, to show him just once that he was worthy of his respect, was much stronger. Maybe he wouldn't be chosen, maybe she wouldn't even give him a second glance, but one thing he was certain of; he had to try.

The sound of the wooden chair legs scraping against the stone floor interrupted the quarreling and drew his parents' eyes to him. Thane stood, staring hard at his father and for once letting him see the anger and resentment that he had felt for so many years. "I volunteer," he declared, his tone like steel.

"Now you listen here, boy..." Baran pointed an accusing finger in his son's direction, his tolerance for being contradicted this evening running dangerously short. "I won't deny that Jorna Hailstone has heart, but she's still only a woman and she's just going to get someone killed!" He ignored the sharp intake of air and the glower coming from his wife, his unleashed temper making him forget how sorry he'd be for making such a comment about women in front of her.

"It's not her place to gallivant around on quests, no matter if she is a shaman. She calls it duty, but it's just the fool notions of a girl who was never taught her place! And you..." he snorted, "you're better off as a nobody."

The General's view on women wasn't unique, there were plenty of other men who were staunch traditionalists of the old law and believed that even though women should learn to fight, they had no business doing so except in defense of their lives, their home, or their children. Most, like Baran's brother Bodrin, thought differently, taking historical accounts of famous female warriors as proof that the old laws, on this subject at least, were not stringent.

Thane had never bothered to decide where he stood on the matter, having little interest in such affairs, but he had realized his rather strong opinion on the subject now. He couldn't tolerate the sight of his father, of the cynical, degrading manner in which he spoke of a woman whose strengths he clearly refused to acknowledge. If only he had chosen to further poke fun at his son, Thane would have simply walked away, but he had finally been pushed too hard.

"You are a narrow-minded old fool," Thane growled without bothering to think the action through. He felt a surge of elation as the words left his lips. So many times he had dreamed of telling Baran what he really thought, but his father's remarks had never stirred his anger enough for Thane to overcome the good sense that always cautioned him to keep his mouth shut.

"You vomit up bile and filth, letting your temper get the better of you and still you think of yourself as such a big, strong man." He barked a laugh. "Once you might have been a great champion, but age has made you as fat, lazy, and spiteful as an old cow. I'm thankful that I am *nothing* like you."

Baran's shock had drained the color from his face, but as his son's words began to sink in, the ugly purple was rapidly returning. "What did you just say to me...?"

Seeing the brief moment of silence as her chance to put an end to this once and for all, Ravika quickly intervened. "That's enough from both of you!" she shouted, her dark eyes fixed sternly on her husband to keep him from interrupting. "You've said plenty, old man! And Thane..." Her gaze flashed to his face, the barest trace of disappointment evident in her expression. "I taught you better than to be so disrespectful, no matter how justified you may think you are! Now, go up to your room!"

Thane knew better than to disobey her, even if he was an adult and had been for over two hundred years now. He would have liked to let the moment unfold without interruption, to see the result of such a confrontation. Decades of being pushed around and berated were itching to break free, but Thane used every bit of his self-control to force them back down.

A large part of him knew that he was playing with fire, knew that if he pushed too hard, he would force the relationship with his father to a dark place that they would never return from. Because of this, Thane stepped away. His heart wasn't ready to give up, not yet, despite how often he had been crushed beneath his father's ridicule.

"You were always a disappointment and you always will be."

Baran's uncharacteristically calm voice caught up to him as the blacksmith reached the door. "Especially now that—" he choked on the words, not because it pained him to inflict the wound on Thane, but due to the stinging reminder of his lost son. "Especially now that Thunar isn't here to cover for your *weakness*."

Thane's shoulders sagged under the weight of those words, inciting the guilt that needed no further excuse to haunt him. Hanging his head in defeat and shame, he pushed open the dining room door and left his parents behind to finish the argument without him.

THE CHAMPION

JORNA WAS NERVOUS AS she allowed Baran to open the door to the war chamber for her and she knew exactly why. She was about to make a decision that may very well spell doom for her people if she got it wrong. She'd be a fool not to feel an anxious churning in the pit of her stomach. It must also be credited to the slightest bit of excitement. She was eager to get going, eager to reach Dwenenar and complete her task. The sooner the book was safe in her possession, the better.

This matter had to be dealt with first and so she tried to put both extremes out of her mind, focusing instead on what the General was saying.

"I found you solid recruits, Princess." His tone was more gruff than she'd ever heard it before. Now that she was paying more attention to him, she could tell he was flustered. The way he held his shoulders and the hard set of his gaze made her think of a wolf with its hackles raised. What was he so tense about? The realization did nothing to ease her own nervousness.

"Thank you, General," she offered, trying to sound as diplomatic as possible. "I'm sure it will be a tough choice." Perhaps if her mood and manner remained light, his would improve as well? She could only hope.

Leaving him at the door, she strolled inside, taking in the surroundings with a quick glance. The chamber was larger than she would have guessed, with plenty of space for twenty or so armored Sarven to stand comfortably, even more if they were packed together.

It had a large, rectangular table, that, judging by the wear marks on the floor rug, was usually placed in the center of the room, but for this, had been shoved against the back wall. Bodrin was sitting atop it, meaty hands folded in his lap. Next to him stood Javrin and King Ulthrac, the latter of which was talking quietly with the Historian. Javrin just looked impatient, as he often did when it came to matters he felt didn't warrant his time or attention. He was probably trying to feign confidence in his sister, though she knew that his faith in her was low.

Seeing that he was also in a grim mood caused Jorna to let out a soft sigh. She had hoped this would be an easy process, but she feared that with everyone in such a foul state of mind, it would drag on much longer than was necessary.

Then it occurred to her. What if she didn't find someone right away? What if there was nobody worthy and willing to put their lives on the line? Not for the first time, she wished her father was here, that his wisdom might bring a solution that would please everyone.

"Well, sister," Javrin muttered to her as she took up a position beside him, "I hope you know what you're doing..."

"Your vote of confidence is appreciated," she replied tightly, finding that her own mood had plummeted considerably since she'd walked into the chamber.

She could feel his piercing stare on her but refused to look at him. His negativity was the last thing she needed and so she was determined not to give him the satisfaction of glaring back at him. They had discussed this matter, arrived at a solution, and both knew full well there was nothing else they could do. This was the best course, whether he believed her capable of fulfilling the task or not. She wasn't about to sway from it.

That cold determination bolstered her resolve but did nothing to change her grumpiness. Even the sight of the four burly, battle hardened warriors being led inside by Baran did nothing to make her feel better. She watched without expression as he lined them up, shoulder-to-shoulder and then turned back to her. With a curt jerk of his head, he indicated that she should join him and so, with arms crossed over her chest, Jorna complied.

"These are four of my best men," he started, "You should be thankful they're standing here. Don't forget that Hamdralg's warriors are no cowards."

She took a deep breath before responding, needing that fraction of a second to keep from snapping at him. "Your warriors honor not only me, but all the Dwenenari. We are grateful," she remarked instead, her tone genuine, though what she really wanted to do was roll her eyes at his sour demeanor.

That would have gained them nothing. The General was sending someone on a dangerous mission, possibly to their death; he had the right to be bothered by that. She would have thought less of him if he wasn't.

Her comments seemed to ease him and he nodded, putting a hand on her shoulder so that he could guide her to the first man. He was the tallest of the bunch, though he remained an inch or two shorter than Baran. "This is Nargith Skullbane of the Ironbear Clan. He's slain a hundred giants and left their skulls shattered on the battlefield."

The brute gave her a curt salute. "It would be my honor to protect you, Princess," he declared in a rumbling voice. "I will see that you leave and return all in one piece."

"Thank you, Nargith." Jorna smiled graciously at him, not belying that she found his vow of protection to be a little upsetting. She wanted someone to fight with her, not for her. She wasn't looking for a babysitter.

Baran led her to the next warrior. He was broad in the shoulders, narrow at the waist, with two large hands that seemed more adequate for breaking skulls than Nargith's. "And this, this is Valrig Tinyfist of the Swifthawk Clan. He is the son of Thredor the Brave, leader of the Swifthawks and has seen his fair share of combat."

"My father always spoke highly of Thredor." Jorna gave Valrig the honor of a bow as she said this. Her father's praise meant a great deal to her, for he did not give it lightly.

"I am grateful, Princess," he answered, bowing back. "You have my sympathies for his loss, I am sorry I did not get the chance to meet King Guldorn. I have heard he was a great and wise man." He bowed again.

Jorna smiled, her heart touched and softened by the compliment. "Yes, he was indeed."

Before she could say more, Baran was leading her on. She tried to listen as he introduced the next warrior, but the sound of the door opening caused her to miss his name. It took all her willpower not to look at who had entered, but instead, to bow to the man in front of her and thank him for being present. As such, she didn't get a glimpse of the newcomer. All she knew was that he had joined the line, so she didn't fret. She'd eventually get to see who had arrived late.

"Gargern the Render of the Blackboar Clan. He stood against an entire tribe of savage orcs and defeated them all." Baran grinned and the fourth warrior pounded his own chest proudly. Jorna was certain that there was plenty of exaggeration, as there often was in the retelling of mighty deeds, but she knew better than to call any warrior out for being boastful.

"An impressive feat," she started to say, but a derisive snort from the latecomer kept her from finishing.

She couldn't help herself anymore. She flicked her gaze to him and gasped openly when she saw who was standing there. She wasn't the only one. Baran's face had turned as red as his hair, his fury unmasked as he stared in outrage, while behind her, the others were muttering quietly. Even the warriors were trying to get a good look at him, and as soon as they realized who he was, they began to laugh.

"Thane Stoutforge," Jorna spoke the name softly, a mix of surprise and pleasure filling her chest. She was glad to see him there, glad to see the proud and determined look in his eyes. She couldn't have said why exactly, all she knew was the sight of him blew away the doubts, the fears, and the crankiness.

Beside her, as she tried to regain control of herself, Baran found his voice again. "You," he bellowed. "You do not belong here, *blacksmith*!" He hurled the word like an insult and indeed to a man whose life had focused around battle, having a son who did not pursue a career as a warrior or who lacked clear ambition was certainly a disgrace.

The other warriors laughed even harder, jeering at Thane in a way that greatly displeased Jorna. She wanted to defend him. She looked back at Bodrin and Ulthrac, hoping one of them might as she had no authority here, but they were watching Thane, no doubt wanting to see how he handled himself first. Though she disliked it, Jorna followed their example, turning her gaze back to the blacksmith to see how he would respond.

Thane drew himself up, his hands clenched into fists, his shoulders squared. "Yes, I'm a blacksmith," he shouted at Baran so loudly the room nearly shook.

Silence fell immediately, though the General was still glaring with fury at his son. "I am a blacksmith, but I am also a Sarven and that means a warrior as well," Thane continued.

Then suddenly, he fixed his eyes onto Jorna and dropped to one knee. "All that I am I pledge to the purpose of Jorna Hailstone. Whether you choose me or not, fair lady, I will serve you even with my dying breath."

Jorna felt a shiver of inspiration as she stared back into his unwavering gaze. There was no doubt in that moment, no uncertainty. Perhaps he was only a blacksmith, but of every man in this room, he alone had fought the same monsters and survived. Besides, when she looked into his eyes, she saw a man desperate to prove his worth and she found kinship in that desire.

"I accept." The words fell softly from her lips, drawing everyone's gaze to her, but Jorna ignored them and smiled at Thane. "Thane Stoutforge will be my champion."

All at once the room erupted. The warriors were suddenly outraged that they had been upstaged by a blacksmith. Baran was bellowing at Thane incoherently, he was so furious now, while Bodrin in turn was yelling at Baran for being so harsh on his son. Ulthrac was the only one who remained quiet, watching the events unfold with the expression of a man discerning every detail.

Javrin suddenly appeared at Jorna's side, grabbing her arm roughly and spinning her to face him. The look in his eyes was frightening, wild and hateful. "You fool! I forbid you to journey anywhere with that *failure*," he hissed, squeezing her arm even tighter. "If you are so incompetent, woman, I will make the selection for you!"

She had never seen her brother act so hostile toward her. The shock of his seething outburst gave her pause, but only for a moment. "No, you won't!" Jorna's own temper flared and she shoved her brother away. "Enough! Enough, all of you!" She moved to stand in front of Baran, blocking his path to Thane. "It is my decision alone and I have made it! I choose Thane Stoutforge!"

With the room quieting down again, Ulthrac finally stepped in. "Perhaps they would understand better, if you explained why." His voice and demeanor were both kind, as though he had already perceived the answer. It gave Jorna courage to see that the king at least supported her. No matter what anyone else thought, Ulthrac's voice carried the most weight.

"Because he..." She half turned, glancing back at Thane as she tried to find the words. She knew what she wanted to say but was certain nobody would understand her feelings. They needed hard facts, something to make them think she wasn't being a sentimental fool but had actually thought the decision out logically. That she felt a sense of common ground with him simply didn't matter. "He's faced these creatures before and lived. Of the warriors here, that feat tops the rest."

Her confidence in the decision swelled the more she spoke. "You have killed giants and savages, but have you killed a monster straight from nightmare? Thane Stoutforge has." She fixed her gaze on Baran, daring him to contradict her. "He *is* a warrior and now, he will be my champion."

Before anyone could object, Ulthrac clapped his hands together and spoke in a commanding tone, a tone that left no room for further argument. "Then it is decided. Warriors, your willingness does you honor, and though you were not chosen, know that your king has seen the mettle in your hearts." He motioned toward the door. "You may leave now."

The room was filled with stony silence as the four rather perplexed and annoyed men, filed out. Jorna could only imagine the discussion they would have as they returned to their stations and the gossip that would spread throughout Hamdralg. Whatever was said, whatever anyone else thought, she remained confident in her decision.

"Well, Thane Stoutforge," the king continued once the chamber had been sealed again, "you have taken on a heavy responsibility. Accompany Bodrin; he will provide you with information regarding your quest. Prepare yourself, you leave at dawn tomorrow."

Ulthrac shifted his gaze from Thane to Baran and then Javrin in turn. "I would like to speak with Jorna alone," was all he needed to say to dismiss them along with the others.

Jorna could feel her brother's eyes on her, but she refused to look at him. Whatever had come over him, causing him to treat her as he had just moments ago, she would not simply forget. It was true that he was under an enormous strain and sitting back while she took action must have been driving Javrin mad, but that was no excuse for his behavior.

With the room empty of all except herself and King Ulthrac, Jorna allowed the tension to leave her body. It was a subtle change, the slightest relaxing of her shoulders as the door clicked shut.

"I have known your father for many, many years," Ulthrac began. His eyes searched her face, his expression intent, but not stern. "I know the depth of his pride and faith in you, which is a large part of why I have agreed to this quest. Guldorn was not an easy man to impress and though you are his daughter, he was not blindly biased toward anyone." He laid a gentle hand on her shoulder. "However, I would be remiss if I did not caution you."

She nodded, indicating that she was listening.

"Your journey will be dangerous and your supplies limited. This is no task for the faint of heart. Keep your wits about you, trust nothing save yourself and your champion. And," he reached into an inner fold of his shirt and produced a worn, folded piece of parchment, "you can trust this. It is an old map of the Beldrath from the time of the Giant Wars, but it contains scout's markers that indicate shelters and dangers. My ancestor was a scout during the Wars; this map kept him alive and has since become an heirloom of my family."

Ulthrac extended the map to Jorna, who took it with a deep bow. "Thank you, good king," she bestowed him with a smile. "I will heed its wisdom and return it to you once my quest has reached its end. Thank you, for all that you have done for me and my people." She bowed again.

The king squeezed her shoulder. "Go now, tomorrow comes swiftly."

BLUEBERRIES

EVEN WITH ALL HE had to accomplish, the day passed far too slowly for Thane. He was eager to leave Hamdralg, to put distance between himself and his father until the aftermath of their fight had blown over.

Baran had refused to speak another word, for that much he was grateful, but the silence was somehow worse. Thankfully they didn't see much of each other, for the General was still needed at the palace and Thane had preparations to make in order to close the forge while he was gone.

That night, when they were in the same room together, the very air felt thick with the unexpressed anger and hurt, despite the womenfolk trying to help the two stubborn men patch things up.

Ravika especially did her best to get them talking, as though she were desperate for her family to be on good terms before her son departed on a dangerous quest. If she wasn't stressing the importance of mending hurt feelings with his father, then she was practically begging

Thane not to go.

He knew she was only worried for his safety, afraid of losing another child, but he couldn't let that weaken his resolve. Instead, he did his best to assure his mother that he would take care of himself, though he wisely refrained from promising to return home alive. He felt certain that doing so would only invite disaster.

The next morning, Thane awoke earlier than the rest of his family. He dressed quietly in his room, fighting the nagging voice in his mind that told him over and over that he was heading toward failure. He wasn't good enough to be chosen for this sort of task, not skilled or brave enough to be of any use to anyone, much less a princess.

These doubts continued to nip at him as he gathered the leather satchel of his personal belongings, then chased him out the door and down the hall. More than once he nearly turned back, his father's voice ringing loudly in his ears that he would never amount to anything. He was a useless lump, he was weak, he was nobody...

His pace faltered on the stairs as he trudged slowly down them until he was forcing himself to keep going, one more step, then one more and one more after that. It would be so easy to turn around, to return upstairs and slip back into his room. He could fall into bed, pull the blankets up over his head, and shut out the cruel, cold, pointless world. When he came to the final step, he ground to a halt, one foot partially extended, frozen in place as if he were pausing on the edge of oblivion.

A part of him just wanted life to return to an easier time, when his brother was alive and nobody had any real expectations of him or even knew he existed. He liked it that way, liked being left alone to his daily routine of rise, eat, work, eat, sleep, repeat. Every second of every day was the same, no change, no spontaneity, just the blissful surety of convention.

For a second, he was decided. He settled his foot back on the step and let his pack slip from his shoulder. He was determined to remain home and focus his energies on getting his life in proper order once again. Not to mention forgetting entirely about the fair Dwenenari princess, who... He didn't even let himself finish the thought.

The abrupt reminder of Jorna made him realize just how unhappy he had been before. His life was dull, empty, meaningless until she appeared and gave him a purpose. This was his chance to do something worthwhile, to break out of the tired, old rut that he'd been digging for as long as he could remember. She had given him a chance to be something *more* and he found, for the first time in his life, he actually wanted more.

Thane's feet made up his mind, stepping off the last step and carrying him toward the front door that was just at the end of the hallway. Conviction tightened around his heart, fortifying his resolve to boldly face whatever challenges he was walking into. Not for his sake or for glory or honor, but for the benefit of one woman who was brave enough to put her duty above her own safety. If she could find such courage, then he could as well.

"Thane?"

The voice stopped him dead in his tracks, just a couple of paces from the door. Frantically he tried to find an escape, wondering if he could sprint out of the house and believably pretend he hadn't heard his name being called. His new resolution made him ready to face anything. Except his brother's wife.

"I was hoping to catch you," Makira continued to say, her voice hushed so as not to disturb the rest of the household. "I feel like you've been avoiding me since..." She trailed off.

Thane half turned to face her, taking in her appearance with a glance. She had a crochet blanket wrapped tightly around her shoulders, the one Ravika had made for her as a gift after she and Thunar had announced their marriage. Her golden hair was disheveled, belying that she had spent the night tossing and turning, and her soft, hazel eyes were rimmed with red. She looked tired and not because of the early hour; he had often noticed how run down she seemed, even in the middle of the day.

He tore his gaze away, guilt and sorrow ripping at his heart. He was too ashamed to look into her face, afraid of what he might find staring back at him. In his mind he could hear his brother's voice, lovingly whispering her name as his life ebbed and he wished that he was strong enough to tell her just how much her husband had adored her, but he couldn't form the words.

I should have been the one to die...

Makira took a step closer, her desire to reconcile whatever was wrong between them written clearly on her face. "I have missed you," she told him gently. "Have you forgotten that you are my brother, too?"

All he could do was shake his head, his tongue feeling too heavy and thick to form coherent speech.

She studied him closely for a long moment. He could feel her sad eyes searching his face, though he still dared not look at her. Finally she gave up waiting for him to answer and began to muse aloud, her voice tinged with melancholy. "I will never forget the day I met Thunar. I was working in the merchant quarter with my parents, and he wandered up to the stall, trying to charm me. He was so handsome." She trailed off for a moment, losing herself in the memory. "He was also very arrogant, too sure of himself, always bragging, and I refused to court him for those reasons. But, day after day, he kept coming back. He'd buy a basket of blueberries from my father and spend the next several minutes trying to woo me..."

Thane knew this story he'd heard them tell it over and over again to anyone who would listen. He also vividly remembered the span of over a month where the only fruit the family seemed to eat was blueberries and nobody could figure out why.

Ravika claimed they simply appeared in the kitchen one afternoon, then again the next day and the next day until eventually she was warning them all that if she ever saw another blueberry again, she'd lose her mind.

When they learned that it was due to Thunar's most recent crush, nobody was impressed. He had such a habit of becoming infatuated with a new girl every so often that their parents were beginning to think he would never be able to settle down with anyone.

"It wasn't until I saw him with you, that I realized there was more to him than what he tried to show me," Makira continued on, having recovered from a lapse of silence. "I was always taught to chose a man based on how he treated his family, and I knew when I saw the two of you together that I was seeing the real Thunar at last."

Tears sparkled in her eyes and her voice cracked, but she managed to confess, "I never told him why I eventually said yes to his advances. It had become a joke between us. He would try to guess, but he was always so wrong." She hung her head, no doubt to hide the tears she couldn't hold back any longer. "I always thought that someday, when he least expected it, I would tell him the real reason..."

If she was trying to comfort him, she was doing a terrible job of it, Thane thought. All she had done was make him feel worse, adding fuel to the already blazing fire of guilt. Despite this, he listened anyway, knowing that her words could have been much, much worse.

Composing herself, Makira reached out for him, her hand gripping his arm as the other swiped at the trails of moisture on her cheeks. "He was always proud of you, always faithful that someday you'd find your way, that all you really needed was time."

Thane squeezed his eyes shut, feeling that he didn't deserve the kind things she was telling him. Let her scream and yell, let her berate and ridicule him for failing to bring her husband home, that he was prepared for, not this, not this at all.

"I know that deep down Baran blames himself. He gave Thunar that assignment, trying to test his resolve, trying to prove that he would never show favoritism, even to his own son." She spoke with confidence, though this could only have been based on a woman's intuition.

"It's a truth he can't deal with yet and so he wrongly blames you for something that was not your fault. That you refuse to look at me, even now, tells me that you blame yourself as well." He felt her fingers on his chin, lifting his head so that his face was no longer hidden. "Look at me," she pleaded softly.

Thane finally relented, opening his eyes so that he could meet her gaze. He expected to see the exhaustion and sorrow but found himself surprised by the deep sense of caring. Immediately, he realized Makira held no ill feelings toward him and probably never had, instead she had taken it upon herself to watch over him in Thunar's place. They were kin, brother and sister as surely as if they were related by blood and nothing would ever change that.

"My husband loved his family more than he loved himself, a fact he proved when he gave his own life for yours," she told him sternly. "Perhaps, if you hadn't been there, he might have lived, none of us can say for certain. What I do know is this..." She moved her hand to his shoulder, squeezing it meaningfully as she continued, "Had he died as just another fallen warrior, his death would have meant *nothing*. At least this way, his death was worth something."

They stared at one another for a long moment, her words wrapping themselves around Thane's heart and protecting him against all the doubt and despair that had plagued him since that fateful day. She had given him a sense of relief he didn't feel he quite deserved, but he was grateful to her nonetheless.

"Be safe," her voice was hushed once again, barely above a whisper, "and let your deeds honor his name." Her hand fell away as she turned from him, having said everything she needed to. The rest would be up to Thane.

This was a fact he very well knew; it shed his impending quest in a whole new light. Now he wasn't just going to help a princess, he was going to find the part of himself that his brother had always known was there and that his sister had just put her faith in. Like her words, that faith was a gift, a beacon of hope that perhaps he could finally find a way to succeed in the task that he was undertaking. He owed her far more than he could ever truly repay her for, which meant he would need to start immediately.

Catching her arm, Thane drew Makira into a tight hug, burying his face in her shoulder as a child would when seeking comfort. He felt her arms return the embrace, heard her sniffling back a new wave of tears as he whispered, "Goodbye, sister."

8

STEPS OF BULVAI

NOW THAT JORNA HAD made her decision, King Ulthrac wasted no time in supplying the promised provisions. He even included a little surprise for her: three of the finest Sarven muskox in Hamdralg. They were very similar to the wild muskox found in this mountain range, but these had been bred for generations to be bigger and even more hardy than their cousins.

During the Giant Wars, they were used to travel over the harsh peaks, carrying siege equipment and supplies to the various battle-fields. Many were also trained to act as battle mounts, bearing Sarven warriors into combat. Those days may have been long ago, but the muskox were still essential to Sarven living. Whether carrying a rider or pulling a cart, the shaggy animal remained the primary beasts of burden in the underground society.

The three given to Jorna by Ulthrac varied only slightly in color. The one that had already been loaded with their supplies was closer to black, while the other two were dark brown. These were riding muskox, trained to carry a rider anywhere, even into battle. The only distinction between them was that one had more blond along his back.

This was the one Jorna selected, drawn to his intelligent eyes and the sweet gray muzzle that sniffed curiously at the shaman's approach. Letting the muskox inspect her, she gently scratched around his ears until the beast had decided she was no longer of interest. With the introduction finished, she moved around to check that the plain saddle, laden with a couple extra fur blankets and water skins, was secure.

Much to her relief, Thane had arrived at the top of the staircase on the surface level only a couple minutes after her. He was carrying a satchel of personal essentials that he attached to the pack animal before gathering up the lead rope. Once his own checks were finished, he gave her a slight nod to let her know he was ready whenever she was.

She opened her mouth, about to call out to him, when the sound of Javrin speaking her name took her by surprise. "Leaving without a goodbye, sister?" His voice sounded cordial enough, but to someone who knew him as well as she did, she could sense the distance between them.

"Javrin," she greeted him, looking at him for the first time since his outburst the day before. "If you have come to argue, then you have wasted the trip."

She wasn't sure what it was about her decision that had upset him or if that even had anything to do with his treatment of her since their arrival in Hamdralg. Perhaps it was the weight of his new responsibilities as leader of the Dwenenari people, perhaps it was something else entirely. Whatever it was, it would have been better for him to confide it in her, rather than allowing his feelings to fester.

She saw his jaw clench beneath his beard and braced for another outburst, but a second later he let out a sigh. The act seemed to deflate him, his shoulders slouching and an expression of concern taking over his features.

"Forgive me, Jorna." He stepped closer. "I do not wish you to depart this way. I am sorry for my manner, but I have often felt..." He put a hand on her shoulder and squeezed it gently. "I worry for you," Javrin finally confessed.

Jorna let her face soften, knowing it must have been difficult for him to admit such a thing to her. "That worry does you a disservice. I will return in no time; you'll barely notice I was gone. Especially as I'm sure caring for our people will keep you very busy." She gave his hand a soft pat. "I must go, you must remain. That is the lot fate has carved for us, brother."

"Yes, I know. But knowing and accepting are two different things." Javrin leaned over and placed a soft kiss on her forehead, his expression turning somber and his gaze belying a touch of fear.

For a moment he looked as though he had something to say, but he must have thought better of it. Giving her shoulder a final squeeze, he turned toward Thane, who was waiting patiently near his mount.

She thought about intercepting him, uncertain what Javrin was considering, but in the time it took for her to weigh the action, he had already skirted around her and was standing at Thane's side.

"A word, blacksmith." Javrin's tone was tight, leaving no room for the other man to refuse. He didn't wait for a response; he dropped his voice to a menacing whisper so that Jorna couldn't hear what he was about to say.

Frowning, she strained to hear but couldn't make out his words. The exchange was brief enough that she had little time to interject before Javrin spun on his heel and walked back to her. "Be safe and good luck." He kissed her forehead one last time.

Echoing his words, Jorna watched him stroll away, wondering what he'd said to her companion. One look at Thane told her that he wouldn't be sharing any details as he was already leading the two muskox toward the gates.

In truth, she had a good idea what sorts of things her protective older brother might have muttered in her defense, but she had a strong feeling that the reminder wouldn't be necessary. With a shrug, she put it behind her and hurried to catch up to Thane.

This level acted as a sort of entryway for the rest of the city. There weren't any buildings, just a broad hallway lined with tapestries depicting ancient battles and heroes. The only other passage was to their right and led upward to the Vista of Kings where an open balcony overlooked the beautiful, snowy landscape of the Beldrath mountain range, home to the Sarvens' underground realms. That place was reserved for only the most special of occasions, namely for crowning kings and royal celebrations such as marriages or the birth of a ruler's first born.

The observatory was not their destination; they were headed for the front gates. Like all Sarven kingdoms, the doors to their city were a reflection of the people who had built them. The Gates to Hamdralg were massive, heavy slabs of stone cut directly out of the mountain. No man could open those doors on his own. It required using a clever mechanism akin to a pulley to part the large rock.

Beyond the gates, the roadway leading up the side of the mountain was little more than a rocky slope. It had been a source of great frustration to merchants and farmers attempting to guide wagons of produce or merchandise to the city long ago. The good thing about it, in fact, the only reason that it hadn't been improved, was that in all the centuries since Hamdralg was built not a single army had made it to the gates.

The Sarven had built in many defense mechanisms to render the slope nigh impassable in times of imminent invasion. Unfortunately, once those defenses had been put into place, all those inside were pretty much stuck there. As a result, the homes and farms built in the valley beneath the gates, having little by way of defense, had been completely destroyed a number of times in Hamdralg's history before eventually being abandoned. Now that the Sarven were entirely self-sufficient and didn't need to rely on surface-grown crops, few of their citizens cared to leave the mountain's comfort and protection.

Stepping over the threshold nearly blinded Jorna, who raised an arm to block out the vast brightness of the outside world. It had been many years since her last excursion to the surface. She scarcely remembered it and so the assault of new smells and sounds came as a bit of a shock. The air was fresh and crisp, tickling her lungs as she inhaled. Beneath her feet, the snow crunched with every step she took and a sharp wind nipped at her exposed skin. It was invigorating and overwhelming all at once.

As soon as her eyes had adjusted to the glaring brightness, she glanced up into the sky, meaning to gauge what the weather might be like, but she soon wished she hadn't. A wave of dizziness slammed into her, causing her to stagger a step as she reached out to steady herself.

She tangled her fingers into the muskox's fur, letting the coarseness anchor her until she was able to regain her reeling senses. The sky was so vast and endless, not dark and solid like the rocky ceiling of her underground home and would certainly take some getting used to.

The steep roadway was covered in a thin layer of fine, white snow, making it a bit more treacherous than it might have been during more mild seasons. Thankfully the wind kept the path from becoming too piled up, which was a huge benefit considering nobody maintained it otherwise. They waited until they were further outside to mount up, trusting the rocky path to the muskoxen who were built for easily traversing ground under such conditions.

Jorna turned abruptly at the rumbling sound of the gates being shut behind them. On the outside, they blended almost perfectly into the side of the mountain, unadorned and naturally camouflaged as added protection against invaders.

Dwenenar had not taken this approach. Its doors were ornate, reflecting the considerable wealth of the city below, but perhaps that was part of the problem. They had been so casual in flaunting their assets instead of remaining humble. She almost wanted to add, like the people of Hamdralg, but she knew the only reason they hadn't done the same. In a time when they were the sole civilization of Sarven, with no allies except the humans and elves, they had chosen practicality over all else.

"Are you ready?" Thane's deep voice pulled her from her thoughts.

A shiver of unease ran down her spine, as her eyes fell to the path that stretched out before them. It certainly would have been easier to travel to Dwenenar by the same route that her people had taken to reach Hamdralg, but the fear that those passages were being watched kept her from using them. If there was to be any hope of success, she would need the element of surprise in order to reach the vault unseen.

"Yes," she finally answered, drawing her cloak tighter around her shoulders as she urged her mount to start down the road.

For the better part of the day, they remained in the foothills, following a trail marked on the old map that Ulthrac had given Jorna. The snow wasn't very deep here, which allowed them to travel at a decent pace.

They stopped around midday to share a quick meal of bread and cheese and to let the muskoxen rest before pushing forward.

When the sun began to set a handful of hours later, they took shelter from the wind in a dense grove of snow-laden pines. The air was a few degrees cooler beneath them, but that didn't matter much once night set in. A small fire was all they dared to make and so they sat huddled close to it, eating a brothy potato soup that didn't quite fill Jorna up.

While Thane cleaned up the remnants of their dinner and made sure the muskoxen were settled in, Jorna boiled snow to replenish the water they'd used. For the last hour before sleep, the pair sat in silence across the fire from each other, neither one certain what to say and so they languished in the uncomfortable quietude.

When Thane finally spoke, offering to take the first watch, she assured him in a soft voice, "Don't worry, I have placed runes around the camp. If anything comes near, we will know. Rest, while you can."

He didn't seem to fully trust the arrangement. Like most men, the shamanic ways eluded him and probably always would unless he saw their results firsthand. Jorna was fairly certain that he'd have that chance at some point. She knew better than to expect a smooth journey and should they be backed into a corner, she would be ready to unleash her power to save them if that's what it took. She was glad when Thane conceded and laid down to sleep, putting trust in her if not her mysterious ways.

The ground was hard and cold, very unlike the comfortable bed she was used to. Jorna spent far too long struggling to fall asleep, envying Thane for how quickly he drifted off. His quiet snoring had started mere minutes after he'd settled down. Staring up at the stars above didn't help, it only made her feel as though she'd been lost in a sea of inky blackness, so she turned onto her side placing her back to the fire.

At some point after that she finally drifted to sleep, but it was fitful and light. Every little thing disturbed her, from a gust of wind to the hoot of an owl somewhere in the distance. There was so much going on out here, even at night, that she couldn't fathom how anyone managed to live on the surface their entire lives. She knew that many ages ago the Sarven had, before delving underground to search for precious gems and metals, yet she found it difficult to picture.

When the first rays of light began to color the sky, fading out the pinpoints of star light, Jorna gave up grasping for a few final minutes of rest and started preparing breakfast.

It wasn't anything special, just more soup and bread, which was pretty much the bulk of what they had brought. She knew there were a few goose eggs, rolled protectively in cloth to keep them from being broken, but she intended to save those to add a bit of variety here and there.

Thane stirred a few minutes before it was finished cooking and took the spare moments to gather up his bedding. By the time he was done, Jorna was handing him a full bowl and a hunk of bread. Like the night before, they ate in silence, having little to say to one another, more because they were uncertain than from a lack of desire. Every time their eyes met across the campfire, Jorna felt a surge of elation, but the right words simply wouldn't come.

An hour after waking, they were ready to continue, the camp picked up and the muskoxen taken care of. Like the day before, it unfolded quietly as they rode in single file, Jorna leading the way and Thane just behind her with the pack animal in tow. The snow started to get a little deeper as they trudged upward and the wind's bite grew more fierce the higher they traveled along the path. Not seeming to mind the increasing cold, the muskoxen continued their plodding pace.

By midmorning they'd reached the jagged pass known as the Steps of Bulvai, which changed the trail from a mere upward slant to a winding pathway chiseled along the mountain. It stretched up and around out of sight from their low vantage point, but they knew by looking at Ulthrac's map that it would take them to the Icedrift Steppes and beyond that to the Whitetop Peaks, which marked the location of Dwenenar from the surface.

"I'll go first and pick a safe route along the path," Thane broke the silence that had stretched for hours now.

Jorna frowned up at him and was about to protest that she was just as capable as he was, when she caught herself. He was here to protect her after all and if that included making sure she didn't fall to her death, then she shouldn't argue. Besides, so far Thane hadn't done anything to treat her like she wasn't capable; she had no reason to feel self-conscious about it.

"Okay," she conceded. "I'll stay well back."

With that decided, they began their tedious ascent.

The Working

For two days, they toiled on the steps, their travel time doubled as they were forced to continuously stop and clear fallen rock chunks or snow drifts from the path. At least the brutality of the wind was not so bad as they wove their way up the mountainside.

Even still, Jorna caught herself slipping her gloved hands into the muskox's fur for the extra warmth: the beast didn't even seem to notice. The nights were spent on snow-covered rocky shelves, huddled close to the fire. Each morning they packed up quickly, eager to get moving and put the treacherous stairs behind them for good.

On the third day, the narrow path finally gave way to a rocky mountain passage. The snow was at least two feet deep here, the trail weaving through a tangle of jagged stones and outcroppings. Once it may have been actively traversed, but those days had long since fallen into history, leaving their route nearly impassable.

They took turns leading the way, checking beneath the snow for any sharp rocks that might injure the livestock as they slowly pressed onward. The wind quickly became a problem, blowing through the pass in strong, freezing gusts that pierced straight through the layers of clothing they wore as though they were trudging through the mountains completely naked. The only reprieve they got was at night, when they made camp behind the very rubble that during the day impeded their progress and even then, it only protected them from the brunt of the icy gales.

On the fourth day since leaving the steps, they got lucky and came across a shallow cave around late afternoon. It was just big enough to fit the two Sarven and the three muskoxen comfortably. Normally they would travel a bit further before stopping, but given the circumstances, they decided to seize the opportunity to get out of the elements for a night.

Slowly adapting to the surface, Jorna was still struggling to relax. Thane could feel her restlessness across the fire every time she shifted or turned over. The weather was doing little to help. He heard her gasp awake sometime after midnight, startled by a furious howling of the wind. With his eyes cracked open, Thane watched as she simply pulled the blanket tighter over her head and tried to block it out. Despite wanting to comfort her, he thought better of it and allowed himself to drift off again.

Thane woke a few hours later, but not to the smell of cooking food as he did most mornings. His eyes fell to Jorna as she sat perfectly still on her bedroll, one of the extra furs wrapped around her shoulders. She was staring intensely outside.

For a moment, he seemed uncertain of what to do, if he should rise and start making them something to eat or wait to be sure he wouldn't disturb her. After a few minutes, he did sit up, deciding that if she didn't respond to that simple motion, then he'd go about his morning routine, albeit as quietly as possible.

"Good morning." Jorna's voice startled him. "No need to rush, the storm is only growing stronger." A worried frown had creased her brow.

Now that he was fully aware, Thane could sense its wrath as well. He joined the shaman in watching as the dense flakes of snow poured down and angry gusts stirred the mixture into an even greater tempest. After a moment, he shook the unease it gave him away and stood up from his bedroll.

"Hungry," he grunted, moving to gather what he would need to prepare them food.

While he did that, the shaman pulled herself from the warmth of her bedding and tended to the muskoxen. It was just as well as they were starting to get impatient for their own breakfast. Just because they were being delayed didn't mean the chores could be put off as well.

With the furry beasts munching happily, she moved to help Thane with the cooking. He'd started a pan of potatoes and goose eggs, but it was starting to burn, so she took over tending it and asked him to finish with the animals.

Once they sat down to eat, Jorna went back to observing the storm, which was only getting worse. She picked at her food in silence, her expression pensive and a little uncertain.

Thane flicked his gaze to the cave entrance again, wondering if she was concerned that if something wasn't done, they may end up snowed into the cave. Already a deep drift was piling up in the opening and he knew it was possible for the storm to rage for days, which only made it worse. Leaving during a blizzard, especially one as fierce as this, would have been a death sentence, but what other options were there?

"You have to eat." Thane had moved to stand over her, a disapproving expression on his face as he peered down at her plate of untouched food.

She nodded, impaling a hunk of potato with her fork and popping it into her mouth to show that she was eating, just slowly. With him watching over her, she was able to focus on her meal and cleared her plate, clearly savoring the last of the goose eggs.

When she was finished, she helped Thane clean up the cookware and repack it, then suddenly she stopped him with a hand on his arm. "Do you trust me?" she asked, her entire demeanor becoming very somber.

Thane took his time considering the question, thinking that she was going to press him to travel despite the storm, and though he didn't fully understand its power, he wasn't so ignorant that he couldn't see it was bad. He glanced down at the hand still resting on his arm. He could feel the warmth of her touch even through the layers of his winter clothing or at least he imagined he could.

More than anything, he wanted to say he trusted her, it was the truth after all, but, while this may have been her quest, he was tasked with keeping her safe. He was quite certain that included preventing her from getting herself frozen to death in a blizzard.

"I think we should wait out the storm," he said, providing no actual response to her question. How she took the comment would determine whether or not he answered it at all.

"We will." She gave his arm a meaningful squeeze, her eyes locking with his. "But I need you to do something for me and I must know that you trust me first."

Nodding slowly, his concern abated with her first two words and then returned all the stronger as she explained further. Before, he'd had an inkling of what she might be planning, but her assurances left him with nothing and that didn't sit any better in his gut.

If it weren't for her confidence, the unwavering certainty that whatever she was considering was the right thing to do, he wouldn't have put blind faith in her, no matter how much he may have wanted to. That was not the case and so he conceded his true answer without any further delays. "Yes, I trust you."

This brought a smile to her face, the only indication she gave that she had heard him. A second later she was moving to where their gear was stashed against the back wall, speaking as she dug through her satchel for a few pouches and a sheathed knife before collecting her glaive from where it leaned against the craggy surface. She explained in detail what she was about to do, all the while moving about.

"I need you to sit on your bedroll. Do not speak, do not move." She paused and turned back to him, her expression stern as though she were giving instructions to a child known for misbehaving. "No matter what you see or think you see, you *cannot move*. Trust *me*, trust only my voice and my commands. Can you do this?"

Thane's feelings of trepidation only intensified the more she said. Like most men, he didn't fully understand the way of magic that was innate mainly to women. Shamanism was as much a part of his culture as any other Sarven and yet he found himself distrusting it, despite his faith in Jorna's abilities. He had never personally witnessed a working and that trepidation weighed on him. His breakfast squirmed uncomfortably in his belly the more he thought about it.

Despite all of this, he caught himself nodding, felt his lips form the words, "If that's what you need, yes." He sincerely hoped that phrase wouldn't be his last as he sat down on the bed of furs, facing the cave entrance so he could watch her actions.

Satisfied with his response, Jorna went about her preparations, laying her supplies out in front of the crackling fire. Kneeling on the ground, with Thane on her left, she slipped the small knife free of its sheath and placed it so the blade was horizontal. Then she took the worn, leather pouch, collected a pinch of the pine needles contained within and sprinkled them over the stone ground. With the components spread out, her eyes fell closed and she began a quiet chant, a song to the spirits and elements that echoed over the surface of their world.

She had explained that inciting those spirits was the easy part; calling upon the *right* spirits was much more difficult. The dried pine needles were only a start, the greeting line of a letter and her rhythmic chant conveyed intent, binding the other pieces to the parameters of her desire. Next came the hardest part to accomplish properly: the actual message.

This came in the form of runes, carved into the ground with a special blade made of silver. Delicately she plucked the small knife up and began to scratch away at the soft stone, inscribing a sequence of blocky markings around the scattered needles. Not wanting to completely destroy the tool, she kept them shallow, barely visible in the flickering firelight. That would be enough, it was the drawing of the runes that mattered, not that they were visible to the mortal eye.

Once that was done, she leaned back, flexing her fingers around the knife's handle as she raised her other hand over the workings. Still chanting she pressed the dulled blade tip into her palm, just below her index finger and slit a thin cut all the way to the heel. Her voice wavered a little and she winced at the streak of pain that throbbed in her hand, but with a deep breath, she refocused on finishing this stage of the rite.

Still watching, it took all of Thane's self-control not to bolt from the bedroll and put an end to what she was doing the moment she harmed herself. That was not something she had warned him about.

No matter what you see... The words echoed in his mind, words that he had vowed to obey without question. He knew with a distasteful clarity why she had not spoken of her intentions and why she'd bound him to a promise first. If he had been given forewarning, he would have stopped her.

Unaware of his thoughts and seeming to forget entirely that he was even there, Jorna continued her work. Laying the knife down out of her way, she held her wounded hand with the palm facing up, allowing the blood to pool. She dabbed the red liquid onto her fingertips and leaned back over, coating the runes in her life essence.

"This is the final piece of the message," she whispered an explanation. "It's a signature to identify who is sending the letter in the first place. It ties my shamanic powers to the elements I have appealed to."

Rising to her feet, the Sarven woman clutched the pole of her glaive in her still bleeding hand and began to pace back and forth. Her chanting grew louder, red streaks running in rivulets down the wooden haft as she knocked the bottom against the ground in a rapid succession of three beats - three sets of three to reflect the total of nine runes she'd carved.

For what felt like hours, she repeated this process, ever chanting and beating. Thane could see her strength waning, her power being sapped not only to send her message, but by the elements as payment for agreeing to her terms. It was a test, a challenge to be certain she possessed the resolve to handle the spirits that she'd summoned. If she wavered or was interrupted at this critical stage, it could have serious ramifications, the least of which was her ritual failing and the most extreme being death. The first lesson she had ever learned she'd told Thane earlier: spirits were not to be trifled with.

It wasn't until she looked ready to collapse from dehydration and exhaustion that they received a sign of success. The squalling noise of the blizzard suddenly died down, reduced from a furious roar to a whining howl in the span of a mere second. Forcing herself to concentrate for a few moments longer, Jorna finished the verse before letting her aching voice lapse into silence.

All at once the efforts of her rite crashed down upon her, causing her to slip weakly to the ground, her glaive clattering against the stone at her side.

Her eyes flashed to Thane, who was watching her with an unreadable expression on his face. When he realized this was not part of her ritual, he started to move and then thought better of it, his body jerking as he forcibly kept himself sitting.

Her expression softened with pleasure that he continued to heed her words, but otherwise she seemed too exhausted to do much else. Thane wanted to rush to her, but he kept himself firmly rooted in place. It wasn't until she called to him, her voice cracking on his name, that he felt free to move.

Thane was on his feet in the blink of an eye, his knees protesting the sudden action after remaining in the same position for so long. He grit his teeth against the stiffness, helping Jorna to stand once he reached her side. She was incredibly unsteady, leaning heavily against him as she tried to walk under her own power. Exhaustion was written plainly in her features, but also a determination to do as much for herself as possible. He respected her for that, but he also recognized that pride for what it was: Sarven stubbornness.

Without effort, he swept her into his arms, inciting a disapproving gasp that he ignored as he carried her to the fire and sat her gently down on the bed of furs. Wrapping one of the spare blankets around her shoulders he retrieved her water skin and helped hold it up to her lips. She drank greedily, a trickle running down her chin and dripping onto brown fur.

Leaving the skin where she could reach it, Thane moved to their equipment and grabbed the satchel of healing supplies before returning to sit beside her. Jorna started to protest when he clasped her wrist in a gentle grip, pulling her injured hand closer so that he could inspect it. One stern look dissipated the words before she even fully formed them. He had trusted her, now she must trust him in kind.

Jorna watched him tend to her wound, her gaze flicking between his hands and his face when her eyes weren't drooping from the weight of her exhaustion. To his knowledge, this was normal, though he suspected it was also heightened by the difficulty she'd had resting in general.

They wouldn't be able to travel right away. The storm had slowed, but it still was not safe and wouldn't be until at least the following morning. Thane hoped she could use that time to recover her strength and perhaps even make up for the lack of sleep over the last week.

Thane started tying off the bandage, the wound having been cleaned and cared for already, when Jorna let out a small wince. "Sorry," he apologized softly. "I'm afraid I have a blacksmith's touch."

"I don't mind," she whispered back.

Thane didn't look up at her, his eyes remained on her hand, which he was still holding in both of his own. Her skin was so much lighter than his, porcelain to his caramel, her fingers long and slender. Every spot that her skin touched burned with a pleasant warmth. He felt guilty for not stopping her from harming herself, even though he knew it was all part of the working.

He had a lot of questions and even more concerns about what he had witnessed. Glancing at the entrance of the cave, he could see the blizzard had shifted. Whatever she'd done, it had worked, but at what cost?

"Will you be okay?" he asked instead, deciding that everything else could wait until she was stronger.

"Yes," Jorna gave him a faint grin, "just tired."

"Then rest." He pushed her hand back beneath the fur blanket and started to rise, but Jorna kept a light hold of him.

She stared up into his dark eyes, appearing as though she wanted to say something more, but couldn't quite find the right words. In the end, all she whispered was, "Thank you."

Thane gave her a reassuring squeeze. "We can talk later. Please, rest."

She gave him a final, weak nod before sinking backward onto the bedroll.

While Jorna slept, Thane kept a close watch over her, afraid something bad, something he couldn't fathom might befall her. He knew little about shamanic workings, only that they existed for those women with the insight to learn. None in his family had ever taken up the art, but he knew several prominent families that were known for producing gifted daughters.

He recognized those powers for what they were, a part of Sarven culture that he may not have understood, but that he accepted as a piece of what made him who he was. That wasn't the issue. His only problem was the realization that those powers were *real*, tangible, and for the last few hours he had witnessed them being put into action. It was a sobering experience to say the least.

Stepping over to where she had begun her ritual, he studied the runes and blood. After a moment, he shivered. This was beyond his ability to grasp. Not only that, it was an art that was best practiced by a woman, like blacksmithing belonged in the hands of a man. It was one of the lines drawn long ago and comfortably maintained by tradition. If there was one thing Sarven disliked most, it was change.

Briefly he considered cleaning up the mess, but he immediately thought better of it, not daring to touch the remnants of the working. Instead he returned to his own bedroll and sat heavily upon it. There was little he could do at this point except wait for Jorna to wake and he suspected that would not happen for many hours.

10

OLD ENEMIES

Jorna awoke with a start, uncertain what had disturbed her and not knowing how long she'd been asleep. She glanced around the small cave, the scent of fresh bread wafting to her and drawing her attention to the fire.

Thane was crouched beside it, tending something with his back to her, unaware that she was awake. Sitting up slowly, she flicked her gaze to the entrance and noted that there was no light coming from outside.

She found the water skin still lying beside her bedroll and reached for it, her mouth and throat incredibly dry. The refreshing wetness went a long way in chasing the last bits of fog from her mind, revitalizing what sleep hadn't been able to.

"You're awake."

Thane's voice startled her, causing her to dribble water down her front as she tugged the skin from her lips. She nodded, swiping at her chin. "How long did I sleep?"

"Most of the day and evening," he answered, offering her a plate of fried bread.

Realizing how hungry she was, Jorna gladly accepted it, devouring the food as though she hadn't eaten in weeks. When she was finished, she noticed that Thane was sitting next to her, watching her with a mix of curiosity and... something she couldn't quite work out.

She set her empty plate to the side, swallowing the last bite that she'd been savoring. "What's wrong?" she ventured.

He shook his head, seeming to struggle with putting his concerns into words. All he knew for certain was that he worried about possible repercussions to her health more than anything else.

Jorna read enough of his thoughts on his face that she was able to give him a response before he could speak. "The act is done, the power is gone," she recited, reaching out to pat his arm soothingly. "I will have fully recovered by morning and then we will be able to travel safely in whatever remains of the storm."

"Very well," Thane conceded and gave a slight nod.

She wanted to speak further words of comfort, but the urge to rest fell over her again. Now that she had tended to her body's needs, it was once again pulled toward sleep. Grudgingly, she settled back down, but her hand sought Thane.

"Stay beside me?" The question left her lips before she could stop it. Her cheeks flushed, but to her relief, Thane did not ridicule her.

His fingers wrapped around her hand, holding firmly. "I'm not going anywhere," he vowed.

Despite her exhaustion, Thane's reassurance put a smile on her face.

They started out the next morning as planned, re-packing all of their equipment and loading up the muskoxen. Jorna found that she had slept well through the night. In fact, her unease at being on the surface seemed to have lifted since performing the storm ritual and she was finally able to relax. The unusual noises and vast, empty sky no longer weighed down on her mind; the biting chill of the wind didn't even bother her as much now.

Unfortunately the last leg of the pass was harder to complete after the storm. The snow was deeper and it only kept falling, accompanied by the occasional squall. She walked with her glaive, using it to support herself while she led the brown muskox behind her. Just ahead was the pack animal, trailing after Thane's mount as he waded through the snow, picking their path around jagged rocks and potholes. Of course she had offered to go first, but he hadn't allowed it and she knew he was still concerned.

Her palm ached today, throbbing painfully each time she bumped it against the reins or gripped the pole of her glaive too tightly. She tried to put it out of her mind but when their progress was so agonizingly slow, it became all she could think about.

Waiting for Thane to start forward again, she glanced down at the bandage and had to resist the urge to lift the wrapping to inspect the wound for herself. Twice now he had cared for it without letting her get a good look, which normally wouldn't have bothered her, but she couldn't help but worry that she was allowing him to care for her too much. The last thing she wanted was to be viewed as weak, by anyone but especially those who might judge her actions during this quest, such as King Ulthrac and her brothers.

The crunch of snow drew her from such contemplations, and she glanced up, expecting to see the muskox had moved, only it was still patiently waiting. A frown creased her brow as she flicked her gaze around the beast to Thane, but he continued the pattern of searching for a safe path - the noise had not come from him. A sudden sense of foreboding caused her to scan the surrounding area, her gray-blue eyes searching the pass for anything that was out of place.

That was the only warning they got. A second later, a heart stopping battle call split the air, followed by the rhythmic beat of drums; giants were upon them.

Thane immediately drew his axe, dropping the lead ropes from his hand and joining Jorna in searching for where the behemoths were going to strike first. The answer to that was all around, behind them and ahead. A dozen great, tall men with massive clubs, axes and broad swords that they brandished threateningly.

Their blue skin was pale, like the color of a glacier, and they had long white hair that hung in scraggly lumps from broad heads and wide jaws. They wore mammoth pelts as loincloths, their thick, muscular chests bare to the elements. Mountain giants were impervious to the cold, their true weakness, the Sarven had learned long ago, was fire.

Packed around them were roughly six silver-coated beasts, their hackles raised as they paced on wide, feline paws, their stubby tails twitching anxiously. Saber cats were the pet of choice for giants, fighting with them in battle and protecting their dwellings. Like their masters, they were quite large, easily twice the size of a tiger and even more tenacious than its wild cat cousins.

A single giant and saber pair would have been enough of a challenge for the two Sarven, but in these numbers, they knew right away that fighting was not a plausible option.

Inching her way closer to Thane, Jorna was thankful that the Sarven muskoxen were bred for courage as well as labor. Any other beast may have tried to run, but these stood their ground, moving close together for more protection. She gently patted her muskox's shoulder as he bumped into her. She could feel him trembling beneath her hand.

Exchanging a glance with Thane, she passed her weapon to him and took a few steps closer to the giants who had closed in. If the giants wanted to attack, they could have easily overrun them, but they hadn't, which meant they were willing to talk. There was a chance that Jorna could negotiate with them.

It's certainly worth a shot. What other choice do we have?

"We mean no harm," Jorna called into the wind, raising her hands to show that she was unarmed and passive. "We are mere travelers, passing through to the Whitetops."

A booming laugh echoed through the pass as the giant leader took a step closer, bending forward so he could peer down at her more closely. "Peaceful Sarven, there is no such thing!" He thundered in a deep voice that seemed to shake the very mountains. "Your kind are loud and violent, a swarm of biting insects!"

"Yes," she agreed sadly, "we were very hot-blooded in our youth, but wisdom has come with age. We do not seek conflict as we once did."

"Hah! Pretty words from a lying tongue," he growled, his face contorting with suspicious outrage. "It was not so long ago you tried to tame these mountains, destroying our dwellings, slaughtering our children. We have not forgotten the battles fought across the Beldrath slopes! The only reason we have not cut you down is because your knowledge holds value. Now tell me, how many more follow you?"

Jorna shook her head, scarcely able to believe that they really thought the Sarven were about to invade again. The wars he spoke of were thousands of years old, from a time before cities like Hamdralg had been built. Why waste resources fighting to claim a harsh, unforgiving land when they could rule unopposed in their own realm beneath the earth? One glance at the chieftain and she knew he would never believe her. The giants were convinced that their old enemies were resurfacing and they didn't seem to care if the notion was preposterous or not.

"We are travelers, not scouts," she tried again. "We carry food and provisions for our journey alone and we have armed ourselves for defense. We are not your enemies."

"Sarven lies!" Rage darkened his face, and he took a sinister step closer, his massive fist tightening on the grip of his club. "I should pummel you where you stand!"

Thane stepped closer to Jorna, a warning glare on his face. "You would only die trying!" he challenged, his voice every bit as strong as the chieftain's, even if it was not as deep.

This caused a stir among the giants, who roared and stomped at the audacity of their captive. Sensing the growing tension only made the saber cats quiver with a barely contained frenzy. The racket forced their chieftain to shout in order to be heard above the din. "Strong words from a runt! Like all your kin, your mouth is better than your skill!"

Putting a hand on Thane's arm to prevent him from rising to the bait, Jorna tried to calm the situation. "Please, he meant no offense. Surely you understand the importance of duty and his is to protect me." For a fleeting moment, as the commotion died down, she thought perhaps she'd managed to reach a common enough ground to keep from becoming prisoners. She opened her mouth to elaborate further, but the chieftain interrupted her.

"A single traveler? With an armed guard?" His eyes narrowed to mere slits, his voice grating like gravel as he rumbled. "Do you think me dim? What are you called, little Sarven woman? Who are you?"

She briefly considered lying, but after being accused of it, knew to do so would be nothing short of foolish. There was a slim chance that he wouldn't recognize her name. After all, the Sarven had little presence on the surface and yet it was not uncommon for other nations to keep track of rulers and their possible heirs. She had no doubt that her name was known among the humans and elves; the question was whether or not the giants knew it as well.

"I am Jorna Hailstone of the Silverwolf clan," she answered after a pause and immediately she wished she'd given any other name but that one.

Outrage spread among the giants, causing a ruckus that was louder and fiercer than the previous one. They recognized her as the daughter of a king and many of them cried for her blood to be spilled, others that she be ransomed.

Sharing that knowledge had only made their situation worse. Their captors were prepared to use it to gain more information or even as an excuse to slay them outright, and given the rough terrain, there was no chance for them to escape by running and no hope to survive a direct assault under these conditions.

Thane took that moment to assert himself again, pushing Jorna behind him protectively, more as a gesture than because it would do any good. He thundered above the noise, "I challenge you to single combat! Stand against me or forever be a coward!"

That got everyone's attention, especially Jorna's. She tugged his arm, trying to pull him back, but Thane would not budge. His eyes never wavered from the chieftain's, which were aglow with indignant rage. No doubt he didn't appreciate being challenged by someone he viewed as beneath his might, but whether he liked it or not, he couldn't say no without appearing weak.

"I, Drogthul, accept. What are your terms, runt?" the chieftain finally conceded.

"When I win," Thane boasted, flashing a daring grin, "you allow us to leave with what belongs to us and promise not to interfere with our journey again."

Baring his teeth threateningly, the giant leader countered, "When I have broken every bone in your body, then I will be free to do as I please with the daughter of King Guldorn." He waved his club above his head and bellowed to his men, "Take them! We march to Velknair!"

Not needing to be told twice, the giant warriors lunged into action. They gathered up the muskoxen, one man each leading the startled beasts behind them as they plowed a path by kicking rocks and snow out of the way with massive feet. Thane was marched forward just behind the animals, prodded along with rough jabs in the back and snarling jeers, while Jorna was scooped up by the chieftain and carried over his broad shoulder, despite her protests. The saber cats prowled around the outside edge of the procession, hungry blue eyes flashing to the muskoxen and prisoners, thirsting for the taste of blood.

THE CHALLENGE

WITH THE GIANTS MAKING a path, the trek out of the pass went considerably faster than before. In no time at all, they were being led north-west in the opposite direction of where they needed to go.

Soon after that, the foggy lines of smoke appeared, spiraling into the sky above the hills - no, not hills, *tents*. Made of white mammoth pelts, they blended almost perfectly into the snowy landscape, but the closer one looked, the easier it was to distinguish between the two. It helped that the rest of the encampment that made up Velknair also began to take shape, revealing mammoth pens, weapon racks, heating pits covered with bone gratings and of course, the giants themselves moving about.

Children nearly as tall as Jorna scurried through the tents while their parents worked to prepare food and repair tools and weapons or perform other necessary tasks. At the sight of their warriors returning, all of this activity came to an end as they gathered to see what was going on and who they had brought with them.

Chieftain Drogthul proudly boasted of their success in capturing quite the prize, inciting a roar of approval and support from the rest of the camp as Jorna was presented to them.

Ever dignified, she raised her head against the bloodthirsty jeers and insults, refusing to allow hateful words to affect her. Instead, she remembered who she was. Though it meant something different to her captors, she embraced that identity to mean she must always remain serene, especially in the face of opposition.

A giantess, tall and beautiful in her own right, with a wide sloping forehead and sparkling eyes, stepped up to Jorna at Drogthul's command. Spitting at the Sarven noble's feet, she roughly grabbed her hands and bound her wrists with a coarse rope. The chieftain was telling the masses about the champion of the king's daughter and his challenge, a challenge that by honor must be answered.

That was all he needed to say, and his people flew into action. The muskoxen were herded into a pen with the mammoths by the children, while Jorna and Thane were hurried to the center of the camp where a massive pit had been dug. Blood stained the trampled snow at the bottom of the crater, belying the outcome of past battles fought within its depths.

Thane was shoved into the pit and barely managed to stay on his feet as he landed. He immediately drew his axe, scanning the crowd of pale blue giants that now packed around the outside of the sparring ring. His eyes found Jorna as she was being lifted from the ground, fighting as the giantess who had bound her hands now hung her from those same bonds.

The thick wooden post looked as though it were meant to specifically hold giant prisoners. The iron hook was placed nearly ten feet from the ground, high enough that a giant could stand with his arms above his head. Jorna, who wasn't even six feet tall, dangled from that height, her boots such a distance from the ground that it might as well have been miles instead of feet.

A hot rage boiled in his chest that spurred Thane toward her, demanding that she be let down, that she deserved more dignity than that. This only provoked a chorus of laughter and further ridicule, but he did not regret speaking for her, nor would he regret fighting to free her either.

"Jorna Hailstone," he called above the crowd, halting in his tracks. He felt the ground rumble as Drogthul dropped into the pit behind him like a boulder, but he did not turn or stop speaking and his eyes remained on her face. "I'm coming to get you, right after I pound this giant bastard into the ground!"

Her grin was all he needed to bolster his courage as he finally spun to face the massive chieftain, his axe catching a glint of light from the sun trying to peek through the lingering storm clouds. Like a furious bull, Drogthul charged toward him, club held in front of him like a battering ram, forcing Thane to leap out of the way or be crushed.

It was strange to fight someone that was so much bigger and bulkier than he was. Even Thunar at almost seven feet had not been so large. Agility wasn't a tactic that had ever worked against his brother, but he knew right away it was going to be the best option for this fight. Drogthul depended too much on his strength and size to intimidate lesser foes; he expected for Thane to be shaken by that brute ferocity as well, another weakness the Sarven was more than willing to use in his own favor.

At first, he acted afraid, all but running from the hulking giant every time he tried to engage. Each time he was rushed, he took the minimal action to avoid the attack, retaining as much of his own stamina as he could, while working to drain Drogthul's energy. When the giant began to slow, Thane's focus changed. No longer did he simply duck or dodge out of the way. He used those actions to get passed his opponent's defenses. The blows were meant more to harry and frustrate than to cripple, though if he got the chance, he wouldn't be above inflicting more serious damage - the point was to win after all, and the giant certainly wasn't pulling any punches.

"Stop fighting like a cowardly runt!" Drogthul bellowed, growing tired of the glancing cuts that now lined his lower back and legs. One particularly nasty laceration was trickling blood into the already stained slush at his feet; he had been favoring that leg.

Thane didn't give him any response. Instead he lunged forward, feigning for the wounded leg when his real target was the other one. Staggering back, trying to protect his weak spot, the giant didn't see the shift in direction until it was too late. The blade of Thane's axe bit into his bare thigh, oozing rivulets of blood from the deep slash that pattered into the snow. A howl of pained rage chased the Sarven as he danced out of reach, though it wasn't entirely necessary to back off as far as he did.

Drogthul crashed to his knees, a hand reaching down to stem the flow of red liquid that began to gush from the fresh wound. He still held his club in one enormous fist, which was the only reason Thane now kept his distance. Even if the giant was crippled, momentarily at least, he could still gravely injure anyone with that cudgel.

"You are beaten!" Thane cried, ignoring the angry shouts of the other giants. "Yield and honor the terms of our fight!"

Angry white eyes glowered at the Sarven as Drogthul struggled to rise, using his weapon as a crutch to steady himself. He slipped in the bloody slush beneath him and tumbled back to the ground, growling furiously. After a pause, he spat a guttural word that Thane didn't understand. At first he thought it was a concession, but he realized far too late that it wasn't even close.

Something large and heavy slammed into Thane without warning, knocking him off his feet. He felt the axe haft slip from his fingers and heard it clattering out of sight as the mass leaped away from him.

Trying to shake away the surprise and get back up, Thane could just make out Jorna's distressed voice among the cheering and roaring of the giant community. He struggled to regain his focus, searching now for the thing that had struck him from out of nowhere. It couldn't have been Drogthul, he'd been looking *right at him,* and yet he knew the chieftain had cheated rather than keep his end of the bargain.

The truth of that became very clear as his brown eyes caught the glimmer of silver fur. He twisted to face the saber cat, just as it lunged for him again. All he could manage to do was throw his arms up in defense of his face and neck. The ground rushed up to meet him as the beast crashed into him, this time meaning to do more harm than simply knocking the Sarven into the dirt. He felt its hot breath, reeking of rotten meat, as the feline opened its mouth, yellow fangs flashing.

Desperate to keep those teeth from clamping down on something he'd rather not have punctured, Thane grabbed one of the long front canines and tried to push the cat's face away. Growling and hissing, the saber fought to free itself, which was something of an improvement over it attempting to gore him with the same fangs that Thane now clung to for dear life.

Shanik

Jorna hated being stuck on the sidelines while her companion was busy fighting in her name. That was something she got from her father, a need to stand on her own and fight for the things she cared most about.

She was alleviated to see Thane beat the giant, impressed with his prowess and grasp of tactics. It was hard to believe that was the same man who claimed to be only a blacksmith. When they made it out of this mess, she would have to remind him that any Sarven worth his beard was not only the profession he claimed for himself, but a warrior as well.

Her relief was short lived. Jorna glanced away for no more than a second and when she looked again, Thane was being attacked by Drogthul's pet. A surge of panic and outrage gripped her stomach, but she quickly pushed them aside, deciding she'd been a spectator long enough. Wiggling and twisting, she fought to free her hands from the tight bonds, ignoring the pinching burn as the ropes grated against her pale skin.

The giantess heard her struggling grunts and hurried to keep her from slipping free, but Jorna saw her coming. As soon as the tall beauty was in range, the Sarven swung her feet up, planting both of her boots into the other woman's surprised face.

With a startled cry, she reeled backward, red blood gushing from her wide nostrils and oozing down her chin to splatter onto her bare chest. In the time it took for her to blink the tears out of her eyes and shake off the stunned pain, Jorna had finally managed to slip her bonds.

She fell into the snow piled around the base of the log, landing on her feet, but the inertia threw her forward so that she ended up on her hands and knees. In the back of her mind, she knew that later she'd feel the ache of a dozen stiff joints, bruises, and scrapes. For the moment she was focused only on reaching Thane, who was pinned beneath the large mound of fur and claws. Already she was running, her sore feet forgotten as she bounded into the fray.

A battle cry tore from her lips as she scooped up Thane's axe. Not breaking stride she raised the weapon above her head. She felt the ground beneath her, the snow now soaked with blood, and she called to it, gathering the reddened flakes into the air in front of her like an icy shield.

When she was nearly upon the struggling pair, she envisioned the snow rushing forward, becoming a raging tempest and slamming into the unsuspecting feline. That was all it took. The whirling flurry answered, carrying out her desire so that the saber cat was thrown several feet across the pit.

Jorna reached Thane in the next instant, dragging him off the ground even as their foe recovered. Passing him the axe, she stayed in front of him, though he put a hand on her shoulder in an attempt to push her out of the way. Her eyes went to the snarling saber cat that prowled closer to them, hesitating to attack for some reason that became clear a split second later.

"It's too late," Drogthul rumbled, the snap of his fingers calling the feline to his side. "Your champion was defeated." If saying those words made him happy, he didn't show it.

"Only because you cheated!" Thane proclaimed, the fact that he'd been robbed of victory seething in his eyes.

The giants shouted angrily at the accusation, their voices raising to defend the chieftain's actions. It was true that their culture believed their saber cat companions were a part of their souls. They lived in their dwellings, ate just as well as their children, and were considered an outside extension of their giant masters, but using the feline in single combat was a stretch of that law to anyone who was not part of their society.

Jorna realized painfully that Drogthul had never intended to give Thane a fair fight. He'd kept his cat in reserve on the off chance that he started to lose and now claimed it was his right. Since they were in his village, surrounded by his kin, there was quite literally nothing they could do, no higher authority to appeal to. There was no way either of them were going to walk out of that camp unless they were bound in ropes. All Thane had really managed to do was prolong them being stuffed into cages.

With the spar concluded, that's exactly what happened. The two Sarven were dragged out of the pit, the giantess glowering maliciously at Jorna, who flashed a crooked grin as she was led away. The cage they were pushed into was made of strong leather and even stronger mammoth bones. It had been placed in the middle of their encampment where everyone could watch them slowly freeze to death - though the process was hastened by the top layer of their clothing being confiscated along with the rest of their belongings.

Thrown together in one cage barely large enough to fit a grown female giant, the pair would at least have some measure of shared body heat to help against the cold. Hopefully that would be enough to keep them alive until they could find a way to escape.

Night fell a few hours later, causing the giants to retreat into their tents. It was the first time the prisoners had been left alone since being forced into the bone cage. Their captors had taken turns jeering at them, gathering in small groups to shout and sneer insults at the trapped Sarven.

With their tormentors gone, the encampment was peaceful and serene, the only giants in sight being the guards who patrolled by intermittently. Had it not been for the drop in temperature and the cruel wind (or the obvious fact that they were stuffed inside a cage) the evening would have almost been pleasant.

Shivering against the cold, Jorna moved a little closer to Thane for warmth, certain she wouldn't be able to fall asleep even if she tried. Not just because of the cold, but more from the sense of dread that had settled at the bottom of her hungry stomach like a heavy stone.

Several times they'd tested the cage door, trying to break it open when the guards were nowhere to be seen and still it held fast. Eventually they'd given up and were sitting side-by-side as far from the door as they could get, their backs pressing against the solid bone wall. Now that they weren't shifting about, the air felt even chillier than before.

Showing his concern for her well-being, Thane reached for Jorna's hands, covering her soft fingers in an attempt to keep them warm. His eyes fell to the angry red rope burns ringing her wrists and an expression of guilt passed over his face. "I'm sorry, my lady," he rumbled quietly, his voice tinged with shame. "I failed you."

"No." Jorna didn't even hesitate, knowing with surprising clarity that the last thing Thane had done was fail her. "You honored me today. You fought in my name with bravery and cunning..." When she saw where his eyes had fallen, she squeezed his hand gently, drawing his gaze to her face. "Do not allow the dishonor of your opponent to sour a well-earned victory."

Her words brought a rare smile to his face, that in spite of being faint was full of meaning. It was the expression in his dark eyes that Jorna had trouble reading as he raised a hand to her cheek and tenderly caressed her smooth skin. "I promise you, I will do everything in my power to keep you from harm," he said breathily.

Aware of just how close they were, Jorna felt her cheeks flush and hoped he wouldn't notice their sudden rosiness. The soft manner in which he touched her, regarded her, made her heart tremble with warm emotions. She knew just by his tone of voice and the certainty in his eyes that his oath had nothing to do with being chosen to help with her quest.

Caught up in the swirling sensations, Jorna abruptly pressed against him, laying her head on his shoulder. She felt his arm tighten around her, holding her close, and caught herself wishing they could be anywhere but trapped in this cage.

At the unbidden reminder of their plight, Jorna couldn't help but shiver as unpleasant feelings pushed aside the inner warmth she'd been basking in.

"I'm afraid," she whispered, surprising herself by sharing the sort of thing that she had always been taught to keep to herself. Pulling from him enough that she could see his face, she was momentarily concerned that he would think her weak for such an admission, but she saw right away that her concern was unnecessary.

Thane gently drew her close again, his arms wrapping protectively around her shoulders as he tilted his head to respond in a quiet tone, "I am, too."

They lapsed into silence, both aware of the reason they clung to the other, but making themselves believe it was to combat the cold night. Though she hadn't thought it possible earlier, Jorna drifted into a light sleep.

She still felt the occasional chill as a gust of wind blew through the camp and she was dimly aware that Thane was dozing as well, his head leaned back against the cage. Her mind fought to shut out the cold and instead focus on the pleasing heat that grew between her body and Thane's.

She had almost fallen deeper when she felt an insistent tapping on her shoulder that startled her awake. Letting out a soft gasp, she turned, pulling slightly from Thane, to see a slender, black reptilian tail withdrawing.

Her wide eyes followed it to where a small dragon, no more than three feet long from snout to tail tip, clung to the bone bars of the cage. His wings were folded tightly against his obsidian flanks, a crest of horns arranged regally on his head, and proper talons on the end of every digit, of which there were four per foot. His sapphire eyes gleamed in the dark, their depths belying the creature's age.

She was baffled by his size. All the stories she'd heard about dragons claimed that they were huge, bigger even than houses, and yet this one was so little!

Everyone knew that dragons had once walked Talaris, long ago when the three races were still very young. They also knew that the great wyrms had disappeared and not been seen for more years than even history could count. It was for this reason that Jorna just sat there, stunned into complete silence, unable to believe her eyes.

"Don't you recognize a jail break when you see one?" he rasped in a sarcastic tone. "Stop gawking and get moving before the guards come back!"

She was drawn to one of his four feet, which was shaking a jagged bone key at her impatiently. The sight of it drove away the stunned fog clouding her mind, snapping her into action as a surge of delight brought a grin to her face. Sitting the rest of the way up, she reached out to awaken Thane, but her movement had already done so. She expected for him to give her a quizzical look, but when she glanced at his face, she saw that his eyes were fixed at a point over her head. He had just seen the dragon.

Jorna grabbed his shoulder, jostling him until he brought his gaze to the same key, which she was holding just in front of his nose. Slowly a grin captured his features as he realized what she had a few moments ago; they were free!

Passing him the key, she allowed him to precede her to the cage door. She watched over his shoulder as he stuck his arm through the bone sections and worked the key into the lock. The scraping noise as it turned over caused them both to tense. Jorna cast a quick glance around to be certain the guards weren't coming. A second later the door popped open, its hinges creaking as bone rubbed against bone.

Thane was the first one to crawl out, ever alert for signs of their captors. Once satisfied that it was still clear, he turned around and helped Jorna to her feet. He frowned as the black dragon scuttled around the cage and leaped to the shaman's shoulder.

Momentarily startled, she gave the creature a curious look, but all he did was stare blankly at her as though he had no idea what the fuss was about. Letting it go for the moment, the two Sarven moved closer so they could converse in hushed whispers.

"We need our supplies," Jorna commented, knowing they wouldn't make it more than a few days if they tried to escape without food or tools.

"Agreed," her fellow Sarven nodded slowly, then started in the direction of the mammoth pens. Jorna didn't waste a moment, following right behind him.

Their trek across the camp was slower than either of them would have liked. More than once they had to hide in order to avoid being seen by one of the patrolling guards, hoping that they wouldn't wander by the cage and notice their prisoners were missing.

At least not until they had reached their muskoxen and were long gone. The longer it took for their escape to be discovered, the better chances they had of actually making it away from the giants' camp and not being recaptured.

Once they made it to the pens, their new dragon friend, if that was the correct term, left his perch on Jorna's shoulder, disappearing into the dark sky so he could keep watch. While he circled above, invisible to the naked eye, the Sarven snuck into the pen that held the muskoxen.

The poor beasts were very pleased to see their masters, no doubt highly uncomfortable in the strange surroundings with nothing familiar but each other. Doing her best to keep them quiet, Jorna was pleased to see that none of their belongings had been tampered with. At least not yet; she figured the fight between Thane and Drogthul had distracted the giants from sorting through their gear.

That was their last shred of luck however. No sooner were they leading the muskoxen out of the pen that the dragon suddenly dipped back down, whispering from the sky like a shadow to land on Jorna's shoulder again. "Hurry," he hissed, "someone's coming!"

The color drained out of Jorna's face. Now that she paused, she could hear the sound of giggling and talking. With one glance at Thane, she saw that he had heard it as well. He was already swinging into the saddle, the lead rope for the pack animal gripped in his hand. She followed his example, not bothering to shut the pen as she climbed up.

Barely having a chance to get her backside settled, a pair of young giants rounded a tent, their hands clasped together, smiling and fawning over each other. It took them the span of a single heartbeat to realize they weren't alone. They saw the Sarven atop their muskoxen, saw the pen gate swinging lazily as the wind toyed with it and recognized that they'd just caught the prisoners trying to escape.

The girl let out an ear-splitting shriek that could have stirred the dead, backpedaling with such dramatic force that all she managed to do was trip herself. Handling the situation with a bit more decorum, the boy staggered away, pausing to drag his lover back to her feet as he shouted needlessly for the guards.

"An otherwise flawless escape, foiled by a pair of courting teenagers!" the dragon huffed disgustedly. "What are you waiting for? Run!" He launched himself again into the air, just as Jorna spurred her mount into motion.

WORM FIELDS

WITH THE DRAGON LEADING the way, they bolted through the camp, which was rapidly coming alive. At first the giants started to gather around the young couple, giving Jorna and Thane a small head start, but as soon as word spread that the prisoners were getting away, it didn't take the giant warriors long to begin a pursuit.

While a handful of men began the chase on foot, the rest prepared the mammoths. Drogthul was helped onto the back of a great white beast, his bandaged leg giving him some trouble until he was seated. With a dozen riders and saber cats behind him, the chieftain led the charge, his mount releasing an echoing trumpet of excitement.

The muskoxen could easily outrun the giants who were on foot, but there was no way they would be able to stay ahead of the mammoths. They could hear them coming now, thundering across the snow-covered ground so that the mountains seemed to tremble all around them.

Jorna started to slow, looking for some other means in which to evade the angry behemoths. The dragon's voice called down to her, shouting for her to keep moving, that he had their back. Having few other options, the shaman could only trust him. With renewed urgency she pushed her muskox once again to its full speed.

Fire lit up the night, raining from the sky in raging balls that slammed into the ground just in front of the giants, causing them to stop short as they hunted for the source. Fearful of fire and having little resistance against heat, their mad dash after the two Sarven slowed to a halt. Though they searched the sky, they couldn't see where the attacks were coming from. The dragon's agile flying making him near impossible to track. All that could be seen were the blazing fireballs.

Drogthul's anger overpowered his unease, and he bellowed a war cry that echoed through the night. He pressed his warriors to pursue their prey once more, reason giving way to blind rage.

Heading northeast, Jorna could see the open steppes in the distance, close enough to reach in a matter of minutes at this speed. Not that reaching them would do much good under the current circumstances. There was no shelter, no place to lose the giants that were doggedly following them, nothing except a flat expanse of snow drifts. She could feel her muskox tiring and knew they wouldn't be able to keep this pace up for much longer. They had put some distance between themselves and their pursuers, but that advantage would swiftly be whittled away by the larger mounts.

She'd seen the horde chasing them; fighting was not a viable option either. It would buy them a few minutes at best and then they would either be slain or taken captive once more. A shiver of despair ran down her spine. To have come this far only to fail was a thought that didn't sit right with her, not in the least. Her family, her people, were counting on her to succeed, she couldn't bear to let them down...

Jorna pulled her mount to a sliding halt, the poor beast breathing hard, grateful for a pause in their headlong flight. Confused, Thane did the same, coming up beside her as his muskox grunted its own relief.

"What's wrong?" he exclaimed, glancing nervously over his shoulder.

"We can't outrun them forever," she responded with an irritated shake of her head, her blond hair rippling with the motion. "We need a plan, some way to make them stop chasing us!"

The dragon swooped down, circling around the pair lazily as he listened closely to their exchange. "I can handle that," he interjected, cutting across Thane who was just opening his mouth to comment.

"Haven't you done enough?" the blacksmith growled. His distrust of their new acquaintance was easy for Jorna to read, even in the heat of the moment. The mere thought of what a dragon might want from a Sarven princess must be making him very uncomfortable.

Muttering something unintelligible, the black dragon soared off, leaving them to stare after him until it became too difficult to follow him against the dark sky. For a moment, Jorna wasn't sure if he was still going to help or not, until she saw a streak of flames burning toward the giants.

She watched in fascination as the dragon zipped around them, seeing his movements not because she saw *him*, but because she noted where the fireballs came from. All he seemed to be accomplishing was to stir them up, infuriating them more and more. Then she saw a burst of fire that was nowhere near the giants...

There was a rumble, deep and quivering, that turned into an echoing crack. The peaks that protruded from the landscape between the giants and fleeing Sarven, covered in deep snow that had been collecting since the start of winter, began to shed their white cloaks.

It took several seconds for the giants to figure out what was going on and by then the waves of snow were already crashing toward them.

Panicked shouts went up, those with mounts racing to get out of the avalanche's path before it buried them alive.

"Run!" Jorna shouted, spinning her muskox toward the steppes and urging it into a swift gallop. She heard Thane behind her, rushing to keep up as they hurried to stay ahead of the same avalanche that was now swallowing up the giants who had been on foot. They both had the good sense not to turn and watch or even slow down until the ground stopped shaking and the rumbling of snow fell silent. Even then, they didn't halt. Their dash became less desperate, but they did not pause to celebrate their escape just yet.

When the dragon joined them again, he was humming proudly to himself, bobbing in the air closest to Jorna. If he was expecting praise from either of them, he would be disappointed. At the moment, all either one could think about was putting the giants as far behind them as they could.

As Jorna had thought, they made it to the steppes moments later, though she immediately began to miss the protection of the hills they'd just left. The wind lashed across the open expanse, nasty and biting and utterly cold. There was nothing to act as a buffer, so at times it felt as though a particularly strong gust might send them flying. Jorna had no idea how the dragon managed to stay aloft or why he didn't seem bothered by the chilly squalls. Whatever his secret, she sorely wished it was something he could share.

Not for the first time she missed home. She missed being beneath the earth in a city of stone and rock. Closing her eyes, she could almost see the sharp curves of the palace she'd grown up in, but a sudden fear forced her to push the memory away.

She had not stopped to consider what state her home would be in when she arrived. What would have become of the dead? Would she find their remains, her father's remains, desecrated and left to rot? The idea made her heart sick and she hung her head against a different sort of chill.

Misreading the drop of her head, Thane called out from behind her. "We should stop for a bit; we could all use a break, especially the muskoxen."

Jorna just nodded. They hadn't stopped, even as the sun rose above the horizon, wanting to put as much distance between themselves and the giants as possible. It was a safe bet their foes were still digging their kin out of the snow, but just in case, there was no point in betting their lives on such an assumption. Thane was right, though. They had pushed on long enough and could all benefit from a little rest.

She started to look around the area for some place to camp, but as her eyes scanned the empty plain of snow, she realized the effort was futile. There was no place that she would call suitable, no place to protect them from the brutal wind. It made her instantly hope they could put the endless tundra behind them soon.

Coming to a halt, Thane and Jorna worked together without a word, each having grown used to setting up camp together. Though at this point they didn't unpack all the gear, not when they would only be staying long enough to care for the muskoxen, satisfy their own hunger, and regain some strength. This far north, in the dead of winter, there was precious little daylight. The shorter their stop, the further they could travel before nightfall.

Besides, there was another matter Jorna wanted to attend to: finding out more about the new addition to their party. Once she and Thane had eaten some bread and the last of their cheese, she turned to the dragon, who was perched like a statue on top of her saddle.

"I suppose an expression of gratitude is in order," she began. "Thank you, for helping us to escape." She paused, giving him a chance to volunteer the information himself, but when all he did was lazily sniff at the air, she asked outright, "Who are you?"

Rolling his shoulders in a motion not unlike an anthropoid shrug, the dragon turned his bright blue gaze to her, staring for a long moment before answering in exasperation, "You may call me Shanik."

"Why did you help us?" she pressed, unperturbed by his apparent annoyance at being questioned.

"Must I have a reason?" His raspy voice took on a different tone, somewhat softer, but still possessing an irritated edge.

Thane took the opportunity to interject before Jorna could answer. "Dragons are a subject of legend. Many doubt you ever existed, but here you are, in the wastes of the Beldrath, just in the nick of time to help a Sarven princess escape death and ruin at the hands of a giant tribe... Yet you claim there's no motives for your actions? I'll buy that, *lizard*, just as soon as my muskox sprouts wings and flies," he finished with a scoff.

Emitting a flustered *tsk*, Shanik turned his head away, refusing to look at the Sarven for several long moments. Even in miniature, the creature possessed all the legendary pride of its larger brethren. "I am not a lizard," was the only answer he gave.

"Oh come now, we are not fools." Thane's patience was wearing thin, and it echoed in his tone. "Dragons, even small ones, have never come to the aide of common mortals unless there is something to be gained. As proven in every historical account of your kind."

"Interrogating me after all the trouble I endured to help you escape?" The dragon bristled, almost like a bird ruffling its feathers, but Jorna couldn't quite tell if he was truly offended or not as his tone of voice was dripping with sarcasm, contradicting the gesture. "Really, what more does one expect from an uncivilized Sarven? I'm sure your mother would be appalled at your manners!"

Already tired of the bickering, Jorna put a hand on Thane's shoulder to keep him from delivering the scathing comment that had no doubt been on the tip of his tongue. "We are grateful for your assistance, Shanik, but I must ask if there is something you wish for in return?"

Shanik sighed dramatically, his eyes never leaving the blacksmith as he responded, "I happened by as you were being ambushed. It's that simple." He sniffed at the air again before adding, "And just because you don't see dragons, doesn't mean we've gone extinct."

"Great, thanks." Thane glowered, clearly not convinced of his story. "Now shove off, we can take it from here." He folded his arms across his chest, his glare darkening the longer Shanik simply sat there.

It was Jorna who broke the stare down, stepping in front of Thane and drawing him a few feet away from the dragon. She could understand his distrust, but she wasn't quite convinced that sending such a powerful ally away was a good idea, not when he could come in handy later.

In a soft whisper, she said as much to her companion, hoping he would see the logic. "He could be very beneficial if we run into more trouble. Legends tell us that dragons were capable of great feats of magic, magic that the other races could only dream of. We would be foolish to turn that sort of assistance away, don't you think?"

She saw the struggle on his face and understood the war that must be going on in his mind. Trusting a stranger was difficult, especially when that stranger was straight out of myth.

In the end, he let out a sigh and gave her a slow nod. "I believe you are wise. As such, I will trust your judgment, but," he paused as if to consider his word, "I will be watching him closely. One false move, one trick or threat against your life, and I will not hesitate to do what must be done."

Jorna felt her heart swell with emotion at the thought. She knew she had made the right decision then, that there was indeed more to Thane than others believed. If he took his duty so seriously that he was willing to protect her, even if it brought him face-to-face with a dragon, then he was the furthest thing from a coward.

She rewarded him with a soft smile, squeezed his arm, and then turned to regard Shanik. "We have business in Dwenenar and we would be honored if you joined us."

The dragon's scaly lips curled up, revealing sharp fangs as he smiled. "I thought you'd never ask."

They didn't rest much longer, all of them feeling a sense of urgency to continue moving. When they did finally stop, it wasn't until well after dark. One good thing about being on the tundra was that it was smooth and well lit. The rays of moonlight were cast fully on the sparkling snow, illuminating their path. The downside was the lack of shelter; there was no place for them to get out of the elements, not even anything to block the wind, which was much colder at night.

Jorna did what she could to brace them against the chill, but her wards weren't capable of blocking it out entirely. It made them all very grateful for the extra blankets. Though it may not have been entirely appropriate, they followed the example of the muskoxen and slept close together.

Shanik curled up beside the shaman, covering his stubby snout with his tail to keep it from getting too cold, while Thane insisted that Jorna sleep between him and the fire. She knew better than to argue with him when it came to matters regarding her well-being and so she complied without a fuss.

The next morning, they got started early, before the sun had even started to rise. This high in the mountains, the amount of daylight they got was minimal during the winter, and their progress would have been far too slow if they traveled only by day. In the pass, that had been much, much more difficult and so they'd not bothered, but here, on the steppes, they got in a full day. Two full days in fact.

Early on the third morning after their escape from the giants, the sunlight barely peeking from over the distant Whitetops, they reached the worm fields.

Few ventured this far over the mountains and even fewer returned to speak of their journey. That was for one reason alone: the worm fields. Named for the large ice worms that inhabited the deep, labyrinthine network of snow tunnels, the fields were incredibly dangerous.

Not just because of the worms that lurked beneath the surface, but for the sinkholes that they used to trap prey and defend their territory. One false step and a traveler was as good as dead, falling into the impossibly deep drifts to become worm food. It was risky coming this way, but it was also the shortest route to the Whitetops and comparatively less dangerous considering what other creatures stalked the Beldrath wilderness.

The best way to cross the field was to fan out, keeping the muskoxen at maximum distance while Jorna and Thane tested the ground, picking their way carefully across. It was the same tediousness that had made traveling this far take as long as it had, but if they wanted to reach the other side, they wouldn't rush. At the same time, neither one of them wanted to spend the night out here, so there was a great deal of incentive not to dally.

Before they got started, Thane tied the pack animal to his mount, keeping them close together so they wouldn't wander and end up going down a sinkhole, but allowing himself enough room to safely test the ground. This left Jorna with only her own mount to contend with, which is exactly the way he liked it.

For the better part of the morning their progress was steady and though they got hungry around midday, they silently agreed not to stop for food. Above them, Shanik did his best to scout their paths, looking for signs of sinkholes, though they weren't always visible to the naked eye. Even if that eye belonged to a dragon.

Using her glaive to test the snow's integrity, Jorna was quite confident in her own abilities, trusting that her shamanic insight would serve her well in distinguishing a good route.

Unfortunately, determining sinkholes was not an exact science. A method that might reveal one wouldn't work on another. It depended on several factors, such as the size of the worm who made it and if they were older with more experience at hiding their traps. This one fit that description, for she had no idea she'd mis-stepped until it was too late.

One second she was making good progress, she took a few steps and was about to begin checking the next patch, when the sound of shifting snow alerted her to the grave mistake she'd just made. All she had was a second, a heartbeat, to react.

Her eyes flashed to Thane, who had also heard the noise and froze, afraid it had come from beneath him. He was just figuring out that it was Jorna when she called his name, her mind reeling for some solution to her dire plight.

Thane turned just in time to see the snow give out from beneath the shaman, causing her to cry out as she fell with the crumbling ground.

14

BLACKSMITH'S GRIEF

His impulse was to rush to her, to try and do something, *anything*, to save her from being swallowed up, but his instincts kicked in and prevented him from acting. One false step, he reminded himself. He wouldn't be able to help Jorna if he got himself into trouble by being rash.

Still, he called her name, slowly, painstakingly, starting to work his way to the dark pit where she'd disappeared. He hoped that she had found something to hang onto, that she wasn't lost to him. The thought that he had just found her, that she meant so much to him and what his world might be like without her in it, tried to claw at him, but he shoved it aside, focusing all his strength on simply getting to her.

Shanik flew up out of the hole as Thane was nearing it, his glossy black scales catching the sunlight as he hovered in the air near the Sarven. His face was unreadable, but his voice belied his worry. "I don't see her," he reported, "The hole is deep. Even if there isn't a worm down there, she would never..." he choked on the words, but forced himself to say it anyway, "she wouldn't survive that fall."

"No!" Thane refused to believe it. He swatted the dragon away from himself, kneeling down as close to the edge of the sinkhole as he dared to get and desperately called for Jorna. When she didn't answer, he waited a few moments and tried again and again and again, longing to hear her voice shout up at him, telling him she was all right. It never happened. No matter how many times he yelled her name, no matter how badly he wished or hoped, Jorna didn't answer.

Thane was relieved to reach the other side of the sinkholes, glad that he would not have to spend a night wondering if a giant worm was going to come up beneath him and swallow him whole. But he was also sorrowful, missing Jorna and wishing once again that he could switch places with the dead.

Now that they were relatively safe, he collapsed to the ground, allowing the three muskoxen to wander off to dig for food. They wouldn't go too far from their master.

This was the first chance he'd gotten to really think in the last few hours. He'd forced himself to focus on traversing the dangerous ground and pushed aside everything else. Part of him wanted to believe that Jorna was still alive, trapped beneath the snow and ice, struggling for a way to get back to him. It had all happened so fast, much faster than when Thunar had died, surely there was some hope?

Shanik said there wasn't. Over and over again, he reminded the Sarven that she was gone. But what did a dragon know? He also urged

Thane to continue her quest, to recover the book in her name, for the sake of her honor, and for her people.

Thane knew that should be his main concern now, but all he wanted was to curl into a ball on the snow and let the unforgiving weather leech the life out of his body until all that remained was an empty husk. Not only was someone he cared about gone, likely dead, but he had failed to save her and he'd allowed himself to be led away without recovering her body.

"There was nothing you could have done," Shanik cut into his thoughts in another attempt to comfort him. "Even if she were alive, you couldn't have helped her. The hole was just too deep."

Thane's head knew it was true, but his heart... his heart refused to believe that someone else he loved had been ripped away.

He frowned suddenly, realizing that he'd used a word to describe his feelings that couldn't possibly make sense. The painful wrenching in his chest said otherwise, forcing him to see a wonderful, terrible truth.

He was in love with Jorna and he was never going to see her again. Never going to get the opportunity to tell her just how much she meant to him. A mirthless laugh tore from his lips as he realized what that meant. He was a Sarven, his heart had been given whether he was aware of it or not, there was no going back. He had finally found a woman he could love, a woman whose name he wanted to be the last word he spoke, a woman to bear his children, to fight alongside, to grow old with, and she was dead. Jorna was dead.

The laugh turned into an agonized sob, his heart feeling as though it had just been crushed by a massive fist. It was like the pain he'd felt at losing his brother, only a hundred times deeper. He couldn't imagine feeling anything worse, but he was certain he deserved this pain, for it was the same heartache that Makira endured every day since her husband's death. This knowledge only made his guilt and grief stronger, crippling him as surely as though someone had severed his legs clean from his body.

Through these muddied, sluggish thoughts, he was dimly aware of Shanik screaming his name, of the ground shaking beneath him and the frightened cries of the muskoxen. The only sensible part of him that remained urged him to get a grip, that if he died here then Jorna's quest would fall to ruin.

Had it not been for that single truth, he would have ignored what was going on around him and let whatever this new evil was simply take him. But he could not dishonor her memory by giving up. He knew that Jorna would never quit, she was far too stubborn, and so he wouldn't either.

The memory of that night in the giant camp, of how she had whispered that she was afraid, trusting him with her deepest feelings, came to him suddenly. He hoped wherever she was now that her fear was gone, that she was warm and comfortable. He imagined also that she was with Thunar and her father, sharing drinks and tales in the presence of all the great warriors who had come before her...

He held onto to that image as he dragged himself to his feet, pulling his focus to what was going on in the moment. In a flash, his dark gaze took in everything. The first thing he saw was the worm, massive and armored with thick bone plates resembling chunks of lavender ice that protected it not only from the cold, but from weapons as well.

It had burst out of the packed snow and gone for the muskoxen at first. It may have managed to gobble up at least one or two had it not been for the dragon's fast thinking. He was hurling bolts of fire at the glistening worm, doing his best to keep it interested in him, though the fussing of the animals made them far more appealing than an annoying black dot fluttering about its wide, round head.

Taking a deep breath that chilled his lungs, Thane sprang into action, hurrying to the muskoxen so that he could retrieve his axe. Once he had it in hand, he sent them running in the safest direction possible, away from the worm and the fields.

They didn't go far, frightened of the hungry creature, but even more frightened of getting lost in an area that was so unfamiliar. That sort of instinct was exactly why the Sarven valued the beasts as mounts and pack animals over other livestock. They were hardy and not at all flighty, which made them perfect for the sort of lifestyle led by Sarven of old.

Thane pushed away such thoughts, focusing instead on how the two of them were going to defeat the hungry worm. Jorna may have been gone and he may have wanted nothing more than to join her, she and Thunar both, but he refused to let go of life without one hell of a fight.

Winter's Spirit

Jorna awoke to a feeling of being trapped and cold. She was stuck in darkness, her fingers felt stiff, and her entire body was shivering. It took her a few moments to remember what had happened, the ground giving out beneath her feet, falling an impossible distance, and then nothing but blackness.

As she chased the last few remnants of fog from her mind, she knew that she was buried in snow and that if she didn't get up and start moving around, she could very well freeze to death. The question was: could she get up?

If she were buried in a lot of snow, she might not be able to get to the top of it. She was pretty sure nothing was broken, but her limbs were so cold she might have gone numb to the pain.

Determined to at least try, she began to push with her shoulders, freeing her arms, both of which seemed uninjured. Clawing and pushing, she fought her way out from the pile of snow, relieved to discover that she was only a couple feet beneath the top.

It was still dark. Above her head she could distantly see a dim shaft of light, no doubt the very hole she'd fallen through. She saw right away that it was far, far too high up to attempt climbing, but staying put wasn't a good option either, not when there was the danger of a worm coming along to eat her. At the same time, wandering off in a random direction could be just as dangerous. She eyed the path running across where she'd fallen, certain that one end of it had to lead to the worm's nest.

For a long while she sat on the mound of snow, straining for any sound from the surface, any indication that Shanik and Thane were trying to rescue her. Either they had given her up for dead, which she wouldn't blame them if they had, or it was so far up she couldn't hear them. She frowned as she realized just how long a drop it'd been. Had it not been for the soft powdery snow at the bottom, she likely would have been injured.

Gathering herself up, she decided to move on, to try and find her way back up. Surely there were tunnels leading to the surface? The worms didn't always stay burrowed underground, did they? Picking which way to go was the hard part and she found herself wishing more than anything for a sign pointing her in the right direction.

No sooner had the thought entered her mind than she heard the crunch of snow underfoot behind her. Fearing that a worm had just come for its snack, she spun, thankful that she'd been able to retrieve her glaive, and held it out in front of her, prepared to fight for her life. What she saw standing atop the pile of snow was nothing of the sort.

Radiating a soft, shimmering light of its own, a pure silver-white wolf stared keenly at her with knowing, icy blue eyes. She recognized it immediately for what it was, the manifestation of a spirit. A creature, pure and divine, formed from the very earth. The wolf's expression changed as Jorna's mind coursed through a thousand different notions at once, almost as though she could read the Sarven's thoughts. A gasp escaped her and she knew that was exactly what the spirit was doing, reading her like an open book.

Jorna started to speak, wanting to ask why she was here, hoping her purpose was to help, but the wolf was already answering, the words appearing in Jorna's mind. *"I am Firodel, a spirit of winter, and yes, I have come to help you out of your predicament."*

Smiling softly, the Sarven nodded, allowing Firodel to take the next step, which she did quite gladly. Leaping down off the snow, she trotted past Jorna, glancing back to make sure she would follow, before leading the way down the tunnel. The aura of light was enough for her to see by as she followed after the wolf, keeping her senses on alert for any signs of approaching danger.

She couldn't help but think a thousand questions, wondering why a spirit had come to her without being summoned through a ritual, which was the accepted method of communing with them. It struck her as a bit odd, not that she wasn't grateful, she was ecstatic and honored. She also remembered the things her mother had told her when she was teaching her the shamanic ways.

Spirits never did anything without getting something in return; whether it was a taste of mortal energy or some sort of favor, they weren't in the business of charity.

Firodel was aware of all of this and flashed Jorna with a sparkling glance, reminding her of when someone smiled and their eyes lit up. *"We've been watching you, shaman, especially since you beseeched us to calm the snowstorm. As for our motives, you will discover that soon enough."*

Jorna frowned, not sure she liked the idea of such uncertain terms. She didn't want to have anything like that hanging over her head.

"Do not fear. We seek the same end."

She couldn't imagine what that might be, probably not the Gold-steel book. It wasn't exactly something related to spirits, nor did it benefit them. If Firodel had any insight on that, however, she declined to share it.

Instead, there was nothing but silence, well, not so much a silence as the sense that the conversation had ended. She knew Firodel was still aware of her mind, but not actively tapping into it, which was a strange sensation she had to admit.

The idea slipped from her the longer they walked, following a network of tunnels that Jorna hoped would eventually lead them up again. She wondered what time it was and she worried for her companions, especially Thane.

She could only imagine how awful he must be feeling, cut off from her, not knowing if she was alive or dead, fearing the worst... A sudden, strong longing to be there for him and tell him that everything would be all right nearly overpowered her. She didn't want him to be upset; the thought of him mourning her was almost too much to bear. It only increased her urgency to reunite with them.

Shanik, I barely know, but Thane...

A soft smile touched her lips as she thought of him. That night as the giants' prisoners, sitting together in the bone cage, came to mind. The way he had looked at her with his dark eyes had made something inside of her come alive.

Never before had she trusted someone with the softer side of herself, allowing them to see things that were meant to be kept private. With Thane, she felt she could share anything. He didn't judge her or look down on her and even though he was incredibly protective, he didn't smother her in order to keep her safe. That was something she could respect, and he was someone she could admire, trust and care for; she knew without a doubt that she already did.

On and on the tunnels stretched, Firodel leading the way through them as though she'd been raised within their labyrinth. Several times, Jorna could distantly hear the smooth scraping of a worm's hard shell against the icy walls, but the wolf was smart and cunning. She kept them well away from the hungry creatures that wouldn't hesitate to make supper out of a lone Sarven.

She also noticed that in the spirit's presence she wasn't nearly so cold, or perhaps that had something to do with being out of the wind, which was so brutal on the surface. Whatever the cause, she was quite happy for the reprieve, though at first the tingling in her hands and feet was a bit unpleasant as warmth returned slowly to her extremities.

After what felt like hours, they turned down a different passage and Jorna noted almost immediately that it had a subtle incline. The further along it they traveled, the steeper it became, and her heart soared with excitement. She was quite eager to return to her companions and she couldn't shake the feeling that she was only getting closer and closer to seeing them again, to seeing Thane again.

"You care a great deal for the warrior." Firodel's soft voice flitted into her mind as the wolf paused to shoot her a knowing glance.

There was no denying that Jorna did, though she was far too uncertain of their relationship to put words to what that meant exactly. Instead, she grasped at something else, something that was less invasive; the spirit had referred to Thane as a warrior. Not even Thane himself claimed that title, though Jorna could see that he had the heart of a fighter, as all good Sarven did.

This seemed to amuse Firodel. *"Always he has separately defined warrior and blacksmith, but one day he will learn these parts of himself are the same. Soon, the world will know this as well."*

Frowning at the cryptic prediction, Jorna tried to hold back the first thought that came forward, but unlike her tongue, her mind was not so easily controlled. She wanted to know what it meant, if the wolf was speaking of their journey to Dwenenar or of something else. Young she might have been, but Jorna was no fool. She was astute enough to figure out what Firodel *wasn't* saying.

Thane was important, which meant everything they did now was also important. *Why* was the question. Because of the horrific creatures that nobody had ever seen before? She opened herself to the possibility that Dwenenar and the book were small, tiny pieces to a much larger picture and once she did, she didn't need Firodel to answer any questions.

It was no coincidence that the nightmarish fiends had come to conquer her city not long after human dignitaries had come seeking to negotiate for the secrets of Goldsteel. In the back of her mind, Jorna had always suspected that somehow those two things were connected, but she hadn't wanted to see it for herself, not when such a possibility was so terrifying. Even now, she hoped it was only a fear.

If it wasn't, then this epiphany made her task of retrieving the book even more dire. It had always been a danger for those creatures to get their hands on it, but realizing that the secret could be used to destroy the world as she knew it made her sick to her stomach.

She also knew, without a doubt, that this was merely the beginning of the journey. Even if she succeeded, and she was quite determined not to fail, the winged monsters weren't going to simply go away. Something would have to be done about them and about the humans who were now in league with them. That was the larger picture. The idea that she and Thane might have parts to play in saving their world from certain destruction only served to unsettle her further.

"You are wise, shaman, but fear not your future trials." These words were soft and reassuring. *"A great darkness waits in Dwenenar, an evil and a truth that will test the resolve of your heart. When this trial comes,*

remember your allies. Trust the dragon, trust your guardian, and trust yourself. Your courage will come when you have need of it."

She heaved a sigh, remembering what her mother had told her about foresight. A glimpse into the future was a gift, a curse, and not to be trusted or ignored. Time was fluid, ever shifting and changing like the flow of a river. Only the moment was certain, the choice you made or didn't make was all that you could trust, but those glimpses were good for one thing and one thing alone: they were a warning. A caution, a small piece of what was to come, reminding you that all of your choices mattered and that taking the time to weigh them was necessary.

These thoughts followed her out of the tunnels, where a cruel gust of wind reminded her just how much she missed home. At least she was safely on the other side of the worms, but her relief was short lived. She could tell right away that it was almost dark, the sun nearly hidden behind the mountains now.

Firodel trotted north, pausing to glance over her snowy white shoulder to be certain that her charge was still following. *"Hurry now, something foul is on the air..."*

Gripping her glaive more tightly, Jorna didn't hesitate. She ignored the nipping wind and trudged along behind the wolf. They hadn't made it far when she caught the sound of shouting voices, and in the falling darkness, flashes of orange light glaring across the distant sky. Straining to catch a glimpse of what was happening, she stopped beside the spirit, a frown knitting her soft brow.

"Your warrior's mettle is being tested once more," Firodel answered the unspoken question, seemingly unaffected by the sudden rush of frigid air that ruffled her shaggy fur. *"Go now, you are beyond the worm traps. Go and follow your path to its conclusion."*

Jorna looked down at her guide, her expression a mix of gratitude and rising determination. Gathering up her strength, she turned from the white wolf spirit and raced toward the noise of battle.

16

THE FROST WORM

THE CLOSER JORNA GOT, the more she was able to make out what was happening. She saw the worm looming against the horizon, its shining carapace catching the last rays of light as the sun disappeared behind the mountains. She could also make out Thane, his axe in hand, and Shanik breathing fire in an attempt to drive the creature away.

They were holding their own, keeping it from advancing toward the muskoxen, which seemed to be what it really wanted, but they weren't succeeding in scaring it off or breaking through its armor. Even Shanik's fire was barely doing any damage. All they'd really done was made it angrier and meaner, a consequence that would soon bite them both in the rear - literally.

Jorna let out a shout, calling to get their attention as she closed the remaining distance. A smile might have been on her face, had the circumstances been different, especially as she saw the expression on Thane's.

The moment he saw her running toward him, his eyes grew wide and his brows shot up in stunned surprise. She could see the mix of emotions behind his gaze, confirming that they had thought her dead after all. It felt good to show him that assumption was wrong, but that would have to wait. Right now, they had a worm to deal with.

"To me!" she instructed, heading toward where the muskoxen were worrying the ground. "Draw it this way!"

It didn't take them but a second to realize what she was trying to do and even less than that for them to leap into action to help her achieve the goal. Together the three of them dragged the unsuspecting creature away from the fields, watching as it was forced to slither further and further out of its hole, its own fury working against its instincts. The process was not swift, it was slow, but steady. Inch after inch, the tapered tail cleared the hole and the worm shot toward them, spurred by the full might of its rage.

As soon as she felt the solid ice beneath her feet, Jorna began to flank the worm, needing to get in behind it so that it couldn't escape back to the safety of its burrows. "I need fire!" she shouted at the dragon, whose face she imagined held a bewildered expression. "Trust me!"

A second later she got her wish. Shanik hurled a blast of flames in her direction, a little off to the side of her. Jorna raised her glaive, which was no ordinary weapon. It was a shaman's staff, imbued with magic power that made it nigh indestructible, and also acted as a vessel to host elements. A common weapon couldn't be used in her rituals, no matter how powerful she might be, and the process to bond with a staff was tedious but worth it.

That rite had been one of passage, marking her as a full-fledged shaman, though she'd chosen a less than traditional weapon. Most practitioners used a wooden staff, adorned with beads or feathers or other such objects that held personal significance. Jorna was a warrior in her heart, just as Thane was, and so she'd chosen a glaive.

The fire connected with the shaft just above her hand and spread the length of the pole, all the way to the tip of the glaive head. She wasn't harmed, as the staff protected her against any ill effects that might be caused in this situation, as opposed to if she were to attempt grasping an open flame. She could feel its warmth, its power, far stronger than that of ordinary fire: there was special magic in a dragon's inferno.

Jorna didn't stop moving, twirling the glaive in her hands as she planted herself firmly behind the worm. The creature was unaware of her intentions as it was too focused protecting its other flank from Thane. If it was beginning to realize its mistake, then it was far too late to do anything to save itself.

Slamming the end of the haft against the ground, Jorna incited a wall of flames that arced over the ground, cutting off the creature's escape just as she had planned. The fire rose into the air, lighting up the dark night, and causing the worm to release a squeal of fear. Now it beheld its doom. Frantically the creature tried to flee, trying to skirt the blazing wall and plow passed Jorna, but more fire spread out around the shaman, blocking its path.

While she continued to keep it from running away, Thane and Shanik took on a new strategy, deciding without words what had to be done. Later, once the danger was over, they would think back on this and wonder how they had ever managed to share a moment of such camaraderie, but neither one would ever admit that it simply felt natural. As though they had known one another for years and didn't need words to communicate what must be done. Instead, they would always claim it was a happy coincidence, that they simply had the same thought at the same time because it was really the most logical solution.

They had already seen that the worm's armor was nearly impenetrable, but no matter how tough or thick, nothing in the world could repel both Sarven crafted weapons and dragon fire indefinitely, especially when both of those things were aimed at the same location.

Hacking gracelessly at the worm's back, Thane threw all of his strength into the first three blows he was able to land. He paused then, hoping to see that he'd at least made a dent, but he wasn't able to get a good look. Reminded of his presence and its anger, the worm lashed out with its tail, whipping it around to send the Sarven flying.

Skidding across the snow and ice, Thane focused on not accidentally chopping a limb off with his axe and hoped he wouldn't crash into anything that would cause him serious harm. Once he'd slid to a stop, he quickly regained his feet, shaking the snow off his shoulders as best he could before rushing back into the fray.

Meanwhile, Jorna was pleased to see Shanik's balls of fire hitting the same armor segment, which now seemed to be a serious issue for the worm. It was flailing and fighting wildly, not sure who to attack as it was having a hard time tracking Shanik and it seemed to know that Jorna was not responsible for the painful blasts. The shaman was trying to draw its attention though, hurling fire from her staff at its gaping maw, which served to keep it in a state of confusion.

Thane was the least of its concerns right now, forgotten as it tried to fend off the other two attackers whose fire was a much greater threat. In a way, Jorna almost felt sorry for the creature; it had only been after a meal. It wasn't an evil monster, merely a predator that had picked the wrong prey.

Even still there was no course for mercy, not against a creature driven by sheer instinct. If they let it go, there was no guarantee that it wouldn't reach its burrow and continue the fight where it had the advantage. The only way to be certain that the worm couldn't hurt them or their animals was to slay it.

Thane brought his axe down on the weakened armor segment and heard the satisfying crack as the carapace was finally shattered. A shrieking howl echoed as the desperate worm spun toward the Sarven, its mandibles snapping with harmful intent at any part of him that it could grab.

He rolled out of its way just as a flash of dragon fire streaked across the sky above him. Without needing to look, he knew by the cry of agony that the blaze had reached its mark, dripping through the broken armor to scorch the tender flesh beneath. Mountain creatures might have had a natural fortitude against cold, but that made them even more susceptible to heat. Because of this, the fire spread, burning the worm from the inside and filling the air with the scent of charred meat.

It was over in a matter of seconds. The night grew silent save for the roar of the nearby fire walls and the panting of the three companions. Nearby, the muskoxen shook themselves, acting as though nothing had ever happened. They lazily wandered closer to their masters. Thane picked himself up off the ground again, brushing snow off his clothes before turning to watch the smoldering remains as they continued to burn.

Shanik dropped down from the sky, landing on the unmarred segment of armor next to the one they had shattered. The dragon seemed to be eying something within the fatal wound. After a moment, he reached down, tearing a chunk of scorched flesh out of the hole. He sniffed it suspiciously, gave it a tentative lick, and with a shrug, popped it into his mouth. For a long moment he sat there chewing thoughtfully, perfectly aware that Thane was watching him with an expression of disgust. Finally, he swallowed and declared matter-of-factly, "It just needs a touch of salt."

Rolling his eyes, the Sarven turned away from the dragon, looking for Jorna.

The shaman was standing a few meters away, leaning heavily on her glaive, which was no longer blazing with fire. She'd released the magic, allowing it to simply dissipate, and now that she had, she was feeling incredibly exhausted. Such practices were quite draining, leaving her head swimming and her eyes droopy. All she wanted to do was collapse into the snow and take a very long nap, despite the dangers.

Suddenly aware of Thane's gaze on her, she glanced over to him and remembered in a rush how they had been separated.

Now she let herself smile, forgetting about the tiredness that edged her vision and dragged on her limbs. She was overcome with a sudden joy, and she could see by the light in his eyes that Thane was, too.

She took a tentative step toward him, wanting to close the distance so she could be near him, whispering that everything would be alright but also feeling a bit of uncertainty. Why she didn't fully know, perhaps it was her upbringing, the propriety she'd been taught reminding her that she could not simply rush into any man's arms. She was a princess, her actions reflected her family and most importantly her family's position as leader of a kingdom.

She quickly reminded herself that she was not in Dwenenar, or even Hamdralg. She was in the middle of the wilderness, she'd cheated death, returned to her companions, and helped them to defeat a great ice worm.

Before she realized it, she was moving freely, the inhibitions driven away by a rush of desire. She let the glaive slip from her fingers as she hurried to Thane before some unbidden notion could stop her. It felt like an entire continent separated them, as though it took forever for that gap to close, despite Thane rushing to meet her. She let her emotions guide her actions, and once she was finally close to him,

Jorna threw her arms around his neck, not caring if the entire world bore witness.

REUNION

LIFTING JORNA OFF THE ground, Thane felt as though he were caught in a waking dream. He distantly wondered if he was still laying on the ground just beyond the worm fields, becoming delusional as he froze to death. The warmth of Jorna's body, which fit perfectly against his own, was fair proof that what he was experiencing was real. She was real and more than that, she was alive. His heart sang with joy as a grin nearly split his face in half. By the way she clung to him, her arms tight around his shoulders and her cheek pressing against his, she was every bit as happy to see him as he was to see her.

"I thought..." he started to say, but his voice cracked as he remembered the intense pain he'd felt when he believed her dead. "I thought I had lost you," he finally managed the words.

Jorna pulled back, not far, just enough so that she was peering compassionately into his face, her gray-blue eyes soft with an emotion he couldn't name. He was reminded of the first time he'd seen her, strolling with confidence into a king's war chamber, proving with her regal bearing that she more than belonged there. He knew that's when he had fallen, the moment her beautiful gaze touched him. That day had changed the entire course of his life, taking him down a path he would never have thought he could walk, and she'd been beside him through it all.

"Thane..."

Her voice drew his dark gaze to her pale lips. He couldn't help but wonder what they would feel like against his own. The notion brought with it an overwhelming desire to find out. He saw her cheeks flush and knew his intent was written plainly on his face. He also knew that Jorna had not stepped away. She was still pressed tightly against his chest, her hands on his shoulders; he could feel the trembling puffs of her breath against his beard.

Gently he brushed hair back from her face, letting his fingers caress her ear as he leaned down and brushed his lips against hers. For a brief moment, he feared he'd overstepped, that he'd read her wrong and just offended a princess, but then he felt her kiss him back.

An elated surge shot through his heart, obliterating any remaining tendrils of pain from when he'd thought her gone. Never before had he known such joy as he did in that moment, holding the woman of his affection in his arms, tasting the sweetness of her kiss for the very first time.

It was over far, far too quickly. Her nose bumped against his as their mouths parted, making him smile more freely than he had in what seemed like a lifetime. "I wouldn't go anywhere without you," she was whispering, her flush deepening with embarrassment. "Is that a foolish thing to say?"

"No," he answered, shaking his head, "I never want to go anywhere without you either."

A sound, much like someone retching, prevented Jorna from replying further and drew their attention to Shanik, who was still perched on the dead worm. "This is your only warning! Stop being utterly repulsive or next time I may actually vomit on you instead of just mimicking the sound!"

"Sorry," Thane grunted sarcastically and not at all with any real remorse. "I forgot you even existed, lizard."

Puffing out his scaly chest, Shanik's entire demeanor belied his indignation. His wings ruffled and his nose went into the air, his sapphire eyes narrowed to mere slits. "That's not surprising; having an empty head makes it difficult to keep important things from simply falling out," he quipped curtly.

Thane released an unamused growl, wanting nothing more than to pummel the mouthy dragon into silence so that he could return to his moment with Jorna. Unfortunately, it had passed. He realized that as soon as he felt her step away, though the way she squeezed his hand told him that it was not the end of their exchange.

Still glowering at Shanik, he turned to go fetch the muskoxen, who were nosing around in the snow a short distance away.

"We shouldn't linger here," he heard Jorna say behind him, "I'm sure there's some sort of predator or another that would like to make a meal out of a worm. At the very least scavengers. It's better if we've moved on before the feast begins."

Shanik glanced up at the sky, his expression neutral now that they were discussing serious matters. "The moon is veiled. It's not a good evening to travel too far, but I agree it's most wise to put some distance between us and the remains."

Returning with the muskoxen to where they were standing, Thane couldn't argue that they had a point. He wasn't particularly keen to hang around the fresh kill either and even less inclined to bury it to keep it from drawing out predators and scavengers. It was far better to simply move on and leave the corpse to feed the wild creatures that inhabited the mountains.

Without saying much else, the three companions set off, determined to travel for a couple hours more before making camp. Thane and Jorna rode beside one another, flashing each other significant glances and coy smiles as their mounts plodded along, the pack animal in tow. Ahead of them, Shanik bobbed up and down with the currents of the wind, happy to keep the pair of Sarven behind him so he didn't have to witness their fawning.

As planned, they made camp a little while later, not long after coming to the edge of a forest filled with snow-laden pine trees. It was nice to get out of the beating wind, to have some buffer against its cruel gusts and simply to have some measure of being in an enclosed space again. The vast emptiness of the steppes was even worse than just being on the surface and both Sarven were very thankful to officially put it behind them.

Tired from the exertion of all they'd been through, they set right to work in dealing with the chores that came with making camp: tending the muskoxen, preparing food for themselves, cleaning up afterward, laying out their bedrolls.

The meal was not eaten in silence as it often had been since their journey's start. Jorna shared her story, telling of how she'd met Firodel and been guided back to her companions by the white wolf. She left out a few details, namely the cryptic comments that she felt neither of them would understand, but nearly everything else was divulged around her supper. Thane and Shanik both listened intently until she was done. The dragon seemed to be full of questions, most of which she answered easily, but Thane seemed content with all she had shared.

When it was time for sleep, she and Thane laid their beds a little closer together than the previous nights, even though it was no longer necessary to have them side-by-side now that they were more protected from the icy wind.

While Shanik perched up in a tree, muttering something about keeping watch, the pair settled under the fur blankets, facing one another. When he could take being separate from her no longer, Thane lifted the edge of his furs, beckoning Jorna to come closer. Her cheeks flushed, but after a second's hesitation she shifted from her bedroll to his.

Thane secured the blanket and his arm around her shoulders, thrilled at the wave of heat that her body sent washing over him. He held her close, breathing in her scent and soaking up her warmth. There were so many things he wanted to tell her, but whenever he tried, the words wouldn't come. So he settled for just holding her and hoping she could feel how much he cared in his touch.

18

DRAGON MAGIC

THOUGH THE GROUP AWAKENED before dawn, they did not resume traveling until much later. Instead they took their time with the morning chores, preparing to go as soon as the first rays of light showed themselves over the Whitetop peaks.

Even after they were ready to get moving, Jorna took a fair amount of time going over the map, confused by the existence of a forest that was not at all indicated on the worn parchment. The Icedrifts should have given way to the Whitetops, leading them directly to the door into the mountains.

Draped around her shoulders, Shanik sniffed dubiously at the map, then offered another of his odd shrugs. "Maybe the map-maker just ran out of parchment," he rasped sarcastically, earning himself a stern look from the shaman.

"The reality…" Thane interjected from where he was standing near the muskoxen, eager to be under way, "Whoever created the map probably never made it past the worm fields."

Jorna could certainly buy that. The Sarven had been fighting a war with every creature that inhabited the Beldrath range; it stood to reason that they wouldn't have committed the manpower or resources to exploring beyond the worm fields when they were so consumed with fighting the giants. That meant the map was made partly from assumption, at least this far from Hamdralg where few had dared to tread.

Even when her people had left the Sarven kingdom, they certainly hadn't departed via the surface. They remained underground except when building the two outside entrances to Dwenenar, the back door being unknown to those who were not among the royal family or highest ranking nobles and advisers. It was meant as an escape route should all other entrances be under siege.

Thinking about it, Jorna was quite glad that when fleeing to Hamdralg, the refugees weren't forced to escape to the surface. They surely would have frozen to death or died at the hands of giants or the hungry maw of an ice worm.

"We need to move while we have the light," Thane broke into her thoughts, his voice sounding uneasy. Like most Sarven, he did not trust the woods.

Rising off the fallen tree she'd been using as a seat, Jorna folded up the map and stuffed it back into her belt as she moved to join him. He was right, there was something about this forest that unsettled her, especially during the day. It was far too silent, too empty, despite the thick clumping of the trees and underbrush. Even the muskoxen seemed a touch nervous this morning, as though they were expecting something to jump out at them. It was a sensation that she understood quite well, for she too felt as though they were being watched.

Despite their misgivings, the three companions started deeper into the forest, traveling without stop since there was only a limited num-

ber of hours that the sun would illuminate their path. From what they
could see of the mountains in the distance, it would only take them
a few days to reach their destination, though they could have easily
fit that time into one or two days were it not for the overwhelming
darkness of winter.

They pushed on as long as they could, waiting to make camp until the
light was almost completely gone. Thane took his axe and ventured
a short distance away to fetch firewood, leaving Jorna to settle in the
muskoxen, which she tethered to a nearby tree. She was nervous about
any of them going too far away from the camp, but she knew Thane
could handle himself. After all, they'd come across no signs suggesting
that anything at all lived in this forest, not even woodland creatures.
This made her feel even more on edge, but she did her best to push it
out of her mind.

When she was finished with their animals, she laid out the cookware, setting up a spot for a fire and then laying out their bedrolls. By
the time she was starting on the latter, Thane had returned, his arms
laden down with branches and sticks, his axe still strapped securely to
his back where he could easily get to it. He set to work preparing the
fire, or more accurately, goading Shanik into setting it for him - a fact
the dragon realized a little too late.

Turning away as Shanik began his outcry, Thane moved to Jorna,
ignoring the dragon entirely. She straightened from smoothing out the
furs and was surprised to see him standing so close. Surprised, but also
pleased. She would have greeted him, she opened her mouth to do just

that, but the expression on his face told her that he had something on his mind.

"I have something for you," he finally commented, reaching for his belt.

"Oh?" She searched his face for some clue as to what it might be before glancing down to see what it was he had held out to her. When she did, all she could do was stare.

Resting lightly on his wide palm was a small, pale blue, delicate wildflower that she recognized as a frost flower. It was soft, with round petals and a white stamen. The stem was not the typical green of most flora, instead it was a dark blue. They were known for their beauty and fortitude, for the frost flower only grew in winter and could only be found in the coldest of places.

"I found a bunch of them and I thought of you," he started to explain when all she did was stare at his hand. There was a faint hint of uncertainty tightening his bearded jaw, belying his nervousness.

His words, sweet and hopeful, brought a warm, honest smile to her lips. The gesture might have seemed out of place to anyone who didn't know the best kept Sarven secret of all time. To Jorna, who had often listened as a child to tales of how her father had won her mother's heart, it was exactly the sort of gesture she had always dreamed of. Still smiling, Jorna gladly accepted the flower and told him breathily, "Thank you, Thane. It's quite lovely."

"Bah, it's just a silly plant," Shanik interjected scathingly, attempting to reclaim Thane's attention. "I demand a measure of respect, Sarven. I am a dragon, not your personal flint and steel!"

Pleased that Jorna had liked his gift, the blacksmith wasn't at all bothered by the continued tirade and even managed to grin as he turned back to face the still fussing dragon. "Poor little lizard, did I bruise your delicate ego by outwitting you?"

"This has nothing to do with my ego, it has to do with respect!" Shanik retorted haughtily, sitting back on his haunches and crossing his front legs over his chest in a very anthropoid manner.

While the two of them renewed their squabble, Jorna took a step away, announcing softly that she'd return in a moment. Neither of them really seemed to notice her departure. She needed to think, and she couldn't do that with the two of them bickering. Nor did she want to risk that one of them might notice something was wrong. The last thing she wanted to deal with was having her current frame of mind pried into.

She didn't go too far away from the camp, she could still distantly hear them talking and see the glow of the fire as she stopped, moving to press her back against the nearest tree. With a sigh, she slid down to the snowy earth between its protruding roots, feeling less uneasy with her back against something solid.

It was strangely comforting, almost as though that tree had formed in such a manner in preparation for this very moment. Such a thought was quite fanciful, but that didn't make it any less nice to consider.

Jorna waited until then to let the feelings inside of her take over. Perhaps it was silly to hide herself away, but she couldn't fight her upbringing any more than she could fight the air. Tears of joy or tears of sorrow, it didn't matter, they must still be shed in private and for Jorna they were a mix of both.

She was happy to have found Thane, her feelings for him continued to grow and she knew without a doubt that her future would be spent with him. That was the way of their society, the way of the Sarven heart. Finding it now made the experience bittersweet, for she had always expected her family, her whole family, to share in her joys. The thought of her father never meeting the man she cared for, never getting to see his grandchildren, tore at her heart, casting a shadow over what should have been nothing but bliss.

She looked down through tear blurred eyes at her hands, where the blue frost flower lay against her palm, and she couldn't help but smile as warmth battled the sorrow in her heart. There had been other suitors. As an eligible princess, she was often the object of infatuation. These other men had tried to gain her favor by presenting expensive, lavish gifts, hoping to prove their worth with all sorts of useless trinkets or pointless feats of strength.

Not Thane Stoutforge. He had tried to woo her affections with nothing more than a single, beautiful flower - a simple token, but one that was more powerful than all the combined riches of the world.

Reaching up to brush the tears from her eyes, she smiled to herself, confident that her father would applaud Thane's choice. He would have also been proud of hers, whether he was there to tell her or not.

These thoughts were still in her mind when a raspy voice startled her. "So this is where you wandered off to!"

Sitting upright, Jorna quickly composed herself, wiping away the last tears from her face. "Yes, sorry!" She turned her head to where Shanik was sitting stoically on one of the raised roots. "Where's Thane? Is everything all right?" she asked, mildly alarmed when she saw that she'd been gone for more than just the intended few minutes. Judging by how cold she felt anyway.

"Oh, don't worry about the hairy ape." Shanik sniffed disdainfully. "He's straining himself to make supper... Something brown that smells worse than he does!" He reached a clawed foot up to rub at his temples, as though he were suffering from a headache.

Giving him a slight smile, Jorna reached out and idly scratched under his chin as her thoughts drifted to other matters that were more important than the squabbles of her companions. The reminder of their argument, however, brought to mind another problem. She had no place safe to put her flower.

She glanced down into her hand at the delicate frost flower; already it was starting to show signs of withering, its soft petals drooping ever so slightly. It probably would have lasted longer had it not been confined to her hands or a pocket or pouch, but no matter where she tucked it, it would only get damaged. She held on her palm the most precious, special gift she had ever received, and it was soon going to die.

That thought caused her brow to furrow deeply. She had no way of protecting it herself, not out here on the road. If she had a book, she could have pressed it, but there was no book because there was no reason to bring one along and that meant there was nothing that could save her beautiful flower from its troublesome fate.

"Please tell me you're not actually attached to that weed..." Shanik had been watching her closely and in fact, he'd taken a couple minutes initially to observe her long before he'd spoken, startling her from her contemplations. When she didn't answer him right away, he arched his scaly eyebrow. "What is it that has you so enthralled? It's just a silly flower, there are dozens upon dozens in these mountains, no doubt!"

"Yes, but this one is special," she answered weightily, her voice tinged with worry. "It's proof that he thought of me, at a time when I wasn't there, when I shouldn't have been on his mind... He saw this flower and thought of *me*."

Jorna didn't notice it at the time, she was too consumed in her own plight to have been aware of the dragon's sudden shift in demeanor, but a day would come when she would look back at that moment and realize how melancholy he became. He dropped his head, staring hard at the root he was sitting on, his shoulders and wings slumped.

"That does make it special," he conceded gently, his voice unusually hollow. "Is that not good?"

She nodded without any hesitation. She knew it was most certainly good. Whatever lay ahead for them, there was nothing that could sully his gift, except perhaps having to watch it wither away.

"Then..." Shanik looked up at her, his reptilian features tinged with curiosity. "Why are you so sad?"

Turning her gray-blue gaze to him, the Sarven didn't care how silly it might sound, she blurted, "Because it's going to die!"

"Ahh..." Understanding flashed across his face, and he nodded slowly, reaching a talon up to rub thoughtfully at his chin. "That is very unfortunate..." He fell silent for several moments, while Jorna dropped her gaze away from him in defeat, resigned to being incapable of changing that awful fact. Then abruptly he held out his claw to her. "Let me have it."

She frowned uncertainly, having no idea what was going on inside the dragon's mind and that made her very hesitant to relinquish her new treasure. Finally, she decided to trust him and if he did anything terrible... she'd let Thane deal with him. "Be careful with it..." There was a threatening edge to her tone as she laid the delicate flower in his outstretched claw.

Shanik gave her an exasperated look, wondering for a brief moment if she really thought he might damage it on purpose. He told himself that was unlikely, she was just being protective of something that meant a great deal to her, and though he saw no worth in a mere flower, he could understand that, in her eyes, it was priceless.

Carefully he closed his digits around the frost flower, shutting his sapphire eyes as he muttered a string of ancient draconian words. Magic had always come naturally to dragons in a way that most mortal creatures couldn't even fathom. The three races were capable of performing certain kinds of magic, magic that was unique to their people, but their gifts barely scratched the surface of what was almost second nature to a dragon.

The trickiest bit was restoring some of the flower's radiance, making the petals crisp and fresh, as they had been when Thane first plucked the small token. Anything much bigger and he may not have been able to pull it off, such magic was the most difficult to perform after all, but he managed it quite well in this instance.

Next, was the easiest and best part, a simple charm that would forever preserve it so that it would not decay, followed by a protection spell that would prevent it from becoming damaged. Once he finished weaving his magic, a person could take a knife or club to Jorna's flower and not a single petal, nor mere inch of stem, would be ruined.

"There..." he said softly, a pleased expression forming on his face as he held out the improved token to her. "Impervious and eternal."

Gingerly she accepted it, turning it over in her fingers, inspecting it closely. Right away she could tell it was no longer starting to wilt, but she had her doubts that it would stay that way. To her senses it was exactly the same, a delicate, beautiful flower.

"You don't believe me..." Shanik's eyes glittered. "If you want proof, try to pinch a tiny bit off the stem with your fingernail."

Her expression was dubious, but she couldn't see the harm in demonstrating that the dragon was not as clever as he seemed to think. Besides, a little sliver removed would not matter in a few days when it was brown and dead.

Carefully, she pinched the bottom of the stem between her finger and thumbnail. When it didn't break off, she squeezed harder and harder, but still it was undamaged. She couldn't even see a mark where her nail had pressed!

Jorna beamed a grin at Shanik, pleased with the results of his magic. "You're a good friend," she told him, leaning over to place a kiss on the end of his snout, whether he liked it or not. If dragons could blush, she was certain he would have turned bright red. The way that he ruffled his wings and glanced away was more than enough to betray his embarrassment.

Still smiling, the Sarven came to her feet, plucking Shanik off the root and holding him up so that he could crawl onto her shoulders, which he did contently. Without another word she headed back to camp, feeling much better than when she had left.

AMBUSH

As HE SAT WAITING on his mount, Thane's gaze wandered to the shaman, who was standing beside her own muskox, Shanik draped around her shoulders, that specific location having become his usual perch.

She was dirty and disheveled from traveling, her green dress creased with wrinkles where it got bunched up while riding. Her pale hair had been divided into twin braids, though it was grimy from lack of being washed and mussed around her head from being slept upon but not brushed. Yet to his eyes she was every bit as beautiful as the first day he had met her in the palace.

Feeling his eyes on her, Jorna turned a curious expression to Thane that he quickly shrugged away. She must have decided not to press the matter, for she simply gave him a warm smile and then returned her attention to packing the last of her belongings.

He watched her for a moment longer, caught off guard by the familiar warmth in his chest, a sensation that he had come to associate as his feelings for the Dwenenari princess.

Thane was so distracted by his companion that it took him a moment to realize something was wrong with their surroundings. Had it not been for a hiss from the dragon, they would have had no warning at all, but thanks to Shanik's keen sense of smell, they knew that danger was near.

A moment later, an odd trilling flitted over the air, summoning another growl from Shanik. Quickly, Thane scanned the immediate area, looking for any sign of what could have caused such a noise, a noise that he had never heard from an animal before. There was nothing, no people, no creatures, absolutely nothing except the wind as it whistled through the pine and birch trees cluttered around them.

Then the source finally appeared. Tall and dark, they seemed to spring from the ground as though it had just given birth to fully grown and primitively armed orc men. Their earthy brown skin was smeared with white paint, and they wore clothes made of fur and hide, no doubt to aid them in blending in with their surroundings.

One among them, with a headdress of sun-washed bones and gold-dyed wooden beads, stood out among the rest, drawing Thane's gaze by merely staring intently at him.

The brief exchange of two warriors staring one another down lasted only seconds, giving the companions just enough time to ready themselves before the primitives rushed them. Rolling out of the saddle, Thane pulled his axe free and brought it up to meet the crude spear of a painted man, knocking the other weapon out of the way.

Taking advantage of the exposed flank, the Sarven swung the haft around and walloped the man's ribs with the hard wood, forcing him to stagger into the stone as he was thrown off balance by the sheer force of the blow. He wasn't given a reprieve as several more of the savages came flying at him, targeting the bigger, stronger Sarven as the most dangerous.

Jorna soon made them regret the assumption that she was weak because she was a woman. "For Guldorn!" The battle cry tore from her lips as she danced into the fray, her glaive tripping one of the orcs who was preparing to leap at Thane's back. She dared not use fire, afraid of setting the trees aflame and causing them all problems they didn't need, so she did not call for Shanik to once again imbue her weapon. Instead, she summoned what came naturally and what was already plentiful.

Planting the bottom of her glaive into the snow, she gathered the pristine flakes, drawing them up so that they circled around the silver shaft, the blade glistening as though it were encrusted with ice.

Two of the men watched, horror on their faces. They didn't dare to attack her and instead they tried to flee. She let them go, turning as she grasped the glaive in both of her hands and took up a position beside Thane. There was a cut on his shoulder from a savage who had got lucky, but he didn't seem to notice it. He flashed her a grin and brandished his axe, daring the orcs to attack again.

By now however, they had all stopped their assault and were rallying around their leader, the man with the bone headdress. The ones who had been foolish enough to try stealing the muskoxen were limping or holding burn wounds. Shanik had taken it upon himself to protect the animals, though when threatened they had done what was necessary to defend themselves. The group's ability to hold its own was not what stopped them - it was Jorna's magic.

The leader stepped forward, his dark gaze turning to Thane. Slowly he began to speak, forming words that were barely understandable, not because they were poorly articulated, but because they were an ancient Sarven dialect. No doubt these primitives were remnants of conquered slaves that had been used during the Giant Wars and either thought dead or left behind when the Sarven retreated. That was the only explanation Thane could think of that made any sense for a tribe of orcs to be here. Being far less familiar with the old tongue than Jorna, no doubt part of her education as a princess had been learning it, Thane glanced over to her, silently asking for help with his response.

She blushed at first but translated word for word. "He says, your woman commands the winter and he extends his remorse at mistaking us for enemies. He's inviting us to share his lodgings and food, that he may honor us..." She trailed off, her brow creased with uncertainty. Finally, she added simply, "They believe we're gods..."

NEW ALLIES

THEIR WALK TO THE village was slow and casual, the leader doing his best to chatter with Thane, though the Sarven had difficulty at first to understand him. With Jorna's help and a bit of patience, he was beginning to comprehend the strange, yet familiar words of long ago.

The orc warriors, who called themselves the Boesh, led them northward to where their encampment was nestled in a stand of birch trees, the fur lodgings built in such a way that they seemed to have grown directly from the foliage.

It wasn't the most defensible location, considering the primitives were bunched together. Any great number of men could overcome them, set fire to the surrounding trees, which would spread to their homes, and then easily slaughter every single one of them during the ensuing chaos.

Their one advantage was the ability to see such dangers from the tops of the trees as they approached, a notion that the Boesh must also have been aware of, for Thane was certain he'd seen painted sentries sliding to the ground as they came down the snowy trail.

Warning must have been given to the tribe that their warriors were returning, for every woman, child, man, and elder came forward to greet them and, Thane suspected, to inspect their visitors.

They all possessed the same muddy, brown skin, only the warriors painted theirs white, and their hair color seemed to range from a sooty-brown to darkest black. It was worn long by the women, while most of the men kept theirs short or completely shaved off. The women were dressed in light deer hides with crude jewelry adorning their wrists, ankles and necks, while the children wore fur clothes that were similar to that of the men - leggings and loincloths for the boys and simple hide dresses for the girls.

It seemed to be a statement of strength among them to wear little protection against the cold, though after countless generations of living in such a harsh environment there was no doubt that they had developed as much resistance as the other creatures and beings who inhabited the Beldrath mountains.

They all pressed close, chattering in their unfamiliar language too quickly for either Sarven to fully understand, their hands outstretched so that they could touch the newcomers as they were led further into the village.

Thane felt fingers stroke his hair, a palm brush across his shoulder, and even one elderly woman grabbed his backside. Face flushed red with embarrassment, the blacksmith glanced to his companions, hoping that neither had seen. He could just imagine that Shanik especially would never let him live it down, but he was instantly perplexed.

None of the orcs were touching Jorna; in fact they respectfully kept their distance as though they didn't wish to offend her. They bowed and whispered reverently, while the princess, accustomed to such behavior, graciously thanked them for the honor they bestowed upon her.

"Yes, Sarven, I saw that." Shanik's raspy voice, thick with sarcasm, drew Thane's attention before he could give the strange actions of their hosts any more thought. "You should find out which tent is hers. I bet she'd make you lovely children."

Scowling, Thane fought the urge to push the last few invasive hands away from his arms and back. He was just about to deliver a scathing response to the dragon, when the warrior leader, who they knew now to be called Ikta, brought them to a halt.

When the gathering had given him their attention, he began to speak, welcoming their honored guests and explaining that they would soon dine together. He then presented his sister, a younger woman with the same dark skin and bead-decorated, black hair as her older brother.

Ulta, as was her name, smiled and extended her hand out to the shaman, who hesitantly took it and started to follow. When she realized that Thane and the other men were not accompanying them, she stopped abruptly, turning back. She started to ask why they were being separated, but Shanik whispered something in her ear, which seemed to allay her reluctance. Jorna quickly flashed Thane a parting smile before continuing on with Ulta and the other women of the tribe.

Thane was equally concerned, but Ikta's strong hand on his shoulder drew him away from the retreating form of his companions and back to the warrior who stood beside him. Flashing a toothy grin, he beckoned the Sarven toward a big tent near the center of the village, conveying with a few guttural words that they would see the others again soon, that meals were taken apart.

Nodding slowly, Thane made no comment but followed after his guide. He quickly noted that none of the women had stayed with them. Their entire group was made up entirely of men and, much to his surprise, boys. So that was what he had meant when he told Thane they ate separately; he had been referring to the difference in gender and not something in direct regards to Thane or his companions.

A sly smirk appeared beneath his thick, black mustache for a moment as he imagined Shanik's reaction to being the only male in Jorna's group. Apparently the orcs saw him more as a pet than an individual, a fact which would undoubtedly fluster the dragon to no end!

The tent that Thane was led to was made of hides and fur, mostly elk and bison if Thane had to guess, all stitched together and spread out over a light, wooden frame. Not the most sturdy of shelters and highly flammable, not to mention the whole lodging had a strange, oily scent to it, but Thane wasn't about to complain; it was better than nothing, after all.

Inside was an older man, easily two hundred years old or more, judging by the sheer number of wrinkles that covered his leathery face. His once black hair had turned a dull shade of gray and hung in a myriad of thin braids down his hunched back to pool on the blanket-covered ground where he sat.

When the group entered, he glanced up, one watery eye a warm brown and the other a milky blue. Clearly, he was blind in that eye, no doubt from the same blow that had left a gnarled scar from his bushy gray eyebrow to his craggy cheek. Thane glanced quickly away and hoped nobody noticed his staring.

As the elderly leader began to speak, his voice quiet and shaky, Ikta moved to his side, dragging Thane along. He offered the elder's name, Kelkta, and identified him as his father, before pushing the Sarven into a seated position next to the old man. The odd smell he'd detected upon entering wafted over to him, more strongly than before, making Thane almost certain that the source wasn't the hides, but the elder.

He really hoped they didn't expect him to eat here; he wasn't sure if he could stomach that smell while trying to do so, not when it was so absolutely overwhelming.

And I thought humans stunk the worst when they sweat... he thought, mentally grimacing at the idea of what the old man might smell like were he to exert himself.

Around them the other men filed in, taking up seats on the ground with their legs crossed. Some of the young boys were held on the laps of their fathers, while the older children sat in small groups. Everyone was packed into the tent, leaving very little space to walk.

After a few minutes, which most everyone spent conversing quietly in their foreign dialect, two elderly women came into the tent, bearing bowls of food in their arms. They started with the youngest of the children, bringing in two to three bowls at a time until all the boys had been given their portion.

Much to Thane's surprise he was next. The old woman, her wizened face smiling down at him, passed him a warm wooden bowl that was filled to the brim with what looked like a thick, goat meat stew.

The spicy scent of it filled Thane's nostrils, overpowering the oily smell of the old man next to him and causing his stomach to grumble in anticipation. He gave her a nod of thanks, knowing he had been honored by being offered food even before their elder, who was served directly after the Sarven and just before his son. After that, the rest of the men were given their meal according to their social ranking. When the task was finished, the two women departed without a word.

Once the gathering had begun to eat, Thane started as well, digging into the hot food with the wooden utensil that had been passed out already stuck in the bowl's contents. The stew slowly became more spicy the more of it he crammed into his mouth, heating his tongue and lips and forcing him to pause in between bites.

It was this action that prompted Kelkta to begin speaking, as he believed Thane was giving him an opening for conversation. His words weren't much better than his son's, but it was his soft tone that made him somewhat difficult to understand. Even still, he shared with the Sarven many tales of his youth, from when he had undergone a rite of passage to becoming a man and how he'd lost sight in his left eye during a great battle with a rival tribe.

There was a great deal Thane knew he was missing in the translation, but he gathered that once he'd held the same position as Ikta, leader and warrior, then the position had fallen to his first born and he became the tribe's Elder. From what he understood, being Elder didn't hold very many duties; it was a position of honor and respect, a way for him to impart his wisdom upon younger generations that were more able-bodied.

The conversation carried on until the three of them were done eating. Once everyone was finished with their meal the men began to leave and Ikta signaled Thane to join him as he, accompanied by his father, moved to depart as well. It was quickly explained that each evening, as the sun was setting, the warriors of the tribe would perform a ritual to ward them against the night so that they could endure safely until morning.

The way they spoke of the darkness, the tightness that was evident in Ikta's tone, told Thane that they were terrified of it, though he could not have said why. When dawn came the women (usually wives, daughters or sisters to the warriors) would undergo a similar rite to welcome the sun's return to power and rejoice in the tribe's survival of the night. Everyone, from the very youngest to those of the most advanced age, observed these ceremonies and so the three companions were expected to also partake in it.

They came to the most eastern side of the camp where a large circle had been formed by white, painted stones with a massive bonfire at its center. The fire was just starting to burn, growing in size and intensity, causing the wood to crack and smoke.

Already most of the women had gathered, mingling with the handful of men who had arrived first. No doubt they were finding their families before taking up positions on the ground, just inside the ring of stones.

Thane glanced about for his companions as he was led to a position that was clearly reserved for the leader and Elder and once again he was bade to sit with the two men. He knew he couldn't really refuse, but he did pause, opening his mouth with the intention of inquiring about Jorna, when her familiar voice called out to him.

Spinning to face the way they had come, he was about to offer a greeting, but was once more interrupted, this time by the mere sight of her.

When she had been led away by the womenfolk, he simply thought she'd be looked after, fed as he was and little else, but apparently they had done quite a bit more for her. The first thing he noticed was that she had bathed. Her unbound, platinum hair glistened in the waning sunlight and the smudges of grime were gone from her pale skin. Of course, it made sense that they would have given her new clothes, since her dress had clearly been dirty, but he would not have expected for the deer hide clothing to suit her so well.

The cream-colored hides that were customarily worn by the Boesh women now clung to her form (he noticed, not for the first time, that her body was quite curvaceous) leaving her arms and belly completely bare. The slitted, lightweight skirt swished around her legs as she hurried toward him, revealing flashes of the form-fitting leggings that were tucked into her familiar worn boots. Ever present were her silver arm bands; polished and sparkling, they fit perfectly with the rest of her attire.

For several long seconds, all he could do was stare, at a complete loss for words. He had known she was beautiful before that moment, but his attraction to her was wholly renewed. Now, when he gazed down into the icy depths of her shining eyes, his heart hammered furiously in his chest and his palms suddenly felt sweaty.

She touched his arm, her expression turning to concern. "Are you alright?"

Thane's mouth felt incredibly dry all of a sudden, his heart racing faster at the warmth of her hand. "Yes," he finally croaked, trying to shake himself free of the wonderful, frightful way he felt. Slowly, his mind cleared and he realized that Shanik wasn't with her. "Where's the runt?"

A sly smile turned up the corners of her pale lips as she turned and indicated Shanik's location with a flick of her gaze. He wasn't far behind Jorna, coming with the last of the stragglers in a manner that brought a beaming, impish grin to Thane's face.

A young girl, no older than three or four years, was cradling the dragon in her arms like a reptilian doll, cooing in the tribe's native tongue as she trotted beside her mother. Shanik looked quite unimpressed and more than a little ruffled by the whole ordeal, but he graciously allowed her to do as she pleased without the slightest fuss. Even when she lost her grip on his haunches (she would have dropped him completely had she not latched onto his throat with her hand) stepping on his tail, which had dangled to the ground, he did nothing more than release a strangled yelp.

Taking pity on the poor dragon, Jorna moved to the girl and gently coaxed her into giving him back. It took a bit of convincing and even then, her mother had to assist, but she finally relinquished Shanik to the shaman to his never ending relief!

With a muttering hiss, he allowed Jorna to hold him against her chest, being far too concerned with his trodden tail. He took hold of it in his front feet, gingerly massaging it, an expression of remorse and irritation on his scaly face. When he caught the two of them watching him, the dragon flashed a scathing glower and snarled, "We will never speak of this."

"I make no promises," Thane answered, still grinning as he returned to where he had been instructed to sit earlier.

Now that he had been reunited with his companions, he settled into the position gladly, feeling strangely better for having them at his side. Jorna sat close to him, her leg pressed against his once she was comfortable. It brought to his mind the feel of her warm body in his arms as they had kissed on the windy steppes and he longed to draw her close again, to renew the spark of blissful emotion they had shared.

She must have felt the same, for a moment later she shifted closer, elbowing his arm out of the way so that she could lean against his side, her head resting on his shoulder. Taking the obvious hint, Thane wrapped his arm around her shoulders, squeezing her gently as contentment settled over him.

The ritual began a short while later, as the warriors took up positions around the now blazing bonfire. Their guttural language sounded even more foreign as they began to chant, their voices booming in rhythm with the almost urgent motion of their dance. As the sun continued to fade below the horizon and the moon rose to take its place, their pace changed, became slower and softer. Their sorrow could be heard through the wailing of their song and seen in the intensity of their swaying bodies.

To Thane it seemed like a lot of pointless nonsense, there was no power in such traditions, at least he didn't personally believe in such things. No amount of whooping and hollering was going to keep anyone safe.

There would always be dangers, no matter the time of day, and the only way to defend against them was to be vigilant. He knew it wasn't right for him to judge, the Sarven had traditions and superstitions of their own that could be seen as pointless by those who didn't understand them, but he had no intention of allowing their fears to taint his senses.

The truth was the only time he ever felt uneasy in the forest was during the day and he attributed that to the Boesh who no doubt had been watching them long before they made their attack.

It was fully dark when the ritual reached its conclusion and by then most of the younger children had fallen asleep in their parents' arms. Slowly, the families headed for their tents, children in tow or carried, still sleeping, by their mothers or fathers. Ulta led the three companions to a small tent that had been prepared for them and after being certain that their guests would be comfortable, she departed to join her own family.

Once they were alone, the three companions looked over everything that was in their lodging. Their packs had been brought in and sat beside the wide bed made of furs, no doubt by whoever was taking care of their muskoxen. It seemed the Boesh had mistaken the relationship between them, assuming that since she was not his kin, she was his wife because they traveled together. This left the two of them standing there, both suddenly too shy to voice their thoughts or come up with a solution.

Not having any qualm with the sleeping arrangement at all, Shanik had settled right down on the furs, but the tension in the air and the uncomfortable silence was enough to keep him from falling asleep. With a sigh, he raised his head, glancing between the two Sarven before rasping, "You were just displaying your affection in front of strangers, you kissed the other day, you've been sleeping inches from one another... What's the problem here?"

They both answered at the same time, or at least tried to, but all that came out was stuttering and stammering. Jorna tried to say it wouldn't be proper, while Thane rattled off inane comments that had nothing to do with the fact he feared he was inadequate for a king's daughter.

The dragon might have found it comical had he not been keen on getting a good night's sleep, so he waved them to silence. "Since you two seem to have become imbeciles, I'm going to save us all some time and cut right to the end. Jorna, he thinks himself inferior and beneath a woman of your breeding. Thane, she's bound by the silly notion of propriety and is waiting for you to stop being a coward and *claim her as your own*. See, that wasn't so hard, was it?"

Instead of being embarrassed, Thane glowered at the dragon, wishing he'd kept his snout shut and allowed them to work through it without interference. Unfortunately it was too late for that; it was also too late for him to simply offer to sleep on the ground or to go fetch his bedroll. The time had come for him to either claim Jorna or let her go.

The mere thought of the latter made him sick, his heart clenching painfully as he imagined a life without her in it. He knew that wasn't the answer, but he didn't like being put on the spot. He wanted what he had to tell her to come naturally, when the time was perfect... It struck him that the time may never be *perfect*.

Thane turned to look at her and could tell by the tension in her shoulders that she was anxiously waiting for him to say something. With a sigh, he reached for her arm, his fingers brushing her soft skin as he stepped closer and leaned down to whisper, "Could you ever come to love a simple blacksmith?"

Her lips tugged up into a faint grin as she cast her gray-blue gaze to his face and answered, "Only if his name is Thane Stoutforge."

Her confession sent pleasant tingling down his arms and brought to life a heat in his groin that was both eager and demanding. Without taking his eyes off of Jorna, he told Shanik, "It's time for you to leave, lizard."

Shanik sniffed at the air and nodded. "I quite concur. I'll go check on the muskoxen." With that, he ducked out of the tent and disappeared, leaving the pair of Sarven alone.

21

THE CLAIMING

JORNA'S CHEEKS WERE BURNING with embarrassment from what Shanik had said. Is that really what the dragon thought? Were they so obvious together? More importantly, did she really want Thane to *claim* her?

Emphatically, yes...

Now that they were alone, the redness in Jorna's cheeks did not fade. Her heart was hammering in her chest as she waited apprehensively for Thane to make the first move. She wanted to encourage him, give him some indication that she wanted him as much as he seemed to want her, but all she could manage was to smile weakly in his direction, her eyes aglow with desire.

That was all she had to do. Thane read the invitation on her face and closed the distance between them so suddenly, Jorna barely saw him move. In the next instant, his mouth was against hers, crushing and wanton, much unlike the chaste kiss he'd given her after they had slain the worm together.

Powerful longing ached in Jorna's core, filling her with an almost overwhelming sensation of heat and lust. As Thane's hands roamed her back and hips, she could feel his arousal pressed against her belly and the sudden realization that it wouldn't be long before it was penetrating her depths sent a hot jolt through her.

Caught up in the moment, Jorna began tugging at Thane's clothes, remembering the chiseled chest from when they had first met. She wanted to put her mouth on his hard pectorals, wanted to outline every perfect muscle with her fingertips. All propriety was forgotten the second her hands came into contact with his caramel skin.

A moan escaped and Jorna blushed, pulling from the passionate kiss so she could turn her face away. "I'm sorry," she whispered, her breath coming in shallow pants. "I'm being too forward, aren't I?"

"Not at all," Thane answered, his tone equally breathy, but firm. "Your boldness excites me, Princess." Gently, he spun her around so that her back was pressed to his chest. "I would ask though, what's the rush? We have all night..." As he spoke, he began to undress her, each motion antagonizing and slow. If any skin became exposed in the process, he would place a delicate kiss on it before continuing on until Jorna was standing against him entirely naked.

Jorna shivered, not because she was cold, but because she had never felt so exposed. "Thane..." she said his name with a hint of the uncertainty that had crept into her mind.

He didn't increase his pace, but he didn't stop either. Thane's hands moved over her bare, hot skin, leaving tingles in their wake. Meanwhile, his lips found her neck and alternated between kissing, nibbling, and sucking at the sensitive flesh.

She jumped when his thumb and finger captured a hardened nipple, then twisted sensually until she rewarded his efforts with a trembling moan. His other hand traveled lower, to the center of her arousal.

The noise she released elicited a chuckle from Thane as he touched her in a way no other ever had before.

"I'm going to make you mine tonight, Princess." Thane's husky voice caused Jorna to shudder or perhaps it was the way his thumb swirled lightly over her nub, while a finger slid easily between the moist folds. "This is your last chance to save yourself. Tell me to stop, Jorna. Do it now, before I lose all control."

Jorna shook her head immediately. Despite what his fingers were doing to her, she managed to gasp, "Don't stop, Thane..."

At this, he growled in her ear and walked her carefully to the pile of furs that made up their shared bed. "On your back," he commanded, and she eagerly obeyed, though her cheeks were once again flushed pink.

Thane paused, his eyes roaming over her naked figure the entire time he took to remove his own clothing. Jorna watched in turn, her rosy cheeks getting rosier at the sight of his unleashed manhood.

Was it supposed to be that large? She'd overheard married women gossiping about how well-endowed Sarven men were, but she had never imagined what that meant exactly. A lash of trepidation chilled her skin, but before she could even consider what came next, Thane was kneeling on the furs, his hands spreading her thighs open.

She whimpered uncertainly, but to her relief, he bent low and placed his face between her exposed legs. The sudden sensation of his tongue slipping between her folds erased every thought from her mind and reignited the heat that now flared through every inch of her.

Jorna reached down, her slender fingers tangling in Thane's long, curly black hair. Moments later his hand returned, one digit pushing inside her and making her groan. On and on he went, playing her like she was a delicate instrument that could only make music for him. His touch, persistent and firm, drove her higher and higher until she gladly fell over the edge of ecstasy for the very first time.

Warmth and fuzziness settled over Jorna's body and mind, making her feel energized and wrung out all at once. She was still in a state of euphoria as Thane directed her to roll onto her belly. She obeyed without wondering what he was doing or what was coming next. The soft bed of furs brushed against her skin and face, making her feel even more cozy.

"Thane?" she called, distantly aware that he was still there and that he had lifted her hips up. "What about—" A sharp intake of breath drove the words from her mind at the sudden pressure of Thane's hardness as it found her soaked entrance. A second later and Thane was inside her.

A cry broke from Jorna as she was stretched to capacity. There was a strange, sharp pain that was offset by a burning desire for more. She whimpered and bucked against him, wanting the bliss of her orgasm to return, but also wanting relief from the almost uncomfortable stretch as well.

"Thane..." Jorna moaned as he pulled back.

He leaned closer so he could whisper in her ear as he thrust slowly into her again. "You belong to me now, Princess. No other man will ever touch you but me..."

Jorna bit her lip, her hands clutching at the furs beneath her naked body. She squirmed beneath Thane as he held himself in place. Why was he moving so slow? She wanted to feel the friction of his strokes now that she was adjusting to his girth. Her body ached for *more* of him, for the feeling of completion to never end.

"Harder," she begged, blushing at the wanton edge in her own voice.

To her relief, Thane quickened his pace with a soft growl.

She lost herself to his stroking rhythm, the euphoria returning and building once again. Jorna focused on Thane's ragged breathing, her mind keenly aware of his fingers digging into her hips the faster he went and of the hot slapping of skin against skin. Her body sang with ecstasy as another orgasm crashed into her, drawing loud cries from her wide open mouth.

"You have never looked so beautiful than when you come undone beneath me," Thane grunted, his tone sending shivers over her flesh. His verbosity pleased her, excited her, in ways she hadn't known was possible. She had gotten used to his silent nature and now, hearing his inner thoughts so easily expressed buzzed through Jorna to ignite her passions once again.

To her surprise, Thane abruptly pulled out. Before she could do more than whimper a protest, he had adjusted her hips again, straddling one of her legs while he wrapped the other around his hip. Then he plunged into her again, his groan of satisfaction echoing in the otherwise quiet tent.

He leaned in close, capturing her lip between his teeth and giving it a soft tug. She sighed and his tongue slipped inside the soft cavern of her mouth to tangle with her own. All the while he kept moving, his movements becoming more frantic as his orgasm built. Thane groaned her name against her lips, clutching her, filling her until all that remained was the two of them, their sweat-slicked bodies, and the furs beneath them.

Another toe-curling orgasm shook through Jorna, ripping a cry of ecstasy from her throat before she collapsed from where she was straddling Thane onto his chest.

"Now I'm torn..." Thane's voice guided her back down to earth. His fingers were caressing her back, even as he panted from the exertion of their love making. "You're quite beautiful when you're coming undone on top of me, too."

She giggled and swatted playfully at him before placing a teasing kiss on his mouth.

It was well into the night and Jorna couldn't remember stealing more than a few moments of sleep in between their bouts of passion. In fact, sleep was the furthest thing on her mind right then. She didn't want the night to end, for the morning would bring duty and peril once again.

Her arms tightened around Thane, and she buried her face in his chest, enjoying the tickle of his chest hair on her cheeks. "I wish morning wouldn't come..." she lamented, her voice partially muffled.

Thane ran his fingers through her unbound hair and sighed his agreement. "This has been a most pleasant night..."

Silence fell between them as they laid there together, just content to exist with and explore one another. Doubts began to creep into Jorna's mind about the following day and all it would bring. Without realizing it, her body tensed as the weight of her task and how close she was to returning home began to weigh on her.

"Jorna," Thane whispered her name, guiding her chin up so that he could look into her eyes. "Let tomorrow unfold as it will and rest tonight."

"But what if—"

He pressed a finger to her lips to quiet her and then drew her into a tender kiss. When the tip of his tongue teased her mouth open, she forgot her worries entirely as desire warmed her body and drove the doubt away.

Dwenenar

Dwenenar

Iᴋᴛᴀ ᴄᴀᴍᴇ ꜰᴀʀ ᴛᴏᴏ early to collect Thane the next morning. Jorna was loathe to see him leave, but he promised to return to her as soon as he could. Shortly thereafter, Ulta showed up to wake Jorna for breakfast, so she wasn't able to catch any extra sleep either.

They ate in the same fashion as the day before, with the men separate from the women and then rejoining around dawn to celebrate the coming of the sun.

It was tempting to stay another day or two, just to have a chance to recharge and put off her quest a little longer. Shanik was the one who gave her a stern talking to, pointing out that they didn't belong with the Boesh no matter how welcoming they were. Strangely enough, Thane agreed with the dragon.

"It's better that we keep moving, lest we bring misfortune to these orcs," were his exact words.

In the end, Jorna's own sense of duty prevailed as well. They said goodbye to the Boesh shortly after dawn, loaded their belongings onto the muskoxen and started the last leg of their journey to the secret entrance.

The sun had not yet set by the time they reached the hidden entrance into Dwenenar. It was far different than the main gates of Hamdralg, not blended into the side of the mountain, but set apart from it for those who knew what they were looking at.

An arch of golden runes were carved into the rock at eye level, sparkling in the waning moonlight. Only a Sarven with stone sense would be able to figure out the opening mechanism and gain entrance. If they were lucky, they'd also be able to see the traps before setting it off. In Jorna's case, she knew about them in advance and was privy to the information needed to turn them off safely.

That was getting a little ahead of themselves though; they still had a few preparations to take care of before they went inside. The first thing Jorna worried about were the muskoxen. She knew they wouldn't be able to sneak across the city with them in tow, no matter how good they were. That left her with only one option and that was to set them free and allow them to return to safety on their own.

As she slid out of the saddle and started to remove the tack, she could feel Thane watching her. She glanced over her shoulder at him and patiently explained, adding a small reassurance, "They should make it back to the Boesh safely at least, if not return to Hamdralg."

"Ha! They'll probably just eat them," Shanik chortled, dipping down low enough so that he could easily be heard.

Ignoring the dragon's quips, Thane followed Jorna's example. Though he did add under his breath, "Good luck getting through all that hair..."

Once the muskoxen were free of their tack, Jorna spoke softly to them, not wanting them to be afraid of heading into the wilderness on their own. Her quiet order to return the way they had came seemed to be enough to get them moving, and as they headed southward, she hoped they would be okay. Sure, they were just beasts of burden, but they had served her well on this quest. Without them, they surely would not have made it so far.

Approaching the carved stone, the shaman inspected it closely, recalling what her father had said when teaching her the secret of opening the back door. He had put it into a limerick for her, Javrin, and Jalrik, all three of whom had been taught at an early age should they need to use the door without their parents being present. It had been a precaution, one of many that Guldorn had taken to instill in his children.

As she went through the steps, she spoke the limerick aloud, hearing her father's voice in her ear as though he were standing beside her, testing her to see if she really remembered it. Faintly she could hear the mechanism clicking and whirring, the gears shifting until the lock was undone. With the final line, she slipped her index finger into a slight crevice that was just above waist height and found the lever to disable the traps.

When she was done, she caught Thane giving her a bemused grin and shrugged in response. "Father didn't want us to forget," was the only explanation she gave.

"Fair enough," he replied stepping back so that she could have the honor of pushing open the door herself; this was her kingdom after all.

It only took a bit of a push for the door to shudder open, giving them just enough space to slip inside if they turned sideways. Jorna was sure it opened more than that, but she didn't see the point in bothering to make it wider when they were just going to shut it again in a moment. She went in first, followed closely by Thane who was every bit as eager as she was to be out of the elements and finally underground again.

The familiar scents and feeling of being secure beneath the rock caused Jorna to release tension that had been pent up since setting foot on the surface. She paused just inside, running her hand against the stone as she breathed deep the stale air.

Thane laid his palm over the hand that was still on the wall, smiling meaningfully at her as she raised her gaze up to meet his. She knew that being home wouldn't have felt so wonderful if he wasn't there to share the moment with. She was looking forward to all the other moments that were soon to come, once this foul business was concluded. With a single glance at his face, Jorna could tell that Thane felt the same way.

Their hands fell away from the stone as they focused once again on their quest. Jorna reached into her pack and pulled out the two glowstones that had been inside of it. In the dimness of the tunnel, the glowstones did exactly as their name implied, giving off a faint white-blue light that illuminated the darkness. It wasn't very much, but more than enough for them to travel by and of course, there was the added benefit that they wouldn't cast so much light as to draw unwanted attention.

A grunted huff pulled their attention, drawing their eyes back to the entrance, where a (much to their surprise) larger Shanik was attempting to squeeze himself through the opening. Clawing and wiggling, puffing and growling, he finally managed to succeed, flopping into a heap just inside. Swearing indignantly, the dragon picked himself up, shaking out his wings and then smoothing them delicately against his flanks, which glistened as the light of the glowstones caught his obsidian hide.

"You're... bigger," Jorna commented, raising her eyebrow quizzically. Where before he had been the perfect size to fit on her shoulder, he was now the height of a large dog, coming to about mid-thigh on her.

The dragon's sapphire gaze glinted as he replied in a tone that suggested he felt what he had to say should have been obvious, "I didn't want to get stepped on in the dark." He sniffed at the air and shuddered uncomfortably. "This place has a foul odor."

Thane took a deep breath, seeming to enjoy the scent of rock and earth. Though he could no doubt also make out the stale aroma of dust and a faint trace of mold, those details did little to spoil the overall experience - at least for Jorna.

There was something wonderful about being inside a mountain, the way the air felt, the comforting sense of being surrounded by hard, dense stone... She had been born deep within Dwenenar, had lived the whole of her life underground and hoped that when death finally came to claim her, her last breaths would be filled with the familiar, comforting scent of stone.

"I just smell home," Jorna responded, a content smile tugging at her lips. Thane gave her a startled look and she wondered if perhaps she had spoken his thoughts aloud.

"Of course you do. A Sarven's nose is no match for that of a dragon's!" Shanik huffed. "Those *creatures* still dwell here, I'm sure of it. We should be very careful." His voice held an edge of unease as he spoke the last, his wings ruffling with discomfort.

"That's our plan." Jorna knew exactly what had the dragon so on edge, but it was clear she wasn't about to let it demoralize them. They had come this far, faced so many hurdles... there was no turning back now.

Their descent into Dwenenar went much faster than the vast majority of the previous legs of their journey. Though this path had not been used for a very long time, it had been built to last by the finest Sarven masons and therefore it remained solid even thousands of years later. The walk down went silently, as there was a bit of anxiousness hanging in the air. Though Jorna was sure that nobody would know of this tunnel, they still feared bumping into one of the hellish creatures.

They stopped after a couple hours to eat and rest. Thane and Jorna hadn't had a whole lot of sleep the night before, and that coupled with traveling on foot had worn them both out.

Shuffling drew her attention to where Shanik was rising off the stone ground, his wings rustling as he shook them slightly. She watched his movements, taking in details of his reptilian physique that she hadn't noticed when he was smaller. Mostly it was the pattern of his scales, how some were smaller along his legs and shoulders, but larger across his chest and belly; the perfect arrangement for keeping him adequately protected. Every now and then, she thought they cast the faintest hint of sapphire, but whenever she tried to get a closer look, it appeared to only be a trick of the glowstones.

The dragon must have caught her staring for he sniffed. "Something the matter, shaman?"

Jorna quickly shook her head and offered a sheepish smile. "Not at all." Her voice was barely above a whisper. "I have never seen a dragon in such detail. I was admiring how sleek your scales are. I apologize if I offended you."

"Ahh, yes." Shanik puffed himself out and instantly Jorna knew he was not at all offended. On the contrary, he was letting her remarks go to his head. "I *am* rather glorious…"

Thane let out a noise that sounded like a stifled bark of laughter. "I've seen prettier chickens."

Now Shanik was offended. He raised himself to his full height, which was much more impressive due to his shifted size, and took a deep breath in preparation for a long winded rebuke. Jorna deflated him instantly with a finger pressed against his snout for she feared he would forget where they were and speak in a raised voice.

The dragon was still displeased. He flashed Thane a withering glare and then pointedly refused to acknowledge him for the rest of the day. Jorna had grown so used to their bickering that she felt relieved. They were acting normally and that went a long way to making her feel as though they weren't headed toward doom.

Shortly after that they carried on, Jorna feeling certain that they were nearing the city proper, specifically the noble district. The tunnel should have come out in the cellar of a house, the one that belonged to one of her father's most trusted advisers. Her heart twisted with grief as she remembered this man was also gone, one of the first to have fallen when the siege began.

Dathor Ironkeg had been like kin, especially to Guldorn who did not have any siblings. Jorna remembered growing up with his children, learning to fight under his tutelage… She also remembered that her father had wept upon hearing the news that his brother in arms had died. It was the only time she had ever seen him display such emotions. It would be strange to go through Dathor's house and find it empty, but he was the one man who Guldorn had trusted to safeguard the entrance. She was certain he would not mind.

They reached the end of the hidden passage, which was little more than a ladder leading up to a covered trapdoor in the floor of the unassuming larder. Thane went up first, holding the glowstone so that only a peel of light seeped into the small room. When he determined that it was empty, save for some undisturbed dust, he quietly shoved the door open further, an annoying task as the rug hiding it from view had slid down and wadded up, blocking the hinges.

After a bit of manhandling and forcing, he had it so that he could fit his broad frame through the gap, which he did with a grunt. Next up came Jorna, who took her companion's offered hand, more for his peace of mind than because she needed assistance. Lastly, Shanik scrambled out of the tunnel with an indignant ruffling of his wings. He was no doubt grateful to be out of the cramped space.

Speaking in a soft whisper, Thane informed his companions that he was going to check the next room to be sure it was clear before they ventured out. The wooden door leading out of the cellar was tightly sealed and clearly hadn't been used since the recent fall of Dwenenar, a sign that made them hope the rest of the dwelling was equally abandoned.

Cracking the door open, he once again shone just a sliver of the glowstone into the next room. When he saw nothing, he made the opening a little wider, flashing a bit more light and was pleased to find that the house was indeed uninhabited.

"It's clear!" he whispered back to Jorna and Shanik, motioning them to join him as he pushed the door open the rest of the way and started out.

They didn't hesitate, in fact, Jorna felt a strange mix of eagerness and dread, scarcely able to believe that they could be so close to reaching their goal. In her mind, she was already laying out the route from here to the palace district and from there into the palace itself and finally to the treasury.

If they were very lucky and very careful, they would be able to make it there and then out the western gates without being seen, then it would just be a matter of going with all haste back to Hamdralg. She would have been ecstatic were it not for Firodel's words echoing in her thoughts, reminding her that something unpleasant was just ahead of her.

Cautiously they worked their way through the house, though they were all fairly certain that the dwelling was deserted. If the dark creatures were still in Dwenenar, then they must have been using other lodgings or perhaps they simply didn't sleep; nothing about them could surprise Jorna at this point.

Peeking through the window at the streets, she could tell that nothing was happening, as they too were empty. This more than the abandoned house caused her to shiver with uncertainty. It seemed so wrong for her home to be so quiet and lifeless, as though it too had been slain.

Thane was opening the door, intending to proceed her outside, but Jorna stopped him, telling him with a look that she needed to lead the way. Not because she wanted to be in charge or didn't trust him, she just wanted to have some measure of normalcy and being protected in what should have been her home was making the situation harder to bear.

She had known this would be difficult, but as she walked out onto the road, the scent of fires and death washed over her, marring the beautiful city that she had always loved. Staggering, she reached for Thane and found that he was barely a step behind her, ready to offer his hand so that she had something with which to anchor herself. She clasped him tightly, grateful for his support, for the warmth of his skin. Taking a deep breath, she composed her reeling mind and started once again down the street.

Everywhere they walked, it was the same, empty and defiled, barren of the lives that had given the city its pulse. The closer they came to the heart of the city, to the center where the palace had once stood tall and proud, the more destruction there was. Some of it, the burned buildings and toppled statues were scars from the battle itself, but then there were the defaced monuments and structures that had been sullied for the mere amusement of the conquerors. Worst of all was not the wounds of Dwenenar, but the broken, decaying bodies that littered the roadway.

It took all of Jorna's strength not to lose her stomach as they passed the remnants of the carnage. Instead she turned that agony, that sorrow into a pure, white-hot rage that settled comfortably in the pit of her belly like a smoldering stone. She silently vowed to make those who had desecrated her home pay dearly, if not this day, then at another time and place. It didn't matter how long she had to wait, she would see the monstrous fiends suffer for their sins and if the humans were behind their actions here, then they too would face her wrath.

"I promise, Jorna, when we return to Hamdralg I will speak with my father and we will do all we can to make this right," Thane was whispering, his voice heavy with sorrow as he no doubt recalled his own hellish experience when his brother had perished. "Even if we only hold Dwenenar for a day, at least we can care for the dead."

The princess shook her head slowly, rustling her platinum hair. "I fear that Dwenenar will have to wait, that Hamdralg's warriors may be needed elsewhere." She gave him a significant glance, telling him with that one look that this was only the beginning of their fight.

Reclaiming a lost city was not as high a priority as defending kingdoms that still stood. Someday her people would return to their stolen home, but until then, they would endeavor to make certain nobody else suffered the same injustice.

They crossed into the palace district a few minutes later with mixed feelings about having not run into any patrols or guards. All of them were certain that the city was not wholly empty. The evil creatures had to be here somewhere, and the fact that they still hadn't seen them was more unsettling than if they had come across hundreds of them.

Without any opposition or sign of anything living, they arrived at the palace far more quickly than Jorna might have guessed, which did nothing for her growing unease. The vast mansion stretched out before them, reaching up toward the stone ceiling high above and spread out across the ground much further than the light from the glowstones suggested.

Not a lot of detail could be seen in the dark, but Jorna knew the structure had been crafted with only the finest materials and as such was nothing short of resplendent. She stood before the golden, spiral gates, remembering them as she'd known them in her youth. Now they were broken inward and destroyed, leaving just enough space for a single armored soldier to slip through.

They beckoned to the trio, urging them to go inside, but a sliver of fear and uncertainty kept all three of them rooted in place. Something was very wrong here.

"Please tell me I'm not the only one thinking this is far too easy," Shanik whispered from beside Jorna, his voice sounding uncharacteristically timid as though he feared something sinister might overhear.

The shaman just nodded, knowing exactly how the dragon felt and wishing there was another way through the wall. Once they were beyond the gate, she intended to go through the servant's entrance, certain that they were less likely to get caught that way. The fact that proceeding any further at all just seemed so wrong didn't encourage her to move though, despite the weight of her quest and how close she was to being done. That they hadn't come across a single living creature did not bode well.

Thane put his hand gently on her shoulder, to assure her or draw her out of her contemplations she wasn't sure, but she was thankful for both. Glancing up at him, she saw that her concerns were mirrored on his face, that he wasn't particularly comfortable with how this was playing out either.

So, they were all in agreement: they had to go forward, but they would do so with the utmost caution.

Jorna took the first step, letting the reassuring warmth of Thane's hand slip away as she approached the eerily inviting gate. With each step, she feared that an ambush would be sprung, that the terrible monsters responsible for the fall of her city would appear from the darkness and slay them all.

She remembered seeing their front lines destroyed by the blood-thirsty ferocity of the fiends, remembered the screams of a dozen dying men and the heavy scent of ash and gore. Those smells echoed inside her, like the cries of the dead whispered through the still air, warning her to stay away, to run while she could.

Against every fiber of her being, Jorna strolled through the palace gates, aware of her companions filing in behind her. She couldn't help but jump when Shanik bumped against her leg, her nerves and senses strained to the max. From the corner of her eye, she thought she saw the shadows shifting, but when she whipped her head around, there was nothing.

Shivering as a sudden chill ran down her spine, she shook off the uncanny sensation of being watched and ignored the tingle on the back of her neck that told her they weren't alone.

DRAGON FIRE

ALL THREE OF THEM remained on high alert, proceeding at a slower pace than they might have had they not been certain they were walking into a trap. The further they got into the palace, the more certain they became that they were being tracked. Jorna especially knew that the noises they kept hearing were not natural for the building. She had grown up here after all; she was intimately familiar with every sound, every smell, every corridor.

This place, with its thick stench of death and ruin, the plush carpeting laid over the smooth marble floors ripped and torn, the statues, tapestries and other adornments defaced, this was not her home. Everywhere she looked she saw something new that broke her heart, something that destroyed the fond memories of her childhood and made her wish that the task to retrieve the book had not fallen to her. She wanted to remember Dwenenar as it had been, not what it had become.

Going through the servant's entrance had been the worst. It appeared that a handful of maids had tried to hole up in one of the cellars but were discovered at some point. Their deaths had been slow and gruesome, that much was evident from the sheer amount of blood and gore that would forever stain the stone floors and walls. It had taken every ounce of Jorna's strength not to crumble to her knees and weep endlessly. She had known those women, at least the ones who were still recognizable, and it pained her that they must now be counted among the victims.

She was grateful for Thane and Shanik. Without their silent understanding and support, she would not have endured the horrific scene or had the will to press further into the palace. It was the reminder of their presence, of everything they had accomplished together in their short days as a team that kept her from turning around and running back to Hamdralg like a frightened child. So long as the three of them were together she knew they would make it through whatever trials were thrown at them.

They took the most direct route, the fastest route, through the palace, all of them eager to get the book and leave as quickly as possible despite the unspoken reality that whatever it was lurking in the shadows would unlikely allow things to unfold in such a straightforward manner. The walk seemed to take forever, feeling as though it would never end, so that when it finally did, the three companions couldn't help but release a collective sigh of relief.

The door to the treasury was untouched, the twin lock hadn't been tampered with or forced open; there were simply no signs that anyone had even come near it since the siege. Frowning, knowing this was not good news, Jorna reached into a pouch on her belt and withdrew two keys that were identical except that one was gold and the other was silver.

The latter she handed to Thane, motioning for him to mimic her movements as she slipped her golden key into the bottom lock. When his was in place in the top lock, she indicated which direction he needed to turn it, then held up her free hand to count so that they could turn them at the same time. Three short seconds later, the scraping of metal against metal preceded the tell-tale sound of a tumbler unlocking.

Jorna cracked open the door before retrieving the keys and securing them once again in her belt pouch. She then pushed the door in the rest of the way and cautiously slipped inside. None of the treasure had been touched either, but that was expected since the door was still intact.

The light of the glowstones caught the sparkling gems and gold ingots that were stored here, casting strange, bluish shadows on the walls. She recalled the first time she had been brought here, hand held firmly in her father's as he explained the importance of Dwenenar's wealth and that the treasury existed not to make her life luxurious, but to be used to make the lives of their people more comfortable. It was a lesson she had taken to heart and, like so many others, would never forget.

"Are you alright?" Thane whispered into her ear, his tone belying his concern.

She realized she had stopped abruptly and was staring blankly at the wall ahead, losing herself in a moment that was now long gone. "Yes, we're almost there," she answered, moving forward with purpose as she raised the glowstone above her head to better illuminate their path.

This was not the only treasury in the palace; in fact, it was one of six. All the others had much more complex locking mechanisms and were much larger on top of it. This one had been cut in half to house the special vault at the back of the room, the front portion filled with only a fraction of what the 'real' vaults protected. The light in her hand splashed across the thick, impenetrable doors of the true repository, the one that held Dwenenar's most prized possession: the book of Grefjein Goldsteel.

Jorna stopped just in front of it, her eyes sweeping the familiar runic carvings that adorned the solid, stone doors from ceiling to floor. Every inch was covered in them, the meaning of those letters known to only three living people in all of Talaris. Their meaning floated in her mind, sung in the voice of her father who had taught her their power when she was little more than a teenager. That was the first time she had ever been permitted to see the Goldsteel book. She remembered being giddy with excitement, barely able to contain herself as she waited for the song to end so that she could finally set foot in the forbidden room.

She let her eyes fall closed, let the memory wash over her like a rush of warm air...

'Stop bouncing, Jorna,' her father had chided, putting his hand on her shoulder, *'Listen to me, you must remember these words. Never forget the importance of this book. Its secret gives us strength, but in the hands of our enemies, it would be our downfall. It is our duty as the ruling family to protect it, no matter the cost. Do you understand?'*

The intensity in his gaze had dampened her excitement, making her realize just how serious and important their duty was. She'd never fully understood until then, but that moment had taught her more than just how to open a magical door; it had given her a perspective of life that she lived by, even now.

It was for that reason alone that she had come here, through great peril and risk, to fulfill a promise made by countless kings before her, a promise that her father had made and that she silently made as a knobby-kneed teenager. She vowed to protect their most precious secret and by doing so ensure the safety of the Dwenenari people.

Another shiver tingled down her spine as she heard the strange noises again, much closer than before. Where before the sounds had unsettled her, now they incited her wrath, reminding her of every injustice her people had suffered, every man, woman and child who lay dead in the once great city, for the many more who now begged for scraps from their brother kingdom.

Their home had been desecrated, destroyed, overrun with filthy, abhorrent monsters like it was little more than a worthless shack. And now, these *things* thought they could outsmart her? That she was too foolish and ignorant to sense their presence, to know that they were only waiting for her to open that door, to practically hand them the most priceless artifact in the Sarven kingdoms, past and present, combined.

Shaking her head, Jorna barked a mirthless, harsh laugh, turning so abruptly that both of her companions jumped, confused and uncertain what had caused her to change. She knew they trusted her enough to stay silent, to not interfere and so she didn't bother to stop and inform them of her sudden clarity of the situation. She dropped the glowstone, leaving it in her wake as she strolled to the middle of the treasury and then stopped, planting her glaive firmly on the ground next to her feet.

"I am Jorna Hailstone," she called, her commanding voice echoing off the stone ceiling as it carried into the hallway. "I am the daughter of King Guldorn Oathbinder, the daughter of a great line of kings. I am a shaman, a vessel of magic and voice to the spirits of Talaris. I alone have the power to unlock this door, to retrieve the book of Grefjein Goldsteel, but I will not. Not today, not tomorrow. Not so long as such darkness and evil crawls through the glorious halls of my ancestors like vermin! Come out of the shadows and face me now, that I may cut you down and reclaim *my* city!"

Her challenge was met with scraping and scuffling, then a shrill cry that caused her heart to tremor as she recalled the bloodthirsty scream of the hellish fiends. She had been right, they were there, lurking and waiting for her to make a fatal mistake. Now that she wasn't cooperating, she feared the worst, feared that they would see no point in keeping her alive. It didn't matter, she decided an instant later, watching as the shadows in the hallway began to shift like wild, untamed beasts. Just as her father and his brave warriors had not so long ago, she would fight them to whatever end.

Blazing fire roared, almost deafening in the small treasury, its flames painting the stone walls a chilling mix of blue and violet. When the fighting had broken out, the first thing Shanik had done was coat the floor in front of the door with a wall of fire, which Jorna had promptly used to imbue her glaive.

Now they stood together behind it, battling the hellish creatures that pushed and shoved into the room. Some were capable of withstanding the flames long enough to surpass it as though they had some sort of natural resistance. A few were not so lucky and quickly succumbed to the blaze.

Those that did make it into the room were met by the three companions, who by now were quite comfortable working together in a fight. Without needing to verbally communicate, they moved as one, defending each other's weak spots and preventing the fiends from overwhelming them. Jorna and Shanik each took a side, with Thane in the middle. Fire from the dragon and shaman acted as a protective wall to prevent them from getting flanked while they funneled foes into the blacksmith's waiting axe.

The door acted as a choke point, keeping the monsters from overwhelming them like they surely would have had they been fighting out in the open. The low ceiling also deterred them from using their wings to get behind them or resort to dirty tactics like those Thane had described them using at the watch post. Because of this they were able to stand their ground for much longer than they might have under different circumstances.

The only thing that worked against them now was the sheer numbers of their enemy. They came at them in an endless swarm. No sooner had they vanquished one did another brave the fire wall to take its place. Between the heat of the roaring flames and the exertion of battle, they wouldn't be able to keep up the defense for much longer and though shutting the door would buy them a reprieve, it would do little more than stave off the inevitable.

They didn't have enough food to last indefinitely, which meant they would have to face the creatures again or simply starve. If they were going to die, they all silently agreed that falling in the heat of a glorious battle was better than slowly wasting away.

The onslaught continued to rage, the hideous reptilian bodies of their fiendish enemy piling up, forcing them to give ground so that they weren't in danger of tripping over a lifeless limb. Jorna could feel her body weakening. The energy it took to keep her weapon imbued was immense, she knew it was only a matter of time before she had to release the stored element or risk burning up herself. The only downside was once she did that, her exhaustion would no longer be held back, she would feel the full brunt of it and become utterly useless. She pushed the thought from her mind, preferring to burn, to take her enemies and half the city of Dwenenar with her to the grave.

Instinctively she felt Shanik shift, moving to set fire to the corpses that littered the floor in front of them. She and Thane immediately compensated, protecting him while he blew a gust of molten flames from his gaping maw. The creatures may have had some resistance, but it was not infinite protection, especially against dragon fire. Their remains ignited as the inferno lashed over them, filling the treasury with the sickening smell of charred flesh and smoldering hair.

Not at all deterred by the flaming bodies of their fallen sisters, the other fiends continued to rush in, picking their way through the newest obstacles as they tenaciously lunged at their prey. Any normal soldier would have at least been enraged at the sight, at the audacity of their enemy to desecrate their dead, but these hellish monsters were so single-minded in their assault that they seemed to not even notice.

This, more than the scent of death coupled with the rising heat, made Jorna sick to her stomach. She couldn't imagine feeling so little for the people who fought at your side that you could crawl over their burning corpse and not be disheartened.

The realization that her opponents were so incredibly bestial made it a great deal easier to slay them, not only for Jorna but her companions as well. Renewed, they redoubled their efforts, fending off the new wave of snapping, shrieking hags as though it were the first and not the most recent in a never-ending stream. They were prepared for the next, ready, even eager, to deliver their deaths, but the limitless tide had come to a jarring, unsettling halt.

Not one of them rejoiced or even hoped that this was the end. They could sense that something was holding the creatures back and the thought of what horrible thing might possibly be able to control them sent a shiver of fear through each one of their hearts.

"Whatever comes through that door," Jorna said softly, her breath ragged, "whatever happens next, it was an honor to fight beside you both." She threw Thane and Shanik each a significant look, letting it say the rest of what she did not put to words.

Despite the aching in her muscles, the streams of sweat that she could feel sliding down her back and beading on her forehead and the exhaustion that clawed at her mind, Jorna raised her fiery glaive into the air and shouted at the top of her lungs, "For Dwenenar! For Guldorn!" Her battle cry was joined by Thane's deep voice as he called his own and by Shanik's mighty roar, their collective shouts shaking the entire room as they dared the dark monsters to send their worst.

A single, slender form appeared on the other side of the fire wall, indistinguishable through the flames. Hissed words, inaudible until the three companions calls tapered off, drifted over the crackling magical inferno, the voice that spoke them sounding masculine. The figure held something above his head, a vial perhaps, and with a final, definitive word, he threw it into the fire with a dramatic flourish.

Sensing the human magic, Shanik barely managed to growl a single word before the gust of enchanted wind came hurling toward them. Fortunately all he needed was one, for dragon magic, far superior than anything the lesser mortals could conjure, was not overly verbose. The howling squall snuffed out the smoldering fires in its path, picking up the lifeless, charred bodies and dragging them along like rag dolls. Had it not been for the dragon's quick reaction and spell of dissipation, they would have been slammed into the vault door with enough force to break bone, then crushed beneath the weight of a dozen corpses. As it was, the violent gust became a strong breeze that blew by them harmlessly, the only evidence of its passing the rattling and clinking of disturbed treasure.

Through the sudden quiet the sound of slow, deliberate clapping was all that could be heard. After a brief second, it was joined by the whisper of boots over the stone, which was swept clean thanks to the unnatural wind. "Quite the riveting performance," purred the man's voice as he stepped from the shadows into the faint light of Jorna's still inflamed staff. His pointed features and sunken eyes appeared ghastly in the fire glow. His smile might have been charming were it not for the chilling cruelty behind his pale green gaze. Straight, brown hair streaked with just a touch of gray was slicked back from his narrow face, falling in greasy strands to brush the nape of his neck and curling around his ears to end on his bony jawline.

"The delusional princess with her brainless oaf and pet dragon, making their final stand against a horde of single-minded monsters... It's so noble and pathetic all at once." He chuckled mockingly to himself, as though he'd told a joke only he could understand, and perhaps in his own mind, he had.

Jorna strode boldly to stand in front of her companions, raising her chin defiantly in spite of his obvious insults. "You know who we are. Who are you?" she asked pointedly, having no patience or time for games or nonsense. "And what are you doing in *my* city?" She was running out of time, her imbued glaive continued to sap her strength, though now that she wasn't using it, the drain on her was significantly reduced.

"Your city?" His thin eyebrows shot up, the motion spreading lines across his forehead. "No, no, you are mistaken, this city belongs to the humans of Ardon now. Its former inhabitants scurried away like frightened rats at the mere sight of my beautiful pets." He raised a hand so bony that it hardly had any flesh at all and snapped his thin fingers once.

The sound brought a single of the fiends through the treasury door. She was barely visible in the dim light. All they could really distinguish was that she was larger than her sisters, taller and no doubt had a broader wingspan. Her bright, violet eyes glinted through the darkness, belying her malicious, unquenchable rage. At the sight of her, the three companions prepared themselves, ready to resume the fight should either of their enemies cease to simply stand there.

"Now, now." The human sounded a touch cross. "There's no point in getting violent. You've already lost. I have you outnumbered and overpowered. Lay down your weapons and surrender to my custody. I give you my word that you will not be slain." He pursed his lips, as though considering something, then added nonchalantly, "Well, not immediately..."

A rush of seething fury ignited in Jorna's eyes at the mere notion of willingly giving herself over to anyone, let alone her worst enemy. She would rather die fighting than wait to be executed and she knew with great clarity that Thane and Shanik felt the same way. With an echoing cry, she lunged forward, bringing her fiery glaive around in preparation for a killing blow.

She didn't make it even two steps before a blinding hot pain stopped her. For a moment she feared that she had waited too long to release the fire element, that in the next second she would be consumed by it and fall into oblivion. When that didn't happen, she glanced up and saw the man staring at her, his face split in a ghastly grin. She noticed that he was holding something between his bony fingers and at a second glance she identified it as a talisman, no doubt made of components that conflicted with her power and most importantly her weapon.

Cold fear washed over her as she realized he somehow knew her greatest weakness, the one thing that could actually destroy her glaive. All it took were a few words, the right words and the magic that coursed through the weapon would overpower the wards that kept her from being harmed by that same magic, both mentally and physically. She had one choice and only a split instant to make it.

Fighting back the increasing pain that shot through every inch of her body, Jorna let go of the element, allowing it to seep out of her glaive. Instantly she was assailed with the wave of debilitating exhaustion that she'd known would come. It drove her to her knees as black spots invaded her vision. She was dimly aware of the weapon still in her hands, her arms too tired to hold it, but even if she'd tried, she knew she wouldn't be able to drop it.

Somewhere above she could hear his wispy voice, the jagged shamanic words he spoke in complete contrast. Though she wanted to fight, to rise off the floor and destroy him, all she could do was sit there, blinking back the darkness and watching as the shaft of her glaive splintered, then shattered into tiny pieces. Agony, like nothing she had ever experienced before, wracked her body, forcing out an involuntary scream as the backlash of power from her broken weapon crashed over her. She had always been cautioned that should her staff be forcibly destroyed, it would be most unpleasant, but experiencing it, feeling it firsthand, she came to realize it was much, much worse.

Jorna lost awareness of everything outside her body. She no longer heard the man's whispers or knew where her companions were at. She didn't see Shanik throw himself protectively over her convulsing body or hear Thane's thundering commands for the human to stop whatever he was doing. Between the pain and fatigue, her mind simply couldn't focus on any one thing. Within a matter of seconds, she had collapsed completely to the stone, the gnawing blackness that consumed her good for only one thing: blocking out the tormenting pain.

24

PRISONERS

THANE AND JORNA WERE separated from Shanik, much to their dismay. The blacksmith tried to insist that they remain together, but the human simply ignored him. They had exchanged a glance, deciding without the need to debate that for now they would go along, they would wait for Jorna to return to consciousness, and when the time was right, they would act together.

Refusing to allow the fiends to touch his charge, Thane scooped her limp form off the floor, alarmed at how hot her skin felt as her forehead brushed his cheek. He glanced at the fragmented remains of her glaive, wondering if he should find a way to reclaim them for her in the off chance that they might be useful later, but something told him that was not the case. Besides, he had more important things to worry about, like where their captors were taking them and what dark things they might have planned.

As he was led through the abandoned palace, he could hear Shanik somewhere behind him, growling and hissing threateningly. He remained in the chamber long enough to watch as they had secured chains around the dragon's neck, bound his wings to his flanks and muzzled him so that he couldn't speak or breathe fire.

Thane couldn't be sure, not knowing Shanik's age, if he was in any real danger or not. Older dragons, it was said anyway, were nearly impervious to weapons and were entirely immune to harmful spells or curses; it would take a great deal of effort to slay one. One a few thousand years younger, however, could very easily be slain.

Hoping that for now at least Shanik would be relatively safe, Thane allowed himself to focus all of his thoughts on looking after Jorna. There was no denying that he worried for her. After what they had witnessed, he feared she would never awaken or if she did that she wouldn't be the same woman. He had no idea what to expect; he knew so little about her shamanic ways that all he could really do was wait and see. It wasn't exactly ideal, he hated waiting, then again nothing about their current predicament was anywhere close to ideal.

A sharp jab in the middle of his back reminded him of just how dire things had become. The fiendish creatures seemed barely able to contain their desire to maim and kill. Each one he passed looked at him with an expression of unrestrained hostility. He was certain that escaping them would be difficult. If escape was even possible, he thought bitterly. Chasing the doubt from his mind, he convinced himself that no matter how difficult it was, they would find a way to reclaim the book and make it safely back to Hamdralg.

The group of fiends took him down into the dungeons, which reeked with a noxious odor, a mix of unwashed bodies, bile, and death. He nearly choked on the pungent concoction as it coated his nose and mouth, but he quickly forgot about it when he heard the sound of someone coughing, followed by the rustling of movement from inside one of the cells up ahead. Could they have truly taken prisoners?

Half afraid and half eager, Thane allowed himself to be pushed over the threshold and down the row of iron cages. Once they were passed the inner stone wall, he glanced into the first set of cells and saw that there were a few dirty, starving Sarven men held inside.

They stared out at him, mirroring the shock that was on his bearded face, but they didn't move. They stayed away from the doors, out of reach of the creatures. Sweeping his gaze to the end of the aisle, he made a rough count of nearly twenty, all of them men and by their attire all warriors, too.

Thane was brought to a stop about halfway down the row, their captors moving cautiously as they opened the cell door. One stood by with a pole weapon, ready to thrust it through the bars in order to fend off any of the prisoners who dared try to escape. Shoving roughly at the blacksmith, the creatures made him hurry inside and then sealed the door shut so swiftly behind him that his back was nearly closed in it.

He could hear them leaving, pausing to torment some of the other men before the leader of their group snarled something unintelligible at the rest. The heavy iron gate slammed shut in their wake, the screeching sound of the lock echoing in the dank dungeon.

Through it all, Thane stood with his gaze fixed on the pair of men he had been put with, unwilling to blindly trust them. Slowly he started to move for the nearest corner, intending to prop Jorna against the back wall, which unlike the sides and front of the cell was made of solid stone.

The intensity of his gaze caused the two men to shift out of his way, the older of the pair seeming almost curious, while the younger was on the verge of taking offense. In their eyes, they were all Sarven, there was no point in distrusting one another, not in the face of such terrible monsters. Thane knew this, but he also knew that it was his duty to protect Jorna and after everything they'd been through, he wasn't about to let his guard down now.

Gently he set her down, leaning her against the wall and then pulling off his heavy outer shirt so that he had something to cover her with. It was rather chilly down here, but nowhere near as cold as their trek over the mountains.

Using the back of his hand, he tried to gauge her temperature, concerned that she might have a fever. With a sigh, he found that her skin was still too hot, unnaturally hot, which made him think that it had something to do with the fire she was using with her staff.

Being so unfamiliar with her magic put him at a great disadvantage. He had no way of knowing how to help her or if she even needed assistance at all. He could only keep her covered up as best as possible and hope she pulled through.

Scraping behind him drew Thane's attention back to his cellmates. The older one was trying to see around him, a frown on his filthy, haggard face. "Bless my beard," he whispered, his tone almost reverent as the glance he'd stolen confirmed his suspicions. "The princess! She shouldn't be here!"

His exclamations drew attention from the occupants of the cells that flanked theirs. Within seconds whispers were floating through the dungeon as the men spread the word that one of the new captives was Princess Jorna. Thane watched with growing unease, glad that his back at least was protected by the solid wall. He hovered protectively over the unconscious shaman, watching the other Sarven closely.

"Easy now, lad," the elder said, his bushy eyebrows knitted in a sympathetic frown. He wasn't really that old, save for a touch of gray at the roots of his auburn hair and below his lip; he could have been Thane's age for all he could tell. Over a month of living in squalor, eating just enough to stay alive, had taken its toll on every warrior he looked upon in their dark hell. "My name is Renarn and this here is Rulvon. I promise we mean no harm to her or you…"

Rulvon snorted, still seeming annoyed at Thane's distrust. He looked a lot like Renarn, though his eyes were a bit of a lighter blue. The two could have easily been brothers. "If anyone should be suspicious, we should be suspicious of him," he declared in a thick Dwenenari accent. "I have never seen this man in my life and yet here he is with the princess. How do we know he didn't try to hand her over to those creatures?"

Releasing a sigh, Renarn threw the other man a significant look, clearly telling him to keep his mouth shut. "Forgive my brother, being trapped here has done little for his temper." When Thane did not speak, but simply continued to glance between them, he went on to comment, "You must be from Hamdralg. I take it the refugees arrived there safely?"

Thane allowed himself to relax, if only a fraction. He could certainly sympathize with their situation, being trapped and at the mercy of those fiends, cut off from their families, not knowing if they had survived or suffered some other horrible fate. If he were in their position, he would be desperate for news. Flicking his gaze to the still motionless Jorna, he reminded himself that these were her kin and that the least he could do was ease some of their concerns.

"I am Thane and yes, I am from Hamdralg," he answered softly, leaning back and settling himself against the wall beside Jorna. He wanted to hold her close, needing the firmness of her body to assure him that she was going to be fine, but he remembered his place and settled for keeping a watchful eye on her. "I'm afraid I don't know much about the refugees, but I will tell you what I can…"

THE SUMMONS

JORNA AWOKE TO THE steady sound of water dripping nearby and the muffled noise of people talking. Her body felt stiff and sore, her limbs heavy. She could tell that she was not fully recovered from overexerting herself or from the negative side effects of having her staff broken. She felt the desire to sleep for an eternity, despite having just regained consciousness. She knew that the best remedy for her recovery was a good meal and plenty of rest. Unfortunately she had a sinking feeling that both of those things would have to wait.

Forcing her eyes open, she took in her surroundings with a blurry gaze, blinking to clear it so that she could make out finer details. The first thing she saw was Thane's concerned face, and behind him, the unmistakable view of bleak, smelly dungeons. That made plenty of sense, she decided, where else would their captors put them if not in the palace holding cells?

Tentatively she reached up, rubbing at her forehead to ease the throbbing pressure as she muttered quietly that she was all right. The statement was mostly true; she certainly would *be* all right, even if at the moment she didn't feel so great.

As Thane settled back down beside her, his worried brown eyes never straying from her face, she was able to see a broader view of where they were at. It took her mind a few seconds to register that they weren't alone. When she'd first regained consciousness, she had assumed Thane was speaking to Shanik, but the dragon was nowhere to be found.

Instead, there were Sarven, more than a dozen of them by a hasty count. All of them Dwenenari warriors, but more than that, these were men from the rear guard, the brave souls who had covered the escape of the refugees, willingly sacrificing their lives... Only they were not dead. They were sitting all around her, staring as their princess came back to her senses, and though they looked like they'd been through hell, there was a gleam of hope behind every gaze she met.

"Renarn," she said the name as a greeting, remembering him as one of Dathor's captains.

The man bowed his head respectfully, his thick brows brushing together as he frowned. "Princess, we're very glad you're awake. You had us all worried."

"I'm fine," she reiterated, glancing about for some source of drinkable water, but it seemed that the prisoners were deprived of constant access to this basic necessity.

Turning to Thane, she offered him the most reassuring smile she could manage, reaching out to brush her fingers against his hand. "Where's Shanik?" She whispered the question, fearing the worst.

His expression grim, Thane slowly shook his head. "They took him somewhere else."

Jorna didn't bother to keep the concern off her face. Whatever they had planned for Shanik, it couldn't be good. She hoped that they would be able to get out of this new predicament and help the dragon before anything terrible befell any of them.

"How long has it been?"

"Just overnight," Thane answered. She could suddenly see that he was tired. No doubt he hadn't slept at all, having been too busy watching over her. This brought a smile to her lips and had it not been for their audience, she would have touched his hand or shoulder to further reassure and praise him.

"Well, that explains why I'm so hungry." She rubbed her belly.

Renarn chimed in again, his tone apologetic, "They don't feed us often I'm afraid. Once every few days if we're very lucky."

Nodding to let him know that she had heard him, Jorna's mind drifted away. She found herself wondering if their supplies were still in the treasury, though if they were she couldn't imagine what good that did them now.

The meager food they had left was barely enough for the pair of them to return to Hamdralg on, let alone feed twenty starving men. Her stomach growled in discontent and she decided that even a small snack would have been better than nothing.

After a few minutes, she was drawn into a conversation with the two brothers, both of whom curious as to why she had returned to Dwenenar. In fact, everyone had crowded as close as they could get to hear her answer, even those on the other side of the dimly lit aisle. She spoke up so that they could hear, explaining that she had come to secretly recover the Goldsteel book, but that the creatures were laying in wait. With Thane's help, she did her best to describe the battle and all that happened with the human afterward.

"His name is Stefan," Rulvon commented bitterly, his jaw clenching beneath his scraggly, unkempt beard. "He's an Arcanist."

That made a lot of sense, Jorna thought, remembering how he

had conjured the gust of wind. The humans practiced a peculiar sort of magic, a magic that was more a science, steeped in equations and formulas. They didn't have rituals or cast spells. They created potions, scribed scrolls, imbued weapons with enchantments and some rumors suggested that they were capable of much darker deeds.

"He's a cruel, uncaring bastard is what he is," one man corrected, making it apparent that this Stefan had won no popularity contest among the Sarven survivors. None of them were afraid to share what horrible acts they had seen him commit. When they had been taken captive, they numbered just under thirty and now there were precisely twenty-three.

Stefan had taken some of the men away, done things with them, changing them into mere shadows of their former selves until they were so crazed and paranoid that he ordered them 'put down'.

Hearing this made Jorna sick, physically and emotionally. She hated seeing her people, good, brave warriors, tormented by a sadistic bastard. It also worried her for Shanik, who she hoped was not being subjected to the same treatments. If by some unlucky stroke of fate he was, then she prayed his draconic nature would serve to protect him against Stefan's experiments.

She caught the men watching her and realized that her concern must have been written on her face. Since they did not know of Shanik, they had misinterpreted her worry. She quickly sought a way to ease their trepidations. Forcing herself to relax, though it was the last thing she wanted to do, she would much rather be hanging on the door, demanding to see Stefan, she began to tell of their journey.

Jorna shared everything, their encounter with the short-tempered giants, how they crossed the worm fields, their battle with the worm itself and how they were welcomed by a savage tribe of orcs. Thane helped to elaborate on certain points, giving details that Jorna couldn't or that she might have forgotten. He seemed quite proud to share of his battle against Drogthul, despite the giant's cheating that had caused him to lose.

By the time they were done with the long story and the flurry of questions that followed, they knew it was well into the night. The survivors urged them to rest while they could, warning them that Stefan might send his hellish pets to fetch a new specimen as he seemed to prefer working at night. With little else to do for the moment except wait for their 'host' to send them an invitation, Jorna and Thane silently decided to rest.

Jorna settled back against the cell wall, sitting so that she was only inches from touching Thane's side with her own. Perhaps it was the exhaustion pulling at her, but she oddly did not care if her closeness to him was inappropriate. He was warm, his presence comforting. She couldn't stop herself from resting her head against his shoulder as her eyes drifted closed. It reminded her of their night together in the giant camp, what now felt like a lifetime ago. Her heart swelled with the memory and with something else that she was too tired to put a name to.

This thought carried her into a deep sleep, the result of still being exhausted more than because she was comfortable enough to let her guard down. In the last month, she had slept in far worse places; at least here she was surrounded by allies and most important of all, she had Thane at her side.

The cell block was mostly silent now, save for the consistent dripping of water that echoed in the stone chamber. None of the Sarven slept well enough or deep enough to actually snore, most simply dozed, all of them on alert for the abrupt sound of the dungeon door being thrust open.

With a ringing clatter, this happened only a handful of hours later.

In an instant the men moved, getting as far away from the aisle as possible. Jorna was jostled awake by Thane and just about to ask what was wrong when she heard the sound of approaching footsteps, of talons clacking against stone. Immediately on edge, she glanced up just in time to see four of the fiends come into view.

They didn't glance into a single one of the cells or stop to harass the inhabitants. They strode with purpose to the middle door which held their newest prisoners. Clearly they were in a hurry, no doubt having been sent with all haste so that Stefan wasn't kept waiting too long. Glaring with baleful eyes into the cage, their leader hissed, raising her taloned finger to point right at Jorna.

This action incited the Sarven into action, inspiring them to overcome their fear of the creatures so that they could shout in protest. Many of them flew against the iron bars, their deep voices reverberating against the walls so that it was nearly impossible to make out what they were saying. Not that it was at all necessary in order for their intentions to be clear. They were trying to protect their princess, offering themselves in her place, begging the monsters to have mercy.

Snarling and snapping, they didn't oblige. They slammed their weapons against the bars, beating at the arms and hands of any Sarven who didn't get their limbs out of the way fast enough. Rulvon and Renarn backed away from the iron door, but they stayed blocking the path to Jorna, their fists raised threateningly as they hurled insults, daring their captors to even try getting passed them.

The whole ruckus made the throbbing in Jorna's head worse. She glanced to Thane, hoping he would help her to get control, but with a single glance she could tell he would be just as stubborn. Already he was posed in front of her, an expression on his face that promised violence to anyone or anything that even thought about touching the one he was sworn to protect.

A part of her found his brazen willingness to defend her endearing, but the more sensible part of her knew that it would accomplish nothing. She needed to speak with Stefan, to learn more about him, specifically to learn his weaknesses so that she could use them to get them all out of Dwenenar alive.

"Silence!" Jorna's voice rang above the din, immediately hushing the warriors and drawing everyone's attention to her. She gave them all a stern glance, a glance that clearly stated she was capable of handling herself, and then she started forward, answering the crude summons of the creature.

Thane gently grabbed her arm, opening his mouth to voice concern. She saw on his face everything he was going to say, every argument he was going to make, and she silenced him by placing her hand firmly on his chest. She could faintly feel the rapid beating of his heart against her palm and willed it to still.

Jorna fixed him with a determined gaze, letting him know that she would not be swayed. He did nothing to hide his disapproval, but after all they had been through, he must have known he had little choice but to trust her judgment.

The slightest lowering of his chin was the only sign he gave of backing down. A moment later he released her arm, though with obvious reluctance. Jorna allowed her hand to linger a heartbeat longer, then turned to face the impatient monster and stepped over the threshold.

26

THE ARCANIST

Jorna was certain of her destination the moment they turned down the hallway from the dungeons. There were many reasons to head in this direction, but since the vault holding Goldsteel's book was the other way, she guessed that this was more of an introductory meeting and not yet an effort to force her into opening the door.

Or they already have the book... No! That's not possible, I would have felt it if the seals were broken.

From what the warriors had told her of the arrogant Stefan, it made perfect sense that he would make the throne room his base of operations, for it was the most grand room in the palace.

She could feel her memories swimming around, coming to the forefront of her mind, and she pushed them aside. This meeting was going to take all of her strength, all her wit and cunning simply to survive.

She was hoping to get some information about Shanik, to find out if her friend was safe or not, but doing so would be difficult. She couldn't outright ask; to place that much value on him would make him a target, of that she was certain. Being straightforward wouldn't work at all. She would have to be cautious, aware of his words and any possible double meanings, while conveying her own goals in the same fashion.

Her father had told her this was the biggest downside to being a ruler, finding a way to endure the politics. He'd said it with such irritation, but all the times she had observed him in discussions with nobles or other dignitaries, he made it look incredibly easy.

It didn't take long to reach the throne room, the creatures pushed her to walk fast, which took a conscious effort on her part. Were her mother to catch her moving so swiftly, she would have undoubtedly been scolded and reminded that she must exercise control at all times. Those lessons had been hard to learn as a child, but by the time she was older, they were ingrained, a habit, something she did without thought. Her escorts would never have understood this, so she said nothing and followed along at the pace they set.

When they came to the wide double doors, which once had been awe-inspiring as they were intricately inlaid with shimmering gold designs, her heart sank; the gold had been stripped, leaving them bare and ugly. Glancing down at her feet, she noticed that the velvet carpet was torn and stained with dark blotches, mud or dried blood she couldn't tell. She could only imagine what horrific state the throne room was in. She took a deep breath as the doors were carelessly shoved open, dreading the sight that was about to meet her eyes.

A sharp jab in her lower back sent her over the threshold. She released the air in a quiet sigh, her gaze sweeping the well-lit chamber. To her surprise it was mostly untouched save for the defacing of a few statues and the destructive removal of the Sarven tapestries. The room's gold ornamentation was perfectly intact, though it could have used a good polish. The carpet was still dirty from being trod upon by those who simply didn't care to keep it in presentable condition. The servants would have been more than a little annoyed, that was for sure.

Additions had been made, she saw that the moment they cleared the six pillars that swept outward from the doors. Tables had been brought in and crammed together just below the raised dais, blocking from sight the last few steps leading to the throne. They were littered with strange instruments and vials, sheets of scattered parchment and a handful of worn tomes, some of which lay open.

Her gaze was quickly drawn from what was clearly a workstation to the rightmost gallery, where an answer to her concerns regarding Shanik was plainly provided.

He was bolted to the floor with heavy iron chains that were normally used in the mines for hauling up loads of ore. The dragon did not appear to be harmed, though she couldn't imagine that he was at all comfortable. It took all of her control not to demand he be released. She knew such a demand would do no good, so she bit it back, flashing Shanik a sympathetic glance as he had seen her only a second after she had seen him.

"Ah here she is…" The familiar voice of the arcanist flitted down to her from the gold and stone throne. He was lazily reclining upon it, his special "pet" as he had called her, standing beside him like a fetid shadow. No doubt he had chosen that position to infuriate her, a tactic that absolutely succeeded, not that she let it show on her face.

"Jorna Hailstone, the shaman princess formerly of Dwenenar, it is an honor to have you in *my* hall."

The creatures stopped her in front of a narrow walkway, the only free space left by the tables. The pair that had been leading her stepped back, but she didn't doubt that they were ready to spring on her if she made any sudden movements. She pointedly put them out of her mind, ignoring the sensation of unease that their seething eyes gave her. The real monster was sitting in her father's seat.

"Stefan." She raised her voice, grasping onto every shred of dignity that she could. "I don't advise you to get too comfortable up there." A little smirk twisted her lips.

The rattling of a chain drew her attention from her adversary, causing her to glance in Shanik's direction, but she immediately saw he was not the source. She did her best not to frown, wondering if perhaps she was going mad, until shuffling and more clinking finally betrayed where the initial noise had come from.

Tilting her head to get a better view, she caught a mere glimpse of matted, straw blond hair from around the table before the rest of the head poked itself above the surface. Jorna felt as though a musk ox had just sat down on her chest.

Her breath caught in her throat, and though she tried to keep her expression neutral, the familiar, haggard face of Guldorn Oathbinder was a sight she would have never guessed she might see again. He looked filthy, worn down, and his eyes were wild, unfocused, but there he was, alive and breathing just a few steps from where she was standing.

Slowly she rounded the table, her eyes needing to be certain before the rest of her could react. She swept her gaze over his filthy clothes, catching a whiff of his unwashed odor even this far away from him, and though he looked so different from the man in her memories, she knew without a doubt that *he* was truly her father. As this realization finally hit her, Jorna forgot where she was, she forgot the pretense of strength she was supposed to be maintaining and in a rush of exhilarated joy, she bounded to him.

Guldorn jumped, a startled expression on his face as the young woman fell to her knees in front of him and threw her arms around his shoulders. For a moment it seemed that he might return the gesture, but an expression of confusion spread over his features and with a frightened cry, he shoved her back, scuttling frantically across the floor to get away from her.

"Father?" she breathed, fighting a wave of tears at the lack of recognition. How could he not know her, his own flesh and blood? "Father, it's me, it's Jorna," she tried to press, unable to keep the pain out of her voice. "It's your daughter..."

His dry, crusty lips mouthed the name as though he were scrambling to recall what it meant, but after a few moments he gave up the attempt, sulking back to the floor in defeat. Jorna tried to scoot closer to him, just a few inches to see if he would allow it, and when he didn't seem scared, she carefully closed the distance. She laid a hand on his arm, her mind struggling to catch up, struggling to process that her father was alive, but the joy was soured by the horrible state he was in.

A cruel laugh reminded her of Stefan and the aching pain in her chest instantly turned to a seething, burning fury. No longer did she care about pretenses or veiled words, of hiding her motives or intentions. She wanted this man, who was every bit as evil and twisted as the creatures that served him, to know he had crossed the final line. He would be given no quarter, no mercy. She wanted him to know that eventually she would escape his clutches and when she did, she was going to kill him.

Raising her eyes, Jorna allowed him to see every ounce of her contempt in the cold depths of her gray-blue gaze. "What have you done to him?" she demanded, her voice ringing with power.

"Oh, you look angry. That's not very becoming on a princess," he teased mockingly, not seeming at all bothered by the death glare she fixed him with. He held her gaze, searching her, musing within himself at what lengths she might really go to if he pushed her hard enough.

He whispered a word and in a sudden flash, Jorna was granted insight into Stefan's mind. She saw what he had done to her father, how he had tested his limits, picked at his resolve until the king's mind had broken under the pressure.

This he had achieved through a mix of careful torture and hallucinogenic poisons that had left his victims either screaming in terror as they believed they were assailed by the most terrible of monsters or weeping, begging, pleading as they imagined their loved ones suffering the cruelest fates.

He had no plans to do this to Jorna directly. He was going to use the twenty odd warriors rotting away in the dungeons and force her to witness the unraveling of their minds until she gave him the secret to recovering Goldsteel's book from the vault.

He had learned his lesson with Guldorn, having meant only to torture him until he got what he wanted, but he'd gone too far and now he was little more than a drooling mute who didn't even know his own name. The thought of his failure made him bristle, but it also reminded him that he needed to begin breaking down the shaman's defenses now, softening her up so that she would be susceptible to the suffering of her kinfolk.

While he personally enjoyed the process of breaking a person's mind, Dwenenar was growing dull. He needed the book and its secret so he could return to his plush home and grand laboratory in Hewshire...

Jorna let out an involuntary gasp as their brief mental link was severed. She was confident he had not seen into her own, only shared what was sitting upon the surface of his mind. Still, it was not an experience she was keen to experience again. She felt dirty and even more angry at the intimate nature of such a connection. She squared her shoulders, summoning resolve as she once again hardened her gaze.

"Answer me, swine." Jorna's defiant voice broke the quiet that had fallen and instantly put an annoyed frown on his face. "What have you done to my father?"

"Patience," he hissed, motioning to the four guards that it was time for the captive to move away from his chained pet. "I'll show you the exact process soon enough. If you behave, I might even let you pick the first subject." His thin lips curled into a sinister grin.

Jorna resisted the two monsters who approached her to take her away from Guldorn. She did not want to be parted from him, but that didn't matter to them. Each grabbed hold of an arm and together they yanked her off the floor so hard she thought they might just rip her arms clean out of the sockets. Even then she didn't make their task easy. She fought them with every step until they had brought her back to the other side of the tables. Once they let her go, she remained still, her eyes once again seeking her enemy, perched atop his stolen throne like a twisted peacock.

"I am not sure which is fouler, the creatures or the man they serve," she shot at him, openly insulting him now, testing to see if he was quick to lose his temper or not.

Stefan brushed the offense off, proving he was not easily rattled. "It is true, the old saying; 'beauty is in the eye of the beholder'," he mused aloud, shifting his position slightly so that he was sitting up a bit straighter.

"These beautiful creatures are my legacy. If I were a sentimental man, I might even label them my children. They are a living testament to my arcane prowess for I created them with a touch of magic and a few other, special ingredients." He gave her another ghastly grin. "I call them wyrmkin for their draconic appearance. Don't you think it suits them? It was the Sarven after all, who in their ignorance gave the moniker to the dragons of old…"

He was watching her intently for any reaction, the slightest tick or shift that mIght belie how she took this revelation.

Jorna refused to give him the satisfaction and maintained the defiant, contemptuous expression. "They are abhorrent abominations and I promise you, I will do everything in my power to wipe their kind from the face of this world," she spat, her tone commanding and thick with passion. "Now I demand that you release us, *all* of us, including my father and the dragon. You had no right to take us as prisoners. This is *our* home and you are *not* welcome here."

Chuckling in genuine amusement, Stefan raised a dubious eyebrow in her direction. "You certainly have an abundance of spirit," he mused, shaking his head and mockingly repeating her words as though she had just told the sort of joke that was so terrible it deserved a small laugh anyway.

Whether intentional or not, she had given him a perfect opening to direct the conversation to exactly where he wanted it to be. Otherwise he would not have taken her comments so jovially. "Well, he did warn me that you were a handful..." He delivered the phrase like it was meant to hold some importance, letting it trail off as he turned his face away and sniffed at the air, purposely ignoring her.

Already needled by his reaction to her demands, Jorna didn't much care for the game he was playing; she was not so oblivious she couldn't see that he was toying with her. She very nearly didn't ask the obvious question, wanting to see if he was annoyed by her subtle refusal, but she couldn't deny that she was curious.

Her father would not have had given him any information. She knew for certain he would have died first. Someone must have told him something about her. Otherwise he wouldn't have been able to destroy her glaive and weaken her magic. Whoever it was, she needed to know their name so that she could be sure they paid for their betrayal.

"And who might that have been?" she finally asked after making him wait a few long moments. "I would even wager it's the same person who gave you my secrets."

"Oh, you mean my informant?" He shrugged noncommittally at first, clearly attempting to see just how badly she wanted to know. When she simply stared blankly at him, he adjusted on the throne, his gaze drifting to Guldorn, the green depths glinting with an unmasked viciousness.

"I do wish," he commented softly, almost to himself, "that I could say it was your father who gave me the knowledge to undo the magic of your staff... I wonder, how that would affect you, how deeply you would feel such a betrayal."

A nasty, cold grin revealed his teeth as he paused to imagine all the interesting possibilities. It was quite clear that she adored her father, most daughters did; knowing that he betrayed the values he had spent years teaching her would surely destroy whatever strength and resolve she might have.

"Alas," he pulled himself out of his daydreams and back to the moment, "your father told me nothing." He allowed her that small victory, let it sink in that her father had not broken and watched with glee as the faintest of grins quirked her lips; then he stole it away.

"I spent weeks torturing him, taking him to new heights of physical and emotional agony until his mind broke. Perhaps, if he had a greater mental fortitude, he could have held out until you arrived. Or perhaps if you had returned sooner..." He trailed off, his callous eyes goading her.

Jorna clenched her jaw, fighting to keep herself from rushing up the stone steps and strangling him with her bare hands. A single shred of her good sense was all that held her back, telling her that she would not have gotten more than a few feet before the wyrmkin had restrained or slain her.

It didn't stop her from imagining how good it would feel to force the life out of his scrawny, worthless body, to feel his futile struggling begin to wane as he succumbed to death... Taking a few calming breaths, the shaman carefully reined in her temper until the proper time and place when she could unleash it on her enemies.

"If not my father," she commented once she finally had full control of her mouth again, "then who? Or would you rather play more silly games before telling me?"

"Aww," he mocked a crestfallen expression, "don't you like our games, Princess?"

"Said the cat to the mouse," she answered dryly.

Chuckling coldly, Stefan studied her for a moment before heaving a disappointed sigh. "Oh very well, since you seem so keen to know the truth." He couldn't help smiling, perhaps the most honest and malicious smile he had ever expressed in her presence.

"This man was singularly instrumental in all of my plans here in Dwenenar, from the initial invasion to your capture at my hands. I might have accomplished these tasks on my own, but not with nearly the same efficiency or delight." He straightened on the throne, leaning forward to rest his elbows on his knees as he eagerly continued, "I must profess, I am greatly enjoying this moment, though I do regret that you will not appreciate it nearly as much. Most individuals balk at being the bearer of ill news, but I find it quite refreshing!"

"Get to the point already," Jorna snapped, her meager patience stretched to breaking. The more words that came from his vile lips, the more her skin crawled. She couldn't imagine how someone could go through life with that much darkness clouding their hearts. Even with everything she and her people had endured, she could still feel hope and love and light. It made her wonder what sort of evil could taint a person so completely.

"Now, now," Stefan chided crossly, "such asperity is unbecoming of a princess." When all she did was glare more harshly at him, he released a displeased *tsk*, giving up the notion that she might apologize for her coarseness and opened his mouth to continue what he had originally been saying. "Minister Prowd came here to re-negotiate the peace treaties of our two nations, but as you know the king turned him away without even granting him an audience. He was—"

"He came to strong arm my father into giving him the secret of Goldsteel," Jorna sternly corrected, remembering exactly what had happened and why the minister was turned away.

The treaties had expired months before, when for thousands of years they were renewed well in advance with little to no alterations. Guldorn had suspected that the humans let them run out on purpose so that he would have cause to negotiate entirely new treaties or face the threat of future invasion. It had been a risk, refusing to see the visiting dignitary, but the king had wanted to send a clear message that the Sarven would not be bullied.

As she considered all the pieces that were now falling into place, Jorna was certain that these *wyrmkin* creatures were exactly why the minister was so boldly going against the old alliances. They were counting on the fiends to bring the Sarven and elven nations to their knees without Ardon having to lift a finger to aide in any of the fighting that ensued. This realization was just another plank of wood on the fire rising in her belly and further motivation to put an end to what was turning out to be nothing but a wicked, greedy plot.

Clearing his throat irritably, for he greatly disliked being interrupted or contradicted, especially at the same time, Stefan fixed her with a hard stare until he was certain that she was finished being rude.

"As I was saying," he grated with emphasis. "He was quite surprised when a member of the royal family approached him on the eve of his return to Ardon. *Quiet*," he growled, stopping Jorna before she could do much more than open her mouth to protest that none of her relatives would ever do such a thing, that Stefan was lying.

"I know you were taught better manners, Princess. I know this because your brother Javrin's were quite exceptional. Unlike his stubborn, boorish father, he saw the wisdom of the minister's words and negotiated on behalf of Dwenenar."

SHAMAN'S DEAL

"You're lying!" Jorna proclaimed, her temper flaring hot, her gaze burning as she glowered at the nasty wretch of a man. "Javrin would never betray his family or his people, and for what? Scraps from a human minister? He would rather rot!"

Stefan only laughed at her, clearly reveling in the trouble he had caused, in how she could barely keep herself from trembling. It didn't take another glimpse into his mind for her to know what he was thinking. He wanted her to argue, to defend her brother's honor. He was still toying with her, and for the first time a sinking feeling churned in the pit of her stomach. Did Stefan have proof? Had Javrin really betrayed them? But why?

"Oh, not for scraps," he finally answered, his voice almost a purr. "His price was much, much higher than that..." He paused for dramatic effect, studying her intently as he finally whispered, "He wanted *your* throne."

Her lips parted, more angry denials ready to spill off her tongue, but she stopped abruptly, a frown creasing her soft brow. Had Stefan just made a blunder? What he had just said made no sense! She didn't have a throne! Jorna was the second born; the throne already belonged to Javrin.

She let her anger melt away as a victorious grin lit up her face. It seemed that Stefan had indeed made a mistake. He had tried to throw her off balance but had gotten his facts wrong. "Javrin is first in line to be king, not me," she informed him smugly, her eyes dancing with triumphant. "Your story isn't adding up, Stefan."

"Oh?" Stefan looked genuinely surprised, then he began to laugh to himself, muttering excitedly. It was not the response she had expected.

"Oh, poor, poor, Jorna," he cackled without the least bit of pity or remorse in his tone, "nobody told you?" He forcibly composed himself, though he continued to watch her with unbridled glee. "Guldorn was naming *you* as his heir! Much to the disapproval of your brother, who felt that you had stolen away his birthright. He delivered you to us so that I could use you to recover the book and with you dead and your parents all dead, he was free to take the throne unopposed."

Jorna shook her head, refusing to believe anything he said. It simply wasn't possible. Her father would have told her about a decision that important. He didn't have any reason not to! Just like he had no reason to choose her over Javrin; he was every bit as capable, strong and willing to be king. Besides, he was the firstborn and by tradition it was his right. Very rarely did a ruling king or queen name a younger child heir when their older brother or sister was alive and perfectly suited to the task. It was all but unheard of. Guldorn would have needed a very good reason to get the other nobles to agree...

She frowned, wondering if perhaps he hadn't told her because he hadn't yet broken the news to them, or if he had, that they weren't all in agreement yet. Either of those would be good reasons to wait before sharing his plan with her, but why would he tell Javrin if that were the case? Unless it had merely been a test to see what measures his son would take, if any, to earn the throne over his younger sister. But no, that was a silly notion. Guldorn was not the sort to play those games, especially when it meant pitting his children against one another.

No, the whole thing was wrong. It was Stefan, he was twisting her up, making her question her family and all that they stood for, to what dark end she didn't know, but she refused to let him get to her.

"You're still lying," she told him, her voice every bit as forceful as the last time, but it lacked the distinct edge of true conviction. Whether she liked it or not, a part of her couldn't help but doubt, speculating that perhaps the idea of being Guldorn's named heir was not so ludicrous after all.

"Come now, Princess," Stefan goaded, sitting up straight so that he could stare disapprovingly down the length of his nose at her, "surely you can put all the pieces together on your own."

When she set her jaw in a show of stubbornness, he huffed and folded his long, thin arms across his narrow chest. "He has always been so cold around you, hasn't he? It's because he's jealous of the bond you had with your father. You were always Guldorn's favorite. You have so many of the qualities your father values, and Javrin... Well, he's sly and scheming, traits that are deemed dishonorable by most Sarven standards."

Fighting against his words, Jorna turned her face away, hating that he made sense. Her relationship with Javrin had been strained since they became teenagers. Where once they had played together and gotten into mischief together, a day had come when it felt as though a continent separated them.

Even so, she didn't want to believe it was possible for him to be so angry that he could be party to killing his own family! Javrin had come to see her before she left, had told her all the things a brother should when his sister was embarking on a perilous quest... Had it all been a lie? Had he knowingly let her walk into a waiting trap, hoping she would never return? She squeezed her eyes shut, her attempts at pushing out the sound of Stefan's voice in vain.

"Really, you must put yourself in his shoes and try to understand how he feels," the man was musing, once again leaning back in the throne, this time rubbing thoughtfully at his pointed chin. "An outcast among his family, in a society where family is second only to one's loyalty to the ruling king. Never quite managing to be even adequate let alone equal to his little sister. It's no wonder he snapped when he heard the news that he would never be good enough for the throne."

Jorna's eyes flew open, and she glared hotly, her hands balling into fists at her sides. She was struggling harder than ever not to lose control, not to give in to the famous Sarven temper that edged her vision with a haze of red. "Enough," she snapped, "you have made your point and I still do not believe you! I will never believe you!"

He nodded slowly, pursing his thin lips into a near non-existent line as he pondered his next words carefully. "I see you require proof," he said with an absent, lazy wave of his fingers that signaled the large wyrmkin to his side. He waited to speak until she was nearly in front of the seething princess, then continued in a mockingly sympathetic tone.

"Thankfully I have our signed contract detailing his part and ours in bringing about the downfall of your family. Dwenenar and its citizens I'm afraid were collateral damage, but imagine how heroic and worthy Javrin will appear when he leads Hamdralg's finest troops to drive out the dark conquerors and reclaim the lost city for his people."

Stefan let out a delighted sigh, no doubt pleased at just how perfectly the evil plot was unfolding. "All I have left to do is get the book.

Then I will depart, leaving a number of my pets behind in Dwenenar - not so many as to make the prince's task overly difficult, but just enough to make his performance believable..."

The wyrmkin was standing right in front of Jorna, who glared unwavering into those baleful eyes. She held out a document, clutched in her taloned hands, for Jorna to take. Not breaking their stare down, she took the rolled-up parchment, being careful not to touch the blackened fingers in the process. Their exchange lasted only a brief second longer and then Stefan's pet turned sharply away and returned to her place near her master.

Jorna unfurled the scroll and began to read. The script that outlined the stipulations and details was small and square, penned by a proper scribe who was used to not only fitting a great deal on a single page, but in making sure it was legible. Below the block of contractual text were three scrawling signatures: Minister Roland Prowd, Stefan's as a witness, and Prince Javrin's. There was no denying that the document was real for it also bore the distinct seals of the Ardon ministration and Sarven royal family, both of which were irrefutable.

Jorna just stared at it, dumbfounded, feeling as though someone had just kicked her in the gut. Even now she wanted to believe that Javrin couldn't have possibly done this, that if he had it was under some sort of distress, but she wasn't stupid.

Here was his name, written in his own hand, with the seal of their family to prove that he had betrayed not only his own blood, but all the people of Dwenenar. Men, women and children lay dead, their bodies defiled and broken in the streets of their once prosperous and beautiful city as though they had meant nothing and for what? The greedy ambitions of an entitled prince.

She dropped her head, casting her gray-blue eyes to the floor in shame, shame that was not her own, but felt for the terrible sins of her brother. She could hear Stefan speaking again, but this time she succeeded in ignoring him, needing to be inside her own mind so that she could process this horrible truth without his twisted, cruel words clawing through her thoughts.

The slight sound of a heavy chain rattling caused her gaze to flick to the right, where Shanik lay motionless, facing her. She kept her head down, hiding the fact that she was looking to her friend, gaining silent support from his presence alone. In all this time, she had forgotten he was there, having been entirely consumed with the battle of words she was fighting with the arcanist. The dragon's sapphire eyes caught her, filled with sympathy and understanding, but also the assurance that everything would be all right.

She didn't know how Shanik could be so sure of that; after all, he was bolted to the floor, bound and helpless like an animal. It was a wonder he felt anything except despair. The situation felt entirely hopeless. They were on their own, their enemy had the upper hand, and this time there would be no wolves or dragons swooping in to save them at the last second. This time their efforts would simply fail.

The thought of wolves triggered something in the back of Jorna's mind, forcing her to remember what Firodel had told her only a few days earlier. She had told her that she must learn a terrible truth, but that she could endure so long as she trusted herself and her friends.

At the time she hadn't even fathomed that she would discover her brother was a traitor. She had assumed the spirit meant that finding the hellish fiends in Dwenenar, in seeing all the destruction would be the truth she had described. This was exactly what Firodel had been trying to prepare her for, and in doing so she had also given her the solution, the way out of their hopeless predicament.

Flashing Shanik a meaningful smile, the expression was gone from her face by the time she raised her head up, her eyes fixing immediately on Stefan. For now she forgot Javrin's treachery, pushing it to the back of her mind where it could be dealt with later.

What she needed to do now was simply survive and ensure that all the people she cared about survived with her. As far as she could see, there was only one way to do that. "I will not freely give you the book," she declared, her voice ringing with strength once again, "no matter what you do to me or to the other prisoners. However," she paused, seeming to hesitate, though she was in truth absolute in her new path, "I will bargain with you."

It was clear that her sudden words startled the human, making him pause in what he had been in the middle of saying. For a moment, he simply stared at her, curious but also cautious as to what sort of deal she might offer. Cocking an eyebrow, he asked sarcastically, "Whatever happened to *never* opening the door?"

"We are done mincing words and playing games, Stefan," she answered without skipping a beat, "Do you want to hear my offer or not?"

His curiosity got the better of him, especially since he had expected her to be much more distraught. The fact that whatever she had concocted was enough to make her forget, even temporarily, her brother's heinous crimes made him even more interested to hear what she had to say.

"I'm listening," he prompted, drawing his elbows up so that they were resting on the arms of the throne, his long, bony fingers steepled in front of his chest.

"You know my terms. I want my life and the lives of the dragon, my father, and every warrior in the dungeon," she started slowly. "I also know your terms. You want the secret of Goldsteel. We could spend the next days, weeks, months fighting one another, and I *will* fight, longer and harder than even my father. Or we can both get what we want."

"Intriguing," he breathed, his eyes belying that he was keenly interested. "But there's one small problem. I already have a contract with your brother, and it demands your death."

She shook her head, letting a wicked little grin curl up her lips. "Oh no, Javrin had a contract with the minister, and you are not the minister, you are merely his agent. You are bound by no contract, only by your duty to obtain the book, am I correct in that assumption?"

Stefan's head was bobbing in agreement, his eyes lighting up as he realized what thoughts – or what his twisted mind believed were her thoughts – had given her such ideas. Instead of breaking down, she had turned the crushing blow into her own weapon, using it to fuel a campaign of destruction against her brother. The notion that he may have managed to start a civil war brought a gleefully cruel grin to his face.

"My reputation would be tarnished, failing to manage all parts of my assigned task..." He may have liked her idea, but he wasn't about to just give in without making her work for it.

"Why would the minister care about the hurt feelings of a spoiled Sarven prince?" Jorna watched as he ate up her words. No doubt he was thinking he had somehow corrupted her and was reveling in the now tainted princess's dark scheming. "You would return victorious, telling your superiors and colleagues alike that you will go to any length to achieve your goals. A fine promise to some and a bold warning to others."

That caused his grin to grow wider, stretching across his thin, sunken face as his eyes sparkled with evil delight. "So, you would give me the book in exchange for your freedom and the freedom of your comrades? Just like that?"

"No, not quite so easily." Jorna shook her head, coming to her favorite part of the deal. "Goldsteel's book has been protected by kings since its creation. Only a handful of the best, most trusted craftsmen have ever learned its secret. I would dishonor them by giving the book to just anybody. You will have to prove that you are worthy first."

"Sarven traditions..." he muttered irritably, appearing crestfallen that he was being subjected to them. "Must we really waste time with this?"

"I'm afraid so," Jorna responded without hesitation. "If you want it to seem legitimate—"

"Very well." He waved his hand dismissively. "What does this test entail, then?"

Jorna, well aware that she had turned the tables and taken control of the conversation's direction, made him wait for a few moments before she gave him the answer. "You will choose a champion to fight in your name. If this person defeats me in single, *fair* combat, then the book will be yours."

He regarded her closely for a long moment, considering the offer carefully, weighing it to decide if that effort was going to be worth it. He certainly didn't doubt that any of his pets could defeat the princess. He had taken away the magic that made her a worthy adversary. Besides, win or lose, he would get the book eventually. She may have boasted that she would be difficult to break, but he was certain if she was willing to give up the book now, after a simple test of battle prowess, that in a few days the screams of her tortured men would change her mind.

"A duel would be somewhat entertaining, I suppose," he agreed, masking his eagerness to accept the deal. "I name Giselle as my champion." He indicated the wyrmkin who had long since returned to her master's side, the contract having also been returned to Stefan. "You will begin now."

"No, no," Jorna immediately protested, waving her hands in front of her to emphasize that now certainly wouldn't do. "There must be a measure of ceremony and I did mention fairness. We will do it at dawn, once I have rested and been fed. In fact, I request a gesture of good faith and ask that you provide an adequate meal for all the prisoners."

Sighing dramatically, Stefan nodded to her demands, just wanting to be done with the matter so that he could leave the stuffy, badly decorated Sarven city and return home. "Very well," he started to agree, his voice tinged with annoyance.

"One last thing." She kept her tone even, though she wanted to roll her eyes at his snobbish attitude. "The duel must be witnessed by other Sarven, to protect my integrity and honor. If I am to challenge my brother, I must be able to prove that my actions here were done according to tradition. I will already be frowned upon for agreeing to such a deal and allowing the Goldsteel book to leave Sarven custody. Let the prisoners watch and should your champion win, you and I will go immediately to retrieve the book." She paused, letting her words settle before asking, "Do we have a deal?"

The man leaned forward, resting his lips against his fingers as he contemplated this final request. She watched the wheels turn in his mind. It would be simple enough to have the wyrmkin keep guard, especially if the weakened, half-starved warriors were sufficiently chained so that they couldn't escape.

Even if they did, it would take a matter of minutes to have his pets overpower them. He had done an impeccable job of keeping them malnourished. If this was some kind of ploy, if the princess was trying to orchestrate a jailbreak, she would be sorely disappointed, especially after he made her pay the price for double crossing him.

"Very well." He gave her a sly grin. "We have a deal."

28

WARMAIDENS

STEFAN HAD KEPT HIS word. He dragged the prisoners from the dungeons to the throne room to witness the duel between Jorna and his wyrmkin champion, Giselle. They were escorted in small groups of four to eight, their hands shackled with irons to deter them from trying to escape - if their captors had been wise, they would have also bound their ankles, not that any of the warriors would dare to complain that they weren't thorough enough. Every advantage, no matter how small, was fully embraced, for each one of them knew it could very well be the difference between success and doom.

Once they reached the throne room, the men were forced to their knees in the left galley, their hands still cuffed, with a row of wyrmkin warmaidens standing guard behind each of them. Jorna was the only one who stood apart from them, positioned just below the raised throne, waiting for everyone to be settled in so that the fight could begin.

The first thing she had noticed upon entering was that the tables, along with all their contents, were now gone, most likely at Stefan's behest for he was so confident that he would win that he had already made preparations for his departure. It gave Jorna a great deal of satisfaction, knowing that she was going to be ruining those plans. One way or another, he would never see the book, let alone possess it.

"Well, Princess," Stefan began, a sly smile quirking up his thin lips, "I hope you are well rested, not that it will make much difference. Giselle was bred for one thing and one thing alone: destruction."

To punctuate his words, the wyrmkin spread her ebony wings, and with a powerful leap, she soared to the bottom of the dais, landing heavily a couple feet from Jorna. Rising to her full, terrible height, Giselle towered above the Sarven woman, a hideous monster from her talons all the way to her curved, glossy horns.

She extended something to her opponent as her master explained. "It wouldn't be sporting if you weren't at least armed. I found this weapon quite fitting," he added with a sneer. Jorna knew this because of his tone, as she couldn't actually see him around the creature that was blocking her line of sight.

Jorna glanced down and her heart skipped a beat. Held in the outstretched claws was her father's sword, the blade a polished silver, inlaid with runes and the hilt encrusted with diamonds and sapphires. It was a sword crafted for a king. Stefan had no clue just how perfect it was that he had chosen this weapon, for it was the weapon he was going to die by.

Reaching out, Jorna wrapped her fingers around the grip and waited for the creature to relinquish her grasp. Giselle hissed at her, baring her sharp fangs in warning, telling the Sarven that she had better not try anything, before letting the sword go with a shove. Jorna allowed herself to be pushed back a couple steps, not minding the distance in the least. In fact, she intended to drag the foe back even further once their duel began.

She fought down a sudden surge of fear, knowing this was going to be her last chance to change her mind. For the first time, she felt a shred of temptation to simply give in, to allow the wyrmkin to win and let Stefan take the book. It would be so easy, a voice whispered in her head, so easy to give in. Surely they could recover Goldsteel's book later, and if not, how much harm could they really cause with it? She grit her teeth, shaking away the thoughts and instead tried to focus on the moment. This path might be more difficult, but the honest, virtuous path always was.

Stefan's voice marked the beginning of the fight as he cruelly instructed his pet not to inflict any harm that would prevent her from upholding her end of the bargain.

With a bloodcurdling shriek, Giselle launched toward her prey, drawing a blackened mace from over her shoulder. Rushing to meet her, Jorna cried her father's name, drawing strength from the battle shout, from hearing the word echoing in the throne room as she collided in a mash of iron and sparks with the wyrmkin.

The brute strength of her enemy sent her skidding backward, barely able to maintain her footing as the jar of the impact shook Jorna's body. Without granting her a reprieve, the hellish fiend flew at her again, swinging the mace toward the Sarven woman's torso. She barely had a chance to dodge, leaping back so that the weapon passed a few inches from her ribs, which surely would have broken had the blow connected.

She had to bide her time, to keep the fight interesting and distracting so that when they made their move, they would have a few seconds of surprise on their side. This meant forsaking tactics that would have kept her out of the creature's long reach. Instead she did her best to stand toe-to-toe with her, using her greater agility to keep from getting pummeled by the ferocious blows.

They danced over the stained velvet carpet, the outside world getting blocked out completely as they fought what felt like a battle to the death. It was like Giselle had forgotten she wasn't supposed to kill her opponent.

When Jorna felt that they had put on enough of a show (the sound of the other wyrmkin snarling and hissing for their leader telling her that they were adequately distracted) she stopped playing at defense and took an abrupt offensive approach. She sidestepped a downward swing at the last second, letting Giselle throw herself off balance as she put far too much power into that single blow. A fault she seemed quite prone to. Obviously she had been taught little about the finesse of fighting. Then the Sarven spun around, lashing out with the gleaming blade at the monster's side.

An angry howl of pain told Jorna that she'd made contact, though how much damage she'd done she wasn't quite sure. She was forced to keep moving now as the enraged wyrmkin wildly sought to inflict harm, her motions lacking all predictability and sense.

Taking the opportunity to guide her away from the throne and toward the door, just a few more steps, just enough to give Shanik a clear view of the galley opposite him... Jorna twisted and ducked, jumped and rolled to avoid the flailing, furious creature. The whole while she sought an opening, looking for any possible way to prod at her further, not because she had a death wish, but to keep her reacting as a rabid beast. The wyrmkin was less of an overall threat if she wasn't thinking clearly.

"Stefan!" Jorna shouted, her breath ragged, but her voice still forceful and commanding. She dodged a handful of razor-sharp talons seeking to rake across her face as she told the arcanist in ancient Sarven,

"I'm coming for your heart!"

She was counting on him not understanding the words, though she had no way of knowing immediately if her assumption was correct or not. He had known the powerful words to undo her staff, but that didn't mean he could speak the archaic Sarven tongue in its entirety. Shanik, however, *could* and the warriors knew to expect the phrase, making it the best signal that she could come up with on short notice that wasn't a blatant forewarning that they were about to act.

Shanik was the first. He had been very thoroughly restrained, but his captors had made one very grave mistake - leaving him alive at all. Having his snout muzzled only prevented him from speaking and breathing fire from his mouth; it didn't stop him from shooting fire from his nostrils, which worked just as good to expel flames, especially fireballs. His keen hearing picked up the sound of Thane's voice, instructing the other prisoners to hit the floor and cover their heads, while the wyrmkin guarding them were too occupied watching their leader fight Jorna to notice.

Waiting until the nearly two dozen Sarven flopped onto their stomachs, the dragon sucked in a deep breath through his nose and sent two raging balls of fire streaking across the hall, straight into the unsuspecting creatures.

All but a couple were caught up in the blasts and thrown back against the wall, the heat resistance of some allowing them to survive the initial attack, but not the second and certainly not the third. Thane grabbed the man nearest to him, shouting for the others to claim any weapons they could find and break the chains. The dragon had done an excellent job of keeping the monsters off them, able to tilt his head enough that a well-placed bolt took down any that were missed by his original attacks.

When the fighting broke out, Jorna was granted a reprieve. Giselle stopped her blind attacks and turned to see what the commotion was behind her. The Sarven took the brief opportunity, sliding across the floor until she was beside the wyrmkin champion, her blade seeking the tendons in her leg and severing them with a clean sweep. She rolled to her feet, hearing the shriek of fury and pain behind her as she sprinted toward Shanik.

Stefan saw everything unfold in double motion. He had been baffled by the princess's unintelligible shout and was wondering if she was yielding, but the tone in her voice suggested otherwise, leaving him in a state of confusion. He was still pondering this when the first pair of fireballs flew by and were swiftly followed by another pair and another.

His eyes turned to Jorna immediately, narrowing as a cold rage spread throughout his thin body. He found her just as she was crippling his pet. Trying to regain some measure of control, he predicted where she was headed and swiftly rose from the throne, reaching inside his clothing for the pair of scrolls that in his hands were every bit as deadly as an axe or mace.

He was hurrying down the stairs, his hate-filled eyes fixed on his prey, his mind turning to all the things he would do to make her pay. This insurrection of hers would not last long, he was already certain that more of his Warmaidens were coming, summoned by the mental link shared between them and Giselle, who had no doubt already called for reinforcements.

In minutes a whole swarm of wyrmkin would spill into the room and overcome the troublesome Sarven. Some would die, he would see to it, but their princess, he was going to make her suffer until she *begged* him for mercy and even then, he would not relent. He would *never* relent.

So caught up in thoughts of retribution, the arcanist had completely forgotten the chained Guldorn, who had been riled out of his usual stupor by the fighting. It was true, Guldorn had forgotten his name, had lost himself in a swirling mist of mental ghosts, things that he should have known, but couldn't put his finger on anymore.

Then he had heard his name, heard it shouted by a familiar voice, a voice that he knew belonged to someone important, someone he cared about. It triggered a chain reaction, echoing in his ears as he wallowed on the floor, his mind suddenly assaulted with fragments of memory, the wisps becoming more like blurs with just enough detail that he could recall a handful of important facts.

He sat up slowly, his gaze sweeping over the events unfolding around him. There was fire and fighting. His attention fell to a woman with platinum hair, and he felt a strange mix of familiarity and joy, his eyes pleased to see her, even if he couldn't quite remember why. A furious grumbling drew him to the throne, to the man who was starting down the stairs, his blatant intentions of malice written on every inch of his narrow face. Guldorn recognized him, knew him as his enemy. He also knew that he must protect the woman against him at any cost...

He waited for Stefan to get close, then he pulled the chain that restricted him taut so that it caught the man's leg as he was raising it to take a step. He flailed, the scrolls flying almost comically from his hands into the air as he tried to stop himself from plummeting to the floor headfirst. Stefan was unsuccessful and landed with a sickening crack right on his face, the crack having come from his nose.

Stunned, he could feel the hot rush of blood as his eyes filled with involuntary tears, and his mind reeled to figure out why he'd fallen at all and to determine what injuries he might have suffered.

A rough hand grabbed his shoulder, forcibly turning him onto his back. He was so surprised by the dirty, sunken face of Guldorn that his eyes nearly popped out of their sockets. The Sarven king leered in the arcanist's face. His stench may have been overwhelming had it not been for the fact that all he could smell was his own blood as it flowed from his nostrils.

He felt him rummaging through his pockets, felt them grow lighter as several things were removed. He could only imagine what they were as he struggled to regain himself, though he was next to useless without an instrument of magic. This thought burned his pride, just as being outsmarted by crude, boorish Sarven rankled every fiber of his being.

His renewed rage gave him the strength to call out a single name, signaling Giselle that he needed her assistance. He was dimly aware of Guldorn moving away. He could hear the clinking of the chain as the king freed himself and could only imagine what the deranged man would do to him now that he had the opportunity. It almost made Stefan wish he hadn't been quite so cruel - almost.

Meanwhile, Thane and the other prisoners were just breaking the last of the manacles and had begun to arm themselves with weapons from the fallen wyrmkin.

"We move together!" Thane was shouting. "If you don't have a weapon, stay close to someone who does!" He didn't even realize he was doing it, leading a band of warriors as though it was perfectly natural to do so, and they followed him willingly, rallying at the sound of his voice, listening for his orders.

He was just about to lead everyone to Jorna when Giselle fell on them from above. The tendon in her leg may have been severed, but she still had the full use of her wings. Her razor-sharp talons slashed across one of the unsuspecting warrior's chests, leaving behind deep, red gashes. The others began to scatter, fleeing out of her reach until they could recover and mount a united attack.

A couple were too slow, one caught in the back by her talons, gravely wounded, but not slain. His comrades dragged him away as the fiend caught her other victim, digging her claws into his chest and lifting him up to her height. Her other hand shot out, clutching the top of his head and yanking it back so that his neck was exposed. He fought against her, cursing and sputtering defiant insults into the face of death itself. She laughed at him, baring her fangs before lunging forward and sinking them into his unprotected throat.

THE VAULT

GISELLE WAS PLEASED BY the rush of metallic Sarven blood in her mouth, by the gurgling of her victim as he struggled to breathe and how his attacks became more and more feeble... She paused to savor the kill, clamping her teeth down harder. Distantly she heard his comrades recovering, their leader shouting commands as he tried to orchestrate a counterattack against her. With a moaning growl, disappointed that she had to cut the moment short, Giselle jerked her head back and forth like a dog with a bone, maintaining her grip on his windpipe so that the motion ripped and tore the weak flesh from the now dead warrior.

She spun to face the first wave of attackers and spat the bloody shreds at them, reveling in the horror on their faces before hurling the corpse as well, knocking most of them to the ground with its weight. She released a feral cry, spraying blood as she whirled to meet a second group that was trying to flank her.

They were not deterred, throwing themselves at her as she swatted aside their weapons, her fury helping her to ignore the cuts and scrapes to the skin not protected by black scales or armor. It also helped her to ignore the pain in her leg and the blood that splattered beneath her from the wound. All she saw and heard were her enemies, raging against her like insignificant ants.

Only one thing broke into her frenzy, a weak, strangled voice calling her name, desperation hanging thickly on the word. She didn't hesitate, she couldn't even if she wanted to, the choice of loyalty had long ago been made for her, the word instilled in her mind as a trigger since she was but a child.

Snapping her wings out abruptly, she took a couple of the Sarven warriors by surprise, sending them flying. The creature spun, using the leathery wings to batter any other foes who were too close, careful to make sure she didn't damage herself.

When the area was clear enough, she bounded off her good leg, flapping hard to pull herself into the air so that she was out of reach. Thankfully the throne room ceiling stretched high above, giving her plenty of room to maneuver above the shouting, angry Sarven below. Her eyes swept the floor, seeking Stefan, who was pinned beneath Guldorn. The mad king was poised to strike, a dagger he had stolen from the arcanist raised above his head while the man futilely struggled to get away.

Giselle acted immediately, doing what she had no other choice to do and that was protect her master at all costs. Bending forward and folding her wings behind her, she dove like a plummeting boulder, naturally calculating her rate of velocity and direction so that she wouldn't drop too fast or risk injuring the person she was meant to rescue.

Guldorn glanced up, frowning as he heard her coming but hadn't yet caught sight of her. A second later, she had slammed into him, knocking him backward into the stairs with enough force that had he hit his head it certainly would have shattered his skull.

As it was, he had the wind knocked out of his lungs, felt the pain of a dozen bruises forming along his back and shoulders where the steps had caught his falling body - the velvet carpet helped only marginally to pad the impact.

Trying to regain himself, he didn't bother to look and see who or what had tackled him. His mind may have been fuzzy, but his battle instincts were still keen. He still had the dagger in his hand and wasn't about to wait around for his attacker to make the first move.

He swung it downward for his arm had fallen over his head when he was blindsided. The silver blade got lucky, biting deep into the wyrmkin's flesh, just below her collarbone, in fact, so close that it actually scraped against the bone as he thrust it deeper.

A howl of pain blew her blood-scented, foul breath into his face, but Guldorn didn't remove the weapon. He twisted it, feeling that somehow the act was absolutely deserved. Giselle pulled back, knocking his arm away from her as she reached for the dagger so that she could pull it free. She intended to return the blow, drive the weapon into the troublesome king's heart and watch him die without ever being plagued by even a shred of remorse, but she didn't get the chance.

Shanik was relieved to see Jorna rushing to him, his body aching from being crammed into one position for so long that the thought of getting out of his bonds made him almost giddy. He was eager to be free so that he could unleash his own rage at the number of injustices they had all faced in the last few days.

When she reached his side, he tried to tell her that he wanted his mouth free first, but all that came out was a series of muffled grunts. Fortunately it was adequate to get the point across and she stepped away from the heavy chain that bolted him to the floor long enough to slip the leather strap off his snout.

"Thank you," he grumbled, his voice even raspier than normal as he smacked his lips and worked the stiffness out of his jaws. He coughed up a bit of flames, just to get the stale taste of stagnation out of his mouth. With no water on hand, it was better than nothing.

"Oh, the woes of being a dragon, feared by all for my magnificence and unending talents," he commented dramatically, wiggling as much as he could, which was really only a couple inches. With a disgruntled sigh, he strained against the bonds. "What is taking so long?"

"Be patient," Jorna chastised. "It's not like I have a key." She added after a pause, "Besides, your squirming isn't helping!"

"*Tsk*! My *squirming*?" After days of frustration, he grasped onto the first chance to let off a little steam. Not to mention this was his chance to make up for being gagged for what felt like an eternity.

"Dragons do *not* squirm," he began his indignant tirade, "we are not worms - no matter how you spell it - we are fierce and powerful. Your kind should be in fear and awe of our singular greatness, of our," he frowned as he watched her, but tried to ignore the sight of her struggling against the chain across his shoulders so he could continue his spiel, "...of our per—" He huffed, unable to stand it a second longer. "What *are* you doing?!"

Jorna grunted, trying to lift the heavy chain enough so that she could slide it over his neck and head without crushing either should she drop it. "What does it look like?" she finally responded with a huff of her own, an expression she had no doubt picked up from the dragon.

He frowned, rolling his eyes at her sarcasm. "Well stop it. I'll take care of those; you just focus on freeing my wings!" he told her with an edge of irritation in his voice. "And try not to cut off your fingers or arm or anything. We really don't have time for such nonsense!"

If their situation hadn't been so dire, Jorna may very well have laughed at him referring to a serious injury like getting your arm cut off as nonsense. Instead she simply nodded, giving up on the chains and moving to his flank. His wings had been pinned to his sides with ropes, which were thick, but much easier to deal with than the bulky iron links.

Carefully, so as not to accidentally injure his wings, Jorna slipped the blade of her father's sword between the dragon and the ropes. When it was positioned, she gave the weapon a tug, sawing just enough for the sharp blade to slice in a few inches before cutting easily through the rest of the thick fibers.

The ropes snapped off the dragon, who sighed in relief as he was able to stretch his wings out. He was careful not to open them too far or too fast, mindful that Jorna was close enough that such an action would send her flying. Instead he turned his head to the other side, tilting it and shutting one eye as he took a second to aim at the heavy chain that still kept him pinned to the floor. Shanik opened his mouth with a belch of molten fire, coating the iron in searing flames that ate through the metal in a matter of seconds. Stemming the flow, a satisfied grin spread across his reptilian lips as he flattened and then wiggled his haunches free of the last chain.

The dragon came to his feet, shaking himself violently like a wet animal. He stretched out his legs and back, rustling his wings and rolling his shoulders to work out all the kinks. He was more than a little pleased to finally be out of the evil contraption, but his moment of relief was short lived.

Once the dragon was free, Jorna had turned to what was going on around them. She could tell that the warriors had suffered a couple losses; the bloody remains of a mangled corpse lay beside a second body, this one far less damaged. Her eyes picked Thane out as he was leading them to meet the first handful of wyrmkin reinforcements and a surge of pride filled her heart. She could have stood there for ages and watched him fight, watched him as he commanded the others, keeping their morale high even as more of their brothers fell to the creatures.

Had she not known better, she would never have guessed that he was merely a blacksmith and not an honored champion of Hamdralg. She allowed herself a smile, knowing deep down that a champion's heart beat in his chest.

"Thane! To me!" she shouted, tearing her gaze away to look for her father as she began mapping out in her mind their next steps, but when she found him, she stopped short, fear gripping her chest.

"Father!" Jorna's shout drew the dragon's attention to the dais, where the king was being held against the stairs by the wounded and furious Giselle.

Jorna didn't pause to think. She sprang forward, raising her weapon as she started to shout a challenge at the wyrmkin, but Shanik's voice commanding her to step aside prevented her from doing so. She trusted the dragon without hesitation, dodging to the left just as a blast of fire scorched by her, hurling toward Giselle. A second later the ball slammed into the creature's exposed back, throwing her away from Guldorn and causing her to release a shriek of surprise and discomfort more than pain - her resistance to fire was much greater than that of her common sisters.

"Father!" Jorna shouted again, hearing more than seeing that the others were falling back, covered now by Shanik, who had moved to stand beside the shaman to be close should she need him. "Come with me," she bade, stretching out her hand.

Guldorn saw her as he came shakily to his feet, seeming much more lucid than he had when she had first found him here. His icy blue eyes strayed to Stefan, who was cowering in a ball on the floor, trying to keep a low profile until his pets arrived to protect him.

There was dark intent in that gaze, a desire that Jorna could not fault him for as she felt it strongly herself, but now was not the time. Now they had to get out of this room. It was too big, too hard to defend themselves against the horde of warmaidens that would be upon them any second.

The others were catching up now that they had defeated the first wave of foes, carrying the wounded men among them, forced to leave the dead behind. Those that could still fight and were armed, which was a little over a dozen warriors, broke into two groups, one leading the way to the secondary entrance at the back of the chamber and another group that stayed near Jorna, intending to defend the rear.

"We need to go," Thane pressed, his eyes watching the front doors warily. They could hear the enemy approaching.

There was no more time to dally here. The princess shot forward, closing the distance between herself and Guldorn in a few hurried bounds. Behind him, Giselle was stirring, shaking her horned head as she struggled to rise off the carpet; no doubt her body ached from the combined injuries she had sustained. In a matter of seconds, she would regain herself, remember her fury and be at their throats again. None of them wanted to be around to see the new height of her rage.

Grabbing the king's arm, Jorna gave him a tug. "It's time to go," she urged, not taking no for an answer. Her father didn't say anything. He just nodded slowly, adjusting so that she was holding his hand instead as they rushed to escape with the others.

Stefan started to rise a few heartbeats too early, infuriated that his well-constructed plans had been utterly abolished and by his own gullibility no less! A hateful expression darkened his pointed, blood-soaked face as he started to tell Jorna that she would pay for this outrage.

It wasn't a second later, when she kicked him in the teeth on her way by, that he realized he should have just let her go. As he lay on the floor, pain throbbing in his head like he had never felt before, Stefan vowed to all that was holy that he would make Jorna Hailstone rue the day that she crossed him.

LAST STAND

ONCE EVERYONE HAD MADE it out into the hallway, the unarmed men set about blocking the door with anything and everything they could get their hands on in an attempt to keep the wyrmkin from breaking through too quickly and running them down.

While they worked, Jorna and Thane took stock of the state the other warriors were in. Most of them were fine, emboldened by the heart racing battle and adrenaline that coursed through their veins. They had lost five men and four were injured, one of which probably wouldn't make it if they didn't find a safe place soon to stop his bleeding.

All of this information put the next steps into focus for Jorna, who knew that they couldn't wait around in the hallway or take refuge just anywhere. Besides, they had the book to deal with still and even though she cared a great deal for the men, she had to make that the highest priority.

"This way," she instructed just as soon as the door was as blocked as it was going to get. Leading the way, she headed in the direction of the nearest armory, which was just a couple turns out of their way. They were going to need more weapons for when they inevitably met up with the creatures again; that meant every able warrior needed to be adequately armed.

Their movements were sporadic and cautious, Jorna setting a pace that was hurried but kept them from running headlong into a group of wyrmkin. She was really hoping that they were still flocking to the throne room, that Stefan would hesitate to pursue her, but she knew that was just wishful thinking.

He would know where she was heading and if he was smart, he'd let her get there, but he had been furious with her for breaking their deal and making him look like a fool. If he was acting out of anger, then he may not do what was smart.

Maybe I should have done more than kick him in the face. He can't pursue us if he's dead after all...

The thought didn't sit right with her and so she swept it away. Perhaps she should have had the stomach to kill an unarmed man in this situation, but she hadn't taken the opportunity and wasn't sure if she even could have.

Jorna was greatly relieved when they made it to the armory without encountering any wyrmkin. She sent a few men inside to gather what weapons and supplies they could carry out, while everyone else guarded the hallway. Weapons were quickly distributed amongst the men, some of whom discarded the arms taken from the fiends in favor of Sarven forged equipment. A few other essentials were passed around, including what medical field supplies they could scrounge up, and then they pressed on, leaving the door sealed shut in an attempt to mask their presence.

A few minutes later, Shanik's keen senses came in very handy. Had it not been for his heightened nose they probably would have been caught and their escape turned into a bitter failure. He knew the war-maidens were close, no doubt predicting that the prisoners would try to arm themselves and therefore they were searching the surrounding area. Thankfully it was just a pair of them, and the advanced warning allowed them all to duck into another hallway to wait until they had patrolled by.

"We should have slain them when we had the chance," Rulvon muttered to his brother.

"Better we didn't," Thane cut in, having overheard the remark. "Stealth is our greatest hope for survival; we can't risk being seen at all."

That was enough to silence the impatient hothead.

After that, Shanik took point, keeping alert for any further search parties as they hurried toward the vault, hoping and praying against all reason that they would make it there safely. It took longer than any of them would have liked. They were forced to stop and hide more and more the closer they got to the treasury, which told them that Stefan had predicted they would go there.

Rounding the last corner, they were instantly disappointed when they saw that the doors were being guarded by a group of four war-maidens. They had just passed another patrol, who would undoubt-edly be returning this way in a matter of moments. If they attacked the guards and couldn't take them out before they alerted their sisters, they would risk being overwhelmed just a few feet from their destina-tion.

It wasn't an ideal solution, not in the least, but with a silent glance to Jorna, who nodded to give him the go ahead, Shanik moved to handle the squad ahead. When asked later, he would tell Jorna that he had no qualms killing them.

Stefan might have labeled them as "wyrmkin", but they were no relation to him or his kind, despite their physical traits to the contrary. They were a sad, twisted copy, an insult to the great dragons who were the embodiment of magic itself, and while they were neutral to the troubles of lesser mortals, they were still considered benevolent by those who truly knew them. He was doing the world a favor by exterminating these hellish monsters, a fact he took a great degree of satisfaction from.

He trotted right out to meet them, settling onto his haunches a few feet away and waiting patiently for one of them to notice him. It didn't take long. One of the Warmaidens hissed, turning to face him with her weapon rising into a ready position.

Alerted to his presence, the other three mimicked her actions, all of them preparing to spring on him like a pack of rabid wolves, but Shanik was faster, much faster. A raging inferno of white-hot dragon fire washed over them in a seething spray, scorching their gray flesh in a handful of seconds.

While they fell screaming and writhing to the ground, the Sarven rushed for the door, stepping over what was just flaming corpses by the time they made it that far down the hall. Shanik was still sitting there, a thoughtful expression on his face as the warriors rushed by him and then through the open treasury door. He waited for Jorna to come up beside him, a curious expression spreading across her features, and then he commented, "I'm coming, I just wanted to bask in my superiority a moment."

Rolling her eyes, Jorna didn't waste any more time. She followed the stragglers into the room, waiting to close the doors until Shanik had strolled through behind her. "Barricade these with whatever you can find," she started to say, "it won't be long before they're trying to break them down. Shanik, if you have any magic that can help, now is the perfect time to use it."

She moved to the center of the room, her eyes sweeping the remnants of their first battle here. The wyrmkin bodies were still laying where Stefan's enchanted wind had discarded them and the fragments of her shattered glaive were scattered over the floor as well. When he came up beside her, she could see that Thane had reclaimed his axe from the floor and couldn't help but give him a small grin.

"Make no mistake..." She turned away from the memories clawing at her to face the Sarven warriors. "This is only a reprieve. They will come at us, harder and stronger than ever before and we will have to stand against them. You have already done so much, and I am sorry that I must ask you to fight again, to give your lives when you have already proven your devotion. I have faith in all of you and I know with your courage we will prevail today. Are you with me?"

A cheer rang out as even the wounded men who could barely stand let alone fight shouted that they would have her back, that they would not let the dark creatures win this day. Their loyalty and dedication filled Jorna's heart with strength, reminding her why she had come here, why her father had been so willing to give his life to protect his people. She smiled at them all, letting her bravery and confidence shine through, overpowering the fear and uncertainty that still squirmed in her belly.

"Good, now get to work, we have a lot to accomplish in a short amount of time." She was still grinning as she started to call out orders. The wounded needed to be tended to, the doors secured and barricades erected to protect them as much as possible should the door fail. There weren't a lot of materials to work with, almost everything in the treasury was mostly useless, but there was some furniture and shelving that could be stripped down or pushed to block the doors.

While they set to the task, she moved Guldorn near the vault and sat him down against the wall where she could keep an eye on him. Then she gathered Thane and Renarn off to the side with her so that she could speak to them in private.

"I will be depending on you a great deal in the coming conflict," Jorna started when they were a little ways from the others. The clatter of treasure and scraping of furniture helped to drown out their conversation. "But first, I want to thank you both for your deeds in the throne room. They will not be forgotten."

Thane put his hand on her shoulder and gave it a meaningful squeeze. "Your gratitude is unnecessary. I dare speak for both of us when I say it is our honor to serve you."

Renarn nodded emphatically, in agreement with the blacksmith.

"Renarn, you will lead the men. Keep them back here near the vault doors as much as possible. Should we get overrun we'll fall back inside and shut the wyrmkin out," she cut straight to business after the short preliminary exchange. "Trust Shanik, he'll have your back no matter how much he may complain."

Thane was nodding, though he refused to actually speak his agreement in the event that Shanik were to overhear him. The dragon would never let him live it down if he voiced any sort of confidence in him, though they all knew that any misgivings he had felt before had long since been abolished.

"I'm going to keep Thane here and don't worry about the king. I'll keep him safe," she continued, reaching out to clap the man's shoulder before sending him on his way.

It wasn't much later that the first sounds of movement from behind the door alerted them all that battle was going to be upon them very soon. Their preparations were well worth the effort. The door seemed to be holding well, and the men now waited behind barricades of broken furniture and treasure.

The wounded were furthest from the door, propped up against the wall with weapons in their hands, for Sarven men would not die like helpless infants. Renarn was on the front line with Shanik and his brother, ready to lead by example, the same way he had always seen his general and king lead.

As the pounding only grew louder, Jorna reached for Thane's hand, gripping it tightly. He turned to look at her, silently telling her that he would stand at her side until the very end.

"My oath burns more strongly than ever," Thane whispered. "I will not fail or waiver, my beloved."

Jorna bestowed him with a soft smile before turning her back on the ever growing noise. She put the impending battle and Javrin's betrayal out of her mind as she faced the impenetrable door. She closed her eyes, reaching for the memory where she had first learned how to open it, when she had learned the significance of duty and promised never to forsake hers, no matter what. More than anything, she clung to the recollection of her father, allowing his deep voice to fill her mind.

Quietly at first, her voice rose with the one in her thoughts, singing aloud the powerful chant as she perfectly recalled the words that Guldorn had taught her.

Behind her, the treasury door gave way and the first wave of wyrmkin began fighting their way through the sundered wood. They were met with dragon fire as Shanik began to take out as many as possible before they could get too far over the cluttered threshold. He made his own barricades of fire, a burning maze that held back most of the nightmarish monsters and consumed any that attempted to cross it. A few were able to resist the heat enough to get close, but they were quickly slain by a scorching ball of flames.

In the end, the fire only delayed them. Not only had they seen the tactic used before and apparently had learned from it, but they quickly realized that they wouldn't be able to make it through the inferno, especially with the dragon picking them off. This led them to change how they dealt with the obstacle and within moments they were trying to put out the flames.

Dragon fire was not so easily manipulated, but that didn't mean it was impervious to being doused, only that it was more difficult given its magical nature. Smothering worked eventually, but the flames were so hot, so contagious, that they were set alight if they weren't careful.

That sacrifice proved worthwhile as they fell into a rhythm and cleared a path faster than Shanik could replace the doused blaze. They rushed forward, screeching with excitement as they neared their quarry, the intention to take out their frustrations written plainly on their monstrous faces. With bellowing battle cries, the Sarven warriors rushed to meet them, leaving a handful of men to defend the wounded and the vault should any of the fiends slip past.

The battle was joined in a bloody clash of metal and flesh, the warriors fighting for their lives, for their honor, and their people. They used the power of Jorna's chanting voice to draw strength into their limbs and hearts. They were no longer desperate men as they had been the first time they had met the wyrmkin in combat. They were accepting, knowing that if they died here it would be a glorious end.

Ignoring the rising heat and echoing clang of battle, Jorna did not stop her song as she unsealed the massive door using a series of locks and triggers. Everything had to be done in a specific sequence. If one thing were out of order, then it would cause a whole new set of defenses to activate.

At best she would have to start again; at worst the mechanism would trigger a deadly trap that would surely kill anyone standing in front of the door. She kept these possibilities in the back of her mind, focusing instead on what she was doing so that such thoughts wouldn't become reality.

It took several minutes, but finally the last lock clicked over and Jorna took a tentative step back. For what felt like an eternity, the door remained closed, making her think she had done something wrong, gotten the sequence out of order or that there was another step she just didn't know about.

A frown creased her brow as a growing unease tightened in her stomach and she wracked her memory in an attempt to recall anything she might have missed. She was beginning to give up hope, believing that they had come all this way, overcome so many hurdles only to fail at this critical moment, but then the door began to rumble.

At first, she jumped back, grabbing onto Thane's arm and tugging him along, still afraid that perhaps she had gotten the sequence wrong. It wasn't until the opening started to appear, unleashing a belch of stale air as the door rolled into the wall that she finally relaxed and gave her companion a sheepish glance. He had the good grace not to tease her for being so on edge, though his eyes glittered in a manner that suggested he very well could have.

Reaching out to pat her shoulder, Thane hurried to where Guldorn was sitting on the floor and helped him to his feet. The king had to use the younger man's arm to balance himself as he weaved, the sudden excitement and exertion after sitting idle for so many weeks having tired him.

Jorna preceded them inside, the glow from Shanik's fire the only source of light. It cast strange shadows on the wall as she moved cautiously to where a granite pedestal sat in the middle of the vault. As her eyes adjusted, she could distinguish the outline of a single, thick tome.

She stopped just in front of it, noting that the leather binding was worn with time, that the pages were crisp and aged a faint yellow. It amazed her that one book, one object that seemed so ordinary, could cause so much trouble. That its contents could be so powerful that men would kill and scheme and destroy just to possess its knowledge.

She felt Thane come up beside her after settling the king safely against the wall where he could rest. The blacksmith brushed her knuckles lightly with his own, letting her know that she still had his support. It was an unnecessary gesture, she had come to trust that he would always be there, but the reminder was appreciated all the same.

While she continued to stare at the book, Jorna's mind wandered to the day she had met him. Dirty and grungy from working the forge, he had seemed out of place and uncomfortable in the glamor of the palace. He didn't belonged there, everyone was swift to say, even Thane himself. Over and over again she had been reminded that he was 'only a blacksmith', but something in her gut had told her that he was much more. Thane had gone on to prove himself time and time again, until here they were at last.

Realization filled her and a broad grin swept over her face.

"Do you believe in fate?" She all but whispered the question, her eyes never leaving the aged tome.

ONLY A BLACKSMITH

FROWNING, THANE FLICKED HIS gaze over his shoulder to the battle that still raged. The blazing fires and clash of weapons, the sounds of dying and the acrid scent of smoke and charred flesh stirred inside him, urging him to join the fray.

He trusted Jorna, he trusted her explicitly, but he could not quiet the small voice in his mind that tempted him to get lost in the glorious heat of combat. He was finding that he had a taste for battle after all. More than that, he had an aching desire to *live* and he felt cowardly for leaving that fight to other men while he was relatively safe here.

"We shouldn't linger," he told her softly, trying to remind her that they were pressed for time.

Jorna stubbornly refused to proceed without an answer, so she asked him again, "Do you believe in fate?" This time she turned her gray-blue eyes to him, searching his face as he frowned.

He was trying to figure out why she was being so insistent, why the question held such importance that it couldn't wait until later.

Surely now wasn't the time to discuss such matters? He opened his mouth to ask her that, then saw the expression in her gaze, the need to know written plainly in the cool depths. He still didn't understand the significance, but if it meant so much and if he could ease whatever concerns she might have, then he would do so anyway.

"I didn't," he started to say, his features softening as he reached up to gently touch her cheek. "Until I met you. Luck could never be so keen; it must have been fate."

This brought a flush to her cheeks, her hand rising to caress his before the exchange ended.

"Fate has ruled our lives since our first meeting. It was fate that I chose you over all the warriors and champions in Hamdralg. Fate that we arrived in this place at this precise moment together." The clarity in her voice thickened, her eyes alight with conviction. "This is *your* moment, your fate, your very destiny. You have proven yourself a warrior and now you must prove something else."

With those words she turned from him, leaving Thane to frown after her in confusion as he attempted to understand what she meant. Her boots clicked on the marble floor as she rounded the granite pedestal, her eyes once again on the aged book.

She stopped in front of it, reaching out a hand to reverently caress the old, dry leather with her fingertips, trailing them to the edge of the cover. Carefully, respectfully she eased open the front flap, her other hand rising from her side to collect pinch after pinch of delicate pages, turning them until she arrived at the book's center. The scent of old paper and leather wafted up and she paused, her fingers resting lightly on the turned pages, while her eyes stared in awe at what was contained within.

Nestled in a cut out was a thin stone tablet, no bigger than a handful of inches wide and tall. There was gold lettering chiseled into its surface, enchanted words that appeared to her as mere gibberish. To a smith, their meaning would be evident. The spell was intended as a final precaution against those who were unworthy of learning Goldsteel's secret.

Jorna withdrew the tablet gently, treating it with care because of its age. Once it was in her hands she turned back to Thane, who had been watching her closely. Her eyes never left his face as she extended the precious object to him.

When he only looked at her with uncertainty, she offered a faint, encouraging smile. "Thane Stoutforge, I can think of no greater man to carry this secret. You and all your bloodline will keep this secret in their hearts, vowing to forever protect it for the benefit of all Sarven."

Thane could only stare back at her, worried that he was not worthy of the faith she was placing in him. Doubts and fears swam in his mind, clenching his heart as he scrambled to find a response, to tell her that there had to be other men, greater men, to take on such a task. The last thing he wanted was to let her down, but he was certain, even after all the confidence this quest had given him, that the secret of Goldsteel was far too much for a lowly man such as himself.

Seeming to sense his insecurities, the shaman didn't wait for him to answer. She pushed the tablet into his hands and told him sternly, "This is a secret that *only a blacksmith* can learn. Block out the doubt, block out the past, and listen to what beats in your heart at this very moment." Her voice softened. "Believe in who you have become, not who others thought you were."

For a long moment they gazed intensely at one another, Jorna offering strength and reassurance as Thane struggled to overcome his insecurities. He could see the unwavering faith she had in him and he grasped onto it, letting it guide him to his own self-confidence. This was a great honor, the highest any crafter could hope to achieve. If she believed he was worthy of it, then he would strive to be certain he was. He still had his doubts, he would always have doubts, but he would use them to make himself a better man.

Slowly he nodded, pulling his eyes away from hers and down to the thin tablet in his hands. He heard her say that there was magic in the words, but the rest of her comment was lost as his gaze swept over the gold lettering.

They danced and shimmered before him, blurring on the stone slate until they were illegible. He could feel the words searing in his mind, brightening from gold to a pure, glowing white that flared hot, almost painful before understanding suddenly gripped him.

A laugh nearly escaped as he processed the details, amazed that such a secret hadn't been figured out already. It was such a simple process. He was just about to smile at Jorna, but when he raised his eyes, a wave of dizziness caused his head to swim, ruining the pleased sensation entirely.

Quickly he handed the tablet back to the shaman, reaching a hand up to pinch the bridge of his nose as he fought away the lightheadedness. He started to comment that he would be fine when Jorna's voice, speaking ancient Sarven, cut him off. Forgetting the discomfort, he opened his eyes and dropped his hand, immediately seeking his companion.

She was still standing beside him, but she was not paying attention to Thane any longer. The tablet was in her hands as her low voice chanted a series of clipped words that could only be magic. Knowing better than to interrupt, he watched with growing concern, a feeling of dread worming its way into his heart. Perhaps it was the set of her shoulders, the faint sorrow in her voice or the blank expression in her eyes, but he knew she was about to do something that pained her.

No sooner did the thought cross his mind that the stone in Jorna's pale hands began to crumble, the gold lettering fading away as the slate shifted into dust. She didn't stop speaking the phrase of power until every speck had collected into a pile at her feet.

Now their enemies could never possess the secret. The tome that had held the tablet was but a worthless, old book. Stefan would never know that Thane's mind was the last source of Goldsteel, not that it would matter. Once he learned that she had destroyed it, his anger would surely drive him to exterminate them all.

She exchanged a glance with Thane, who squeezed her shoulder, telling her without the need of words that he understood her actions. It was a tough choice, but a necessary choice all the same.

"Tell them to fall back," she said softly, turning to the empty book in front of her. "Get them all in here and seal the door," she added, reaching out to shut the tome.

Thane didn't need to be told twice. He collected his axe and hurried to the door, shouting before he ever reached it for the warriors to retreat.

With a single sweep of his gaze, he took in the state of the fighting. They were down two more men, but the bodies of the wyrmkin were piled up between the makeshift barricades and treasury door like a dark sea of flesh. Shanik's fire had certainly made the difference in this battle, though all it took was one look to see that the dragon was nearing exhaustion. A being of magic he may be, but even he had his limits.

Renarn heard Thane's shouts and added his own voice, tugging at the men beside him and pushing them in the direction of the vault. Some of them were bloody, a couple clearly wounded, but all of them were ready to fight until the last breath. It took more convincing than should have been necessary to get them all moving. Shanik threw up a new wall of fire to cover their dash to safety before grabbing hold of a man who had just fallen and dragging him along unceremoniously.

When they reached the vault, Jorna was already there, ready to seal them in. She waited until nearly everyone had run by her, except Shanik bringing up the rear with his Sarven-shaped baggage shouting indignantly that he could walk on his own. None of the wyrmkin were fast enough to get through the fire and reach the heavy door before it rumbled closed, shutting the survivors in pitch blackness.

KING'S SACRIFICE

"IT'S DARK IN HERE," someone grunted a few moments later, his voice distracting the others from the pounding noise of the wyrmkin attempting to break in.

"Aye," another, possibly Rulvon, piped up. "Someone get the bloody lizard to belch up some light!"

A chorus of agreement filled the darkness from over a dozen voices, all of them knowing they'd feel a lot better if they could see their surroundings. Shanik's haughty rebuke drown everyone else out, "I am *not* a lizard and I do *not* belch!"

All this did was spur the warriors to deliver more jibes, telling him that he could prove it by providing the room with light, but the dragon only huffed and grumbled, refusing based on principle. It wasn't until Thane growled, "Just do it, sulfur breath!" that he grudgingly relented.

A ball of fire flared to life, the sudden illumination causing the men to cover their eyes until they were able to adjust. The flames stuck to the ceiling of the vault, casting harsh beams of blue across the floor and walls.

Shanik sat back on his haunches, arms across his chest and his nose stuck in the air. "Sulfur breath, indeed," he muttered, his sapphire eyes glaring at Thane.

The Sarven was about to tell him to suck it up when he caught sight of Jorna standing stoically near the door. She hadn't moved since closing it, the sudden light hadn't even fazed her. He left the others to pick good-naturedly at the dragon and carefully approached her, doing his best not to startle her as he stopped at her side.

"Are you alright?" he inquired softly when she didn't acknowledge his presence.

Jorna turned to look at him, her expression grave. In a hushed whisper, she shared what was on her mind, "We're trapped in here. We have no supplies, no food..." She let him draw the inevitable conclusion on his own. They didn't have a lot of options, especially now that the book was gone, at least the real one was. She glanced down to the tome in her arms, her mind weighing the possibilities of what they might be able to accomplish with it, but she doubted that Stefan would be in a bargaining mood.

"We could try to dig our way out," Thane was suggesting. "We might be able to hit another corridor while the enemy is distracted."

She felt Thane's hand on her shoulder, squeezing reassuringly. His faith in her was appreciated, but she feared their luck had finally run out, and no matter how strongly he believed, they weren't going to be getting out of this mess so easily.

At least, she reminded herself, the book was beyond Stefan's reach. Even if they died here, they had insured that its secret could never be used against the Sarven or their allies. They had succeeded in their quest and that was what really mattered now.

On the other side of the door, the frantic clawing and shrieking subsided, though Jorna couldn't say for sure if that made her feel better or worse. She could only imagine what their enemies were in the midst of doing now... She bit her lower lip, knowing there was one significant detail she hadn't shared with the others.

"Food may be the least of our concerns." She didn't bother whispering anymore; there was no point in keeping the truth to herself. The solemn weight of her tone stopped the chattering, casting the vault in a gloomy, dread filled silence. "The book is gone and so is the magic that made this door impenetrable."

Nobody said a word, not even Shanik or Thane. They didn't have to for Jorna to know what they were thinking, for the same things were in her mind. There wasn't much time before the wyrmkin figured out that they could break the door down, and once they did, it wouldn't be long at all before they accomplished the task. They had a couple hours at most if they were extremely fortunate, but if Stefan's arcane abilities allowed him to sense that the magic was gone, that time frame would easily be cut down by a third.

Slowly, quietly the men began to weigh their options, discussing in hushed tones what they might do in order to survive this cruel twist of fate. They demanded help from the dragon, but Shanik could not conjure food or re-enchant the door or make them invisible or do any of the other things they desperately suggested.

He would have gladly done something if he possessed the means; his own life was on the line as much as theirs, a fact he tried to convince them of. They were quite stubborn, insisting that he was holding out. It wasn't until Thane spoke in his defense that they let the matter rest.

It was then they turned to Jorna, looking to her for a solution, though she didn't have one either. Gazing into their dirty, haggard faces, she shared the one idea she had, determined to keep their hope alive, no matter how slim a chance it gave them. "I have this," she indicated the empty book in her arms, "Stefan doesn't know it was just a shell. We may be able to use it to buy time, though I doubt it would be more than a couple minutes before he realized it was blank..."

Despite her efforts, the bleakness of their situation and the lack of any viable path to survival blanketed the room in a fog of despair. Nobody blamed her. Had it not been for the princess, they wouldn't have made it even this far. They would still be trapped in the dungeons, waiting for their captors or hunger to slowly kill them all. She had given them a way to die with dignity, a chance to stand on their feet and face death with their honor intact; for such a gift, they would be eternally grateful.

Just as they were all starting to accept their inevitable and unavoidable fate, a voice cut through the dread. It rang with realization and happiness, a stark contrast to the general mood of everyone else, proclaiming only a single word, "Jorna!"

Every face turned to see Guldorn rising off the floor, his old, tired bones creaking in protest as he excitedly shuffled toward his daughter. The warriors all parted for him, reverently allowing him to pass until he wobbled to a stop in front of the princess.

Recognition shone brightly on his face as he again said her name with ringing clarity, "Jorna!" He reached out, his dirty hand touching her fair cheek as their blue eyes met.

Smiling back at him, Jorna pressed her palm against the back of his hand. She forgot their plight, forgot the wyrmkin who were no doubt plotting ways to get inside the vault, she even forgot the others were staring at them. She was completely consumed with the moment, elated to have her father back, to see the love and pride in his gaze as he peered intently down at her.

It was a brief exchange between father and daughter, brought to an end far sooner than Jorna would have liked as Guldorn pushed something, a scroll by the feel of the parchment, into her free hand.

She glanced down, a slight frown creasing her brow until she realized what it was he had given her. "Javrin's contract with the minister..." She breathed the question, flicking her eyes back to the king's face, "Where did you get this?"

Guldorn merely winked at her, unable to really elaborate, though he would have preferred to do so. The only word his tongue seemed capable of forming properly was her name, otherwise it was entirely useless.

"I suppose it doesn't matter." Her frown returned as she suddenly remembered their dire circumstances. "We're trapped," she told him sorrowfully, "Our chances of making it back to Hamdralg are looking incredibly slim, I'm afraid."

Slowly he nodded, listening to what she had to say with a contemplative expression on his face. He seemed to be struggling with something, trying to recall some detail that was being especially elusive. The more he debated it, the more wrinkled his forehead became until abruptly he snapped his fingers, his features lighting up as he fit the scattered pieces together in his mind. He took hold of Jorna's arm, pulling her along behind him on his way to the back wall.

Baffled, the warriors quickly parted again for their king, watching with eager interest, their hope beginning to stir. If there was one man who could help them out of this mess, it was certainly Guldorn Oathbinder.

Stopping in front of the wall, Guldorn relinquished Jorna's arm, placing his palms against the stone and running them over its smooth surface. He looked like a madman, hair matted and tangled, sticking out in every direction as he groped at the blank wall like a blind man searching the ground for a lost trinket.

For a few minutes, he seemed stumped again, searching frantically, though to the naked eye there was nothing to be found. As the others were slipping back into their well of discouragement, he finally located what his fingers had been fumbling for. He flashed his daughter a beaming grin, watching her face as he triggered the hidden mechanism.

With a groan like distant thunder, the wall began to shudder, the stone shifting back to reveal a dark, gaping passage. Jorna stared into the darkness, her mouth hanging open in dumbfounded shock.

Her father had gone to great lengths to prepare her for anything that might happen; she would have never guessed that there were some secrets he had left to teach. It might have reminded her how their time together had been cut short and how his sudden lucidity might only be temporary, but she was so thrilled at the change of fate that her mind ignored these details.

At her back, she could feel the others pressing in close, their growing excitement and relief charging the air, spreading the elation. It was a chance, nothing more, but it was far better than their lot had been moments before.

"I never thought I'd say this, but bless Sarven paranoia!" Shanik was the first to comment.

This stirred a brief chorus of agreement from several of the warriors, until they realized the veiled insult in the dragon's cleverly spoken words. As Rulvon was opening his mouth to protest the accusation that Sarven were paranoid, Jorna cut across him.

"No time for levity, we need to get as far ahead of the wyrmkin as possible." Her mind was already formulating a course of action. She could feel the time ticking away until their enemies were upon them again and she endeavored to be long gone before they ever came through the door. "Gather the wounded. Shanik, help them light torches. Renarn—"

A hand on her shoulder interrupted her train of thought, drawing her attention to Guldorn's face and then following his gaze to the main door. The vault became silent as the scraping and banging from the treasury grew louder. Whatever Stefan was up to now couldn't be good. If she had to venture a guess, she'd say they were preparing to ram open the door, a process that would be achieved in short order without any magical properties to fortify the stone.

There was no time left. They had to get moving immediately and hope for two things now. Speed to cover enough ground to at least be well away from the palace and that the hidden passage would lead someplace safe. Depending on the latter, they might have a chance to escape the city via the south road, which led through the underground realm to Hamdralg.

If nothing else, they could seek shelter in one of the more intact houses, where they might be able to survive on whatever food might remain in the pantry. After a few days, Stefan and his vile pets may give up, allowing them to safely traverse the city. Whatever happened next at least they had some options, better options than staying here and waiting to be overwhelmed.

Jorna started to press the others, urging them to hurry, but then she caught the expression on her father's face and the words never made it beyond her lips. She knew that look in his eyes and seeing it again made her heart sink all the way down to the floor.

That stubborn determination and fearless resolve was an echo of months past, when a great king had watched a horde of hellish creatures swarming toward his fleeing people. It had taken only a few words to rally more than two dozen volunteers to hold back the nightmare fiends so that the other Dwenenari could escape to safety. Even his daughter had wanted to fight at his side, but he had forbidden it. That was how she knew now that he was staying behind again, sacrificing himself to buy the rest of them enough time to get out of the city.

It was unnecessary and foolish, Jorna decided. She was certain they could make it together, even if it was more of a risk. She grabbed her father's arm, stopping him as he reached out to claim a weapon from one of the warriors who carried two. "You don't need to do this," she urged, trying and failing to keep the emotion out of her voice.

Her words drew the attention of the others who were busy dipping their makeshift torches into the fire that Shanik had set ablaze on the ground. Thane and Renarn were helping to get the wounded ready to be carried or otherwise assisted, but at the distress in Jorna's tone, they also turned to see what was wrong.

Before anyone could comment or Guldorn could do anything to allay his daughter's concerns, something heavy slammed into the vault door from the other side. The entire vault shook and trembled as the impact thundered loudly in their ears. They all knew what it meant. The wyrmkin were using a battering ram, and within minutes the door would crack open, exposing them all.

The vibrations hadn't fully settled before the king was moving. With one hand, he shoved Jorna toward the passage and with the other snatched an axe from a warrior who was startled by the weapon suddenly leaving his grasp. Someone had to stay behind to occupy the wyrmkin and their slippery puppeteer.

He'd be damned before he allowed his daughter to sacrifice herself. His mind was still uncertain of many things, but of this one single moment, of this single thing, he knew absolutely that Jorna had to go on. Perhaps it was fate or perhaps the simple explanation was a parent's desire to ensure the best for his child. Whatever drove him, he would not be swayed from his chosen path.

Instinctively Jorna knew this as well, no matter how much it pained her. She saw with grim clarity that her father's mind was made up. It wasn't fair. She had just gotten him back after losing him the first time and now she was being forced to say goodbye again. Tears stung at her eyes, blurring her vision as she watched Guldorn turn to face the treasury door. Much of his regal bearing had returned, despite the filthy clothes that hung more loosely on his now thinner frame. He was just like the great man in her memories, she realized with a surge of pride, except for one thing...

Jorna drew the beautiful sword, the metal and gems catching the crackling dragon fire, gleaming and glinting brilliantly in the blue flames. She called her father's name, stepping toward him as the vault trembled under another jarring strike and laid the weapon flat on her palms, extending it to the king. "Father, you'll need this."

She stared at him from over the pale, shining gold, watching his grungy face as he peered thoughtfully at the offered sword. With his empty hand he reached out slowly, pausing above the shimmering blade a moment before pushing it back toward her.

"Jorna," he said her name softly, meaningfully, conveying with that single word all the hope and love that he held in his heart for her and for her future.

Relinquishing his weapon to her was symbolic, an ancient tradition born in battle, when a father's last moments of life did not afford him the luxury of drafting legal documents or consulting advisers. With this one act, he was giving her everything he possessed and every eye in the vault bore witness, making it legal. That the law was archaic did not matter; in the eyes of any true Sarven, it was valid.

Sorrow and conflicting emotions stirred in Jorna's chest at the honor being bestowed upon her. She fought to control the rushing torrent, knowing that she couldn't lose herself to such feelings, not yet.

The vault shook again, reminding her that time was short, but she granted herself a second more to embrace Guldorn one last time. She hugged him tightly, whispering, "I love you, Father," before tearing herself away, determined to be strong just a little while longer.

"Renarn, you lead the way." She turned back to the passage that loomed glumly into the unknown, feeling a shiver run down her spine. "Set a brisk pace, we don't have time to dawdle."

That was the only signal that the warriors needed. They gathered up their weapons, men with torches raising them in preparation, but the wounded refused to allow those tasked with aiding them to do so. There were only three of them. One man was hunched over, grasping a bloody stab wound to his ribs that had been hastily treated, while the second seemed to have broken his leg for he couldn't stand without the assistance of the third.

The third was the strongest of the three. His injuries did not seem life threatening, though blood dripped from a wound that was blocked by the warrior he supported.

He raised his chin stubbornly. "Go on without us, we'll only slow you down. Besides..." He turned his gaze to Guldorn and smiled fiercely with pride. "We would rather die fighting at the side of our king than be a burden."

Another thundering slam jolted the room, punctuating his words.

Jorna didn't have time to argue with them. If they wanted to remain behind, that was their choice. She would not taint their sacrifice by wasting the precious minutes they were buying with their very lives and so she clapped him on the shoulder. "You will not be forgotten," she assured them, an edge of conviction strengthening her tone.

Seeing that a decision had been reached, Renarn didn't hesitate, he barked at the other warriors and bolted into the tunnel. The light of his torch licked the walls, casting them in cool shades of blue as he led a string of six men, six warriors being all that remained of the rearguard.

Shanik and Thane waited as Jorna lingered, gazing back to steal one final glance of her father as the room rattled and shuddered again. She felt Thane's hand on her arm, urging her that it was time to go. With a deep breath, she finally turned away and preceded her companions into the passage.

Guldorn waited for the light of the final torch to disappear before he moved to seal the secret door closed. He had been afraid that if she saw him coming, his daughter would refuse to leave without him and so he had waited those few precious moments to be certain she was gone. As it grumbled closed, he turned back to the main door, his eyes fixed on the crack in the stone that had appeared the last time it was struck. Soon now, very soon, their enemies would have it torn down.

Returning to his spot, he paused to retrieve the false book that Jorna had placed back on the pedestal before departing. A plan was already forming in his mind, a short plan that ended in death, but he hoped it would lead to the demise of a certain arcanist as well. With the book in one hand and his weapon in the other, he placed himself beside the still roaring fire, magically started by the dragon. All there was left to do now was wait.

Again the door shuddered, straining against the repeated impact, the crack ever widening with each additional hit.

At his side, the three wounded men waited, looking to him to lead them to a glorious end. He couldn't recall their names, but he knew he cared for them, that was his duty as king after all. They had been with him before, during another battle, a battle that should have claimed their lives. He thanked the stone it hadn't, or his daughter might never have succeeded in her quest without their courage.

It was ironic, he thought, that Stefan had kept them alive to use to his advantage and now that choice was causing him nothing but trouble. No, he decided a second later, not irony; it was pure, sweet justice.

This brought a fierce grin to his sunken face, making him determined to be as big a pain in the ass as he possibly could before the wyrmkin finally killed him. Let Stefan rue the day he ever set his eye on that which belonged to the Sarven. Let him face the wrath of those he had wronged and reap the vile harvest that his greed had sown.

Another bone shattering blow rocked the vault, splintering the stone even further and allowing Guldorn to see the dark shapes of their foes scurrying about on the other side. He could tell they were eager now. The strikes were coming faster, the shouting getting louder and louder. The battering ram landed again, the earth still shaking from the previous assault and then it struck again and again until the door was finally sundered.

It crumbled away, raising dust and grit that danced in the harsh rays of light streaming from the treasury. Dark shapes moved in the beams. The wyrmkin were rushing forward, Guldorn could hear their talons scraping the ground, could almost smell the sulfurous scent of their hellish bodies that was the scent of their sweat. He raised the book over his head, counting on Stefan seeing it, hoping he was overseeing the final slaughter.

A tense heartbeat later, the scrape of claws against stone halted, casting an eerie silence that was interrupted only by the sound of footsteps. As the final particles began to settle, the cloud dissipating,

Guldorn could see the thin outline of Stefan drawing closer.

The man was enraptured with the sight of the book, his eyes fixed on it as he stumbled over the debris of the shattered door and stopped a few feet before the grungy Sarven King.

"Give it here..." he whispered pointedly, never prying his gaze from the ancient tome. "Give it to me and I will spare your lives." His voice was too smooth, belying his true intentions.

Guldorn had many things he wished he could say, but he still found that his ability to speak was impaired, a handicap he had the arcanist to thank for. All he did was grin, his blue eyes gleaming with meaning as he lowered the book, taking pleasure in how his enemy followed the motion, like a dog following a morsel of meat. Slowly he extended it and Stefan leaned ever closer, his hand coming up to accept what he believed was about to be given to him.

An expression of sheer horror washed over his pointed face when the king let the useless tome slide from his fingers, dropping it into the blue flames. The dragon fire quickly began to consume it, eating through the pages like a swarm of locusts.

He watched with satisfaction as Stefan shrieked in despair and anguish, rushing forward without any thought or care in a vain effort to rescue what he believed was a priceless secret lest it be destroyed and lost forever.

He didn't even see Guldorn until it was far too late. The king charged forward, crying the only word he could speak and sinking the blade of his borrowed axe into the human's exposed chest. The last thing that Stefan heard was the ringing clamor of the Sarven warriors taking up their king's battle cry, shouting the name of a princess as they flew into the waiting horde of vile wyrmkin.

On to meet their vile foe.
On to meet their death.

The mighty king, his warriors bold
May song proclaim their worth.

BROTHER'S SIN

A LITTLE OVER A month after Jorna had departed Hamdralg on her quest, Prince Jalrik awoke from his coma and upon learning everything that had transpired demanded an audience with the king. It was the least that he could do, given his sister had left on a suicide mission and so he implored Javrin to see that something was done to help her.

Days passed before Jalrik was well enough to actually see the king. He sat in his quarters, sick with worry that his elder sister was dead. They had already lost so much. To think that she had been safe in Hamdralg only to attempt returning home...

Despair ate at Jalrik, who found little comfort from his brother. Javrin had been cold and distant, rarely coming by to check on him and not staying long when he did. He got the impression that more was going on that Javrin was refusing to admit, but Jalrik's memory was fuzzy and he couldn't pinpoint anything that could explain the strange behavior.

Try as he might, his only memories of the battle were vague. He recalled how he had taken a blow to the head from one of the fiends. It had been Jorna who saved him; he'd heard her strong voice call his name and that was all he could remember.

Javrin did not contradict him, but any time Jalrik mentioned their sister, a strange look came over the other Sarven's face that he tried and failed to hide.

What is he not telling me?

Finally, the day of their meeting with the king came and while it began pleasantly enough, it wasn't long before Javrin had everyone on edge.

"None of us will disagree that her chances of success were always slim," Baran interrupted Jalrik coarsely. "Maybe your brother should have considered that before sending a woman in his place."

Javrin fixed the General with a pointed stare. "Only at her stubborn insistence," he answered evenly. "Had the choice been up to me, I would have gone with a more direct approach to begin with. These creatures are not to be trifled with." He returned his gaze to King Ulthrac. "A mistake that cost my father and many of our kin their lives. The key to defeating them is not defense, it is not subterfuge..." He raised his hands in front of his chest, curling one into a delicate, puny fist. "You must *crush* them before they have a chance to slaughter you!" His words were punctuated by the faint smack of knuckles striking palm.

"As much as I hate to agree with my obtuse brother..." Bodrin didn't waste the opportunity to slip in a quick jab, even when he was proclaiming agreement. "I fail to see how this is our problem. We have already given supplies and support, even one of our own warriors, to aide you in this matter. Now that it has failed, presumably, you want us to give you more? And with no assurances at that."

"Aye!" Baran directed his words to Javrin, though he was glowering at Bodrin. "We can scarcely afford to send one hundred of our warriors to reclaim a fallen city, when we are now tasked with defending our own borders, our own people and homes. Frankly, that you would ask this of us, after all we've done for you already, is quite insulting!" He shook his head, his beard waggling with the motion. "Were you my sons, I'd have strung you up by your ears for such audacity!"

Jalrik frowned, trying to think of a way to get everyone to focus on the real problem, but when he glanced at Javrin, he could see the situation was only about to get worse. It was the General's final comment that pushed Javrin over the edge and caused him to openly glare at the older Sarven.

"Yes, General," Javrin sneered. "Let us discuss your son. How can I be certain that your coward of a son didn't abandon my sister to her death or do only the stone knows what to her before leaving her for dead in the frozen mountains?"

"Because Thane Stoutforge is an honorable man."

The strong, feminine voice that rang through the great hall startled the five men. None had heard the wide doors open through the midst of their heated discussion, and as their eyes took in the disheveled, dirty appearance of Jorna Hailstone, all they could do was stare. She strode out to meet them, the gleaming sword of Guldorn Oathbinder secured over her shoulder and a company of seven Sarven warriors at her back.

Baran was visibly surprised to see his son, equally unkempt, covered in grime and blood, walking alongside the princess, his bearing one of pride and power. If he had not known any better, he almost might have mistaken him for Thunar.

Jalrik's face brightened, and he started toward Jorna so that he could give her a hug, but Javrin took hold of his arm and held him in place.

"Sister," Javrin's voice was steady, though the expression of bewilderment had not left his face. "You are alive after all. We were beginning to fear the worst." His eyes flicked to the warriors behind her and the mere sight of them alone caused his eyebrows to dart upward. "The rearguard... They survived?"

"Aye," Rulvon spat, turning a baleful gaze on the prince, "but we would have surely wasted away or been slain in some twisted experiment were it not for the princess and her champion."

Renarn put a hand on his brother's shoulder, signaling him to silence; this matter had to be settled by Jorna. They were here only to support her claims and to be certain that Javrin wouldn't weasel out of paying for his crimes.

"I smell the stench of sulfur," Baran inserted, ignoring the brewing tension as his eyes searched for the source of the offending odor. He found it a second later in the form of a black, winged lizard that dipped out of the air and perched itself on Jorna's shoulder. "What in the blazes is *that*?!" the General exclaimed, his hand reaching for his weapon as he tried to make sense of what he was seeing. "Is that a... a *dragon*?"

As a chuckle passed through the Dwenenari warriors, Jorna grabbed the opportunity to speak before Shanik managed to say something antagonistic. "Yes, General," she affirmed, gracing him with a slight smile. "Shanik has proven himself to be a friend. Were it not for his aid, we would have surely failed to complete our task."

"You have the book?" Javrin blurted, moving closer to his sister, his eyes glittering hopefully. He might have gone straight up to her, had Thane not taken a threatening step forward, making it very plain that the prince would not be permitted to approach.

"Sister," Javrin sounded hurt and insulted, "will you permit this *dog* to show me such disrespect?"

Jorna ignored his final comment, recognizing it as the bait it was. Instead, she answered his question as though that was all he had said. "I destroyed the book. The secret of Goldsteel is lost."

The chamber erupted in outrage, Baran and Bodrin began to shout, and even Ulthrac was frowning down at her disapprovingly. Javrin alone was silent, though his fury was evident in the wild look that widened his eyes. He seemed to be processing her words, struggling to make sense of such terrible news. No doubt he had dozens upon dozens of questions, but were he to ask even one of them, it would reveal his treachery.

"It was necessary." Jorna raised her hand, trying to quiet the fuming brothers. At first what she said was drowned out, but when he realized she was trying to explain herself, Bodrin shouted Baran into silence.

"Destroying the book was the only way to keep it out of human hands." Her voice remained even and calm; she had no reason to yell or be upset. To lose her composure would only reflect poorly on her and right now it was necessary for Jorna to prove herself. Not to her brother, but to Ulthrac and his advisers.

"You are talking nonsense, sister." Javrin shook his head dubiously. "It was not the humans who overran Dwenenar, it was those *things*."

"They are called wyrmkin," Jorna corrected, "and they attacked Dwenenar on the order of the Ardon minister." She fixed him with a pointed stare, her tone taking on an accusing edge. "But you already knew that, didn't you, brother." It was not a question.

Before the stunned prince could figure out how to respond to her bold statement, King Ulthrac straightened on his throne, clearly unsettled by her implication. "Do you understand the gravity of what you're saying, Princess?"

"Aye, your highness." She didn't even hesitate. "But I do not speak without proof." Jorna reached into the folds of her cloak and withdrew the scroll of parchment that Guldorn had given to her. She carefully watched her brother's expression as she passed the document to Shanik. The dragon lifted off her shoulder with ease and delivered the scroll to Bodrin. The scholar blinked as the dragon hovered before him; it was clear he had never seen one before. It wasn't until Shanik let out an annoyed sniff that Bodrin finally took the scroll, allowing the dragon to return to his perch.

Bodrin flicked a glance to Ulthrac and Baran as he unfurled the parchment, his uncertainty more than apparent. As his eyes skimmed the fine script, they grew wider and wider until what he was seeing sank in and then they narrowed with anger.

"By the stone," Bodrin swore, the document shaking in his hands. "A signed contract, between the minister and Javrin... I don't understand." His forehead wrinkled as his frown deepened. "Why would you trade the secret of Goldsteel, lad, for a throne that was already your birthright?"

A thick silence fell over the gathering as everyone turned an eager gaze to the prince, waiting on bated breath to hear what he had to say for himself. Javrin, however, did not tear his piercing eyes away from Jorna; it was as though she were the only other person in the throne room.

Jalrik was shaking his head, looking between his two siblings as though they had both gone mad. "It can't be true. Say something, brother!"

"Of course, it's not true!" Javrin snapped. His tone was drawn taut with a barely concealed fury. "This contract is a forgery!"

The chamber erupted in angry shouts as the company of Dwenenari warriors rose to defend the honor of their princess. Rulvon looked as though he were about to surge forward and strangle Javrin outright, his eyes nearly popping out of their sockets, his face a deep shade of furious red. His brethren shared his outrage; even Renarn who was usually quite levelheaded appeared to have lost his temper.

Jorna allowed them a couple of moments to express their indignation, her gaze subtly flicking to Thane. The blacksmith was every bit as angry as the others, but he had the good grace not to explode.

"Enough." Jorna did not need to raise her voice in order to be heard. The faint sound of it was more than adequate to quiet her men, a subtle display of power that did not go unnoticed. She reached behind her head, her slender fingers grasping the splendid hilt of Guldorn's sword. With a slow, fluid motion, she drew the blade and held it out for all to see.

"That document only proves Javrin's treachery, but this proves his motive. He learned that our father was going to name *me* as his heir, and like a petulant child, he put his selfish needs above that of his people."

"Lies!" the prince spat, his expression displaying open hostility toward his sister. "Everything she has said is a lie!"

Growing impatient, Ulthrac finally stepped in. "Quiet, boy! I will hear what she has to say."

Jorna graciously thanked the king, pointedly ignoring her brother as he seethed in grudging silence. Knowing better than to waste time, she launched into a more detailed explanation. She started by sharing in vague detail their trek across the mountains, of their encounter with the giants and Thane's brave fight with their chieftain, of how they were separated at the worm fields and their battle with the ice worm. She told them of the hospitable Boesh, and finally that they had released the muskox before entering Dwenenar.

Her audience remained captivated throughout the tale, with only Ulthrac daring to interrupt should he have a question or comment. Even Thane and Shanik, who had lived through everything she described, listened carefully. She realized that this was a gift, that the weight of her speech was a great asset and one of many reasons that Guldorn had chosen her.

Javrin noticed this as well and slowly his expression shifted, his eyes filling with resentment and just a trace of hatred, but Jorna refused to pay him any heed; this was her moment.

Speaking of what they had found in the city was the most difficult part, though she did not hide her sorrow. Only a truly black hearted person would have emerged unscathed from the experiences she described. A display of humility and compassion was not amiss.

The more she spoke of Stefan and his apparent plans, how he had been experimenting on their kin, that he tortured Guldorn to the brink of insanity and most importantly that he had used his dark magic to create the wyrmkin, the paler Javrin's face became. She didn't leave a single detail out, everything she had learned, her ploy to escape and how they had managed to fight their way to the vault; she shared it all. And then, she explained why she chose to destroy the book and that they had all been doomed until Guldorn returned to his senses, showing them the secret passage that had allowed them to flee the city.

"The king and three other men stayed behind to cover our escape." She could not keep the weight of grief out of her voice. "Before sacrificing his life for ours, Guldorn Oathbinder gave me Javrin's contract and, in accordance with the old laws, he bestowed his sword upon me."

As she trailed into silence, the chamber became incredibly still. For several moments nobody dared to speak. For Ulthrac, Baran, and Bodrin, it was clear they were absorbing this information, taking a minute to let it all sink in. Jorna's companions remained quiet out of respect or reflection, or perhaps a bit of both, for they remembered all too well what they had endured in Dwenenar.

Jalrik had inched closer to his sister the more she spoke, though he seemed uncertain of trying to go to her again with Javrin right beside him.

Javrin on the other hand paused not out of reverence, but to decide his next move. One glance at the king and his advisers told him that they had been swayed by his sister's words. There was no refuting the old law or the testimony of eight witnesses who would all swear that Guldorn was lucid in the end and that everything Jorna had shared was the absolute truth. Deep down the prince knew there was no play here, no way for him to reasonably deny these accusations, not only because they *were* true, but because Jorna had simply beaten him.

A bitterness crept into his heart, more intense than any hateful feeling he'd harbored toward his *perfect* younger sibling. What was so damn special about her anyway? He had never seen or understood why she was so popular, why everyone respected her, trusted her, believed in her... She was just a woman in his eyes, a troublesome, ignorant woman. It would not have stung so much had the throne been passed to Jalrik; at least then the throne would have a proper king.

"That's right, *sister*," he sneered the word, not bothering to hide his contempt a moment longer. "There's no point in lying anymore, now is there?" He spun on his heel, glaring balefully up at Ulthrac as his Sarven temper took over his tongue. "Yes, I betrayed Dwenenar, I betrayed my family! I made a pact with the minister to get what was *owed* to me! And then I ensured that I would be put in a position to take control without any interference!" A cruel, satisfied laugh tore from his drawn back lips. "Guldorn got himself out of the way and Jorna," he turned a mirthless, malicious grin to her, "you were meant to die in failure!"

Everyone was shocked by his flurried confessions, by the animosity and loathing he displayed toward family and duty. Even Thane, who had struggled with these issues himself, could not sympathize with a word the crazed prince uttered. It was abhorrent that a man would cause and allow so much devastation and pain, all for his own gain. That he so blatantly and defiantly confessed was a disgrace, an insult, to the Sarven traditions and all that they stood for.

"How could you, Javrin?" Jorna was the first who managed to speak, her voice soft and distant. Only Thane and Shanik were able to pick up the underlying pain that she tried to hide; this was not the time for grief. Though the news had been expected, it still took her off guard. "Your father, your sister... your *people...*"

Javrin barked an icy cackle, watching Jorna's face with outright glee. "I enjoyed every second of your suffering. My only regret would have been not getting to watch you die!"

Succumbing to a surge of anger, Thane stepped forward without warning and slammed a large fist into the prince's mouth. The blow sent him staggering backward, blood splattering from his broken lip as he flailed in an effort to keep from tumbling to the floor. The blacksmith didn't speak a word. He let the action speak for itself instead.

"You should be executed, you despicable whelp!" one of the warriors shouted before Javrin could fully recover enough to speak himself, stirring a chorus of agreement and threats from his fellows.

Glowering from one Sarven to another, the prince dabbed at his bleeding lip, his angry gaze settling on Thane. "Ignorant buffoons," he growled. "Do you really think my dear, perfect sister would allow that to happen? She's too soft!" He laughed as though he thought he had won something, when in reality it didn't matter if he continued breathing or not; his life was still forfeit.

"No offense to the princess," Bodrin cut in, "but that decision rests with the king, I'm afraid. He has the highest authority in Hamdralg and therefore the highest right to declare judgment and punishment."

This caused a slight frown to crease Jorna's brow. "With all due respect, King Ulthrac, I must insist that Javrin's fate remain in my hands. He is of Dwenenar and his heinous crimes were committed in our halls." She closed the distance between them, placing Thane only a step or two at her back.

Staring into her brother's hate darkened eyes, she did not allow him to see beyond the firm, confident mask that dominated her features. From the corner of her gaze, she saw Ulthrac give a slow, understanding nod and took that as her cue to continue speaking.

"You are correct, brother, in that I will not allow your execution." Her words were like stone, hard and heavy. "But you are gravely mistaken if you believe for even a moment that I will not dole out a fitting punishment." She paused, letting her words sink in, letting him see the conviction that burned inside her. "Javrin the Fair, *former* Prince to the kingdom of Dwenenar, your sentence is exile. You will be stripped of your title and possessions, your name stricken from all records and replaced as Javrin the Kinslayer. At dawn you will be given a single pack of provisions, with rations enough for three days and then expelled from the front gates of Hamdralg. Should you return to Sarven lands, you *will* be executed."

As she spoke the smug expression on his narrow face drained away, along with all the color in his cheeks. For a brief moment, there was fear in his eyes; he had never expected Jorna to deliver such a harsh judgment. For a Sarven, death would have been almost kind in comparison to being cast out of not only his family, but the entire society as well.

She had taken everything from him now, his right to rule Dwenenar, his one chance to steal the throne, but worst of all, she had bestowed the cruelest of dishonors. She had shamed him as the Kinslayer for all of history. There was nothing more horrific than being known as the epitome of everything his people despised.

All of a sudden the truth of what he had done slammed into him. The lives that had been lost, his own father killed and his sister nearly following him to the grave... He felt sick all the way down to the core of his being. Sick and twisted. Greed and jealousy had driven him, turning him into a monster.

Lips trembling, he lifted his gaze back to Jorna's face, intending to beg forgiveness, to plead with her to give him one more chance, that he might be able to make amends... but the look in her eyes, that faint trace of love and pity, chased away his shred of remorse and replaced it with a seething fury.

"Don't you dare look at me like that," he growled, his face flushing with anger. "Don't you dare! I don't need your *sympathy*!" he spat, turning himself over to the blind Sarven rage at the mere idea that Jorna would feel sorry for him. "You don't have to pretend, snake! Your doting subjects already believe you're superior, you needn't rub it in my face!"

Jorna took a step back, surprised at the abrupt explosion of his temper. She opened her mouth in an attempt to calm him, but the weight of her sentence and the influence of all his demons sent Javrin completely over the edge.

He reached into the fold of his shirt and withdrew a small dagger, the blade gleaming in the light from the braziers. With a wild howl, he threw himself forward, pulling the dagger back and then swinging with his full might for any part of his sister that he could reach.

Thane started to intervene, grabbing Jorna's arm so that he could tug her out of the way, but a large, burly figure with a shock of flame red hair got to Javrin first.

A fist the size of a mace clobbered the raging man in the side of his head, knocking him clean off the ground so he flew in the air a few feet before dropping to the stone floor in a tumble of fine clothes and flailing limbs. For a long moment he went perfectly still and then slowly, he tried to rise, but it became clear that he was having difficulty.

Jorna, despite his attempt to kill her, started toward him, but Thane tightened his grip on her arm and Baran stepped in front of her, blocking her path. The old General exchanged a glance with his son, who did a very poor job of hiding his concern.

It was Jalrik who made it to Javrin first. He knelt beside him and carefully rolled him onto his back and that's when the hilt of the dagger became visible. The blade was jammed at an awkward angle into Javrin's chest, with thick rivers of blood seeping from the wound.

Now that Javrin had the room, the fallen prince yanked the weapon free of his body. His groan of agony and the fresh stream of blood was more than Jorna could take. She pulled away from Thane and hurried to her brothers. Upon seeing her, anger flashed in Javrin's eyes and he tried to raise the dagger again, intending to strike out at her, but his limbs were growing weaker; he could barely lift his arm at all.

"Enough," Jorna told him softly, laying her hand over the fist clenching the hilt. "Let it go," she urged and after another tense second of hesitation, he loosened his grip, allowing her to take the weapon and place it out of his reach.

"Is he...?" Jalrik, the youngest of three siblings, didn't seem capable of finishing the question. His voice was thick with emotion and concern.

With a glance, Jorna could tell Javrin was not long for this world. He was bleeding too much; even if the healers arrived, they wouldn't be able to stop it before he bled out.

Jorna glanced from his bloody chest to his face and saw that there were tears in his eyes, along with a great deal of fear. Gently she squeezed his hand and remained at his side until death claimed him.

When he was gone, she put her arms around Jalrik and together they wept.

THE RETURN

By the time that Javrin's body had been cleared away, the hour was growing late. Bodrin led the surviving warriors of Dwenenar out of the hall, promising them the finest food and the most luxurious of comforts. Despite the swift approach of dinner, Jorna requested a private discussion with the king and Ulthrac did not turn her down. Once the two of them had gone into the war room, it left Thane and Baran alone.

Thane couldn't remember having spent more than a couple minutes in Baran's presence without someone else there to mediate. He found the silence unbearably uncomfortable, but no matter how hard he tried, he couldn't think of a single appropriate thing to say. Finally, the General broke the heavy quiet by clearing his throat, which drew his son's dark gaze.

"Well, your mother will be relieved to see you back in one piece..." he grunted, scratching awkwardly at his bearded chin. "She's been worried sick, ya know."

Nodding slowly, Thane wasn't sure what to say in response, so he simply let his father continue and hoped the moment would pass without them arguing.

"But she'll uh, she'll be mighty proud of ya." Baran cleared his throat, clearly summoning up the courage to say what was really on his mind. "Now, listen here, Thane," he started gruffly, "this whole nonsense was foolish and impulsive. It's a wonder you weren't minced out there. I'd have bet gold that you and that crazy woman would have frozen to death not two miles from the front gate!" He chuckled nervously, trying and failing to come across jovial.

Thane raised his eyebrow, attempting to see where his father was heading, but having no clue what he was getting at. He could have gotten offended, some men might have, but the blacksmith was used to being insulted by Baran. He knew exactly what that looked like and this... this was something else.

Squaring his shoulders, Baran cleared his throat one last time and blurted, "You did good, son." Then he awkwardly clapped Thane on the back.

When all his son did was stare up at him as though he'd sprouted a second head, Baran barked a laugh and shook his head. "All right, that's enough sappiness..." He started toward the exit. "Now it's time for a fine meal, prepared by the most lovely of Sarven women." He beamed over his shoulder at Thane. "Well, aren't you coming?"

Thane's gaze wandered to the closed door where on the other side Jorna was still speaking with Ulthrac. The temptation of a warm, hot meal of the sort he'd not had since leaving Hamdralg was quite strong, but his desire to remain close to Jorna overpowered it by a very wide margin. "I'll be along later," he answered.

Baran chuckled again, muttered to himself and left the blacksmith alone in the throne room.

Still trying to process what had transpired between him and his father, Thane barely noticed as the minutes quickly ticked by. It wasn't until much later that he realized he had been waiting, pacing a few steps back and forth, for some time now.

Beginning to grow worried, he turned to watch the door and hoped that Jorna would soon be finished with her business with King Ulthrac. Not only were his feet and legs becoming weary of standing, his stomach was rumbling incessantly. The thought of tasting his mother's cooking again was most appealing and had it not been for his devotion to the princess, he might have wavered in his vigil.

Not long later his perseverance was rewarded. The sound of the opening door immediately drew his attention, and he turned just in time to see Jorna, Shanik still perched on her shoulder, exit the war room, followed by Ulthrac. The princess caught his gaze and offered him a soft smile before saying farewell to the king, who strolled out of the hall as she moved to join the blacksmith.

"Sorry to keep you waiting, I had to properly brief Ulthrac about what really happened in Dwenenar," she explained, though Thane had already guessed as much.

"Please," Shanik rasped, tilting his nose up and sniffing at the air. "That took about ten minutes. The rest of the time was spent discussing your coronation."

Jorna immediately blushed as she glanced up at Thane's face, trying to judge his reaction. The slight trace of nervousness slipped away when she saw him grinning, though her pink cheeks shifted to a darker shade.

"It is well deserved," he told her, his voice low as he reached for her hand. "I'm proud of you."

"Of us." She squeezed his fingers. "I could not have done this without you, Thane. Besides, did you forget that we are one now?"

Her assumption was absolutely correct. He had forgotten and so the reminder hit him like a thick slab of stone over the head. For a long moment, all he could do was stare at her, speechless and dumbfounded.

Of course he was honored, flattered even, but he was just a blacksmith. How could she expect him to help her rule a kingdom? That he loved her was irrefutable, but was he capable of what she was expecting? It had all felt so different when she was just a princess, but the realization that she was going to be a *queen* and he would serve as her king made his stomach lurch.

Doubt must have shown on his face, for she reached up and gently caressed his beard. "Jorna..." he started, meaning to explain his misgivings, but her thumb pressed against his lips and silenced him.

"You are strong and wise and you have proven yourself a Champion of Hamdralg. I spoke of your heroic deeds, of your fearless heart and courageous acts and King Ulthrac agrees that you, Thane Stoutforge, are to be honored also. Your name will pass into legend, songs will be sung of our adventures, of our accomplishments and..." She stepped a little bit closer so that her body was just barely touching his. "And of our love."

Thane was just reaching for her, intending to pull her close and kiss her with all the passion he possessed, when Shanik made a mock gagging nose and propelled himself off of Jorna's shoulder. "You two love birds make my scales crawl," he snorted as though to clear an unpleasant stench from his nostrils and headed for the exit.

"Where do you think you're going, lizard?" Thane snapped, annoyed that he had interrupted the moment with Jorna.

"*Tsk.*" The dragon rolled onto his back, hovering for just a moment as he rasped, "I'm going to do dragony things!" With a snap of his wings, he took off, spinning over again in an elegant flourish before disappearing over the threshold.

The two Sarven exchanged a bemused glance, both fully used to their friend's antics. Taking hold of Jorna's hand, Thane pulled her toward the exit. "Come, my mother is probably putting a hot supper on the table right now. Will you share it with me?"

She squeezed his fingers and beamed up at him. "I would be honored."

Being back on the streets of Hamdralg filled Thane with great joy. That Jorna was at his side only made heading home all the sweeter. As they drew closer, he couldn't help but pick up his pace, eager to see his family and hug his mother. His growling stomach did nothing to slow him down either. Understanding his haste, Jorna hurried after him, amused at his childish excitement.

Before long, they had arrived and without knocking, Thane threw open the door and began to shout, making his presence known. Jorna closed the door behind them, smirking to herself as she followed, more slowly and far more quietly.

"Mother! Makira! Everyone! I'm home!" Thane banged loudly into the dining room, grinning from ear to ear at all the surprised faces. Apparently, Baran had kept the news of Thane's return to himself, and given the late hour of their return to the city, the rumors had not quite made it here either.

Tears filled Ravika's eyes as she stared across the room at her youngest son, scarcely able to believe that he was real and she wasn't imagining this moment as she had every night since his departure.

Lucky for Baran, who didn't even look up from his plate of food, she was so consumed by the sight of Thane that she didn't notice his little smirk. He must have been rather proud of himself for "arranging" such a surprise.

"You foolish boy!" The words stumbled past her lips as she sat down the tray of baked potatoes and hurried around the table so that she could crush her son in a tight hug. Makira joined her a second later and together they squeezed Thane until he was sure he would suffocate.

"I hope you're hungry, boy," Ravika said as she pulled away, swiping at her eyes to rid herself of the unshed tears. "Come and sit down!" She started to push him toward his place at the table when she finally caught sight of their guest. "Baran..." she stared at Jorna, her brown eyes inspecting the visitor from head to toe. "Your son brought home a woman!"

"He what?" the older Sarven demanded around an especially large mouthful of meat. He nearly choked when he glanced up and saw Jorna standing next to Thane. "By the stone," the General growled once he'd recovered from coughing. "What is she doing here?"

"I asked Jorna to come," Thane quickly answered, knowing it didn't really make a difference; his mother would never turn anyone away, especially for a meal.

At the revelation of their guest's name, the entire dining room fell silent. Even the two youths had given up their usual antics and were watching curiously. Stealing a glance of her, Thane was quite impressed at the way Jorna handled the attention. He guessed that sort of grace came with being a king's daughter.

He opened his mouth to rescue her, whether or not she really needed it, but was cut off by the cross voice of his mother. The initial surprise was wearing off, the chaos of the room winding up again.

"Jorna? The princess of Dwenenar?" Ravika shot her husband a withering glower, "You knew about this? How come I'm the last to hear about everything?" She was shaking her head as she stepped closer to Jorna. "*Tsk*, stone-brained men, all they're really good for is eating and making babies!" She put a strong hand on the other woman's shoulder, giving her a meaningful push toward the table. "Now come in and get comfortable, lass."

Jorna flashed Thane a bemused look as she allowed herself to be ushered into a seat. He realized with a surge of satisfaction that his mother had placed her between his chair and her own. Remembering his manners, he waited for her to get settled before taking his own place and finally returning her earlier look with an apologetic glance.

Poor Jorna was questioned incessantly by Ravika, who didn't let anything slip her notice in the princess's answers. It was a wonder she had a chance to eat at all, but somehow through the conversation she managed to clean her plate and then, with the same grace and charm he had come to love, she graciously thanked the older Sarven for such a wonderful meal.

"Oh, by the stone," Baran swore again, shaking his fiery head. "No wonder you talked my son into following you all over the Beldrath! With a tongue like that, you can be sure he'll follow you around forever like a little lost pup." Though his tone was gruff, there was a gleam in his eye that belied his teasing manner.

"Baran!" Ravika snapped, clearly won over by Jorna.

Makira smiled across the table at Jorna while the heads of the household began to argue. The look in her eyes was knowing; she'd had the entire evening to see the way that Thane was looking at Jorna and how Jorna was looking back at Thane. She gave her brother the signal to leave while they had the chance, and he nodded his appreciation.

When they rose to leave, however, Ravika certainly noticed and frowned. "Leaving already? We have warm cobbler for desert..." While this announcement got a pair of delighted whoops from Makira's children, Thane and Jorna were set on stealing away.

"Thank you, but I must retire. It's become rather late." Jorna bowed, said her goodbyes to the rest of the family and then followed Thane out of the kitchen. Once in the hall, they grinned at each other and instead of heading for the front door, Thane took her hand and led her upstairs to his room.

Nightmares

ONCE THEY WERE SEALED away in the privacy of Thane's quarters, Jorna smiled softly, happy to finally be alone with him. "Your family is very pleasant," she said, stepping further into the room and taking a casual glance around.

She wouldn't have expected it to be quite so neat and clean, there should have at least been a thin layer of dust collecting on everything, but it seemed that someone had been keeping the room spotless in Thane's absence. She could just imagine his mother, fussing over the small stone carvings with a cloth and tidying the bed, even though nobody had slept there.

So many trinkets and baubles littered what was meant to be a bookcase, no doubt they were mementos of his childhood. There was only one book placed there, an old tome that appeared well used. Tilting her head to the side, she could barely make out the worn, leather binding, which marked it as a collection of children's tales.

Again, she speculated on the past, imagining a young boy seated on his mother's lap, listening intently to his favorite stories, and with this mental picture, her smile widened.

But such thoughts were driven from her mind when she felt Thane's fingers lightly brush through her hair. He had moved with her, stopping at her back when she paused to inspect the shelves in the corner.

She turned her head, gazing up at him. Right away she could see that he was holding back his desires, that all he really wanted was to draw her into his arms and never let go, but something was stopping him.

"What's wrong?" she asked, keeping her voice low so that they wouldn't be overheard.

Shaking his head, the blacksmith continued to stroke her pale hair, clearly enjoying the silky feel of the smooth locks against his skin. "Nothing," he answered just as quietly, "everything is just right."

Jorna turned to face him, raising her hands and pressing her palms lightly against his chest. "Then I believe it's time that you kiss me," she urged, the edge of her mouth quirking into a faint grin. "Haven't we waited long enough for this moment?"

That was all the prompting that Thane needed. He cupped her cheeks gently in his hands, tilting her head back as he leaned down and then placed the lightest of kisses against her full lips.

Immediately she melted against him, her hands falling down his torso as she slid her arms around his waist, holding onto him to keep herself from floating away. Slow and tender, Thane did not rush a single second of that first, delicious embrace. His strong touch turned to velvet as he gathered Jorna more firmly into his arms.

The way he held her, his tender manner, drove away all the darkness in her mind, eliminating the weariness of their journey and the fear she had of what lay ahead. All she knew was his touch, all she needed was his love, which he gave so completely. There was only bliss and magic between them, the swell of heat and desire filling the air like a pleasant, flowery fragrance. Before long that soft kiss had escalated, melding into something hot and wanton.

Jorna sighed as Thane pressed his lips against her smooth neck, his beard tickling her skin and heightening the heat in her belly that only grew warmer with each passing second. His slow, methodical manner was only making her more wild, until she finally could stand it no longer and briefly pulled away from him.

Confusion and uncertainty flashed across his face.

With trembling fingers, Jorna unlaced her dress, loosening it so that she could slip it off her shoulders. The fabric fell slowly off her body, inch by inch revealing her pale, soft skin and ample breasts. Wiggling her hips, she let go of the linen dress and allowed it to flutter the rest of the way to the floor so that she was now standing before him completely naked.

Thane stared with appreciation for a long moment. Then, tenderly he ran his palms up her back, his fingers lightly caressing her spine as he eagerly explored her bare skin.

Jorna leaned up, brushing her lips against his bearded jawline as her own fingers went to work undressing him. In moments, his clothing had joined hers on the floor, leaving him every bit as naked as she was.

"Well then, blacksmith," Jorna's naked breasts were just barely brushing against his chest as she leaned close, her husky voice whispering near his ear, "Will you take me to your bed...?"

There was only one answer to her question. Thane scooped her into his arms, carrying her over to the fur-covered bed and laying her down against the thick pelts. He settled over her, gazing deep into her icy blue eyes, letting her clearly see the unwavering love in his heart. Then slowly he kissed her, groaning as she wrapped her thighs around his waist and tangled her fingers into his long, black hair.

In moments, they were lost together in pure ecstasy, their skin slick with sweat as their bodies moved in perfect tandem. Jorna had to bite her lip to keep from crying out as their passion began to boil. Her hands clutched at Thane's back. She could feel his muscles rippling beneath her palms as he labored above her.

His ragged breathing tickled her neck as his lips nipped their way down to her shoulder. She moaned his name, her nails unintentionally digging into his flesh, as a hot wave of sweet pleasure washed over her, burning sensually beneath her moist skin.

Growling in response to the prick of pain, Thane reveled in the power of her release. How she held him tighter, the quiver in her voice as she whimpered his name... He found her lips with his, kissing her passionately as her blissful climax carried him to his own peak. When their passion was spent, they lay together, faces only inches apart, breathing hard, their hearts pounding as one. For the first time in their lives, the world made perfect sense.

A white mist swirled around Jorna's legs, like steam radiating up from the hard earth beneath her feet. The air around her was nearly black, the only source of light coming from the radiant blade she held in her hands. She could feel more than see the warriors around her, their heavy armor clinking as they cautiously advanced toward some unknown foe.

She had no memory of what she was doing here, of who they were fighting or why, only that their lives hung precariously in the balance. Whatever they were facing, it wanted nothing more than to stamp them out, to tear them apart and leave the bloody, mutilated remains to rot in this barren wasteland. The conviction in her heart told her that this battle was right, that their motives were just and true, but the shiver of fear down her spine reminded her that it would not be an easy day to wi n.

Somewhere nearby a man whispered, but Jorna was unable to make out the phrase. It might have been a question or maybe a hopeful comment that they had been successful... A second later, the desire to puzzle it out vanished from her mind as a terrible screech diverted her gaze to the sky. She half expected some horrible monster to fall upon her from above, but she realized too late that the creature had been aiming for someone else.

There was a terrified scream, the wet, crunching sound of flesh and bone being cleaved and then a whoosh of rushing air. Shouting and yelling could be heard all around as more of the fiends dove from the heavens to strike at the unprotected warriors and then rose back into the air before any sort of counterattack could be mounted against them.

It was different for Jorna. The creature landed in front of her, its shadowy silhouette just outside the ring of soft, blue light from her sword. Slowly, the hideous, scaled beast stepped into the glow, revealing her frightening visage. Black, matted hair hung in ratted clumps down her back and around her narrow, chiseled face and dark, malevolent eyes glittered with malice and cruelty. Jorna realized then that she was holding something in her hand and as her eyes focused on the cluster of round objects, they suddenly came into focus.

Four Sarven heads, held by what was left of their long hair, stared grotesquely back at her, their eyes and mouths gaping, blood dripping from their severed necks. She vaguely recognized the faces, but for some reason she could not put names to them. Disgusted and disheartened, she stumbled back, one hand clutching her stomach as she fought to keep herself from vomiting. As she staggered away, the ring of light shifted as well and the monster was lost to the blackness.

Another hasty step and she tripped over a large, heavy object that was laying still on the ground. Letting out a startled cry, she didn't manage to stop herself from tumbling to the dirt beside it. Fearing the worst, Jorna angled her sword so that the glow illuminated the lump and she discovered, much to her continued horror, that it was a familiar body.

There was no mistaking the broad-shouldered, strong form of Guldorn, who lay broken in front of her. Blood seeped from a massive wound in his chest, staining his once magnificent armor and pooling in the firm dirt around him. Quivering with emotion, Jorna reached out for him, tears welling in her eyes, her heart aching with sorrow and grief. Just as her fingers touched his arm, he shifted and snapped open his eyes, startling her so that she quickly withdrew her hand.

"Jorna..." he choked out her name, coughing up blood. "Beware, Jorna." He forced himself to keep speaking, ignoring the expression of horror on his daughter's face. "The dragon lies beneath the earth. The dragon lies in forgotten shadows. The dragons, Jorna, the dragons hide the truth."

Confusion knitted her brow, but before she could ask any questions, something sharp and hot was plunged through her back, protruding on the other side just below her breastbone. Crying out in pain and shock, she glanced down at the black spearhead, her mind racing as she tried to turn her head so that she could see who had delivered the blow.

A cold laugh told her it was the monster long before the fiend moved around in front of her. Jorna panicked for a moment, for she realized that her father had disappeared, leaving her alone with the murderous hellion. Staring into that crazed, terrible face, she knew deep down that she and her men had failed, that there would be no victory. The world was going to burn.

Jorna woke suddenly with a startled cry, clutching at her chest as she sat up in bed. She was breathing hard and shivering, but she realized with a rush of relief that everything she'd felt and seen had only been part of a dream. A very disturbing dream, but a dream nonetheless.

As she calmed down, she discovered that Thane was sitting beside her. In fact, he had roused her from the depths of her nightmare when she began to cry and toss in her sleep. He gazed at her now with great concern as he gently smoothed damp hair back from her face, silently asking if she would be okay. Leaning into his arms, she rested her head on his shoulder and let out a heavy sigh. Being close to him brought her a great deal of comfort, but the horrible things she had seen refused to leave her mind.

Thane drew her back to the pillows and pulled the furs over them again before wrapping her more securely in his arms. Once she was composed enough, she shakily told him everything she could remember from the nightmare, including the cryptic message from Guldorn. He shifted, clearly as unsettled as she was, but he did a very good job of hiding it for her sake.

He would have offered verbal comfort, but he could see that she was lost in thought and so he simply held her close. Neither one of them fell back asleep, but as morning approached, Jorna found her voice again. She seemed to have shaken away the disturbing visions from her dream as their conversations didn't return to the subject.

When they could finally hear the rest of the house stirring and smell the scent of freshly baked bread and cinnamon, they resigned themselves to starting the day as well. The tantalizing aroma from the kitchen hurried them along, though they were also tempted by the sight of each other. In the end, hunger won over passion and they slipped out of Thane's room and downstairs to join the rest of the family.

As usual the kitchen was buzzing with activity, though far less from the two children, who were gazing bleary-eyed at their plates of food. Makira was telling them if they didn't finish their portions of minced meat, fried potato and eggs that they wouldn't be allowed to have one of the pastries that their grandmother had made. The scent of buttered, flaky dough with cinnamon and sugar drizzled over top was nearly overwhelming this close to the oven, where they sat on a rack to cool.

Baran was grumbling about the lack of gravy with his breakfast and Ravika was busy ignoring him while she finished making a plate of food for herself. Upon seeing Thane, she beamed a grin at him, but it instantly fell from her face as she caught sight of Jorna. It was a wonder she didn't drop the plate in her hand, the expression of utter surprise clearly indicated that she'd been stunned speechless, which was quite impressive.

About this time, the old General noticed that he wasn't being paid enough attention to and became flustered. "Did ya hear me, woman," he grumped, tearing his gaze away from his plate and glancing irritably at his wife. The instant he saw the state she was in, Baran whipped his head around, fearing something was dreadfully wrong.

When all he saw was Thane and Jorna, he simply let out a deep, annoyed sigh and failed to put together what Ravika already had. "You brought her back for breakfast, lad? Why not just marry her and..." Realization struck him as the words tumbled over his lips. Now it was his turn to stare in bewilderment at the pair, his jaw working, but no sound coming out. Finally he blurted, "Well, shave my beard! Now we're stuck with her!"

It was clear from his not-so-gruff tone that he didn't really mean what he'd said. The glance he gave Thane told a different albeit fleeting story. He hadn't held much respect for Jorna not so long ago, but after what she had managed to accomplish, proving to him and so many others that she was capable and wise, his opinion had changed. Not that he would ever admit it aloud; the only acknowledgment he gave was that single glance of approval that only his son witnessed.

Ravika on the other hand had always been far more picky about the woman her youngest child would marry, and now that he had attached himself so suddenly, she felt an even stronger urge to be certain he'd made the right choice. Tension filled the air as she approached the couple, the hard expression on her face conveying quite clearly that she was scrutinizing Jorna very closely.

Despite everything the princess had faced, being stared down by a concerned mother was absolutely her greatest challenge. She knew that to so much as blink or glance away would forever taint Ravika's opinion of her and so she met that dark, penetrating gaze without a trace of the trepidation writhing about in her belly. After a few long, intense moments, the older woman's expression shifted into a beaming grin, and she pulled both Jorna and Thane into a crushing embrace.

With her approval the kitchen returned to its usual state. Makira hugged her brother and new sister, while the children began to squabble. In a rare show of affection, Baran grabbed his wife's arm as she went by and gave the back of her hand a surprisingly gentle kiss that earned him a soft peck on the cheek before she moved to put together a couple more plates of food.

As Thane and Jorna took their places at the table, they exchanged a knowing glance. The warmth of family and kinship filled the room like the glow of a crackling hearth, reminding them that no matter what differences may separate them in the future, no matter what darkness fell upon the outside world, family would always endure.

Vista of Kings

The Vista of Kings was filled to overflowing with well-dressed and nicely groomed Sarven. Even the Dwenenari refugees looked their best in newly acquired formal clothing that had been a gift from the merchants of Hamdralg to celebrate this momentous occasion. Packed in around them were many Hamdralgian nobles, honored crafters, smiths and merchants who had come to witness the crowning of Dwenenar's new queen. Among them were of course her new family and the six Dwenenari survivors, who stood at the front of the crowd, beaming brightly up at the proceedings.

King Ulthrac, flanked as usual by the flame-haired twins Baran and Bodric, was speaking of Jorna's recent accomplishments, of her honor, courage, and daring in uncovering the truth behind the Siege of Dwenenar and Javrin the Kinslayer's foul betrayal. The latter of which was considered most unpleasant and so he only touched on the subject very briefly before launching into further detail about the soon to be queen.

Finally, he turned from the crowd and in a loud, reverberating voice called for Jorna to step forward. The twins fell away from their king's side to allow the princess to join Ulthrac on the dais. Her simple, flowing gown of emerald silk rustled about her legs as she gracefully moved into position.

A light breeze whistled through the balcony, teasing her unbound, creamy hair and causing several of the onlookers to shiver; it was nearly spring now, but the air was still quite chilly. Jorna didn't seem bothered by the cold. She appeared quite beautiful and majestic standing before the assembly.

Speaking in the same commanding tone, Ulthrac began the final litany. "Jorna Hailstone, daughter of Guldorn Oathbinder and Deinri Mistcaller, Princess of Dwenenar, I bestow upon you your father's sword, Hrolduin, as a symbol of your birthright. With this weapon you are sworn to uphold the laws and traditions of the Sarven people, to lead them through war and peace, but most importantly, to honor the kings and queens who came before you."

Thane Stoutforge approached now, delivering Hrolduin to the king so that he could pass the blade to Jorna as the ceremony dictated. Long ago, a proper crown was not always available and so it was commonplace for a weapon, usually a family heirloom, to be used instead. Once this task was done, he returned to the front of the crowd and continued observing.

As Ulthrac extended the sword to Jorna on his palms, she bowed to him, accepting Hrolduin without hesitation. Straightening with the blade in hand, she raised it up so that the turned blade was a mere line in front of her face and recited the words of acceptance in ancient Sarven. When she was finished, she lowered the weapon, flipping it so that the tip rested lightly against the stone floor.

"People of Dwenenar, Citizens of Hamdralg, I present to you Jorna

Hailstone, Queen of Dwenenar!" Ulthrac had turned to the assembly and spoken with a pleased grin. A loud shout echoed over the balcony as the gathered Sarven cheered for the new queen. There was no doubt among any of them that she would make a fine ruler, not when she had already demonstrated her qualities.

When the brief revelry had subsided, Jorna turned to the next part of the ceremony: proclaiming her king. She summoned Thane forward and he complied, moving to kneel in front of her as Ulthrac backed out of the way; this was Jorna's assembly now.

"Blacksmith Thane Stoutforge, son of Baran the Crusher and Ravika Emberspell, it is with great joy that I announce our marriage. Together, we will forge a new alliance between the last of the great Sarven kingdoms, that our people may forever stand united. You have proven your worth, your skill, and your courage. Rise now as the new King of Dwenenar." Jorna was smiling down at him the whole time she was speaking, her gray-blue eyes alight with tender love.

Standing as she had bade, Thane couldn't keep the grin off his face as he took his place at her side. Nothing had ever felt so right and natural to him in all his life. It was almost as though he had been born for this moment alone, to stand next to this woman as her husband and partner, so that they might both be complete at last. She paused to exchange a glance with him, a glance that told him she felt the same way. For just a split second, there was nobody else on the balcony but them.

Unfortunately that feeling was fleeting as duty drew Jorna's attention back to the crowd. Her benevolent gaze had fallen to the six surviving warriors who had stayed behind and nearly been tortured to death by the twisted arcanist, Stefan. Standing beside them was her younger brother, Jalrik, who she had nearly lost as well. This was not part of the coronation, it was something she had wanted to add, a surprise to honor their sacrifice and devotion. Of the twenty warriors who had stayed to fight during Dwenenar's fall, these six were all that remained.

"Renarn Ironbelly," she started to call their names, "Rulvon Firespite, Druln Kilnsmog, Ulvaris the Grim, Kelntarg the Brawler, and Harjein Wintersteel. There is no doubt that the pain and suffering you faced were immeasurable, but your perseverance, your strength, and determination reflect the valor in your hearts." Jorna smiled at each of them in turn. "My first act as queen is to bestow upon you the highest honor by naming you and all the brothers who fell in battle during our escape from Dwenenar Champions of the Stone."

The prestigious title was rarely granted to the living; most of those who obtained it did so by sacrificing their lives in the most selfless and glorious of manners. After discussing it with King Ulthrac, the decision had been made that these six were well deserving of such an honor. They had not only endured hell at the hands of their captors but fought bravely and loyally at Jorna's side when lesser men might have given up.

As the crowd cheered again, the six warriors exchanged surprised glances. They knew that Jorna was planning to grant them all positions as captains or advisers, but the recognition of their deeds was most unexpected. All the same, they bowed low and thanked their queen from the bottom of their massive, Sarven hearts.

"I have one more person to honor," Jorna continued when the balcony had quieted down again. "He is not a Sarven, but he proved to be an invaluable friend and ally. Without the dragon's aid, we would not have reached Dwenenar, let alone returned alive. I not only appoint him as my adviser, but I grant him the Sarven name, Shanik Truefire, as a reflection of his friendship to the Sarven people."

As if on cue, the black dragon, scaled down to his smaller form, swooped from the ceiling above. He glided over the crowd, then came to a graceful landing on Jorna's shoulder, where he perched with all the splendor one might expect of a dragon.

The awe from the gathering was immense as everyone marveled at the sight of an actual dragon, sitting before their eyes as though he were of the utmost importance. Thane had to keep from rolling his eyes, certain that if they really knew Shanik, they wouldn't be any more impressed than he was.

Once the disruption had run its course, Jorna spoke for the last time, bringing the coronation to an end. "As you all know, it is tradition for a new monarch to make an initial decree, a promise of what can be expected from their rule." Her eyes swept the crowd, allowing her words to settle before she pressed on.

"This is my solemn oath: I will not rest, I will not stop until the evil, malicious threat of the wyrmkin has been dealt with, until we stand in Dwenenar once again or until the city has been rebuilt, better and stronger than before. What happened to the Sarven will not happen again. We will prove to the humans, the elves, and the orcs alike that though we might be bloodied, beaten, and weary, we will never yield."

Her impassioned proclamation sent a tremor of shouting and applause through the gathering, louder than the previous cheers. War was coming to Talaris, but it was not a war the Sarven would back down from. They were done secluding themselves away in underground halls. Now it was time to rejoin the world and claim retribution for the wrongs they had been dealt.

Thanks for Reading!

I hope that you found joy, solace, escape, and love within these pages or at least a few hours of delightful distraction. Thank you for walking this journey with me! Becoming an author has always been my greatest dream, but it wouldn't mean anything without amazing readers like you!

If you have a few minutes, it would mean so much to me if you would share an honest review on Amazon and Goodreads! I would love to hear what you thought of *Heralds of Chaos*. Thank you again! TTFN!

MORE BY LUCILLE

ELEMENTS OF CHAOS

Heralds of Chaos

Heir of Dragons

Embers of the Past

PARANORMAL ROMANCE

Hexen Blood: Legacy of Count Dracula

ABOUT THE AUTHOR

Raised in a small town in South Central Alaska, Lucille discovered her passion for writing at a young age and cobbled together a tremendously awful Star Wars fan novel by the time she finished middle school. As an adult, she began her career as a freelance ghostwriter before launching into indie publishing for herself with her debut novel *Hexen Blood: Damnation*. Lucille presently writes and publishes from Missouri.

9 798869 194527